T0209209

LEGEND OF THE MIGHTY SPARROW
PART 2

END OF DAYS, ESCHATOLOGY, THE FINAL
EVENTS OF HISTORY, THE ULTIMATE
HUMAN DESTINY, END OF TIME, AND
ULTIMATE FATE OF THE UNIVERSE

BRYAN FLETCHER

authorHOUSE®

AuthorHouse™
1663 Liberty Drive
Bloomington, IN 47403
www.authorhouse.com
Phone: 1 (800) 839-8640

Published by AuthorHouse   08/17/2016

ISBN: 978-1-5246-2448-4 (sc)
ISBN: 978-1-5246-2446-0 (hc)
ISBN: 978-1-5246-2447-7 (e)

Library of Congress Control Number: 2016913315

Print information available on the last page.

For more information about the Legend of the Mighty Sparrow series visit http://legendofthemightysparrow.com/

CHAPTER 1

In an ultradense forest, which proves difficult to see five feet ahead, Bonnie struggles through.

Moments later, she bumps into a 1,000-pound brown bear with ever so disgusting thick white foam, which drips from the mouth onto the jaw, fur, ground, and her hands.

Then the creature roars with deafening power, so much so Bonnie instantly loses ten years of life—just like that, gone, as the shock denigrates those personal reserves or those ten years instantaneously leap away, and go wherever elusive things travel then eventually find a new home, maybe absorbed back into nature.

Just as importantly, her eyes widen and mouth forms an "Oh" position, as in, "Oh, my God!" then the body repeatedly starts and stops in fits, on where to jump or run, and especially with an impulse to jump or leap, maybe jump up a tree, if that were humanly possible, yet no tree seems close enough, only very tall and ultradense shrubs.

Instead, Bonnie turns then flees, in search of a forest exit, and frantically plows through foliage with a circular arm motion, and often looks back while running—a dangerous practice indeed, especially with the risk of tripping over something, such as a fallen branch or sharp rock.

And as the pace increases, eventually the heart pounds and lungs strain, as well as the chest feels a rush of blood, which now seems palpable, as the taste lingers on the palette, a distinct taste of plasma, as well as a mineral ion feel, and something else—something, maybe a taste of the common, of metal, iron, a transitional metal, and a path, or a path-dependent option.

Regardless, she increases speed, and over ground, which contains mostly fallen crisp brown leaves, twigs and branches that crackle under each stride.

And eventually, beads of sweat form on the forehead, nose, and cheeks.

Just as importantly, events feel quite familiar, yet different, as if in a temporal loop, where events repeat in a distinct circuit, and yet a few aspects change, such as the normal sequence of events are not correctly linked, or as if someone, thing, or it has tampered with the timeline, a history of ideas, or tampered with her mind, with her thalamus.

So, during this escape, she looks about for certain visual reference cues and taps the back of the left hand three times, and again, taps left of right, the left brake, the left-handed material index—well, to see if it creates an instantly awaking moment, in a hospital, sickbay or some other place, such as a limbo, either a secular or sacred version, a purgatory.

Or, she might struggle in an intermediate state, a bardo or liminal state, such as middle ritual, mid threshold or in a special rite of passage, quite possibly atonement, or some other place in the monomyth cycle.

However, cues here and there indicate no such manipulation, and no superimposition, temporal stub, and no sunken kingdom, to reemerge, or different face, different space, or species dysphoria.

Eventually, she sees opportunity then quickly climbs an American sycamore tree, also called an occidental plane.

Yet, twenty feet up, she reaches for the next branch and knocks two bird nests with eggs to the ground, and that accident causes a considerable cringe of "Oh, that's not good! Sorry about that."

Then she carefully scans for that brown bear, which had ever so disgusting thick white foam, which that dripped from the mouth, onto the jaw, fur and ground, and her hands.

As a result, she tries to quickly wipe off every molecule.

"What the heck was that?" and "What's with the foam?" and "Do I need the Milwaukee protocol?"

Not much later, she looks for bird parents, yet finds no activity whatsoever.

In fact, the forest seems exceptionally quiet.

And for certainty, the eyes carefully scan one section at a time, for obvious, as well as subtle, forest aspects.

Yet three minutes later, a profound sense of guilt arrives.

So much so the face cringes with eek then empathy, as an awkward climb down one fragile branch at a time eventually allows her to look for danger at another level then inspect two of the five eggs, which look okay, as they have no cracks or dents, and that generates a sense of relief.

However, three eggs lie at awkward and hard-to-reach places, such as a place where she has to reach, and reach then really stretch, fully extend fingertips, strain and strain, then shimmy the body here and there, wiggle, really wiggle, strain even more, reach and reach, barely touch an egg then rock it with a fingertip, until it moves more, and more, then gains enough rocking momentum and opportunity to grab, "Yes, one small victory, a cosmic egg, transforming from primordial substance into energy, life, spirit and glory, yes, a mystery of resurrection, hermetically sealed, and a new beginning, a temporal adjustment, as well as a certain truth, and rise from this egg, oh noble spirit, rise, rise!"

Each remaining egg proves difficult to reach, yet eventually she secures them then ponders, which egg goes where?

"Oh trouble, big trouble, and will the mamas know the difference? And does it matter to the eastern phoebe, brown-headed cowbird, cuckoo, reed warbler, black-headed duck, dunnock, goldeneye or the sparrow?

"Is it vital to a mother, or essential, in their full arc of existence, and to the universe?

"Is there such a thing as the bird mafia, a revenge thing, when you mess with the mama and her true destiny, and her possibility of true greatness?

"Will you stir a very powerful universal force, the mother?"

Bonnie considers, and eventually thoughts arrive of that bear with disgusting white foam, which causes her to wipe both hands beyond rhythm or reason.

Moments later, she looks around for danger then gathers twigs, fortifies the nests, improves drainage, adds coverage, and makes it "near impossible to dislodge these eggs," as well as adds exceptional style and flair, as compensation, adds an "ultra-retro hip style, and yet fashion-forward, to give both of them a timeless look, because style matters—it really matters?"

Just as significantly, she says, "These modifications make them windproof, stormproof, maybe hurricaneproof—well, maybe not hurricaneproof.

Regardless, these nests and eggs have no significant chance of falling."

Once done, Bonnie says in a fully animated and highly stylized way, yet finishes with a gradual slowdown, as well as an ever so profound realization of *déjà vu*, "Done, as in *finito*. Goodbye, as I will never return, ever, and of equal importance, find a calendar and record this day, as well as time—no, wait, record it in something permanent, yes, for example: chisel it into an enormous block of granite, yes, chip at the stone, at various angles; yes, chisel."

Moments later, and in the distance, something approaches.

In addition, it has a sublime, bizarre, and ruthless aspect, as well as makes a distinct series of creepy sound combinations, which has some resemblance to a Soundsnap website, "Noise Warble Warp B," followed by twelve seconds of sounds, not quite a cross between "Urban Creepy" and chaos, which repeat.

As a result, Bonnie startles, spins, looks about, then flees in the opposite direction and plows through ultradense foliage.

Furthermore with utmost precision to maintain an elusive escape, all of which requires ultraquick timing, she often tacts here and there, as well as must occasionally with world-class Olympic style, with found greatness, hurdle a fallen branch or two and often deflect foliage from the face and eyes, in this bewildering green maze.

Then the sublime, bizarre and ruthless aspect, a weird thing accelerates, as a dangerous mind game, point of no return, max Q, and it plows forward as a true genius beyond description, beyond all words and thoughts, beyond all forms of language.

And without losing speed, she duly notes with a series of rubberneck looks of what-what-what, as breath quickens.

Then she abandons one precise tact after another and plows through wait-a-minute-shrubs, through thorn foliage which grabs, inflicts pain, and causes her to flinch even more so, to protect the face and especially the eyes.

Yet she plows with an efficient technique, a hard-earned lesson, very, to avoid limbs swelling, which would have eventually become grotesque, so much so, and she would have said to herself with a serious plea, "Don't look! Whatever you do, don't look at the limbs!"

However, well, you know human nature, the history of civilization, and the compelling power of impulse to stare at drama, especially an accident, and damage, in search of some great universal truth, a truth that might reveal the mysteries of existence, of the universe.

So, she would have looked and received a shock to her system, the biome, her tree of life, as well as liminal core, which prefers a precise ritual, in certain well-timed stages, and instead would receive a crisis of the self, the coalition, which have quite complex internal agreements, which might null and void at the frontier, such as "You are on your own," well, as a third culture person in a *Weird Tale.*

She avoids all that while running, and moments later the soul shudders and shakes, an Alabama shakes.

Moreover, this chase reveals memories, personal baggage, as well as known flaws and imperfections, which flood her mind with vivid and wholly irrational images as she tries to maintain one long stride after another.

Then with a new forest plow technique, she avoids grotesque swelling, such as the last time, and avoids the mind immediately assigning her a role in life—an outcast, an outsider, and a true freak, which belongs in a classic sideshow, in a new-age combination of P. T. Barnum, claustrophobic microcosm cabinet of curiosities, a decorative *Wunderkammer* facade, Black Scorpion, Jim Rose Circus, as well as a Lollapalooza old time revival—in effect, a show of shows with a colorful and fully animated barker.

Where people can buy a ticket then point and gawk at the human oddities, point at the freaks, the reluctant working acts, and where parents, corporations, and especially governments take mischievous children, to instill fear, maybe the Old Testament version of God, known for fury, vengeance, hellfire, brimstone and suffering—not ordinary suffering, but an eternal suffering, the classic and dramatic version of love, of "Love me completely, with total devotion, or else," and really punish those not in full compliance with an eternal smolder, and crisp: that type of love. Or some other cultural equivalent which uses shame, to wither willful aspects of individuality, and especially wither that part of the mind, body and soul, which generates an impulse to look behind the curtain, the facade, frame of reference, or popular phrase or method, to look for production technique advantages and disadvantages. As well, that system might shame critical objective thinking, to wither that crucial limbic juncture, wither that path into individuality, and instead compel and condition the mind to unconditionally obey, or else.

Regardless, as well as here and now with this new running plow technique, she avoids that type of major damage, yet those thoughts and some damage cause her run too slow then occasionally with odd hobble.

Yet she battles through dense foliage, through a bewildering green maze, as well as thickets, and often hurdles over one fallen branch after another, which often create tremendous stumble, near a sharp rock or two.

Regardless and each time, she quick-twitch recovers and continues to battle forward, which eventually causes her breath to quicken beyond rhythm or reason.

So much so the taste of blood seems palpable—very.

In fact on the palette the taste of blood lingers, a taste of plasma, as well as a mineral ion feel, of iron, a transition metal.

And during this escape, events seem quite familiar, *déjà vu*, as if in a temporal loop, a distinct circuit, superimposition, temporal stub, yet somehow things feel different.

So at the last possible second, she runs hard left, which avoids a complex trap, an ankle snatch to deliberately drag her about, as if she represents a rag doll, and through one wait-a-minute-shrub after another, and over tortuous ground, not the typical "dirt," the type universally found in religious text, and regardless of which religion, regardless of a high, moderate or low church movement, or another cultural equivalent, such as enterprise or some other social construct?

Then at the last possible second, she runs hard right and avoids another ankle snatch, which would have deliberately dragged her over ground that contains danger, prejudice, error, and truly great corruption, then yanked her underground, where the creature or thing would violently bang her about with a whip action, again and again, until her eyes slowly dimmed.

Eventually the mind would fade as emotions drain, until the process creates a blank—a blank verse, a choliambic.

Regardless, if that happened, she would again refuse to surrender, refuse to say that name.

Here and now, still running, and at the last possible second, she avoids one trap after another, which requires a series of quick twitch maneuvers, quite awkward at first, especially balance.

Then eventually her efforts transition into ever so smooth, quite, as a virtuoso with a certain flow, rhythm, style, and *panache* that deploys a last-second sidestep, plow, hard right, plow, hard left, plow, and spin maneuver if need be, to untangle a brier extension, a branch, that pattern, which proves quite effective as she battles towards the forest exit, to freedom.

However, that weird thing, a dangerous mind game, point of no return, max Q, continues to chase her, and it plows forward as a true genius beyond description, beyond all words and thoughts, beyond all forms of language.

As a result, she often looks back to measure distance, which represents a dangerous practice indeed, especially with the risk of tripping over something, such as a fallen branch or sharp rock.

Instead, she impacts against an old-growth tree, with hybrid aspects, which includes traits associated with oak, peach, beech, hazel, ash, eucalyptus, willow, sycamore, almond, baobab and sandalwood, as well as acacia with thorny pods, shevaga, assattha, fig, kalpavriksha, thuja and yew, together with something a person might expect, near a well of souls, a hidden seep, as well as a seep-spring arnica here and there.

Regardless and seconds later, that weird thing risks everything, and rushes into that tree influence, through those stages of, and something an articulate scientist, musician or poet might better describe, and with far more precision regarding all those obvious and subtle aspects, especially as much of that tree system seems to transcend all conventional language and thought.

So, to grab an ankle and quickly drag her out that considerable tree system, it rushes through the region without the proper protocol, without proper phase transitions—those seams, stages, miscibility gaps and degrees associated with liminal, with the structure of identity, time, and common space.

It does so as improper art, which has real implications because the universal entanglement, mostly unseen, as well as the real science and "mythology of lost," because there appears no decent direct route through this complex estate.

Moments later, and with a certain distinct power, control and exceptional flair, a whip action flings the limp body up and into a clear expanse of sky, into the majestic, the exceptionally serene blue expanse.

And as the body soars well above forest, it does so with a certain clear path of freedom, as a damaged being on the rise, which soon travels along a tremendous arc out of the forest.

Not much later, she eventually impacts, a direct hit on the large forest entrance sign, then falls on a pile, on stunned commandos, a half dozen well-armed commandos with the latest body armor and silenced automatic weapon systems.

Just as importantly, these commandos appear to represent BfV, DGSE, DDIS, SAPO, KEMPEI TAI, and SLUZBA BEZPIECZENSTWA services; however, something seems quite odd about their uniform insignias, as well as other subtle things, which that seem, well, for lack of a better phrase, resemble "aesthetic perfections," yet seem artificial and unnatural, something a person such as Franz Kafka, Ludwig Wittgenstein, or Charles John Huffam Dickens might better describe, someone more conscientious, and with exceptionally precise observational skills.

In addition, and underneath them, lay three sprawled and still wet divers in full scuba gear with rebreathers, and at the very bottom of the pile lay a sprawled deep-sea diver in an orange JIM ocean diving suit (ADS).

And moments later, mid pile, an aquatic ape recovers, struggles for freedom, quickly looks about for safety, and then scrambles back into the forest.

CHAPTER 2

Eventually, and after commandos have gone, a dog scratches her back, the same one that often follows.

Again, it scratches her back, to show genuine concern, as that seems the most appropriate thing to do, seems decent, civil, *comme il faut*, at least according to those books, then the dog licks her face.

As a result Bonnie quickly revives then reels from disgust, which creates acute aches, sharp pains, and a series of profound winces, as well as a ghastly grimace that eventually shifts to wholly overwhelmed, bewildered, then fear about serious internal damage.

In addition, it takes a considerable amount of effort to generate a distressed whisper, "Go away. Are you insane? Be gone, you beast," then an effort to wipe away every molecule of dog slobber, causes acute holy smoke distress, as the face and body contorts in an ugly way.

Regardless, eventually and with a whisper, she says, "Don't do that—never, ever. Go- go-go, be gone!"

Nonetheless the dog moves eight feet away, waits, considers then lies facing towards her, with head on extended paws.

And it waits for her and considers, in its own way, *the dramatic potential, that unique human storytelling system to explain life with a panoramic, a special perspective, with context and content, especially regarding appropriate, as well as the ever so long game, of nature, of fetch, the complex systems, most beyond sight and sound, beyond a normal person or canine perspective, and ever changing, yet events seem so familiar.*

And often a minor cue, an incidental, shallow variation often overlooked represents the most important in a shallow language game, then the dog considers *kindred relationships to humans, especially her,* and it considers *semblance.*

Then the dog thinks, *Why do humans show so many mixed signals that lack logic, as well as common sense?*

And they often seem stuck, as well as obsessive, *with so many compound cues, emotions, and dwell on the longest game ever,* the Big Show, monomyth cycle, that great adventure, or *stuck in a niche,* or bubble, *with a certain atmospherics* yet leaky abstraction.

They often appear stuck in some other place, moment, such as *the past,* in an unsolved or *read-ahead loop,* at less according to the dog.

And of greater importance, it seems wholly inappropriate to leave a person in *serious distress, especially near death.*

So, to show full respect and genuine concern, the dog carefully looks at her, measures aspects of that condition, respects boundaries, and waits for a real command, for a real mission, and a command said in the proper way, according to a specialized stack protocol, or one MC full stack alert, or at least one from the prescribed reading list, or with a runtime virtual function signature move, with style, with panache, yes, to open the next major phase.

Yet, in spite of all these internal injuries, Bonnie seems stubborn to a fault, in fact obsessive, which represents a family trait, especially that of her mother, and right now it fuels gameness, fuels grit—raw grit, true grit—which circulates even more particle constructs of power, tenacity, and the impulse to surge forward, particularly from the thought of being pushed around once too often, run off one too many times, bullied through her life for being different, picked on again and again, which triggers genes. Or it could have been from that tremendous impact, or from something else, such as fate, luck, or the randomness of nature, maybe from the thrownness of nature.

Regardless, Bonnie translates it into the personal, very, and seems wholly offended in principle, core then marrow, as well as incorporeal and liminal coil.

Just as importantly, she seems less concerned about risk and more about the bedrock principle, of being treated as "a mere ragdoll, rudely dragged here and there through one punishing menace after another, then summarily slung from the forest, again," as well as "for all those previous slights received over a lifetime, all those pernicious pecks, and especially frustration from lost opportunities, opportunities for a better tomorrow."

As a result, she ignores those dangerous symptoms, eventually rises, barely, and attempts to take a few bold strides, yet staggers and stumbles about. As the body winces, contorts, shows ghastly facial grimaces, which seems overwhelming then bewildering, and eyes roll about in a wholly unnatural way that suggest profound disorientation, and yet she ultimately says, "I'm fine—piece of cake. Shake it off, momma, 'hold on,' as it could be worse, right?"

In addition, she eventually sees a small foreign diplomatic sack with straps, and defies logic, crouches, which creates another holy smokes moment.

So much so the mind, body, and soul undergo a profound mortal suffering, and yet a certain brilliant glory that seems universal, classic, and quite profound, which radiates from her face in a series of very particular expressions and compelling degrees, as if she sits at a fundamental threshold, at the very edge of existence.

However, she deliberately ignores as well the lack of food for several days, and slowly turns, to looks about for more things, more resources for a final showdown, an epic battle.

Regardless, another holy smokes moment arrives.

As a result she staggers about, as a succession of ghastly expressions appears on the face.

Nonetheless she says, "I'm fine," then with a bit of flair and gusto, which requires no significant movement, as well as showing the ability to prevail, to overcome, and to win a decisive victory regardless of the cost, she adds, "No problem. Shake it off, momma, and hold on, Alabama style, as it could be far worse."

However, the full effects of that impact, other cumulative damages, and hunger converge.

So much so dizziness arrives.

Then legs weaken, wildly shake, and knees buckle, and again, which cause an uncharted stagger, a lost fathom, profound mystery, more acute facial grimaces, and balance has a bizarre appearance.

Not much later the full-blown shakes arrive and limbs quiver, in ways that truly unsettle the mind then compel her to one knee, as mental shifts appear on the face, of complete disorientation, confusion, as well as out-of-this-world.

Then something else happens—something.

Still on one knee, near an old growth beech tree, she becomes quite pale and withers as a profound sadness appears on the face, as if truly alone and forsaken.

With this full realization, her soul shivers, and yet eyes widen as if on the very edge of a great cliff, some final precipice of existence, such as a dangerous crag with chasm, which offers a precarious edge of crumble then steep drop, into no more excuses, into the impossible mystery of frontier justice.

Where the possibility of falling causes internal alarms, which petrifies then delivers chills and sends waves of acute anxiety about the cliff, about that precarious edge of existence, as well as the sheer depth below.

So, she looks up to the sky for answers. Then, moments later, a song plays in her mind, which might be "Max Manus OST – 18" by Trond Bjerknes.

However, and more importantly, this song adds to her tremendous sense of alienation, true alienation, as if someone who barely survived a war and still feels numb, then things around become pale, empty, and surreal.

So much so her face shows a distant look—a thousand-yard stare—which suggests an unfocused gaze of a battle-weary soldier or trauma victim who seems despondent, separate, as well as distant from the here and now.

Moments later she remembers her father and how, since the age of three, he called her "Sparrow, the Mighty Sparrow," and did so with such full admiration, and each time his eyes would light up with gratitude, and as if witnessing excellence, then he offered a smile.

In fact he began to glow and glimmer real satisfaction, with all those nuances of a full spectrum event.

The thought of her and that name brought him immense satisfaction, "The Sparrow, the Mighty Sparrow, a good daughter, a truly great daughter, in fact an excellent human being, truly civilized and with an exceptional sense of truth, justice, virtue, creed, culture and gravitas."

However, she never quite understood what he saw, the aspects or totality.

And that happens to many people, as a person often lacks a full and accurate awareness of self, of private and public image, especially the daily interactive persona during various situations, and seam management, the edges in-between strategies, between each gap, and also what others really notice, the idiosyncrasies, the tells, tendencies, and traits, as well as bias and context in relationship to the personality, mindset, schema, atmospherics, and storyline.

And just as importantly, before one script after another load, look in the mirror and occasionally see a stranger.

Yet once found, that version, maybe the true self, submerges, and some other person, persona, or role immediately emerges then acts as if on cue, and does so with a certain script, which often transmits or portrays as a bit disingenuous in those following moments, and it does not act in a convincing or fully committed way for one reason or another. As that substitute persona may not be the original self, the source or creator, and because of all those complex roles a person must live at any given moment with all those obvious and subtle adjustments, which have so many possibilities, endless, and that in total conflict— they will not fully reconcile.

And often a person must live in someone else's storyline or under it, as an extra, a red shirt: a disposable. In addition, a person must often live dozens of roles or storylines at the same time, a metagame, with so many social mandates, a vast number, most hidden, and created by the powerful, as well as tremendously dangerous people, places and things, who believe in MAD—mutual assured destruction—of all in or else, that type of love and devotion, where they set the agenda, the laws, as well as storyline, and demand you live within the escalation, the turmoil, the throughline, and cheer or insult it on a system cue, or else.

So, a passenger tries to safely navigate within, such as avoid one wrong word, a script variation or tonal infraction, something not pitch-perfect, which the powers-that-be view as a serious slight, a serious offense, and because of the all-of-nothing-mechanism, the "all in or out tradition," often based on a whim or myth, which can trigger a major rollback event then removal of insider privilege, a rollback of exceptions, because you are not one of them, not pure. As a system, proxy, or mob might polarize and form, because of the smallest thing, often based on a factoid or rumor, as well as trivia, and very much so, as if much of any given system represents a trivial pursuit with exceptionally dangerous consequences based on minutia, for a small inflection error, from a blink at the wrong time, or failure to cheer loud enough at each slogan of the day, or on cue, on the mark. And it seems quite dangerous, for a very small freedom of expression, and reveals the obsessiveness many systems expect, and yet they often say "*locutions de minimis non curat praetor or de minimis non curat lex,*" that paired opposite, that dynamic of life in a quandary, a catch-22, Cornelian dilemma, no-win situation or Pyrrhic victory-based system.

So the original persona must work under or in back of their role—well, as support, as *The Dresser*, as a theatrical stagehand, and yet a person who deploys a proxy, a spokesperson for the self, to represent this complex stack of roles, and deploys a host, a master of ceremonies or *compère* for the self, which often resembles a reluctant benchwarmer in someone else's storyline, especially on daily as well as frontier aspects, and things not in the script? Yet, much of life is not in the script, and yet any given system requires a person to "stick to the script, the message, protocol, and technique, regardless." Or else, the system will issue a major rollback, or drop something on them, as a lesson to others, drop a metaphorical or literal building on them.

Just as significantly, any given social system often requires a person to respond with a conventional straightforward answer, description, and action, to a very complex question or situation, and requires an answer, which must often quickly fit in an ever so small space, such as "Okay," or fit on a bumper sticker, or squeeze through a small window of time, on cue, such as squeeze a complex subject into a snappy one-liner, for instance, "Bada-bing, bada-boom: life!"

More importantly, her father saw something in her, something exceptional. Then he began to glow and glimmer with real satisfaction, which had all those nuances of a full spectrum event and illuminated soul.

Just the thought of her and that name brought him immense satisfaction, "The Sparrow, the Mighty Sparrow, a good daughter, a truly great daughter, in fact, an excellent human being, truly civilized and with an exceptional sense of truth, justice, virtue, creed, culture and gravitas."

However, and much of her life, she struggled to find something, the right groove, the right mojo, motive, and skill, or memory, dream, genre, situation, as well as high concept adventure then region of stability, to a heal, such as next to an exceptional artesian spring, in a secular or sacred form of Gan Eden, Avalon, Baltia, Shambhala, Beyul or El Dorado, or some other official transcendent paradise with really good water, such as what was loosely described in *The Travels of Sir John Mandeville* or by Juan Ponce de León, the snapback effect of vitality-restoring waters, and that cool sip, which redeems and restores original intent, aspiration, and reserve of spark then sip again, under a tree of life, of knowledge, or as if a localized version, a one-of-a-kind, an idiosyncratic, as no human is exactly the same, the same living tree or rock, with prophetic symbols, as an adaptive regression tree or additive contemplative, yet a place central to everywhere, such as into an exceptional past, present, eternal or future, or all at once.

Regardless, as well as here and now on one knee, she looks toward various aspects of the heavens and searches for an answer.

Yet as she fades from serious internal damage, a song enters the mind, and as if sung in a similar style as Jeannie Carson's, "Ye banks and braes o' bonnie Doon, How ye can bloom so fresh and fair, How can ye chant ye little birds, And I sae weary fu' o' care,

Ye'll break my heart ye warbling birds, That wantons thro' the flowering thorn, Ye mind me o' departed joys, Departed never to return."

Final thoughts arrive and, still barely on one knee, Bonnie looks to the heavens and slowly says in a bare whisper, "Funny, in a sad sort of way, unemployed, bankrupt, homeless, alienated from family and friends, I've become the other."

And for a great number of people it only takes one mistake, one strike, a misspoken word, slip of the tongue, poorly told joke, bad day, the wrong body of politic, or possibly some combination of fate and bad luck, and they quickly become the other, trapped in the underclass.

Moreover, a tremendous number of people remain a paycheck or two away from eviction, bankruptcy, and rapid decline.

Many people and systems do not fully realize the seismic shift underway, a historic employment crisis, a K-wave in the United States of America and especially around the world, the new world order, yet same old-same old, until it affects them, by which time it is often too late, and there is not enough time to adjust before the sudden impact.

Regardless, as well as here and now, her soul shivers, and eyes widen as she kneels on the very edge of existence, and no more excuses, which causes internal alarms that petrify then deliver chills and eventually acute chest anxiety about serious internal injuries, from that tremendous sign, as well as other cumulative damage.

So much so, dizziness arrives and body quivers.

Moments later, something else happens, and it seems quite difficult to describe—something.

And then a breeze arrives, as her face shows a certain majestic sadness, a certain noble suffering, which seems quite profound, poetic, and eternal as the end nears.

Also, her face grows pale as the spirit becomes weaker and weaker, yet a halo forms around her, an aureole of unknown origins, as if a poetic truth, a glory, gloriole, aureole yet nimbus with complex strata, as if a biostratigraphic soul, the core, as well as an under- and over- soul, especially backlit.

Then moments later a significant wind arrives, and it produces *velificatio*, a billow effect.

And that phenomenon often appears in art, the classics, especially during the Renaissance, Renaissance Humanism, Neoclassicism, Age of Enlightenment, and the Romantic era version.

Where a person generates certain truth and or beauty, as a mysterious event, as a definitive state or statement, which has a glory full spectrum, often of completeness, an exceptional totality.

Sometimes it appears as a majestic glory that might appear as square, hexagonal, or three sides, to convey the full power and might of trinity, or double, as with a certain natural duality, which maintains its power and mystery from paired opposites.

On occasion in classic art, it appears as rays of unconditional glory, or powerful harmonic beacons of sapient truth, which that conveys a certain warm, serene and fertile compassion, and from a being, a fertility vessel, a paradise, ripe, passionate, bold and true, and ready, ready to arch, ready to accept, and "Oh! Oh my," and ready to ride the wave and imagine greatness, true greatness, and explore and continue to ride that universal wave, then accept a gift, accept the eternal, which will bloom within, grow and prosper, then become a fully realized redemption, become the source and beam of a truly great culture, become the source of a truly great civilization.

However, right here and now, a breeze produces *velificatio*, a certain billow effect, then as she fades away, another halo forms, a radiance, a harmonic beam of duality, as if from an extraordinary power and glory of paired opposites, from some great secular mystery.

More importantly, her eyes and face conveys a very specific truth, they convey sadness, regret and profound loneliness, and yet it resembles an everlasting glory.

Will she panic from all these grim notices of a pending death and become hysterical?

Of all the possible thoughts, final thoughts to summarize her life, to summarize the entire arc of her existence, will she focus on blame—blame someone, or something, maybe the system, or process, or all of the above, maybe the universe, and how life seems chaotic, unfair, rigged, as well as exceptionally cruel, full of betrayal and all that restless drama?

Will all those powerful feelings stir within the mind, body and soul, and reveal previous wounds that never fully healed, all those slights, and a system that never fully satisfies or resolves?

As death approaches, will she panic, lash out and blame? And who will she blame, the system or the others?

More importantly, will anyone miss her? Will they truly miss her?

At the very end, will she cry? Will she weep in a final purifying-cleanse of a good cry, a final, deep and profound cry, to cleanse the mind, body and soul?

Will she release all of those powerful emotions; finally release them and quiver—yes, quiver—and release that heavy burden?

Will warm tears flow? Will they purify her, redeem her, and will the lower lip quiver, and quiver?

CHAPTER 3

✓ PART 1

Deep inside that forest and well underground, something stirs.

It stirs beyond heavily reinforced concrete walls well over eight feet thick, and inside what might represent a chamber, antechamber, or vestibule.

However, the thing recedes into this room then a series of long chthonic passageways and one fortified bunker after another, and places devoted to Renaissance architecture.

What Marcus Vitruvius Pollio of Rome might describe with the three qualities of *firmitas*, *utilitas,* and *venustas*, or put another way, places that show a prudent, practical, balanced, efficient, and judicious style, a discreet, truly civilized place, with a calm aesthetic, as well as in full harmonic accord with nature, which might stand for a thousand years or more, such as the Tabularium, Curia of Pompey, Roman Forum or Rostra Vetera, and yet here as well as there is a black marble and cement mixture to discourage Sulla aspirations.

In addition, a considerable number of these bunkers have a mobile portion, a section able to quickly detach, and just as importantly, when that thing moves further into the bunker system and through a very long, narrow, dense and claustrophobic tunnel, the path eventually opens into a gauntlet of snakes.

As each snake sits inside its own three-foot square niche, with exceptional ornate and robust inlay, as well as architectural trim made of the finest material, which gives each recess a look of several very complex worlds within one another. And each appears fortified with extraordinary style, elegance, charm, as well as potential, with the back centralmost section a plurisubharmonic function, or unlimited superior.

And yet each niche seems especially designed for the classics, for a study of Renaissance, as well as ancient Mediterranean culture, for a detailed study of "art, architecture, politics, science and literature, especially with a polymath yet moorgate index, a sponsor tag, that perspective, with a commercial break," and "a truly great progenitor" statue would normally sit in the middle of each, a founder, groupoid or abelian group, or more likely a rascal, troublemaker extraordinaire or, wait, a sacred psychonautic, according to western civilization, to tradition.

In addition, each niche stacks in a four high system. Then, the formation curves into a magnificent cerium-blue vaulted ceiling of unquestionable style.

However and of equal importance, these serpents keenly look for opportunity to spit something at anyone who would pass, spit a dense stream at the face, especially the eyes, spit a sagacious stream of truth, a permeation, a fix, the soul of a StreamSQL literary wit, again and again.

And it does so as a ghastly lesson, to create misfortune, cringe and ugly struggle, as a prophetic lesson to a person or system that refuses to honor signs and personal space, for instance the greedy, narrow-minded, common thug or well-educated version, with an insatiable search for beauty and treasure, such as to covet thy neighbor and community with a variety of ways and means, with an excuse, any excuse to justify. For example, act under a bold and colorful banner of God, nation, business, tribe, team, family or freedom of a supreme me, such as me-me-me, with another system to end all other systems, or a grab for principle's sake, to make a point, or an exceedingly stubborn point, of the prickly me, which should send a message to everyone of mine-mine-mine: the dominant aspects of life?

Again, something stirs and quickly recedes further into this room then the next chthonic passageway.

However, a closer look inside the bunker reveals an occasional item interspersed here and there—freakish items, truly freakish, things that would shock the mind.

Meanwhile, this underground forest passageway continues and leads through one heavily fortified bunker after another. Where, content varies and have Renaissance architectural features and items of spectacular style, beauty, elegance, and things associated with discreet and impeccable taste, as well as an unquestionable understanding of art, especially aesthetics according to the ancient Greek term *askēsis*.

However, further into this bunker system, there is an increased amount of content that seems bizarre—very—and as if a strange microcosm of curiosities.

And those things have another world aspect, as well as primordial, yet universal, and some of these aspects maybe alive, maybe creatures and somehow related to humans, just a bit, as in barely, and as if progenitor things, which on the whole gives an overall impression of missing links, of fundamental building blocks from the great philologic scripts, from that vast potential, and well before the age of the super apes and aquatic apes, of evolutional links much further back in time, and those major junctions of alternate biological links, scripts and solutions, yet tampered versions, what-if experiments.

So much so, and further along, the walls and vault ceiling contain dense layers of *Wunderkammer*.

They resemble a Leverian *façade* style, as dense mounted cabinets of mystery, of microcosms within microcosms, or categories and degrees of existence, of crucial stages and craft from certain universal, as well as biological theater, or put another way, devices, tools, agents, Accumulo NoSQL hylomorphisms, hirelings, pawns, spark reserves, as well as a few creepy industrialized sagacious wits who resemble an ecstatic scop or sage, and who use a certain sly as well as malicious propaganda, to insert rot, as a professional political panderer, a deception specialist.

However, a considerable number of things seem transhuman or posthuman, with colorful, irresistible and creepy gravitas, such as slowly back away from them, no sudden moves, and some use Fluorinert, as an experimental liquid breathing system and coolant based on stable fluorocarbon fluid.

Of equal importance, the overall impression consists mostly of things gone wrong, very wrong, especially from experimentation directed by a very wealthy symposiarch or consortium of ultimate insiders who manage one of the nearly one hundred major or minor elite black sites and projects worldwide, and nearly all heavily compartmentalized with ultrasecrecy, especially above and within, and compartmentalized from scrutiny except by a small group at best, which has advantages and not, such as considerable communication problems, from paranoia that often tightly grips without rhythm or reason, grips an idea, or people, places, and things, especially beyond, such as the "back of beyond," or better yet the backstory, or background, foreground, side ground, and post ground property rights, as well as the history of ideas, that infiltration technique. Well, as everyone remains a suspect and should remain ever so vigilant, yet this style has limits, a huge blind side, and lacks a vital something. Because all systems have weaknesses, yet paranoia tends to arrest comprehensive peer reviewable efforts, as well as moderation, and it creates one ever so narrow tunnel after another, with fear as the walls, as containment, reinforcement? And amnesia grows, such as about the comprehensive history of this style, which leads where, to a promised land, to paradise, to a golden age of tranquility, or a small niche among turmoil?

Paranoia polarizes and creates enormous pressure, the blind side, jurisdictional expansion, and obsessive competition to a fault, such as often against the self, that daily systematic grind. Or imagine an ouroboros attacks itself, that form of escalation, as an endless cycle.

Regardless, the end results in these bunkers resemble truly great attempts, yet somehow ultimately translate into an amateur in search of a quick profit, a race to the bottom, a devolution, and a system obsessively tinkering with things, as well as ignoring the fundamental rules of nature, system, symmetry, symbiosis, "set and setting," and to trip, really trip, into a theater of the truly absurd.

This process often occurs in a system that favors yes-men and women, groupthink, and quick agreement with the alpha, or else, or a process hijacked by the need for speed and compliance with the rut, with a system that often methodically runs off a truth-telling sage, advisor then good shepherd, and eventually a wasteland elder?

Free enterprise does great things. In fact, it does truly great things; however, what happens if you remove critical checks and balances, those pesky things, you know, such as real oversight, fresh air, proper sunlight, and instead rely on substitutes, such as forced air, artificial things and symbolic regulation, or oversight by proxies of the self, the insiders, the usual crowd, the ultimate class of insiders who thoroughly and seamlessly rotate between strategic seats of power?

Sometimes a truly great experiment goes wrong—quite. As the system creates a freak, an affront to nature, it creates a gross mockery of natural law, such as an extraordinary freak that resembles a truly sick abomination, a dystopian, yet a creature or thing ahead of the curve, the learning curve, a "curve of fastest ascent," a brachistochrone deixis into the next k-wave plus, and far beyond foresight, and before the system fully realizes the full potential, implication, and sudden impact.

What happens when a creation controls the creator and not vice versa, a situational irony? Where obsessive people ignore the fundamental principles of nature and create a person, place or thing, create a system and entertainment so advanced, complex, compelling and ever changing that it becomes the master, and the science of a truly powerful master, yet a far more complex Orwellian variation of Voyager, *The Thaw.* Where the caretaker, institution or too-big-to-fail system gives us what we want: real entertainment, as well as a compelling and gripping drama with tremendous danger, especially with a mission creep dilemma, such a complex twist or underline twist of separation, and abandon ship, abandon ship!

However, and more importantly, it often creates a Hobbesian trap?

And in search of an enemy, cast the widest possible net in all directions, that escalation technique, and it treats nearly all as suspects, many as third class citizens, such as an entire network of family, friend, tribe, team, employer, town, politic, culture, religion, race, gender or other social constructs, or worse yet, treats them as a thing or an "it," or as a cash cow, inside a rut.

Then the system truly shocks, when a percent of them radicalize from treatment, from enormous pressure and become the enemy, which seems a lesson rarely learned through history.

Enterprise does great things. It does truly great things.

However, in that rush to gain tremendous treasure, a certain dilemma exists when tinkering—and tinkering according to that classic definition, especially on vital systems, fundamental building blocks, and components, as the experimental process— produces a considerable amount of waste and "whatnot."

And this story is about a certain "whatnot," as well as the great biological mystery, and untranslatability functions of nature, beyond all language, often underappreciated by a person, system or set of, in search of a golden age, the next K-wave. And in this case, it results in "dangerously engaging" and "to guard against being sucked into mind games," especially the ultimate mind game, or game theory, of obsession, escalation, paranoia, and purity, a quandary, catch-22, Cornelian dilemma, or Pyrrhic victory-based system, compared to a golden age of peace, prosperity, and tranquility.

✓ PART 2

In another underground room something stirs, and quickly recedes into the next chthonic passageway.

And that passage leads through patches of vapor here and there—fog if you will, yet profoundly hallucinogenic, as well as delphic—then leads past one abrupt raw savage warning and bizarre mystery after another, then through more fortified bunkers all with a mobile portion, and places filled with special experimental attempts, which, well, might truly disturb people.

In fact it might spark bitterness, discord, real criticism and call for a revolution, the type that shouts at the devil or some other equivalent, then lumps all enterprise into a single category, the other.

As a small percent of any population can tarnish an entire industry, government, religion, culture, subset or tribe, because, well, of impossible standards, perfection, or the use of a justification to justify a bias or more, and it is as if most people lack event curiosity to weigh facts, to explore context as well as implications before a definitive blurt. Or, they have been trained as such, on cue, to blurt a slogan, especially a definitive judgment with considerable implications, such as quickly agree to a long term contract, a tether, and that type of shallow memory, mindset and impulse. Or likely, it represents a system conditioning technique, or a stage of life, when a person does not understand subtle things, as well as objective, practical, context, and abstract, those pesky and complex things an average person past the juvenile stage should know quite well.

Regardless, and further along that passage, more bunkers show dense collections of *Wunderkammer* and Leverian that have very complex facades, as well as mounted curiosity cabinets that resemble microcosms within microcosms, worlds within worlds, as in categories and degrees of things gone wrong, very wrong.

And the onlooker would receive an initial thrill, sense of wonder, euphoria and willingness to offer a signature, yet a closer inspection reveals something else—something.

As these things seem so surreal, disjointed, bizarre, lack logic and sanity in one grotesque gallery after another, in real stages of monstrosities, as well as very detailed world within other worlds, and when pure is not good, which gives the full impression of dreamlike, nightmare-inducing then high-octane nightmare fuel, of survival horror, yet not quite Lovecraftian or *Tome of Eldritch*, and based on the science of things not meant to be, or known, at least not this way.

This place represents the distant future, before people can truly grasp the full implications.

Meanwhile, the underground passageway leads to more occasional patches of dense indoor clouds that resemble an experimental Delphic-Bayesian game theory process that hang here and there at various levels, with some very low to the ground, others at medium and ceiling height, and some merge with the wall, as if half inside solid reinforced concrete.

All seem to generate a vivid hallucinogenic effect, as if a Rayleigh wave hierarchy problem based on proximity, or some other process.

Such as, the effect seems to have all those traits and processes that might explain an ocean wave, waves in general, a "Kelvin–Helmholtz instability, Numerical simulation of a temporal Kelvin–Helmholtz instability, Glossary of surfing," yes, of actual surfing as well as what might apply to other states or study fields, yet no water in site, none in the bunker. Plus many of the effects seem hidden from direct view.

And just as importantly these clouds appear quite individual in their own right, as they crackle and spark additive regression kernels.

Moreover, their pace to fathom varies from cool and calm to deliberate insane fury, which tests boundaries of universal law and system theory, as if the universe was a bulkhead or has a series of bulkheads or stack of bulkheads that form a metaverse, or a multiverse, or blank verse, with far more features than transverse and longitude supports, and more than walls within a ship hull or fuselage, those partition elements.

Whereas ones that merge with the wall, half inside solid reinforced Roman hydraulic concrete over eight feet thick, *opus caementicium*, they quietly fathom the insides of sold matter and compare to *De architectura*, and they treat space as a thing, even empty space, such as a vacuum.

And all of these clouds do so as a person might manipulate subspace, the physics, which seems very dangerous and unsettling. Yet, it is as if each of these clouds might be a well-seasoned wit, nonetheless as a juvenile deliberately test the limits, such as "Don't you tell me no truths, I want all of your lies," your algebraic lies, and the history of manifolds, in search of special exceptions within universal law, a search for loopholes, for a technicality compared to "spirit of the law," or done as a protest, with a variety of protest methods, apparently to puncture the great universal fabric, for what "sweet lies?"

And yet it is done as an artist might, with a certain bold style, and each cloud attempts to gain a competitive advantage over the other, which gives the full impression of a very dangerous competition, an obsession, such as when pure is not good.

Soon the underground passageway leads through another series of fortified mobile bunkers that resemble command centers with a sophisticated ultrafuturistic steampunk style, an ultimate retro yet industrial futurism with all those fine details that pays high honor and glory to the golden age of diesel and steampunk, yet the enviable new-age version, as in it was just a matter of time.

However, a closer bunker inspection gives the full impression of maps that could change the world. As some have real-time aspects of map-based controllers, and things associated with control engineering, with guide open source higher-order functions that relate to the theory of categories and exceptions, and all seem more advance than Defense Advanced Research Projects Agency (DARPA), Darktrace, Homeland Security Advanced Research Projects Agency (HSARPA), Intelligence Advanced Research Projects Activity (IARPA), Defence Research and Development Canada, Tekes—the Finnish Funding Agency for Technology and Innovation, as well as Defence Science and Technology Organization, Defence Science and Technology Laboratory, Defence Research and Development Organisation, Defence Science and Technology Organisation, in addition to a few others.

In fact, bunker computer monitors show real-time updates of ultrasecret worldwide projects, show inside their exclusive research laboratories, and done so to maintain the underground system's fifty-year lead, ahead of nation-state efforts, as collectively these projects reveal more than enough.

Beyond that, other fortified mobile command bunkers contain banks of computer systems that monitor other events, and most seem to track a metagame: a grand strategic system against shrewd animals, as in a robust netcentric yet very cold war, and what one expects in truly unconventional and asymmetric warfare, especially the psychological warfare of economics, which focuses on frequent use of thrownness, phase transition, smooth seam management, emergence, swarm behavior, spontaneous symmetry breaks, convection cells, and real-time stochastic calculus.

Moreover, these themes appear on various screens and show "econometric indexes by time series" of the long game, or put another way, differential games, such as the continuous pursuit and evasion, and the play of one game develops the rules for another game, which show as complex nested local and worldwide clusters.

In addition, the screens show each mission, design, function, content, timing, and so forth, such as insider strategy guides, walkthroughs, first mover advantage efforts, as well as prospector techniques.

Most importantly, all of these convey the full impression of a world power, a true superpower, a great sovereign state of unparalleled influence on a global scale, and several advanced stages beyond that classic definition, and more than capable of mutual assured destruction.

Moments later, this bunker system deploys more elaborate short and long games, and does so with one ever so smooth technique after another, not fixated or obsessed, such as on the last war or two, stuck in history, in an aspect of a trouble tree, niche or bubble, and that crude form of escalation, to bang the drum, the bandwagon effect.

And this underground system does not resemble remnants of a great modern or medieval power, a fading glory, to wither from trivial pursuit, to deliberately weaken one vital branch after another, or put another way, one petty pursuit after another, or put another way, add one layer after another of snarl, and all created by an ever so small mind with no vital memory, which represents the hallmark of the human species, a narrow conceptual schema or framework to maneuver in an ever so tight mindset, such as with two-dimensional thought, as well as fit the results on a bumper sticker. Then have a classic thug promote, or mob, or just as often, as the cottage industry of fear, or franchise or a transnational model, to serve as the core economic driver, the upsize that reduces the ability to think, with so many contradictions that draw considerable limits on four-dimensional thought, both obvious and subtle.

And when did "moderation" become a filth word, with no real interest in a true peer reviewable system?

This underground system appears to rely on something other than shortcuts, other than metaheuristic or a new version of *Ars Conjectandi,* Machiavelli products, or some other construct sold as the new normal, to retain power, such as sell a great ugly as vital, in the sense that they are not monarchies yet have a similar technique or two, such as authoritarianism with a cruel method or two, and the art of conflicting principles, said "absolutely necessary" by a noble or carnival barkers, and shortcuts that ironically make a mission more difficult, from a hasty leap to another branch with costly judgment, from reinventing something for the umpteenth time, a human as well as nature, and reliance on the "shallow game," and dereistic, then another hyper metanarrative leap, into the irony of a self-made trap, another quagmire, or same-old, same-old, and often as if a cult, yes, which causes any given system to lose truly great function, mission, voyage, depth, heroes, heroines, especially victims and collateral damage: not that reliance style, not those techniques.

Of equal importance, this "black site" seems to represent a master–slave relationship, or the "drug-to-drug-addict pattern," such as the saying, "Take everything that isn't nailed down, and if it is, check for loose nails or boards," which has mutual cost benefits, and that same true love–hate relationship, with the highest degree of denial at the core, by black site founders who now seem caught in a very quiet cold war with this site, about the last war or two, about founder attempts to deploy proxies worldwide into someone else's dream, and how do you control every dream?

Again, the conflict remains quite cold, as a discreet family thing among ultimate insiders that manage nearly one hundred elite black sites and black projects that often seriously compete against one another, often with bare knuckles, and these projects take on a life of their own, as well as never fully register on the secret accounting books, just appear as a vague category or title, and frequently in a way that might earn a doublespeak, doublethink or a convoluted award, as nearly all of these projects function well below media radar, and the masses.

Aside from that, much of the turmoil in any given system seems based on one manufactured insider crisis after another, by whoever has the skill to conduct a campaign—well, to stir "pent-up mass frustration," create buzz, then focus on a target, frequently rush to the wrong target, that technique, such as to sell "a small ugly or an audacious one," to move a stock price, block a competitor, or sacrifice a generation.

Most of which translate into another revolution, and what feels an endless series of, such as quick and easy to start, yet eventually expensive and time-consuming to resolve.

Meanwhile, that fortified command center bunker tracks dozens of meetings worldwide, which includes a variety of people, innermost circles and coalitions, such as politicians and shadow cabinets, as well as key principal advisors to the president, the United States Global Leadership Coalition, northern K Street members, political action committees and top politico hangouts, also slush funds, corporate interlocks, industrialists, various foundations and federal advisory committees, especially shrewd political animals, the dangerous ones who pull people and systems into very complex mind games, yes, and have the ability to quickly gather sympathizers, also known as groupies, and people prone to shortcuts, to the bandwagon effect, and forty or more cognitive biases, those other systems.

The system also tracks special meetings in other locations, which include hedge fund managers, venture capitalists and bankers, as well as Wall Street quantitative analysts, digeratis, data brokers, as well as elite members of the Russell Aldwych Groups, League of European Research Universities, a few self-confident Sloane Rangers and exceptional meetings in Oslo, Stockholm, Copenhagen, Brussels, Vienna, Prague, Amsterdam, Neuilly sur Seine, Saint Cloud, as well as Strasbourg, Budapest, Madrid, Ingolstadt, Chur, Zurich, Ravensburg, Augsburg, and certain vital aristocrats.

And these bunker systems track informatics of each participant, which includes vital signs like pulse, blood pressure, distribution of body temperature, respiration, weight, as well as ratio of water, fat, and bone.

Apparently it gathers most data from the "internet backbones," also called "principal data routes" managed by commercial, government, academic and other high-capacity network centers, as well as from cell phones and wearable technology traffic, from 24/7 broadcast streams, and relays, such as pride before the fall.

Well, because data systems naturally leak, and most deliberately so, which results in a complex leaky abstraction with profound problematic implications.

Here and now, the bunker systems also show a very precise history of meeting members, show fully "indexed in compendiums" of family, friends, social networks, web browsing cookies, history of cell phone GPS movements, credit card activities, foods purchased with a supermarket discount card, as well as habits, tendencies, mannerisms, tells, likes, dislikes, viewpoints, and other personality traits, vices, virtues, self-perceptions, goals, books read, accomplishments, career, and hobbies, writings, speeches, Freudian quips, credit histories, debt-to-worth ratios, in addition to liquidities, such as a liquid machine states.

It tracks what internet providers, businesses and governments really want from you, a longer term contract regardless of their performance, as well as your informatics in relationship to every possible situation, to people, organizations, locations, conditions, times, sequences, purposes, causes, effects, results, and historical contexts, a comprehensive index of compendiums, a big brother implication, and made easier by credit- as well as debit-based societies, together with cookies, or equivalent, and less real money in circulation, less cash.

All the while, real-time data updates neatly scroll on numerous screens and shows a complex web of a metagame, a grand strategic system and differential game of continuous pursuit and evasion, so the play of one game develops the rules for another game.

Other bunker terminals track the invisible internet, that vast World Wide Web, the main system tree, as well as all those roots and branches that extend, especially activity not visible with traditional web search engines, such as Google, Baidu, Yahoo, Bing, Excite, or Ask, those shown by the internet provider, business and government, with their commercial, economic, and political interest, and what they want you to see, the world, see their worldview, and believe, really believe.

Just as importantly, terminals track those who trigger a major rollback event then removal of insider privilege, that competitive chase, the "competitive exclusion principle" in action, and all those laws and rules, many designed to block a competitor with so many barriers, with entanglements. And the vast majority of people or things might never know; all those rules, laws, and exceptions, with so many wait-on-a-branch techniques, wait in the poorhouse, or in a competitive chase, to find a branch, one sustainable as well as vital. And yet the whole complex process has "a certain" flatness, each worldview. Or, each seems as if a faithfully flat scheme, cohomology, that treats people as if generic property, in a process that demands a faithfully flat fundamental descent that fades into a sober yet ever so complex reality of stuck again, in another quagmire?

Also, another underground bunker system tracks financial markets, especially liquidity in regular, grey, dark and black pools, which stream private security trades not shown to the public, and not through public stock exchanges, as it shows effort to hide by the elite "a-list," by ultimate insiders, such as vital players, families and institutions.

The system shows context as well as real-time insider ways and means, as well as how they secretly communicate.

Another system monitors creeds for sale.

Another one tracks key individuals and systems that create and maintain each vital storyline, each event bubble, bubble physics, as life inside each has a certain dynamics, as well as techniques to sustain, and it tracks how each relates to one another, those dynamics, especially the universe, the ultimate bubble expansion.

Still another underground bunker has a mobile portion that gives the full impression of a directorate that projects a sphere of influence and control inside the forest as it deploys bait in various complex pits and snares, as well as torment of shadow, substance, and other wiles.

As well, some of these bunker systems show far-reaching ability to carefully deliver measured influence overseas, with an exceptional ability to smoothly enter the ways and means of institutional machinery.

In addition, it shows the underground system's ability to quickly buy and sell subtle as well as obvious things, and insert rumor or expose a closely guarded secret, to spark immediate notice and action by government and commercial interest, which includes the media, and especially vigilant outsiders. Or is the word "vigilante," or the Italian word *vigilia,* or "eve of war?"

Moments later, something else happens.

A partial view shows the person or thing known as a Punk Buster.

CHAPTER 4

This creature or thing goes by others names—the Freak, the Psychonautic—and has a certain imperial quality of power and glory, as well as that of an ever so sly trickster, and it takes deep breaths, which seem not quite a Vader breathing style, yet the inhale, hold and exhale have powerful and distinct stages from the back.

It represents the ultimate new-age show of shows, very natural and yet quite artificial, born of borrowed materials and artificially manufactured haste, to generate opportunities and vast fortune.

As the creator sought a decisive victory from obsessively tinkering with things, as well as ignoring the fundamental rules of nature, system, symmetry, symbiosis, "set and setting," as in the term to trip, really trip, trip into a theater of the truly absurd.

This thing or creature sits partially obscured on a throne, a place that gives the full impression of unquestionable glory, with the imperial quality of Napoleon as well as the Imperial Senate throne of Pedro II of Brazil and a secular version of the superstructure and glory behind the chair of Saint Peter in Saint Peter's Basilica, Rome, similar to that golden luminous event of mega, yet a fully functional secular system, as well as with exceptional aesthetics, which that deploys the science of a supreme technocracy, and all that greatness of innovation, of scientism, with a universal applicability of the scientific method.

Of equal importance, this throne gives the full impression of an official residence, yet fortified crown, which seems alive, though not in that classic sense of life, not a carbon-based life form. As carbon represents the key component within all known life on Earth, natural life that is, and yet the throne has a human aspect, as if an evolutionary extension of the mind. Such as the way something might eventually overcome primitive brain structural disadvantages, of originating from a savage species, *ferae naturae*, that primitive structural baggage legacy, as well as that biota coalition within an empire of self; the skittish, jealous, and pettifog beings within, which often impulse a bitter shout at one minor problem after another, or shout at the devil, or some other cultural equivalent, often as a distraction because of procrastination regarding the near and dear issues of self, or a devil created for profit, for employment purposes, yes, for the self, such as a make work program, or a public or private works program, "a shovel-ready project," or to prop up an industry or entire economy. For instance, shout at the cash cows for lack of a better phrase, or monthly income, and often shout at the new-age indentured servants in this brave new world, shout at this stark, cruel and miserable expanse of people in poverty, such as a modern version of the poorhouse, shout at those most vulnerable who greatly suffer.

In addition, this throne shows each new major developmental stage of mind and soul, beyond those traditional brain components, beyond the medulla, pons, cerebellum, midbrain, diencephalon, and beyond the telencephalon expanse, that last great effort, that major system distortion, as if an overgrowth, a bulge, opportunity, port and physical transport layer, as well as the implications of what the telencephalon expanse system will and will not allow, as compared to what another brain aspects might offer if allowed that same opportunity, of a great transformation.

In addition, this throne shows each new brain component expansion and supplements, the what if, as well as beyond those organic devices and natural barriers, to create a large, fortified, detachable aspect of the body, mind and soul within a mobile bunker, all of which give the appearance of tools, which that support extraordinary encephalization quotient and query skills of a resourceful, penetrating, and definitive wit, as implied in *The Nth Degree, Star Trek, The Next Generation* with Lt. Reginald Barclay, though this represents no holographic interface.

It resembles a deep state, in fact a state within the state, as well as shadow governments, yet with brilliant separation of true powers, not a symbolic separation, not a seamless ability to infiltrate and alter a state, or insert proxies, insert cross sight (site) scripting to capture vitals, or insert a proxy-applied filter, copy, redirect, or command for an unconditional surrender with no guarantees, none, as it is not a symbolic check and balance system, as it has no instruments of surrender.

Yet it has the ability to deep-data-dive into foreign systems, into what matters most, into their dreams, into the contemplative tree, belief network, approach techniques and tendencies, for a full exploration, such as into their mindset, schema, and rubric, which also allows the stealing of user credentials, gaining elevated special privileges, establishing command-and-control communications, and moving laterally within an organization, for example branch to branch, that scan ability for options and weaknesses, to power-shell-dive into any given system aspect, well, as a senior executive might, to locate bias and structural defects, to locate token bloat, bloatware, code bloat, or other system bloater forms, or tendencies to chase red herring, or a cat that chases flicker, a phantom.

Or, dive as an executive to search for problems, for Parkinson's Law, or the psake disadvantages, or to find the maximum number of options, including the prospect of a bold system adjustment, such as steer into or out of a quagmire, which requires an active script engine audit that represents no small feat. As a system has certain momentum and resistance to change. In addition, it often has an impulse, of all in, to double down and add another lay on top of other layers, add another construct, such as social construct, other snarl, because if one is good, then two, or better yet, ten, must be great, so the classic "tangled up in blue(s)"?

And of equal importance, from one angle after another this throne has a compelling look, of the most complex being ever, a supreme technocracy, though not carbon-based, not that classic signature of life, not those traditional biogenic substances, and yet it shows a symbiosis, a persistent biological interaction, which maybe mutualistic, commensalistic or parasitic, or something quite different, such as a series of evolutionary updates, and the way it was supposed to evolve before all those evolutionary tendencies, such as from self-created petty distractions, of attacking versions of the self, the others, and done so with such certainty.

However, a closer look reveals an embedded biological component here and there, possibly beings built into the structure, some half inside, some wedged in ever so tight claustrophobic space, some serve as a filter, and they do not resemble ordinary creatures, but some represent unusual category of being, and not a common ratiocination groupoid or abelian group.

Regardless, this throne gives the full impression of effective capital, certain personal privileges and unquestionable glory of a distinguished territorial warlord with a fifty years' lead.

And it has other distinct structural features, which include niches, and each with a world-within-a-world look, those progressions, dozens of them that concave towards the center, as if a farm system, some with a web farm aspect, and each a specialized function, as distinct brain evolutionary expansions, as well as of complex tools and systems, some with whispery bits, and the entire structure has complex atmospherics, which that often crackle and pop as if additive regression kernels.

In addition, each major system segment seems designed to resolve strategic command and control aspects, especially over crude primitive brain functions and impulses—for instance, step on an ant and really mash it, or systematically eliminate the competition, the others, and instead sees them as part of the great quintessential stack, the totality of the universe, whether extinct or current, as localized solutions, and sees them as part of the garden, the farm system: that great dilemma, such as a weed might ultimately represent great opportunity.

Although, and in general, the forest system seems to prefer a specialized feeble, to enfeeble an intruder or sponsor, reduce him or her to a mumble, such as a person or organization that would mostly sit and drool in one form or another, then once in a while have a wild-eyed-fully-animated notion, yet cannot articulate a clear line of effort, and that effort contains very active and colorful delirium, of gestic hallucinations, delusions, disorganizations and confusions about preposition, postposition and circumposition, then the articulation slows to muddled speech, about very complex content, about the next great Zeitgeist or major breakthrough, such as a major mystery, an unsolved problem in physics, mathematics, chemistry, biology, medicine, or about Ludwig Wittgenstein notebooks, or third culture kid, equilibrium types or leaky abstractions. Then as the vital revelation nears, that person reaches a great mental barrier, realizes it then rants with delirium at the wilderness, at the frontier, and that person seems trapped in that endless cycle, of a person kept as a garden vegetable, a trial garden, or much worst.

And this bunker system seems less concerned with retaliation, the wild type, the feud dynamics of escalation, the petty, pettifog of conflict, or worst yet, pleasure from pain, from others that suffer, that crisscross, that mutation, and cackle at severe damage, or just as significantly, indifference, especially to collateral damage, and no idea about the fuss, all of which have a wavelike effect, a ripple.

And equal importance, something circulates between each distinct throne segments, those worlds.

Of which, it gives the full impression of a multiphase liquid, a coolant or highly oxygenated Fluorinert or a similar substance, which may serve as respiration, or aspiration, as well as a system to deliver vital things, which might include sustenance, information, skillsets and descriptivisms, as in the theory of substances and names, and some of which deliver instructions to reduce the fog of war?

Also, a closer inspection of this chthonic throne reveals more distinct sections of depth, fine detail, and advanced technical superstrate exceptionalism, of glory, and none of the whatnot, none of the frivolous things associated with vanity, narcissism, vainglory or bling, or the seven deadly sins, often called capital vices or cardinal sins, included in the mnemonic acronym of SALIGIA.

Yet an even closer throne inspection reveals something else.

A crisis of the self, as certain system aspects require immediate action, something quick, such as an intervention about very particular internal situations, about an "exigent circumstance" here and there, emergency powers, which indicates a serious problem with this rapid evolutionary process, as certain aspects seem stuck in a phase, mid-phase, metaphase, or in the middle-between-phase, or from a phase-lock multibit.

As a result, some internal throne aspects now struggle to escape. And they try a compel underline twist of separation, at that classic dilemma of a bold new frontier, and choice of a natural versus artificial, of organic versus mechanistic, of a new distinct category of being and the next best phase, yet which schema, which fact–value distinction, the distinction between "can be discovered by science, philosophy, or reason, and "what ought to be discovered"?

Then more aspects of this throne, these worlds within worlds, this farm system, seems almost human—confused, disoriented, isolated then forsaken, and in a profound crisis—such as, will they survive from all this experimentation, from this new golden age of biological, chemical, material and subspace manipulation, especially from plastics, the consumption of, and how does a system digest plastics, and think about it, as they seem to circulate everywhere, particularly within the mind, body and soul?

So much so the bunker system undergoes a profound mortal suffering, and yet with a certain brilliant glory that seems universal, classic and profound, which radiates from it in a series of very particular expressions and compelling degrees, as if it sits at some fundamental threshold, at the very edge of existence.

Or, put another way, when a person or thing has a tremendous sense of alienation, as someone who barely survived a war still feels numb, and things around take on a pale, empty and surreal look, then personal demons, painful memories and regrets rush forward along with a full realization. They have become the other, become an it, and have entered the great unknown, that great frontier, and will face a true mystery, which often needs a familiar song, a classic aria, strophic, madrigal, or cue, or something that might resemble "Max Manus OST – 18" by Trond Bjerknes, which might add to the tremendous sense of isolation, and loneliness.

And this frontier problem exists in other areas, fields of studies, such as chemistry, and if a person examines the periodic table of elements with that natural progression of atomic structure, of preferences, and what things can become or not, a pattern exists. It goes from simple to complex, from hydrogen, helium, lithium, beryllium and so forth in a natural progression. Just as importantly, a person can predict the next step or stage, predict size, shape, weight, proportion, distinct energy signature and those complex details of bearing, of how it sits or travel in spacetime, as well as the significance, harmony and durable aspect under tremendous universal forces, especially the mostly hidden. Such as how does something properly sit, move, evolve and become fully realized in universal spacetime, and not drool, not leak, as if a nuclear drip line issue with a weak segment or two, and less concern about vital maintenance, then stumble and disintegrate for refusing to respect the laws of nature, respect the classics, the principle of universal culture with all those pesky checks and balances, which appear to be the price of admission into this great spectacular?

An idea, person, or system undergoes tremendous pressure at the threshold.

Or, put a third way, any given system, mind or idea should not venture into certain configurations, as they disrespect aspects of the universe, aspects of the great string, and a string with a vast number of line segments, such as people, place and thing?

As a result, a thug aspect or some other force will immediately savage, with a certain style and vigor, such as a "curb side stomp, going postal, or paint the town red," as if settling a legal dispute, zoning law and ordinance, as if only certain things may take place under very specific conditions, regardless of what history books say, regardless of those promotional documents. And to add more turmoil, human law often conflicts with natural law, or said another way, with physis, with natural rules, and as if in part, a human justification, a "justification of the state"?

So much so this chthonic throne, as well as being or thing, appears at that odd stage, at the border of a great threshold adventure, and many aspects of this throne and underground system seem in full crisis, as if at an enthalpy threshold, of an identity foreclosure, a critical phase transition during the great identity versus role crisis of the self, at that natural barrier with the mystery of various internal and external separations, as well as all those nuances, and where many things will not reconcile in conventional spacetime.

For instance, when an idea, philosophy, mission statement, party platform, war or system looks and sounds good in the beginning, because it seems attractive or vital, and has a certain gravitas, such as sugar, starch or yeast: however, the deployment represents a very tricky process, a true struggle—which takes on a life of its own, develops mission creep as well as a complex legacy, and requires a complicated process to keep it from bloat, from obsession, as well as distraction, from lack of focus, then sudden impact, and smithereens.

Just as importantly, a closer inspection of this underground system shows other things.

It shows a series of stress fractures, especially this throne and the Punk Buster, also known as the Freak.

Another significant point: both now lack a vital something in relationship to system stability, to endurantism, which better accommodates the theory of special relativity, specifically when any person, place, or thing, even enterprise, takes an idea then applies it to real-life conditions, to dynamics and scalability, the classic problem, those pesky things.

So much so, as well as here and now, that profound crisis spreads within, which resembles an intractable EXPTIME—hard balkanization, manorialism, feudalism, seigneuries, subinfeudation.

And something else happens: a great internal survey, stratified sampling, accidental sampling, and "the grab or power grab" among system aspects, with opportunistic sampling, as well as "dangerously sucked into" a "mind game," the "political mind," political animal, or "the quarterback sneak, a deception play for the ages," a fake team, or permanently embed surveillance, upstream, and intercepting communications at the backbone, and "no morsel too minuscule for all-consuming," just in case, well, because of mission drift and or feature creep, also known as bloat with "ad hoc, informally-specified, bug-ridden, slow implementation," and other unforeseen great adventures within the system, as well as nature, the mostly hidden.

Just as importantly, monitoring a vast numbers of internal throne evolution data points, as well as life beyond the forest, expends a considerable effort.

So much so, it creates tremendous stress within these internal throne containment barriers, in the supreme bulkhead, yet blank verse, which includes far more aspects than transverse and longitude supports, and more than walls within a ship hull or fuselage that partition elements.

In addition, this throne attempts to manipulate subspace, the physics, which seems a very dangerous, unsettling, and deliberate search for limits, as well as to resolve fundamental issues and locate special exceptions within universal law, a search for loopholes, for technicalities, compared to spirit of the law, as a true artist might, with a certain bold style and flair.

Such as to resolve frontier problems, it tests how to move space faster than the speed of light, which appears to have a considerable downside, even over very short distances within this system, such as 1,000th of an inch, cubit, or one yard, especially with distance versus directed distance as well as displacement, and the problem of protein unfolding in real time, as well as an even smaller scale problem of the Nambu–Goto action, a starting point of zero-thickness, of infinitely thin string behavior, and as a special particle sheet travels through spacetime, travels a fraction of an inch or further, such as eject it into ultradeep space: those problems, which could generate malicious internal activities and serious policy violations, such as when an idea seems fine of paper, however.

Moments later, as a human might, the entire throne shudders, and again, then it seems almost human—confused, disoriented, isolated then forsaken, and in a profound crisis from all that threshold experimentation, which produces a tremendous sense of alienation.

Then things around take on a pale, empty, surreal and ugly look, quite so, then personal demons, painful memories and regrets rush forward, along with a full realization that it has become the other; become subhuman, become a thing or an it.

And system aspects panic at that threshold, at that great precipice, that *nonesmanneslond*, then many internal aspects vie for full control over other aspects, as an all-powerful transnational might try to take over a nation-state, or a group of transnationals try to create a New World Order, as if a golden age of the transnational corporation, of how admirably law defines the term "prize," or simply put, how someone might describe a *coup d'état*, or is it just another *coup d'essai*, or more of a *coup de theatre*, as in *stratégie de la corde raide*, which uses a series of faints to provoke other underground system aspects, to overreach, such as the concept in English land law and Law of Property Act 1925, and to gain a decisive victory of one good shot—a third act.

Regardless of all that turmoil, and still partially obscured from full view, the Punk Buster detaches from the throne, from the collective mindstream, alterity and noble savage, from the golden ratio, as well as what could eventually become "the city on the edge of forever." And this detachment causes a considerable number of pressurized hoses to detach then vent various things, maybe atmospherics, plasma, or strange matter, a s*ui generis*, or maybe some new-age sustenance or whatnot, and all the while this thing or creature maintains a keen focus on something, on a system aspect that monitors Bonnie.

In fact it fixates on her, and not on all that turmoil, that *coup d'état* within the underground system, all that extreme confusion, commotion, agitation, polarization and threat of devolution, as well as threat of sudden destruction from internal strife.

Then the fixation translates into a fully absorbed mental loop of immense frustration, smolder, stare, agitation, indignation, spite and thoughts of a pernicious revenge against her.

Moments later, an aspect of the system formulates a very precise solution to Bonnie, the Mighty Sparrow, to a woman who refuses to surrender.

Such is life, as some people refuse to quit, refuse to surrender, and regardless of puzzle, pain and suffering, as well as frustration, want, lack, poverty, danger and fear of destruction.

CHAPTER 5

Outside the forest near a dazed Bonnie on one knee, the forest sign as well as a large old-growth beech tree, the dog notices something, rises, and keenly focuses on distant unseen forest activity, then her.

As a result, the head often tilts here and there to fathom.

Moreover, it waits for a command from her, a real command, a real mission, and a command said in the proper way, such as with that specialized stack protocol, or one MC full stack alert, or at least one from the prescribed reading list, from bookshelf one, two or three, because, well, earlier *she did read the dog tag, seems literate*, and *did not try to distract me with crispy bacon, with a cheap trick.*

However, humans as well as systems often seem a bit *peculiar*— okay, *weird*—and feel exempt from logic and reasonable, then justify. As they often devise an elaborate scenario, a figment in their mental dough, among grey and white fat, as if a distinct variation of state-bound art, or state-dependent memory, and a state-transition equation for *status quo* justification?

Moments later, the dog notices something, shifts demeanor, becomes quite serious then intense.

So much so it gradually edges to a more defensible position, a place more able to protect her then launch a counterattack, and if need be, an epic battle or all-out war, as the first few moments of any battle really matter?

For example, enter the stage in a proper manner, enter the proper venue according to correct terms, at just the right time, motion, and disposition, as well as enter and play the proper part of a continuous action yet discrete set, that mixed signal dilemma played proper, such as according to *Thirty-Six Strategies*, or better yet the dog thinks, *enter as proper art*, which truly represents a lost art form, especially life in general, as well as war as the very last option, a full declaration of war, and enter as a spellbinding event, a being beyond full comprehension, beyond the limits of ordinary experience, such as a Kantian, and act as if the higher calling, a noble being with an exceptional moral duty to the species, to the full outline of history, rather than as an emotional response and the same old story, such as retaliation, the wild type, the feud dynamics of escalation, the petty, pettifog of conflict, or worse yet, pleasure from pain, from others that suffer, that crisscross, and cackle at severe damage, or just as significantly show indifference, especially to collateral damage, and no idea why others fuss, so, if need be, do so as a proper: attack!

However, and with more consideration, it might not qualify as a lost art, for very important reasons. Because, and in general, many consumer-driven systems promote the opposite, with a mass-reach medium of television, as well as the internet. Because the system often campaigns for urgency, for a surge and grab, and does so with a very effective classic "three-time frequency formula," a tried and true system, and these endless series of massive reach-campaigns urge action and often conflict as a solution, and act in a very narrow window of opportunity, a surge, yet another lost opportunity, another lost paradise, so leap or first strike, that foundational style of thinking.

Just as importantly, the system often promotes a main state of mind and mental inertia, and the takeaway message early the next morning is "urgent"; another vital loss, not a state associated with cool and calm under enormous pressure, not positive, high-minded, reserved, balanced, especially the effectiveness of a MacGyver, with a clever understanding of the paradigm shift techniques, or evolution, or kludge, workaround, which often represents an ugly yet practical tool or device, such as a key-recovery advantage. And just as significantly, and much about, sits a tremendous amount of resources already available yet greatly underutilized, such as people, places, and things, which represents a trait of many K-waves, many super cycles, with a special form of inflation, an era of disposables, that form of considerable waste. However, and often, a new idea is needed, new formula, mindset, assumption or method, and often a forgotten one or skill, often mislaid or told to forget, especially during the great rush or obsession, that vacuum, such as forget the simple things, natural, and the vitals, a trace element, trace mineral or two, or biome, or moderation, a balanced approach, way of living, and respect the opposite, respect the symmetrical process, which that has a vital function, or a person could hop on one leg, one idea, philosophy, party platform, war or other system, which is possible: hop, as if who, and on what branch, a *Pinus sylvestris* tree or fingerling?

Just as importantly, enter the stage and battle with exceptional ways and means as if proper art, yet often not because of lack of fundamentals, and because of group think, life in a bubble and urgent need to leap, which was in fact a call for vital nutritional needs, from a starving foundation, from a neglected infrastructure, so a misdirection?

Does proper art represent a greatly underutilized system, with the ability to invoke a state of esthetic arrest, and not the popular usage of arrest, of "Bad boys, bad boys, What'cha gonna do? What'cha gonna do when they come for you," or some other compelling commercial hook, often a hook down, yet some are dragged up for whatever reason, such as an exception, a troublemaker extraordinaire, a genuine rascal of the highest order, wholly unredeemable, and kept afloat then pulled to the top by complex legacy rules, by a scheme or two, quite possibly by a DNA version or scheme-theoretic image thought better universal property. Or put another way, they have the right friend, family, tribe, team, employer, politic, culture, religion, race, gender, or other social construct, or something else, such as a timeless look, golden smile or style, which should lead to a promise land, because style matters—it really matters?

Because, proper refers to the great mystery of equilibrium, of being well-organized.

Proper art represents neither the urge towards nor away from that subject, but instead appears to transfix, mesmerize, or arrest by the sight. In addition, it holds the full attention, and if done quite well, even for those with attention-deficit hyperactivity disorder or "urge to surge," from hormones of a prickly, twitchy, and wholly distracted self, from that classic surge of hormones, from that special biological brew, or crude hormone formula which has not significantly changed for thousands of years, maybe tens of thousands or more, and not updated for one reason or another, and hormones developed for a time, when a person might live to the ripe old age of fourteen. So, this formula had a practical and urgent function, yet every tool and device has a limited range of motion as well as effect, every construct, such as eicosanoids, steroids, amino acid derivatives, peptides and proteins, or "gimme-gimme-gimmie," or what eventually translates into "I must step on an ant." As that phase transition seems quite prone to distractions from a very special and time-tested primal formula of hormones with a few side effects, such as to spark one revolution after another, one meddlesome, petty, personal and insatiable conflict after another. Or a person could think of it as a one-dimensional high-wire act. Or put another way, it represents a crude formulated device that narrows a vast treasure of options into a simple mindset, which that seems to favor one snap decision after another with a dull wit, and it quickly narrows choice into a tight claustrophobic corridor, a place prone to impulse, panic, inflation and hyperbole, prone to surrender, escape or fight, and do it fast, to gain histaminic relief: life?

So, enter the stage or battle as that type of being, or enter the stage or battle with exceptional ways and means, such as if proper art?

Just as importantly, the dog sniffs her for these hormones then thinks, *Here we go again, another war,* and *life as a proxy. If only I had opposable thumbs I'd exit south, to a better life, to a pastoral haven, or a classic hippie haven, yes, or to Balearic Island, an idyll, yes, and live in an exceptional rustic poem under a "tree of contemplative practices" in the spring, and if lucky, lap a golden bock beer, yes, a heavy rich beer, in a big bowl, yes.*

Yet the dog knows limits, knows fact from fiction, and instead descends into a stalk mode line of effort, a low attack posture, and subtle adjustments of ready to launch in a split second with freakish speed, and then it launches with true savage fury, of teeth and pure rage, followed by an abrupt stop, which produces a cloud of dust and swirl, then the dog slowly edges back and returns to that initial low attack position—where it repeats the process of a pure savage attack to forewarn destruction.

And in the distant forest still not visible, death approaches. Moreover, it has a sublime, bizarre, and ruthless aspect, and it makes a distinct series of creepy sound combinations, which have some resemblance to a Soundsnap website, "Noise Warble Warp B," followed by twelve seconds of sounds not quite a cross between "Urban Creepy" and chaos.

It repeats, and some kind of thing rapidly moves through the forest then pass past that huge old-growth tree, the type of tree that seems to have a human aspect to it, and not in a conventional sense of body, mind and soul, but ineffable and primordial, as if a missing link, an unsettling one and yet familiar, even universal, and with hybrid aspects, which include traits associated with oak, peach, beech, hazel, ash, eucalyptus, willow, sycamore, almond, baobab and sandalwood, as well as acacia with thorny pods, shevaga, assattha, fig, kalpavriksha, thuja and yew, together with something a person might expect, near a well of souls, a hidden seep, as well as a seep-spring arnica here and there.

The tree also shows phase transitions—those seams, stages, miscibility gaps and degrees associated with liminal, with the structure of identity, time and common space, such as the axiomatic system, special sets and Cartesian products of both spatial and temporal dimensions concern the moment, period and epoch, and a new way of individuation, as well as aspects that seem constantly stuck or pinned to the here and now.

In addition, this tree has something else not easily quantifiable, for instance sections with matter that seems out of phase, as well as aspects that seem ambiguous and produce a considerable temporal thrownness, as well as disorientation, as if a mid-ritual event, and just after a person or thing exits the original state of identity, time and community; that threshold structure and process of a new way yet not easily quantifiable, and possibly an aspect of subspace, as in some integral part and nuisance location within spacetime; one distinct and yet coexistent with normal space, such as folded space? And from this vantage point, it seems quite difficult to determine the actual processes as well as functions.

Regardless, some tree branches contain what appear as night-flowering jasmine, grape clusters, as well as bonsai attachments, phylogenetic catalysts, and other plants attach in some form of symbiosis, a set of persistent biological interactions maybe mutualistic, commensalistic, parasitic or something else, and yet they all resemble a stockpile of scripts, a series of microcosms or communities, such as community organizations, agents, yes, as if a garden yet theater, which includes an empty set, seat or station to not go beyond, ever.

However, a closer inspection reveals what might represent a heavily fortified vacant station, station port, reference stream, reference point indentation, permanent dwell, and a place for demarcation transactions, for start and end transaction that uses begin, commit, and rollback methods, if need be, such as roll back time, as well as space.

In addition, this tree sits squarely with the four cardinal directions, as if a boxing-the-compass-device.

The tree also shows certain structural and territorial integrity, with a separation of powers, and one side has a well-field schema, altered state, another way or artistic backstory, maybe a mixed selection of, which translates on entrance into this field, as if a complex bilateral language function and tonal adjustment, a prosodic translation, a simultaneous function, and just outside that field a tremendous form of facticity or thrownness.

Just as importantly, that creature or thing with a sublime, bizarre and ruthless aspect plows pass the tree, and does so with certain power and tremendous might, as well as makes a distinct series of creepy sound combinations, which has some resemblance to a Soundsnap website, "Noise Warble Warp B," followed by twelve seconds of sounds not quite a cross between "Urban Creepy" and chaos, which repeat.

However and moments later, it disappears underground.

In fact, things grow quiet then serene.

Just as importantly, nothing moves whatsoever.

Which reveals another strange phenomenon: no insects, none, and how is that possible; no bugs, no annoying insects that pester, and just as significantly, not one foraging bird, rabbit, squirrel or chipmunk that roots among crisp leaves and twigs?

Nonetheless, the dog continues with that restless demeanor, which shifts from serious to intense.

Enough so the dog gradually edges to a more defensible position, and a place more able to protect her and launch a counterattack, and if need be an epic battle or all-out war, or better yet, do so as proper art.

Moments later, it descends into a stalk mode line of effort, a low attack posture, and subtle adjustments of ready to launch in a split second, and with freakish speed, and then it launches with true savage fury, of teeth and pure rage, followed by an abrupt stop, which produces a cloud of dust and swirl, then the dog slowly edges back and returns to that initial low attack position. Where, it repeats the process of a pure savage attack to forewarn utter destruction.

On occasion, the dog carefully studies her unusual behavior, of still barely on one knee yet in a special thought technique, an algebraic technique, to solve the unknown, to unify broken parts.

So much so it puzzles with each and every aspect then eventually turns back towards the forest and descends into a stalk mode line of effort, a low attack posture, and subtle adjustments of ready to launch in a split second, and with freakish speed, and then it launches with true savage fury of teeth and pure rage, followed by an abrupt stop, which produces a cloud of dust and swirl, then the dog slowly edges back and returns to that initial low attack position. Where, it repeats the process of a pure savage attack to forewarn utter destruction.

Moments later, from the south, a massive 1,000-pound brown bear arrives; then one from the north and another emerges at the center. They close possible escape routes, which she fails to notice.

Just as importantly, they harass the dog and Bonnie with malicious snarls and huffs, as well as repeated ground gouges.

So much so the actions rip out large clumps of grass, dirt and rubble, which cause a considerable dust cloud to rise and roll.

Next they edge closer to within killing distance, then collectively roar, which has a deafening effect that eventually causes Bonnie, still barely on one knee, and near an old-growth beech tree, to finally snap out of that deep state, out of that special thought technique, an algebraic, to solve the unknown, to unify broken parts.

And she focuses on current events, which feel quite familiar yet different, as if in a temporal loop, where events repeat in a distinct circuit, a circuit-depth complexity, and yet a few aspects change, such as depth then the normal sequence of events, which are not correctly linked, as if someone, thing, or it has tampered with the timeline, "yes," or tampered with her mind, for example her thalamus, or the universe, such as the master clock or fabric, and as if empty space represents a thing, even once if everything is removed.

And it catches her by surprise; as well, those deafening roars shock the flesh and marrow, the hematopoietic stem cells, the type of roar that causes a person to instantly lose a few years of life, just like that, gone.

Then, one tremendous roar after another blasts away a few more years of her life, bit by bit, and wherever vitality goes, as well as the temporal savings account.

And this process blasts away any remaining charm, wit, dignity, quirk and winsomeness, as well as other indexes of character, such as intangibles, reserves and whatnot, and even aspects of her vast subconscious stockpile disintegrates, bit by bit then one substrate, current, eddy, and long forgotten biological niche after another.

All the while these bears drip thick white foam from the mouth onto jaw, fur and ground. All of which gives the full impression of, well, a truly disgusting sight, and yet it was the least of her concerns.

During all these her eyes widen, very much so.

In addition, the mouth forms an "Oh!" position, as in an "Oh, my God!" yet the petrification process does not allow a complete thought or statement.

Then, three more massive bears emerge from the forest, for a total of six, or put another way, a certain productive group number of equilibrium, of symbolic completeness, and not quite the crossover trial on the sixth hour, yet a secular event.

Then they move to block as many possible escape routes as possible, and all the while they harass both with a malicious air of menace and swipe.

Each time the dog maneuvers with a series of low attack postures, those subtle adjustments associated with a classic stalk mode, of ready to launch in a split second, and with freakish speed, and then it launches with a true savage fury of teeth and pure rage, followed by an abrupt stop, which produces a cloud of dust and swirl, then the dog slowly edges back and returns to that initial low attack position to defend her.

Then it repeats the process of a pure savage attack here and there.

Regardless, the bears edge closer, and closer, then taunt with a series of flinches, as a bully might, to taunt with a known advantage and torment the helpless with threat, coercion, abuse and sheer intimidation, what a person might expect from an authoritarian or totalitarian, such as fascism, or some variation of racial thirst, or a form of imperialism, each designed to force a subject to wither, wither away, wither out of existence, and if possible, as if the subject had never been born, or erased from history, from the very fabric of universal time and space: the classic bully or thug.

Something else happens—something.

So much so the bears stop and turn towards the forest, then they part into two sections, two arcs, as if a parabola, a two-dimensional, mirror-symmetrical curve, and with an axis of symmetry, with a universal parabolic constant that seems to refer to a lodestar, to a guiding principle, to the principle of scientific law, to the freak!

Moments later something rapidly approaches, and it has a sublime, bizarre, and ruthless aspect, and it makes a distinct series of creepy sound combinations, which that has some resemblance to a Soundsnap website, "Noise Warble Warp B," followed by twelve seconds of sounds not quite a cross between "Urban Creepy" and chaos, which repeat.

Again this rattles Bonnie to the core, and feelings intensify then overwhelm, as the heart pounds and pounds, which cause an impulse to jump—or better yet, to leap somewhere, anywhere, and yet everywhere.

And again all this time her eyes widen, very much so. And as before the mouth forms an "Oh!" position, such as "Oh, my God!" or some other cultural equivalent, yet the petrification process does not allow that complete thought or statement.

Moments later, that rapidly approaching thing disappears underground and, sometime after, a massive thing or creature emerges from the forest with bold strides.

✓ PART 2

Then it stops. Standing, it appears well over seven-foot tall, with an overall stoutness of neck, shoulders, chest, waist, arms and legs, as if especially built for a fight, for an epic battle, for the metagame: a grand strategic system against shrewd animals, regardless of a hot or cold war, and whether conventional or asymmetric warfare, even psychological warfare and the long game. Or put another way, the differential game of continuous pursuit and evasion, and the play of one game develops the rules for another game, as well as mission, design, function, content, timing, and so forth.

This thing or creature goes by several names: the Punk Buster, the Psychonautic, and the Neologic Freak; in addition, it resembles an ultimate show of shows, new age creation, artificial and the enviable endgame of free enterprise, such as what happens if you remove critical checks and balances, those pesky things, you know, real oversight, and instead use the symbolic version of self-check, or by proxies of the self, for example the insiders, the usual crowd, the original uber class, not the new age, not the great pretenders.

It shows the dilemma of tinkering with science, really tinkering in that classic definition, especially on the critical frontier issues, such as on crucial systems, on fundamental building blocks, then tinker until you get it just right, or until a truly great experiment goes wrong, really wrong from tinkering with a series of deliberate parity violations, to create a compelling spectacle that sells.

However, it created a freak, and not just some ordinary affront to nature, but something quite artificial and a gross mockery of nature law, a tremendous freak, truly sick abomination, dystopian, thing, creature or whatever, which is so far ahead of everything else, so far beyond foresight, and before anyone fully realizes the potential as well as implications, and when the device gains control over the creator, that irony. As a wealthy creator in search of great fortune ignores the fundamental principles of nature and creates a thing, which becomes so advanced, complex, compelling and ever-changing that the creation becomes the master, as in a variation of *Star Trek: Voyager, The Thaw*.

This neologic freak represents the ultimate new-age show of shows, created with borrowed material and manufactured haste, to generate enormous opportunity and fortune, as in quite natural and yet truly artificial. Where the black site creator sought a decisive victory from obsessively tinkering with things, as well as ignoring the fundamental rules of nature, system, symmetry, symbiosis, "set and setting," then trip, really trip, and trip into a theater of the truly absurd.

Moreover, this creature or thing has an ultimate retro yet industrial futurism style, and with all those fine details, which that pay high honor to the golden age of diesel and steampunk, yet as the enviable new-age thing, as in it was just a matter of time, a neologism, and the darker side of free enterprise, the side system loyalists do not want to talk about.

Just as significantly, this massive creature or thing appears one buttermilk biscuit short of 689 pounds, and gives the full impression of a rock 'em sock 'em, a punk buster, and yet with a great phantasm aspect around it, a secular glory.

In addition, this massive creature or thing wears an unconventional head-to-toe body armor, which consists of ballistic dragon scales made of tunable and nonlinear metamaterials, which adjust radiant properties to absorb electromagnetic energy or project it with great precision, similar to a cuttlefish style and that rapid change of color and light polarization, to camouflage or communicate, as if a chromatophore, and to show images that swirl, mesmerize or mimic things, for instance the surroundings.

Or, with the right scientific technique, it deliberately induces in a victim coma, aestivation, hibernation, brumation, or couch lock, and done by affecting a person's unity of consciousness, the stack, as well as history of ideas, that index, and the brain's ability to create a real-time, in-the-moment binding of events, such as when a person surveys and internally processes within multiple brain aspects.

This technique affects the four major cerebral cortex lobes, the incoming brain-sensory-streams or drafts, especially the visual cortex stream, as well as the mental ability to tag found things then build a mental workspace with them, as it is with an internal visual conversation pit or an internal television if you will, which contains topical things, among others, things of considerable interest, many of which seem as if unresolved problems, or loose ends that need something, for example, bind to a domain index or two, an index node or the end and means.

Regardless, the creature technique causes a person or animal to enter something other than a catatonic state or psychoactive trance, and a particle beam directed at the mind might explain this process, which seems to control neurogenic or bioelectric activity, and this technique is not likely from a psionic event.

All of which, at the minimum, seems to disrupt or modify the thalamus, as if a delta wave event, then that person slips into a profound and persistent vision or shared daydream, yet with paralysis, and not quite a *Star Trek: Voyager*, a *Waking Moments*, *Persistence of Vision* or *Bliss* style event, yet something else, which is the beginning of the end: life!

In addition, the face of this massive creature or thing is covered by the Mask of Eternity, and for all intents and purposes, the Guardian of Forever.

And of considerable interest, whiffs of smoke, plasma or something rise from behind the being, which form a complex backlit Elizabethan purple halo, and as if supreme sumptuary law, not a local legal system, such as small town thug, though of a higher power and true glory, which in some ways resembles a Tyrian nimbus with considerable golden edges that have extraordinary fine details.

All the while, an aureole radiates three aspects of a transcendent secular glory.

And of equal importance, on the chest sits a large dragon symbol, which resembles no known dragon. As, it might represent a combination of *Fucanglong*, *Shenlong* and *Tianlong*, yet one wholly enraged, scary as hell, bug-eyed, quite creepy, especially the face and a few other aspects, which have some human characteristics yet quite unsettling ones, and yet so familiar, even universal, though unlike any known human. And it resembles some type of progenitor being, which gives the full impression of a missing link, a link well before the golden age of the super apes as well as the golden age of the aquatic apes, and as if an evolutionary link much further back in time, at a major junction that represents an exceptional biological foundation or classic prototypical.

Moments later the dragon image fades, as well as the Tyrian nimbus, then the aposematic armor signals utter death and destruction.

Then the creature flashes classic patterns well known in nature, flashes conspicuous images specially formulated by nature to instantly burrow into animal *psyche* then *pneuma*, which advertises zero profit and a gruesome death.

They consist of heinous images that morph, blip and roll, which seem to disrupt the metabolism and overall biology of her, as well as the dog.

And these images often have a lightning bolt effect, a bolt that crackles and crisps internal things then causes alarm, panic, and the mind to disorganize, race about and feel trapped as options narrow to impossible choices, and yet she remains paralyzed for lack of a better phrase.

All of which causes a huge adrenalin dump.

So much so it gives her a feeling of the "outer limits" and Orwellian theme, as well as alternate hot and cold flashes that soon produce profound beads of sweat, as well as wide eyes.

Yet she would never surrender, ever.

Moments later, the body, mind and soul exhaust internal stockpiles.

Then she becomes weak and experiences a slight whole body tremble, disorientation and loss of bearings.

This creature or thing shifts to another mode, to full stealth, which displays the surrounding forest then projects, as a cuttlefish might, bizarre colors and patterns that blip, roll, and flash.

Not much later, these projections evolve into something truly great, even sublime, and as if a living work of art, which create *statikos* in her—and that refers to a state of esthetic arrest, as if viewing proper art, and art well-crafted through very precise negotiation, which forms a treaty according to universal law, if you will, as if a special contract, a reference broadcast time synchronization contract net protocol, and what a classic artist or poet might create to transcend time, space, and all language.

This thing continues to project.

In addition, it evolves into something with certain noble qualities, a majesty, excellence, as if some great experiment, a bold new enterprise or venture, and with a series of universal truths, aspirations, precepts and practices, and all with an exceptional refinement, polish and culture of the classics, as well as great works of visual, literary and performing arts, of celebration and festival then of the ultimate human dignity, freedom and real justice, not the ever so shallow game.

Then the creature transmits exceptional qualities in a bright, vivid and fresh way then reveals a vast treasure of extraordinary frontier ideas, new opportunities, profound mysteries and events, and does so with a considerable poetic greatness both free and fair, as well as with a certain charm, grace, and dignity.

So much so it conveys a restoration, of the way it should have been all along and in the beginning, then it reveals a theory of everything, the ultimate theory, the all-inclusive explanation of the universe, of life, the Grand Unified Theory then Age of Enlightenment, as well as what a person might expect within the golden age of the classical and Renaissance, Renaissance Humanism, Neoclassicism and the Age of Enlightenment, and the Romantic era version, a full restoration of glory, or the original long-lost glory now found.

Moreover, it does so as if a liminal master of ceremony for the phase transition, and with an exceptional nuance of a metaphysical and universal shared wave system that somehow deploys ritualized space, which has all those benefits and natural harmony of a very smooth transition, a true lost art, and one that creates atonement without seams, and all done as if a noble experiment, which that honors the classics, and yet as a bold new frontier of a threshold adventure.

In fact, this projection seems ever so smooth and effortless—well, except for a brief glitch now and again, which hints at an identity crisis of self or system.

However, each glitch is brief yet a telling one, and as if from a system defect, wrong life and body, species dysphoria, leaky abstraction, defective verb or max q of a hidden event, then this creature or thing shifts to other spectacular images, colors and patterns that blip, roll and flash, and all of which convey something truly sublime, as if a living work of art both true and proper.

Where, anything is possible—anything, even exceptional glory and greatest.

However, it eventually devolves into partisan, or partial derivative?

And moments later, a sickly sweet perfume smell arrives, which seems quite unsettling and offers a delayed jolt to her mortal coil then produces a whole body shudder as it mesmerizes her and the dog.

As if the body considers it with primal and long dormant sense, and that sense issues a best-effort warning to locate a clear line of freedom, then compels an underline twist of separation and stampede south.

However, she tries and flinches from internal damage.

Moreover, image projections have a creepy aspect then grotesque, as well as freakish, which resemble a commercial dystopia, and how commercialism can cross that bright redline of being reasonable, then seep into body, mind, soul, spirit and breath, as well as burrow deep into *psyche* then disable various forms of logic, such as inductive, abductive, and deductive.

Of which, these images seem exceptionally cruel, excessive and treacherous, as if a sick abomination contrary to nature law, from a truly great experiment gone wrong, really wrong, and not some ordinary affront to nature but an artificial and a gross mockery of nature law, and as if fueled by a truly sick yet highly educated savage with an unquestionable genius, though driven by high-octane nightmares.

Moments later the Punk Buster speaks, which resembles a deep and powerful fog horn, Tyrannosaurus rex blast of primal fury, then again and again.

So much so nearby foliage moves, and this sound blasts away years of her life, blasts her reserves, which go wherever elusive things travel, such as a new home, or back into the universal superstructure, into that vast hidden domain, or into surrounding milieu, or nearby atoms and quanta, or into dark energy, then dark matter and that cycle, or they simply remain inside the body, in that collective *carroccio* self, yet have been shocked of original intent as well as full potential.

In between each of those powerful blasts, the creature or thing takes one breath after another, which is not quite a Vader breathing style, yet the inhale, hold and exhale have powerful and distinct stages from the back.

Meanwhile, the dog carefully shifts into a more defendable position near her, a position more able to leap as a counterattack, as a noble savage, the well-educated, with an all-out war, yet as an exceptional, then it shows enormous tension and issues a very sinister growl.

Then teeth and gums quiver, and quiver with a certain escalation, as the dog adjusts with a series of subtle stalk attack postures and readies a split-second uncoil with such freakishly feral speed of true noble savage fury.

And it waits for the proper command: "Dog!"

Regardless, the lead bear attacks with electric speed and raw fury.

Just as importantly, and within a split second, the dog adjusts and uncoils a counterattack.

Then both engage in combat with tremendous speed, fury and rage, and with actions that resemble a blur; resemble an aggressive frenzy of savage venom, as both inflict incredible damage in one exchange after another, and all the while, both refuse to give ground regardless of more and more blood, of rich *bluot,* or *bruodher.*

Moments later the Punk Buster speaks. And it blasts a powerful wave again, and again, which causes nearby foliage to move from all of that sound and fury.

Then it attacks, and with a single motion bats aside the dog, which produces a truly disturbing yelp, a call, as if a call agent, for help, call home or copy-restore major SOS: dog!

As a result the dog tumbles forty feet away into the dirt and dust, then eventually resembles a lifeless heap of fur and blood.

Next, the Punk Buster turns towards Bonnie. Then it blasts a powerful wave again and again, which causes nearby foliage to move from all of that sound and fury.

Moments later, it swings around with a 180-degree karate chop style against that nearby old-growth beech tree, with a Jimi Hendrix style chop, as in the Jimi Hendrix Experience's "Voodoo Child (Slight Return)" —"Well, I stand up next to a mountain, and I chop it down with the edge of my hand," then another chop and another on that same old-growth trunk.

So much so the first chop neatly lops off the tree from its roots, the core and foundation, as well as the creeping tree aspects, creeping rootstalks.

And each successive spin maneuver chops off one huge remaining trunk section after another, until the decimated tree eventually surrenders, tips over and thuds to the ground, which causes a considerable amount of debris to swirl, as if a punctuation: life.

However, Bonnie does not unravel, does not become emotional, hysterical or blubber, "Woe is me! The world is out to get me!" or blame the others, but instead remains exceptionally cool and calm then says as eyes widen, "Ah, I see; this must be the place, the great threshold adventure, the savage frontier, a place where anything is possible, anything, even true greatest, and something similar to 'No Woman No Cry.'"

Chapter

Meanwhile, that profound underground throne crisis continues, which resembles an intractable EXPTIME—hard balkanization, manorialism, feudalism, seigneuries, subinfeudation, as well as the great internal survey, stratified sampling, accidental sampling, "the grab" or "power grab," of opportunistic sampling, and "dangerously sucked into" an internal "mind game," the "political mind," political animal, of permanently embedded surveillance, upstream, and intercepting communications at the backbone, and "no morsel too minuscule for all-consuming," just in case, well, because of mission drift or feature creep, also known as bloat, with "ad hoc, informally-specified, bug-ridden, slow implementation," and other unforeseen great adventures of a system, as well as nature, the mostly hidden and profound implications.

And monitoring a vast number of underground forest system evolution data points, as well as life beyond the forest, expends a considerable effort to resolve so much in such a small timespan, which creates tremendous stress within throne aspects, in those worlds within worlds, especially the transhuman and posthuman embedded components with colorful, irresistible and creepy gravitas, such as slowly back away from them, no sudden moves or direct eye contact, and the enormous pressure continues to build in containment barriers that partition throne sections.

And aspects of the throne begin a desperate struggle, as well as effort to manipulate subspace, the physics, which seems quite dangerous, unsettling, and a deliberate search for a way out.

Moments later, the entire throne shudders as a human might; and again, it seems almost human—confused, disoriented, isolated then forsaken, and in a profound crisis from all that threshold experimentation, which produces a tremendous sense of alienation.

Then things around take on a pale, empty, surreal and ugly look, as personal demons, painful memories and regrets rush forward, along with a full realization that the system has become the other, a thing, an "it."

As a result, other system aspects panic at that threshold, at that great precipice, that *nonesmanneslond*, as system stability seems quite elusive in relationship to endurantism, which better accommodates the theory of special relativity, specifically when enterprise takes an idea then applies it to real-life dynamic conditions and scalability, the classic problem and those pesky things.

Then many throne system aspects vie for full control over other sections, especially the weak, the easily overrun, that traditional approach, a power grab based on an exigent circumstance, or whatever, mostly whatever, a construct, and grab with emergency powers, such as "I have the power, so I can change the rules at any time or place," that classic technique.

As a result, large parts of the underground system are under new management, as an all-powerful person, family, tribe, cult, sex, race, religion, economic system or transnational might take over a town, city or nation-state, or a group of transnationals takeover a large nation-state, and often without mainstream awareness, and takeover with a simple maneuver, for yet another New World Order, or some golden age of whatnot, often a hyper as well as desperate fashion of the day, from the fashionista complex that says absolute style, those options yet selected from a short list, a history of constructs, such as a popular linguistic trick, a short cut, which that often yields treat for some and a bitter expanse of poverty for others, for the foreseeable future of slog, a win-lose, to atone with an institution, maybe a transnational enterprise, and how admirably law defines the term "prize," which uses a series of feints to provoke other system aspects to overreach, for example the concept in English land law and

Law of Property Act 1925, to gain a decisive victory of one good shot—a third act, as another war to end all wars, that theme?

This appears especially true for defenseless throne aspects stuck in a phase, mid-phase, metaphase or in the middle-between-phase, or from a phase-lock multibit, and now stuck in the middle of a classic frontier revolution, as a red shirt.

Again, aspects of this throne, in those worlds, seem almost human—confused, disoriented, isolated then forsaken, and in a profound crisis—such as, will they survive from all that experimentation, from this new golden age of biological, chemical, material, and especially plastic, "special purpose plastics," that residual, the taste, well; if you imagine the full implications.

And then things go from bad to worst.

CHAPTER

Meanwhile, on Pennsylvania Ave. SE, Washington, a restaurant employee quietly hands someone three pizzas, a stack with all those mouthwatering notes, also called "the republic with goodness, charm, and delight," yet some people simply call them "Specials" or "the works," and these represent replacements for ones given to a family distress, in serious distress.

And this recipient represents a type of person one reads about in news articles, and is quite possibly a plenipotentiary, or stateless elite, or Davos person, yet not a hard money lender or Young Turk, or thyristor, polysemy, groupoid, or an impossible object, or, well, a hermit, as opposed to an eremitic. He is a person with real wealth, and not stuffy old money, of "Oh my, accept responsibility and please exit my home, turn right after the Rembrandt then left after High Renaissance and right after the Dutch Golden Age." And this person does not represent new money, not a new arrival who has not acclimated—well, to the environment, the atmospherics—and not grasping for stuff, new genes, or new and improved whatnot, whatchamacallit, or for the thingamajig, and is not the frantic me, not raised during the critical childhood years as a cog, or professional grump, or as a glum, grump, gripe, that decimates, as a favorite style, the histaminic, or raised as a tightly wound histone, a repression, or a churn, who specializes in plowing through the surrounding, maybe the poor, middle, or upper class, as a sport, profession, or industry, which might eventually displace a generation or two, for instance "Investment Riches Built on Subprime Auto Loans to Poor," or other classic ways and means to earn, such as by exploiting the weak, or put another way, by stepping on the ants or "hit the monkey, win a cookie."

Regardless, this recipient quietly thanks, confirms full payment for these pizzas, as well as a major community program to revitalize the community then departs towards the great frontier.

CHAPTER 8

Moments later, the Punk Buster has gone, entered the forest, and vegetation sways suggest where.

Just as importantly, the brown bears notice, agitate, frustrate, loathe, snarl, and huff disrespect at Bonnie, as well as maliciously swipe the ground, which sends large clumps of grass, dirt and rubble at her a few times.

Then along separate routes they reluctantly enter the forest.

Meanwhile and deep underground, room after room and the walls, as well as vault ceilings, contain dense layers of *Wunderkammer* that move, and again, as a very complex mystery, of worlds within worlds or microcosms, as categories and degrees of existence, of crucial stages and craft from certain universal, as well as biological theater, and a few things resemble creepy industrialized sagacious wit, such as a scop or sage who uses a certain sly propaganda as a deception specialist.

In addition, more things seem transhuman or posthuman, with colorful, irresistible and creepy gravitas, as well as give the overall impression of things gone wrong, very wrong, yet truly great attempts of a dystopia.

Elsewhere, Bonnie shudders, concerns and puzzles.

Eventually she looks about for a safe haven, gathers strength, rises, and ignores the acute aches, sharp pains and profound winces to collect the dog; the lifeless heap of fur and blood, then stumbles south.

In the meantime and underground, dense patches of indoor clouds form near those compact mysteries—vapor if you will, and they soon resemble an experimental Delphic-Bayesian game theory process, various events, which hang here and there at different levels, with some low to the ground, others at medium and ceiling height, and some merge with the wall, as if half inside solid reinforced concrete eight feet thick and half among a certain microcosm, as a mist among the population, the coalition of the willing at first glance, yet a closer look shows a far more complex situation.

And all these indoor clouds seem to generate a vivid hallucinogenic yet Delphic effect, as a Rayleigh wave hierarchy problem, yet corollary based on proximity, and as if a dream weaver, or dream cast, then an exceptional synectic beam with more than an oblique and lateral strategy, as if to create an exedra or conversation pit effect, or shared state, or ontic wave binding event that tags nearby things in memory, time and space, such as a special workspace, yet not a psionic venture.

Although it has a delta wave feel, which might affect or modify the thalamus?

Moreover, the dense indoor cloud patches try to fathom with various methods, which seem cool and calm, to deliberate insane fury, which tests boundaries of universal law and system theory, as if the universe was a bulkhead or series of complex algebraic stacks, yet the wall versions seem different, and seem to carefully and meticulously fathom through eight feet-thick concrete here and there.

A few of these clouds do so as a person might manipulate subspace, the physics that tests stack theory, which seems very dangerous and unsettling. And they do so as if to create a theory of everything, the ultimate theory, the all-inclusive explanation of the universe, of life, as well as the Grand Unified Theory, of how all those pieces neatly fit in such a small space, such as in the beginning, into that elegant beach ball-size or so universe, and how to fit all ordinary matter inside, all atoms, every star system, as well as dark energy and matter into that ever so small space, that great mystery.

And a few of these dense patches test the ultimate fate of the universal, such as how to rip the fabric of this universe, rip spacetime fabric, to collapse the supreme bulkhead or bulkheads, collapse the supreme algebraic stack, for example how to remove all that space in between everything, and do so faster than the speed of light, with a special warp bubble pierce, for example the harmonics and overtones of deflation, as well as spacetime dependency on symmetrics for an expansion, for example the bell-shaped curve distribution.

They do so as a juvenile might deliberately test limits and fundamental issues in search of special exceptions within universal law, a search for loopholes, or just because, or they sit in a system of addiction, a never satisfied stage, to quench, so construct a stack, as well as protocol, with a procedural method to conduct and experiment, and that product, sequence, timing of an "off-label adventure."

Or they do so as an expendable might, of someone or thing that knows quite well they are disposable, and often told so by the system "that others clamor to take their place," as an expendable in the new studio system and not a super delegate, a special ultimate insider.

Such as, the system can fire a person based on a whim, notion or factoid, which represents how many systems propel their economy based on whim, notion, factoid, and expendables or disposables in the name of something, maybe competition or another construct, such as dispose a person, family, tribe, team, cult, school, politic, enterprise, institution, religion and certain schools of thought, as well as race.

So, close the universe according to that same theme, just because.

And some people, as well as systems, do that, or would do that. They poke and poke at an idea, person, place, thing, or even a system. Or they fiddle with it and fiddle or pick at it, and really pry at something, and pry with an idea, law, process or pry with a crowbar—where a thing might stand for 1,000 years or more as is, but, well, people, human nature, or nature itself pries, with various techniques, such as a rhizome wedge.

And nature has an inherent need to reach for something, for a molecular concern, and regardless of the consequences, as if a "reach-through-claim," or a physics version of product-by-process claim.

Sometimes people tinker for no particular reason, as an impulse or other reasons, because they can, as trivial pursuit, coin, job, or as a servant, maybe a classic or new age debt bondage, as a modern wage slave.

Or, a person pokes in search of an exit from the madhouse, the mental institution or system that has a considerable number of those traits, such as all that restless drama, divisiveness and lack of logic, with a considerable amount preventable, yet much of the system sponsors this style as a lucrative industry for some, as well as "I told you so, told you that a certain class of people are dangerous," such as another gender, race, political party or other social construct. So a person is stuck living in that feedback loop; as a result a person pokes, to protest a system, a status quo of the Big Ugly.

Just as importantly, each cloud attempts to gain competitive power over the other, because a bit of competition seems good, seems beneficial, so the maximum must be great, such as the Old West, the Wild West, or the good old days, or with a temporal shift, to Genghis Khan then Khabul Khan yet Arghun Khan, aka Argon, a devout Buddhist, although said pro-Christian, which again reveals the complex mystery of interconnection, of local yet universal, as well as entanglement, and yet the urgent impulse for another dangerous competition, an obsession, such as to purify beyond rhyme or reason.

As a result, many of these bunker systems begin to clamor and bang about, as pandemonium, as if the capital city of hell or some other cultural equivalent, scientific fact, or constitution, *ultra vires*, a Latin phrase for beyond the powers, or as an abominable fancy yet harrowing event, which resembles more than an intractable EXPTIME—hard balkanization, manorialism, feudalism, seigneuries, and subinfeudation.

And again, other aspects of the throne notices all this bunker bedlam, as if a proxy war, and desperate attempts to manipulate subspace, the physics, which seems a very dangerous, unsettling, and deliberate search for the limit, of "Don't you tell me no truths, I want all of your lies."

Moments later, the entire throne, as well as many bunker residences, shudders again and again, as a human might, and then many aspects seem almost human—confused, disoriented, isolated then forsaken, and in a profound crisis from all that threshold experimentation, which produces a profound sense of alienation.

As a result, other system aspects panic at that threshold, at that great precipice, that *nonesmanneslond*, as system stability seems quite elusive in relationship to endurantism, which better accommodates the theory of special relativity, specifically when enterprise takes an idea then applies it to real-life dynamic conditions and scalability, the classic problem and those pesky things.

Then more throne system aspects vie for full control over other parts, especially the weak, the easy to overrun, with an exigent circumstance, with emergency powers, such as "I can change the rules at any time or place," that top-down style, or just because something has a weakness, so surge or rush based on a natural impulse or obsession, maybe as a control freak.

As a result, large parts of the system are under new management, as an all-powerful sex, family, tribe, religion, economic system, race or transnational might take over a town, city or nation-state, or a group of transnationals take over a large nation-state. Or how someone wins based on a technicality, or receives sixty percent of vote and declares a landslide, a mandate in a gerrymandered system, so celebrate when one great ugly wins over another, as more freedom evaporates.

Then things in this underground system go from bad to worst.

CHAPTER 9

Elsewhere, with the dog, that heap of fur and blood, under an arm, Bonnie stumbles south.

Eventually she notices a forest opportunity well off to the side, one that shows exceptional cover.

And after a stop, careful scan in all directions, she carefully crawls inside while trying not to disturb the ground, such as break twigs or disturb patterns, and anything that might show signs of activity.

Then several shimmy efforts enable movement further inside a dense thicket, which appears to offer safety, seclusion, and stealth.

CHAPTER 10

Meanwhile, the Punk Buster carefully enters a secret underground passage, and things appear normal, in their proper place, as well as a nearby room then one long passageway and fortified bunker after another.

And these places have a Renaissance architecture, what Marcus Vitruvius Pollio of Rome might describe with the three qualities of *firmitas*, *utilitas,* and *venustas*, or put another way, places that show a prudent, practical, balanced, efficient, and judicious style, a discreet, truly civilized place, with a calm aesthetic, as well as in full harmonic accord with nature, which might stand for a thousand years or more, such as the Tabularium, Curia of Pompey, Roman Forum or Rostra Vetera, and yet here as well as there is a black marble and cement mixture to discourage Sulla aspirations.

Then a narrow, dense and claustrophobic tunnel should eventually open into a gauntlet of snakes. And each snake would sit inside its own three-foot square niche with exceptional, ornate and robust inlay, as well as architectural trim made of the finest material, which give each recess a look of several very complex worlds within one another, and stack of four curves into a magnificent cerium blue vaulted ceiling of unquestionable style.

However and more importantly, those dangerous serpents have gone, and each served as a StreamSQL literary wit at each distinct stage, as a polyvalent threshold of life or death.

Then a careful search of another bunker finds normal, and another, even the ones with an increased amount of content, which seems bizarre—very—as if an odd microcosm of curiosities, a dense *Wunderkammer* or complex Leverian.

And many experiments occasionally move, and some seem human, just a bit, as in barely, and as if some represent a progenitor and others as missing links, while a few resemble what-if experiments, CRISPR products, yet done with a technique fifty years ahead and creates things that seem to represent the border between human and everything else, as well as a few ultimate humans, quite, for very specific tasks, for a narrow function, function-behavior-structure ontology, and a functional mock-up interface, especially as it relates to the seven deadly sins, *arishadvargas* or an equivalent.

Regardless, all of these things seem "normal," or more accurately, "usual to these bunker systems," as nothing appears out of place or disrupted, and the experiments continue to evolve.

However, a further search in another passageway eventually shows a room with unparalleled destruction, as equipment smolders, sluggishly burns with a minimum of flame and smoke, yet other sections have damage beyond description, as if by some unknown process, as well as bunker sections that may have a "fractured timeline," or chart of history, or logarithmic scale or K-wave, of certain bits and bytes, for lack of a better phrase, or something is wrong with the room's temporal inflection, bardo, perdurantism, endurantism, alterity or behavioral cusp, something an articulate scientist, musician or poet might better describe and with far more precision regarding all those obvious and subtle aspects, especially when something seems to transcend all conventional language and thought.

Moments later, a few things quickly disappear down the passageway.

CHAPTER

Inside the bunker, and further ahead, a few more things quickly maneuver down the next passageway.

Yet, the Punk Buster immediately repairs then activates a fire suppression system that extinguishes one sluggishly burning equipment flame after another.

Eventually, the smoke rate slows then gradually dissipates.

Enough so, the attention turns from unparalleled destruction to a cautious move inside that passageway, ready for fight, then it motions for one—a real fight—an epic battle of "Come on, right here and now, for the spoils of war!" for the Mask of Eternity, and for all intents and purposes, the Guardian of Forever.

CHAPTER 12

Ａnd yet those other things quickly continue down that narrow passageway, towards the command center then supreme throne.

Regardless, the creature motions for a fight—a real fight—an epic battle of "Come on, right here and now, for the spoils of war!"

Just as significantly, and along this passage, time gradually seems normal, the bardo, the range of threshold transition or behavioral cusp, of new contingencies, new possibilities, and especially the persist and identity aspects, as any person, place, and thing has a distinct temporal part throughout existence, as well as an otherness.

Also, a person, place, and thing has another not so obvious aspect, the alterity or entanglement, maybe part of the quantum entanglement system, a mostly hidden aspect of the universe, the predicament that Albert Einstein described as a "spooky action at a distance," which seems a bit vague for such an incredibly gifted person to have said, yet something another articulate scientist, musician or poet might better describe, a specialist, and with far more precision regarding all those obvious and subtle aspects, especially when something seems to transcend all conventional language and thought.

Nonetheless, as well as further down this passage, all those extremely dangerous and bizarre aspects of time seem normal, seem to flow in the normal direction, with the universal expansion and with the normal range possibilities.

CHAPTER  13

Cautiously, the Punk Buster continues down that narrow passageway and readies for a fight.

And along the way, sections seem normal, of possibilities.

However and ahead, more things quickly maneuver down that passageway, into a bunker, and when the Punk Buster arrives ready to attack, to wage war, the place contains unparalleled destruction.

Where an ultradense cloud patch, a dense mystery, tests something, a spacetime experiment, a superior combination of strategies, of subgame perfect strategies, yet an option that was not thought credible, because to deploy it would harm the player making that attempt, or said another way, a game of chicken, of mutual assured destruction, which represents a military nuclear weapons doctrine, or some other weapon of mass destruction, or mother of all bombs, also known as MOAB, or the insidious neutron bomb. And all serve, in theory, as a powerful deterrent, because no sane person or nation-state, it is believed, would dare cross that bright red line of complete annihilation, that dream of greatness, go out in a blaze of glory, true glory, that form of bitterness, of frenzy, such as all or nothing for both the attacker and the defender, as well as much of a nation or world would become a crisp, become smothering cinders, so, no sane person or nation-state would do it, at least according to a Nash equilibrium.

And yet a few dense clouds do so and surround their respective microcosm, *Wunderkammer* and Leverian aspect, as a mist among each populous, as if a dream cast, a vivid hallucinogenic yet Delphic effect, as if a Rayleigh wave hierarchy problem yet corollary based on proximity, or as an exceptional synectic, an exedra or conversation pit effect, a shared state, possibly an ontic wave binding event, which tags nearby things in memory, time and space, or as if a special workspace.

And the dense indoor cloud patches try to fathom with varies methods, which seem cool and calm to deliberate insane fury, which tests boundaries of universal law and system theory, as if the universe was a bulkhead or series of complex algebraic stacks.

Then they do so to manipulate subspace, the physics, test stack theory, which seems very dangerous and unsettling, a game of chicken, yet to create a theory of everything, the ultimate theory, the all-inclusive explanation of the universe, of life, as well as the Grand Unified Theory, and ultimate fate of the universe.

Moments later, the experiments stop.

And soon, grit settles among the complex Wunderkammer depth, then dust.

Eventually, an ever so peaceful atmosphere arrives, a "peaceful coexistence."

However, these experiments refocus then attempt one technique after another, to rip the fabric of this universe, the fabric of spacetime, to collapse the supreme bulkhead or bulkheads, collapse the supreme stack, such as how to remove all that space in between everything, and do so faster that the speed of light, with a special warp bubble pierce, the harmonics and overtones of deflation, as well as spacetime symmetry.

And they do so as a juvenile might, to deliberately test limits and fundamental issues in search of special exceptions within universal law, a search for loopholes, or just because, or do so as an expendable might, or for any number of other reasons, maybe for freedom, justice, and equality, or mercy, truth, and righteousness, or as a cautionary lesson, of enough is enough, especially to end world suffering, and all that turmoil, that endless petty bickering about the smallest details, and of greater importance, those crimes against humanity, the history of the only remaining human species with a habit of systematic and extrajudicial attacks against people, as well as dehumanization, human experimentation, and extermination.

So, end civilization, collapse the universe, which, in this case, the process would move faster than the speed of light, which in fact represents a humane act, quite.

As the human species has had more than enough time to evolve from the muck, the petty, from cruel and usual, since the Stone Age, the Middle Paleolithic, such as 200,000 years ago, that amount of time, and with social inventions, constructs, or the behaviorally modern human since 40–50,000 years ago, or a bible thumper might say, "10,000 years or so," again more than enough time to evolve into truly civilized, into humanity as a virtue, of love, kindness and exceptional social intelligence, as well as the other virtues in society, science and art, and with cultural branches that reach as well as refine essential ports or portals, as compared to a modern savage, or modern thug, or the well-educated thug, the authoritarian or totalitarian in one configuration or another, again.

Well, because it seems more than enough time has been given the human species for real progress, and why make so many excuses for them, why "grade them on curve," a "bell curve," an education term for "oh my," such slow learners, in fact dense, or said another way, a sluggish, obtuse and foolish mind?

As it often starts with a simple event, such as just because the system can fire a person on a whim, notion or factoid, that style preference, which can have profound implications, and they often propel any given economy based on expendables, on disposables, in the name of something, such as a popular phrase of the day or object, maybe "competition," with a disposable person, family, tribe, team, school, politic, enterprise, institution, religion or certain school of thought, as well as race, disposable when a system, fandom, fan or cult member bristles, and cues a direct or an indirect signal to a mob, horde or swarm: attack then abandon ship, abandon ship!

Or abandon a town, nation or some other construct, and that wake of destruction, that endless loop.

So, close the universe according to that same theme, just because, and no more excuses for the human species, or it represents the most humane act, the most decent thing to do, and decent in every sense of the word, and before the blink of an eye, even quicker, an infinitesimal moment in time, gone: an immediate collapse then eventually into that original beach ball-size or so object, which, in fact, might create a paradise, yes, or the opposite, a tyrant, an absolute ruler, because of dense content, as well as a loss of those branches, and all that context?

Regarding those experiments, a considerable percentage of any population might do that. They poke and poke at an idea, person, place, thing, or system. Or they fiddle with it, and fiddle, or pick at it, and really pry at something, and pry—where a thing might stand for 1,000 years or more as is; however, well, the system, people, human nature, or nature pokes. It tinkers, sometimes for no particular reason other than because it can, such as the freedom to poke, and often on an impulse, or to protest a system, a status quo of the Big Ugly.

Or nature has an inherent need to "aspire," for lack of a better word, or reach for something, for a molecular concern or a nuclear drip line issue, with a weak segment, and regardless of the consequences, as if a "reach-through claim," or a physics version of product-by-process claim, or a very dangerous competition, an obsession, such as when pure competition is not always good.

As a result, each dense cloud patch surrounds a certain microcosm, a *Wunderkammer* and Leverian, as a mist among that populous, as if a dream cast which starts as ever so cool and calm then clamor and bang about, as pandemonium, as if the capital city of hell, or some other cultural equivalent, or a scientific fact, or constitution, *ultra vires*, a Latin phrase for beyond the powers, or as an abominable fancy and yet as a harrowing event, which resembles more than an intractable EXPTIME—hard balkanization, manorialism, feudalism, seigneuries, and subinfeudation, that cycle of ever so cool and calm to pandemonium then the capital city of hell.

All of which produces bedlam, a very dangerous, unsettling, and deliberate search for the endgame, as vivid hallucinogenic yet Delphic effects swirl, as if a Rayleigh wave hierarchy problem, yet corollary based on proximity.

And that greatly affects the Punker Buster, the Super Punk, also known as the Freak, and enough so it drops that one-of-a-kind handheld device, a smartphone-size scanner, then staggers back again and again, from one powerful experimental field to another.

Then moments later and elsewhere, the entire throne and many bunker residences shudder again—and again as a human or a nation might from a profound crisis from all that threshold experimentation, which produces a profound sense of alienation.

As a result, and again, other system aspects panic at that threshold, at that great precipice, that *nonesmanneslond*.

Then more throne system aspects vie for full control over other parts, especially the weak, the easy to overrun, with an exigent circumstance, with emergency powers, such as "I can change the rules at any time or place," and declare a landslide, a mandate, so celebrate even when the choice is between one great ugly or another.

Not soon after, things in this underground system go from bad to worst.

CHAPTER

And each dense indoor cloud patch continues to surround a respective microcosm, a *Wunderkammer* and Leverian, as a mist among that populous, as if a dream cast, a vivid hallucinogenic yet Delphic effect, a Rayleigh wave hierarchy problem, though corollary based on proximity, or as an exceptional synectic, exedra, conversation pit effect, yet powerful ontic wave binding event, which tags nearby things in memory, time and space.

And the clouds continue to alternate from cool and calm to deliberate insane fury, to pandemonium which tests boundaries of universal law and system theory, again as if the universe was a bulkhead or series of complex algebraic stacks.

As a result, these bunker systems clamor and bang about as pandemonium, an intractable, or constitution, *ultra vires*, a Latin phrase for beyond the powers, or as an abominable fancy, and yet as a harrowing event.

And the clouds do so in a desperate effort to manipulate subspace, the physics, which seems a quite dangerous, unsettling, and deliberate search for limits, to puncture the fabric of this universe, the fabric of spacetime, to collapse the supreme bulkhead or metaverse supreme bulkheads, collapse the supreme stack, such as how to remove all that space in between everything.

Just as importantly, this method would do so faster than the speed of light, because space can move much faster than the speed of light, and do so with a special warp bubble pierce, with the harmonics and overtones of deflation, as well as spacetime symmetry.

Which represents how a juvenile savant might with that delicate balance between creativity and mental illness, between true genius and clinical insanity, that ever so careful balance of when to pull back, just in time, at that precarious edge of crumble, where the soul shivers and eyes widen, at that very edge of true greatness, the cliff, or final precipice of existence; such as a dangerous crag with chasm, which offers a precarious edge of crumble then steep-drop into no more excuses, into the impossible mystery of frontier justice that often has no rhyme or reason.

Just as importantly, the Punk Buster weakens under tremendous pressure, which proves vivid, extraordinary, fascinating yet a hallucinogenic mystery, which defies a complete description of nested existence, natural forces, states, and ingenious techniques to establish these events.

As a result, the Punk Buster reels, stumbles back, as if inside an enormous Rayleigh wave hierarchy problem, a synectic, an exedra, shared state, or conversation pit, yet beyond all known language.

As this process manipulates subspace, the physics, tests stack theory, which again seems quite dangerous and unsettling, as a game of chicken yet to create a theory of everything, a full explanation of the universe, the Grand Unified Theory then ultimate fate of the universe, of how to collapse the supreme stack.

This tremendous pressure drives the Punk Buster back again, and again, until it reels, stumbles, and withers from that intense field.

Moments later, a 1,000-pound bear arrives, then another and another, five in total, such as the power of a circle, pentacle or pentagon, and they attack the sources with a savage fury again and again.

In fact, one attack after another happens so fast, as if a savage blur, with truly horrible sounds.

However, and eventually, they wither from those powerful fields of complex pressure and unknown language, as if 50,000 languages spoken at once then directed a universal pressure point, a point particle or universal defect in spacetime.

Soon these bears become overwhelmed, feeble, and lose all vitality then eventually collapse into heaps of fur.

And not much later the Punk Buster grabs a bear foot, drags that creature to safety, then another, until all lie at a considerable distance in a great heap.

Apparently there appears no direct route through this complex state, or state-transition equation, or put another way, state's rights yet the quantum entanglement system, as well as the "mythology of lost," and of the Greek word δρᾶμα, of poetic meter, of set, setting, fundamental rules of nature, system, symmetry, symbiosis, "set and setting," as if the term to trip, really trip, trip into a theater, and that narrow window into, or flash-sideways, yet also known as the issues of a parent, container, or apparent, or visible, yet most sit as a dynamic invisible, for lack of better descriptions.

And if only someone more familiar with the scientific system were here, familiar with history methods and other modes of thought, or a comprehensive outline of thinking techniques, maybe those by Linus Carl Pauling, Nikola Tesla, Michael Faraday, or Eratosthenes of Cyrene, or Franz Kafka, Ludwig Wittgenstein, or a world-class skeptic, maybe Sir Thomas Browne, Benjamin Franklin yet in a David Brinkley review style, and someone quite familiar with the ultimate-inside game, familiar with tricks, as well as cognitive bias, and has "seen it all," so to speak, and just as importantly, is not easily fooled, as life quickly follows desire into a quagmire then niche, into a temporary and narrow haven, whether secular or sacred, then fortifies that position and often by all means necessary: life, a sunken empire continues to emerge from that beach ball-or-so-size object.

Or some other team with other traits might better describe these events, and with more precise observational methods, especially the passage through one segment after another, of complex states, the "mythology of lost," as well as tremendous fields, many with an intractable pandemonium as if the capital city of hell or some other cultural equivalent, or a scientific fact.

Moments later, this tremendous pressure increases, and the Punker Buster experiences a range of emotions, of cringe, distress, ugly struggle, perplex, baffle, concern, worry and trapped, yet curious, in fact fascination with those compelling events, as well as the great foundational mystery.

All of which eventually affects breathing, which now seems wholly unnatural, quite difficult, and quickly spends personal reserves and generates a fight-flight option, and yet with nowhere to go, with no good options, and more importantly with no more excuses, and that causes the Punker Buster to stagger about.

✓ PART 2

However, and with a quick retrieval of that handheld device, which has considerable impact damage yet seems functional, it eventually generates a narrow beam that scans those events for various traits, such as acoustic, biologic, chemical, electrical, magnetic, mechanical, optical, radiological, and thermal.

Moments later, it scans for energy signature, material, thermodynamic, dielectric, luminance, hue-saturation, magnetic field, magnetic flux or permittivity, and then monitors other aspects.

In the meanwhile the bedlam intensifies, as well as alternates from cool and calm to deliberate insane fury, to pandemonium that tests boundaries of universal law and system theory, tests the complex algebraic stacks or supreme stack.

And more bunker systems clamor and bang about as chaos, bedlam, as well as an intractable harrowing of the universal under- and over-soul.

These intense forces cause the Punk Buster to, one by one, drag the 1,000-pound bears further and further back then carefully scout that region, that boundary or boundary conformal field theory, in search of better angles, perspectives, themes, or elements, for better options to maneuver through these intensely complex states and stages, maybe with a series of indirect maneuver through.

And it seems quite important to find a pattern, something that repeats in a predictable routine, such as a template or model, something to infer the common underlying methods to gain a better understanding, then stop this process, this pandemonium, or at least find clues to establish a baseline then compare options.

Moments later an idea arrives, a maybe—maybe things are not what they appear to be.

So the Punk Buster looks about for certain visual reference cues and taps the back of the left hand three times, and again, taps left of right, the left brake, the left-handed material index—well, to see if it creates an instantly awaking moment, in a hospital, sick bay or some other place, such as limbo, or some other secular or sacred version of purgatory or intermediate state, a bardo or liminal state, middle ritual, mid threshold or a special rite of passage, maybe atonement, that cycle of a monomyth.

However, it does not, and it is not an in-the-moment binding of events, such as how someone might tamper with the mental system, for instance during the survey, and when a person looks at events in real-time and multiple brain aspects monitor the sensory streams or drafts, tag things in memory, tag cues in that special workspace in the mind. And how someone outside might tamper with that process, might tamper with firmware for lack of a better phrase, and memory. Of which the observer might enter more than a catatonic state or psychoactive trance, and from the likelihood of a hidden neurogenic or particle beam, and not likely from a psionic event.

All of which, at the minimum, might disrupt or modify the thalamus, or equivalent, as if a delta wave effect, then that person or thing slips into a profound and persistent vision, or shared daydream, or worse yet.

However, subtle cues here and there indicate no such manipulation, and no superimposition, temporal stub, or sunken empire to reemerge, or different face, different space.

Regardless, and with that handheld device, the Punk Buster scans surroundings with a more comprehensive beam, especially the densely managed *Wunderkammer* and Leverian complex, which resemble microcosms within microcosms, then a few things flee into another bunker, which the Punk Buster briefly notes, yet concerns with subtle aspects of time and space as if they represent a localized container, and how a cartographer perceives the natural area code, which includes syntactic relationships, schema, and irrealis mood.

Moreover, the scan slowly looks about for any theatrical cues, show controls, playwright associated with dramaturgy or a temporal subspace mechanic or that boulder creature, yes, which might smolder and shift inside a comprehensive stealth in a distinguished and differentiated subspace domain, or an impluvium of sorts, or portable aedicula paradox, a temporal exception.

All of which seem as if a choice between bad or worse, at least according to the short list, based on priority swapping of dangerous alternatives, of options.

There must be a solution, an exception, maybe look backwards at the problem with a reverse perspective?

Maybe the problem will solve itself.

It might exhaust from built-in universal checks and balances, from built-in limits, from a conservation of matter as well as a localized tendency, such as the reason things naturally individualize, which depend on "location-location-location," and no place in the universe is exactly the same.

Or it might resolve from symmetry, from the universe, which that prefers meticulously selected paired opposites, dynamics, companions and the dependents, of localized nesting events inside the supreme bulkhead, which reveals more about the container.

However, the risk of doing nothing seems quite high, in fact dangerous, as these events cause bedlam and seem to direct what might be 50,000 languages spoken at a universal pressure point, a point particle or universal defect in spacetime, and done so with an unknown focal technique, which might cause a warp bubble pierce, a puncture of the universal spacetime fabric then collapse the supreme bulkhead or bulkheads, or supreme stack, such as how to remove all that space in between everything, and do so faster than the speed of light.

It might happen; maybe not; and maybe this represents just another wild speculation, another spectacle, a show, or show about nothing much, or same-old, same-old. As people often talk about the end of days, especially pundits, critics, as well as people or a system that wants to sell something, such as a used car, or used idea, one tried over and over in a quagmire, or they want to sell a ticket to another quagmire, as if the last few days, final days or eschaton, or end of time, of history, or the ultimate destiny of the human species as well as the universe, with a supreme rollback.

And who could issue a major rollback, a universal event? Maybe a true steward or trustee, or a supreme plenipotentiary, or special stateless elite, or the ultimate Davos person, with an exceptional prerogative, with an exclusive right to force everything to the exit, or the original location, towards the heavily fortified vacant station, station port, reference point indentation, permanent dwell, and a place for demarcated transactions? Such as start and end a transaction that uses begin, commit, and a rollback method if need be, such as rollback space and time, rollback the separation of powers, and the tenacious aspects of the universe, of local events, quantum entanglement, well-field schema and altered states, or put another way, return to the backstory line segment, to the origin, and enter that string then become a collapsed string?

Regardless, the risk of doing nothing seems high, in fact quite dangerous, as these events create an insane fury.

✓ PART 3

The crisis intensifies, as well as alternates from cool and calm to deliberate insane fury, to pandemonium, which tests boundaries of universal law and system theory.

All of which might represent just another shallow event, a wild extravagance, a profound baffle, and it might burn itself out—however, why risk everything?

And moments later, the tremendous pressure increases from this strange event, from 50,000 spoken languages, which causes the Punk Buster to stagger back, as things go from bad to worse, and the bunkers experience a collective identity surge, a shared definition, or use-definition chain, then experience orientation shifts and profound claustrophobia that narrows, overwhelms, and begins to enfeeble from true chaos.

CHAPTER

A gain, chaos radiates as well as pollutes the local timeline, or corrupts the local temporal inflection, or function, and that causes the Punk Buster to stagger further back then lose bearings, and more importantly, lose the history of ideas, as well as context.

As a result, it eventually realizes something else, and one at a time it drags one feeble bear after another to safety.

Just as importantly, it seems unable to find a crisis summary, a resolution with stages, with a MacGyver style or some other method, maybe from oblique strategies, then at the minimum create a kludge, workaround, a great ugly.

Yet the mind seems trapped in a poverty of thought, as if an itinerant, vagrant, vagabond, drifter, then "refuse of the call, refusal of the summons," refuse to bend, as if something has damaged the caudate nucleus, or equivalent, the threshold potential, spatial orientation map, association of ideas, mental workspace, ability to expand an idea and the internal executive function.

However, and eventually, the Punk Buster remembers just enough to adjust the handheld scanner settings, which ultimately sends a tight beam to one event section after another, sends highly specialized particles that attempt to detect the ways and means, especially the techniques.

Again, the chaos quiets, as if to reset, to gain even more true power, true chaos, and ready for the final pierce, to puncture the fabric of this universe, the fabric of spacetime, which should collapse the universe, the supreme bulkhead or bulkheads, collapse the supreme stack, such as how to remove all that space in between everything, and do so faster that the speed of light, with a special warp bubble pierce, with the harmonics and overtones of deflation, as well as spacetime symmetry.

With that, the Punk Buster notices event techniques, as well as hidden cycle, data pattern and subspace cues which launches each escalation stage, and at just the right moment, to stress the fabric, pierce the fabric, the bubble, as the universe might be a complex bubble.

And handheld device modifications eventually transmit a narrow beam, of education to a particular event aspect, and during certain moments between energy cycles, between strategic adjustments, and education done with flair, with style, class, as a true artist might, as a StreamSQL literary wit, a poet, and with a very complex signature of enterprise, of glory and greatness, of true greatness, the way it should be, and not the classic cruel and usual technique, not the crude brute force stage of common or well-educated thug.

And this narrow beam penetrates subspace, and at just the right cyclical moment, between stages, between deployment, and that comprehensive beam educates space, as well as matter, into a charmed set with a special flavor. As if the device creates a lively arch charm of wit, such as a sapient, prudent, shrewd management of practical affairs, a prudent investor of vital circumspection, piquancy and permanence, which helps regulate chaos as well as the normal expansion stage process, and as if with a theatrical cue, on that mark. It does so as a playwright controls the storyline, controls the storytelling system, as well as backstory, especially the under- and over-soul, to work under or over the set, and with the sheer beauty of science, of mathematical beauty, well, as support. And in part, it does so as *The Dresser* might, as not just another theatrical stagehand, another something, a generic, a "could-have-been somebody," yet expected to work as a shadow, or as a nerd, or just another geek, a proxy, yet semiotic, or hermeneutic, and instead work as an elegant spokesperson for the self, yet a mathematical representation of a complex role, a complex stack of deep math, yet a monster group, which that deploys a friendly giant scheme based on string theory, on vertex operator algebra, twisted space, and as a host might, as a master of ceremony or *compère*, and yet often a reluctant benchwarmer in someone else's storyline, especially on daily as well as frontier aspects, and things not in the classic "stall daily script" sold by the system as vital.

However, a vital side note: much of life is not in the script, and yet people are urged to stick to the script, the message and protocol, regardless, or else the system will drop something on them, drop a building on them, a building on fire, well, as a lesson, as "tough love," or so they say in retrospect, when any given system tries to look human, look more humane, and not a common savage, which, regardless, still often appears as if a justification of the classic big ugly, the ugly side of civilization, as well as nature.

As the system, proxy or mob often forms because of the smallest thing, for trivia, and very much so, as in trivial pursuit with exceptionally dangerous consequences, because of minutia, for a small inflective error, from a blink at the wrong time, or failure to perk or cheer loud enough at each slogan of the day or some other repetitive script of hyper gunk—well, depending on the system, for instance gender, tribe, team, politic, enterprise, nation, religion, race, or other cultural or universal construct— at those said vital slogans of the day, which include buzzwords and other chants a person must learn then accurately recite on cue, or else, as in hunks of gunk that follow a person into sleep, into paradise. Or, at the minimum, they follow a person into the great frontier?

And the system, proxy or mob often polarizes and forms because of that cue, on the mark and danger associated with a very small freedom of expression, compared to group think, as well as the obsessiveness many systems expect, and yet often say *"locutions de minimis non curat praetor or de minimis non curat lex"*: that paired opposite, that dynamic, and yet life resembles a quandary, a catch-22, Cornelian dilemma, a no-win situation or Pyrrhic victory system. Just as significantly, any given social system often requires a conventional straightforward description, solution, and action to a very complex question or situation, and often requires answers, which that quickly fit in an ever so small space, such as on a bumper sticker, or one that will squeeze through a very small window, and done so on time, such as squeeze into a narrow mind, squeeze a complex subject into a snappy one-liner, for instance $E = MC^2$, or better yet "Bada-bing bada-boom: life!"

Regardless, as well as here and now, that handheld device transmits a narrow beam to a particular event aspect, and during a certain moment between energy cycles, between strategy adjustments, and does so again and again, as a sagacious stream of truth, a permeation to repair the universal soul, the fabric.

And just as importantly, the beam has an exceptional deep mathematical beauty, succinct and elegant, and directed at a version of monstrous moonshine, at that unexpected connection of monster group and modular functions to what lies under, to the functions that create universal script, the universal building method of nature.

And in distinct stages the beam eventually exhausts the chaos, that deliberate insane fury, which tests boundary of system theory and universal law.

Then each indoor cloud slowly loses their belligerent fathom, as well as crackle and spark, loses their stochastic gradient boost method to incite, to provoke additive regression kernels.

Moreover, and in unusual and distinct stages, they lose their well-seasoned wit then experience a tremendous sense of alienation, true alienation.

Then one by one each grows ever so pure, spotless, stainless, and free from dust, dirt, or taint, which apparently has a cost, regardless of the social construct type, regardless of people, place or thing, as those configurations may have a special cost.

And one at a time, they have a twist of separation from nature, from the universe, and go elsewhere, just like that: gone!

However, one of them escapes down a passageway.

And for the ones determined to stay forever in that state, personal demons, painful memories and regrets "surge" forward, or "rush," along with a full realization that they have become the other, become what they fear most: that loop, that ouroboros process, for lack of a better term, as well as the implications of becoming wholly exclusive in an exceptional niche, or special bubble, yet in a way that does not satisfy, does not fully comfort, in fact the opposite feeling of under siege.

Moments later, something profound happens elsewhere, which cause the Punk Buster to notice, yet not know what, where, or the full implications.

Regardless, a memory sparks about that forest old-growth tree, and it exits the bunker then eventually arrives near that tree, which has a station, port, or portmanteau test, the autocorrelation aspect to test a missing fundamental, or suppress a fundamental, also known as the phantom fundamental, to resolve a frequency and the higher harmonic question, as often life needs a little something extra to find peace and harmony.

However, the tree has a certain structural and territorial integrity, with a separation of powers, and one side has a well-field schema, altered state, another way or artistic backstory which that translates on entrance into this field, as if a complex bilateral language function and tonal adjustment, a prosodic translation, a simultaneous function, and just outside that field, a tremendous form of facticity or thrownness.

As a result, entering that area proves quite a tricky venture, as there is no direct path, no clear route into that sphere of influence, the atmospherics, as one wrong step and a person would trip into the theater, a narrow window or more, or flash-sideways, or lose constructs, frames of reference, a deep belief network, and whole categories of thought, or just as importantly, gain a specie or cloaked shadow, just to name a few potential problems, or worse yet, thrown to the very edge of the universe, to a final frontier, or out of the universe, as a reject or rejection slip, of sail on, sail away.

And once safely inside that field, completely disoriented and now missing so many important aspects from things lost in translation, regardless the Punk Buster eventually scans the tree, as a person might examine a supermarket aisle for vital sustenance, then it locates ingredients, carefully removes various things and all the while avoids inhaling, as a solution for one thing often represents an exceptionally bad idea for another, or worse, such as the pop and crackle of eternal smolder, or conversion to something else, such as dark matter, to part of the universal scaffolding, the foundation.

Just as importantly, and upon eventual return to another deliberate insane fury bunker, it notices a gained specie, a cloaked thing, which closely follows it inside, and inside personal space, yet the Punk Buster does not reveal this understanding, as these types of things often happen in free enterprise, and sometimes they quietly leave after conducting a few secret experiments, such as a variation of *Star Trek: Voyager, Scientific Method*.

And on the Punk Buster, this gained specie secretly conducts a few dangerous tests.

Then that gained specie, in search of something, exits one bunker after another.

Regardless, the Punk Buster records all that activity, replays and carefully examines the data then returns to the early topic, and adjusts the handheld device, carefully loads tree ingredients, which cause the device to examine, glow, and send a beam to that insane fury.

Of which, it cultivates space, the dense cloud atmospherics, as a gardener might, and avoids breathing.

As a result, it begins to transform those dense clouds, as well as what they cover, those Wunderkammer and Leverian aspects.

And it eventually transforms all into a sanctuary, a fair haven if you will, a secular version of *sanctuarium*, idyll, poetic noble *forma relieve* ever so true, and quite so, such as what one might describe as an ever so smooth landing into bliss, yet a strange state of well-being, a best effort under the circumstances.

However, the Punk Buster must quickly exit the bunker, as the atmospherics are customized, and after reaching the next bunker, it finds profound damage, a place filled with unparalleled destruction, smolder, and wisps of smoke that rise, as well as a place with considerable bits of crisp blackened embers, and no replacements for some bunker things, for one-of-a-kind creations.

And that often happens in life, no comparable replacements, such as a lost specie or more, or sibling specie, as ninety-nine percent or so of all species to ever live on Earth are gone, lost, and represent local solutions to a very complex universal system, a puzzle as well as dilemma, and confirm that any given action can have a profound ripple effect.

CHAPTER 16

Elsewhere, and as evening arrives, a woman named Agrippa finishes a fresh vanilla moon pie and enters the town of New Hope, Pennsylvania, then carefully looks for frenemies from the mansion fiasco, and she looks for their Buicks.

Soon after, the former naval commander, of a United States Arleigh Burke-class guided missile destroyer, pushes aside the last empty wrapper while driving down the main street in her tricked-out iridescent burnt orange colored 1954 GMC Deluxe 100 muscle truck, customized, then says, "Let the beatings begin!

"Just as importantly, I need a song," so she turns on the truck media player, spools and looks for something just right, as well as appropriate, for an old-school fistfight.

So much so her eyes narrow and she says, "Something to foreshadow a pernicious attack—yes, something righteous, profound, disproportionate and ugly," as the fully tricked-out truck, a super brute, prowls the streets with a dual muffler system that growls an old-school warning to anyone foolish enough to get in her way.

Elsewhere, and inside a Baron Ferdinand de Rothschild-style country house, similar to the Waddesdon Manor, a woman named Livia phones someone, and in the meanwhile this woman carefully looks in the mirror and studies herself, her properties, or categories of being, as well as metaphors.

And she has a considerable resemblance to Dorian Leigh, similar to that famous 1949 photograph by Richard Avecon of her in a Christian Dior coat as she considered a cigarette, or some other subject, and it gives the impression of detachment, of distance, and cruelty if need be.

However, the similarities end there, as Livia has an exceptional lineage, in fact an impeccable reputation and astute sense of command, which that compliments her extraordinary wealth and all-pervasive influence, and someone to avoid, to not trifle with, as she knows how to deliver a very precise form of retribution, which serves as a special reward, a reward circuit, a complex circuit of shrewd bait, switch, punishment, pain and destruction.

Eventually, an impeccably dressed woman named Mero answers, then Livia demands progress on the Agrippa mansion foreclosure and orders those overpaid lawyers to move even faster. As they must serve additional documents, trash the credit ratings and ability to raise money, as well as press forward on all other fronts, to guarantee a full and systematic destruction of Agrippa.

Of equal importance, both completely agree on the ways and means.

In addition, they formulate more components to this precise and comprehensive plan of misfortune and what will deliver bitter humiliation, untold pain and suffering, as well as utter ruin.

Elsewhere, and unable to locate the Buicks, Agrippa enters a club and carefully scans the crowd for frenemies, yet finds none.

So she considers other options with the help of self-medication, with one quick potent drink after another, with distilled *pneuma*, *psyche* and wit.

And all the while she broods and mumbles about this and that, then eventually exits.

Moreover, this pattern continues through one club after another as she investigates, consumes and embitters with mercurial deliberation and penetrating stare, which resembles a death ray, a beam of destruction to wither and incinerate things on contact, to a crisp.

So much so members of the crowd quickly avoid eye contact and other ways to steer clear of what might become chaos, become a classic ballroom blitz, become the man at the back who said, "Everyone attack and it turned into a ballroom blitz,

And the girl in the corner said, Boy, I wanna warn ya, it'll turn into a ballroom blitz."

Where a person eventually snaps and overturns things in a profound plow action, and over a considerable distance through heavily symbolic goods, services and space of a ballroom blitz!

And this person plows and plows then pauses.

Then in a great proclamation, this person illuminates a brave new world doctrine, a cy-pres—well, because he or she might not make it to the "promised land," which is often the case, as any given human system promises so much yet rarely delivers a fraction?

This sudden vent process often happens to people within their oubliette, epiphanic or cardboard prison, or gerrymandered districts.

However, here, the word "gerrymander" applies to many social systems, constructs, not just political.

It applies to the command and control system, as well as structure, to the regimental style, the top-down system. And tendencies of any given system to entrench then fortify, as well as suppress other options, other forms of recourse, and especially block vital sustenance, the circulation of vital air, water, food and over- and under-soul, and block legitimate interests, concerns and real pressures that should vent, and vent real underlying physics.

And often, these classic blockage efforts use mostly obvious and subtle devices or tricks, such as cheap tricks of the trade to subjugate a class of being, or family, tribe, team, political party, institution, religion, nation, gender, race and other constructs, such as other economic systems, other systems of thought, as well as other species.

They do so to maintain real power, to control destiny, or some people might say, to "decide freedom, fortune and fate," or "determine the course of human events, to write history," which is often written as an aspiration document or promotional device, an advertisement campaign, as fiction, well, to promote fandom, the hype, "to promote exception, privilege and perk" in a niche, or "to promo a bankable star or proxy," for the system, the construct, or better yet promote a superstar, or diva, prima donna, or divo, primo uomo all-stars, with a grand on– and off-stage personality, with style, with an ever so special flair.

Which is how many systems often propel an economy: based on a whim, notion, and factoid, as well as fandom chase, such as rely on the ever-so-skittish in vital, as well as elite positions, especially in key sectors such as the financial district, rely on the difficult to please, the fastidious, those especially breed to recognize something, and who are twitch sensitive, and who sit as a main economic control center, and engine if you will, so twitch?

And will dump and run, in a moment's notice, and yet those complex debt obligations remain, which created tenacious attachments, especially to the expendables, the average person, the less than mobile class, the ones who cannot summer elsewhere, such as ride out the storm elsewhere, in the latest version of paradise, in Oslo, Stockholm, Copenhagen, Brussels, Vienna, Prague, Amsterdam, Neuilly sur Seine, Saint Cloud, or Strasbourg, Budapest, Madrid, Ingolstadt, Chur, Zurich, Ravensburg, Augsburg, or certain aspects of Asia, South America, and Africa, which represents the history of civilization, an outline of history?

Often people awaken inside their oubliette, epiphanic or cardboard prison then realize they represent just another expendable, a disposable in the name of something, such as competition, or put another way, a pawn, sacrificial lamb, scapegoat, and used by warring pairs, tribes, systems, and they often receive a minimum of concern, of maintenance, especially substance, except sugar, starch, yeast and fat products, as well as services.

And a person suddenly snaps then vents.

It happens, and often.

So much so, as well as here and now, in this club, members avoid eye contact with her, and steer clear of what might become chaos, become "the man at the back said, Everyone attack and it turned into a ballroom blitz, And the girl in the corner said, Boy, I wanna warn ya, it'll turn into a ballroom blitz."

Where a person eventually snaps and overturns things in a profound plow action, especially as she self-medicates with one potent drink after another, with distilled *pneuma*, *psyche*, and wit.

And all the while she broods, mumbles, then stares with a death ray, a beam of destruction to wither, crisp and incinerate things on contact.

Just as significantly, even an emperor who claims to be God has done it in the past, as well as various types of kings, such as high king, Adipose Rex, puppet king, rightful king returns, or the king mook, and all those "gods of war," that long "list of war deities": they ballroom-blitz.

It also happened to queens, such as the high queen, queen regnant, queen dowager, queen consort, and even the queen mother, who quietly, and often, considers a ballroom blitz, especially on certain wayward family members, and subjects; well, just discreetly ask the Queen Mum when no one else is looking, and it might surprise you as she discreetly nods, and has often considered a plow through the system, the fallow, or furrow, as well as symbolic goods and space, then the utterly confused asks, "Why now?" and "What the heck was that, Mum?" and "How did that tipping point arrive?"

Worldwide, people live under tremendous pressure, most of it deliberately made so, deliberately made complex as well as artificial, and especially as a person approaches the great frontier, which represents most systems, especially the new age systems, and that approach often requires a new script overlay, such as a social version, or OverlayFS, for lack of a better word, to manage all those internal conflicts within the self, maintain that one-dimensional high-wire act through life, as millions of options exist, yet a system often mandates a very narrow path, as well as style and set of choices, or for instance, attack to civilize, to gain histaminic relief, or surrender, or escape. And most often it requires more digging in the quagmire, or fortify it, such as justify, and do it fast, now—yes, now, go-go-go, or ballroom blitz.

Much later, and with the aid of moonlight, Agrippa eventually finds those parked customized Buicks, a high-gloss amber-red 1949 Buick Roadmaster coupe, as well as two other 1949 Buick Roadmaster coupes, one flat black and the other a high-gloss slightly darker version of Chinese wolfberry. Frenemy cars that have been chopped, lowered, and made into high-performance, high-end muscle cars, into tricked-out super beasts, similar to the Barrett-Jackson Scottsdale 2007 auction of lot 935, though with over 600 horsepower, as in true power, raw power, high-octane industrial might of an old-school savage, with a press-the-gas pedal and the industrial savage will leap.

For her, the mere sight of these tricked-out super beasts creates an adrenaline dump.

So much so the heart pounds and pounds as a realized truth, then the mind repeatedly sparks, crackles and crisps various mental regions as it formulates a pernicious revenge.

Moments later the eyes repeatedly narrow, and with each new formulation she sneers, scorns and smolders, then enters the club.

CHAPTER  17

However, after forty minutes, Agrippa exits that New Hope Pennsylvania club and goes home.

In retrospect, and while in that club, she did not sprint and deliver a flying knee to an opponent jaw, or deliver a spinning back fist, again and again, or deliver a sharp spinning elbow to an opponent eye socket, again and again, or deliver a sharp spinning elbow to an opponent jaw, again and again, or eventually receive black eyes, large ugly purple and yellow contusions, bruised ribs or other damage, which a mild cough or sneeze would create a holy smokes moment, create an acute debilitation, followed by ugly spasms. Then the body contorts in a series of events then eventually withers and wanes into a stupor, as well as produces bizarre hallucinations, because none of those things happened this time.

Because moments before the fight, club security saw her surge inside and that stare designed to disintegrate things, then they discreetly ushered her into a private alcove.

And these upscale security officers applied a special coolant style, which included very specific techniques of subtle gestures, done with an exceptionally serene, steady, and unflappable style.

So much so they quietly deflated each impulse, and wave after wave with nuance adjustments and methods, until her transfixed bug-eyed anger stabilized and settled down in a distinct series of phases, then a durable calm eventually arrived.

All as biological products coursed through her, then eventually settled into less susceptible regions, into places less able to fuel a feral rage, leap, and utter destruct.

Just as importantly, these systematic and exceptional whisperer coolant skills gave the full impression of an art form or natural science, which deployed a calm and sure tone, as well as a series of well-timed coolant cues that included quite civil eye interactions and nuance gestures.

Where, they countered each foreshock or new potential wave at the earliest stage, the stage before she focused and marshaled forces, those internal biological products, before each effort gained momentum from a prepositioning stage.

And their efforts neutralized something each time, and before all those biological substances in her distributed and found the right location, or wrong if you prefer.

In some respects, this skillset and timing resembled early intervention before the Rayleigh–Taylor instability and that hydrodynamics pattern, or something to that effect. As if they addressed the source of all that swirl of turmoil, byproduct and distribution, which may indeed be a lost art, and something rarely taught regarding protest, counterculture, rebellion, herd behavior and crisis management, as well as a daily resource, mainstay or abide, such as being exceptionally cool and calm under enormous pressure.

So much so, and to people, it represents a surprise that families and educators do not teach this coolant skillset as a core requirement, part of the essentials, especially to the very young at those formidable stages.

For example, teach the terrible twos and at other major stages that need vital techniques and tools to cope, to adapt and prosper, and especially teach these things when the mind first creates fundamental structures, scripts and resolution styles, creates the foundation, foundation of the humanities and science, those major categories and peer-to-peer alternatives, peer-to-peer as a meme, as a dynamic yet stable point-to-point communication building block technique.

In addition, advance empirical research might unravel the mystery of prevention, escalation and de-escalation of a panic-prone public with very short attention spans, as well as the distribution of products through the body then social system, and how it relates to biophysics, biochemistry, politic, and other fields that include diet.

Well, maybe not, and society could say no to these special skillsets, particularly the powers-that-be, and not teach them for a very good reason: drama—as drama, smolder, and dysfunction represent a major propellant of many economic systems, as they create turmoil for profit, which include attitude polarization, unrest between the systems, ethnicities, minorities, and other constructs. And they use thrownness, as well as sacred and secular versions of a great apostasy, or to stomp at a primary pillar or twos, or insert a moral hazard here and there, or a tyranny of small decisions, leaky abstractions and other things, which that collectively exhaust the reasonable, as if a *Raisin in the Sun* or some other version, depending on the culture. As they are often given a no-win situation, a choice of "uglies," and frequently absolutes, such as narrow and or binary options, even in an exceptionally complex situation. And this technique applies to gender, race, family, team, tribe, institution, politic and school of thought, as a pawn, sacrificial lamb, scapegoat, and often choices given by warring pairs that often sincerely believe this is the final battle, the war to end all wars, which often creates a theatre of the absurd and the soulless cruel machine aspect, to devalue beauty, spirit and history, along with other deliberately created forms of chaos, which may promote a race to the bottom or decline of a civilization—well, as if a special career path, industry, or done as a classic fundraising tool? Because, chaos sells stuff, such as the big ugly, and the art of imbedding systemic risk to manufacture profit. So the prize of conflict becomes conflict itself, such as "divide and conquer," "decrease and conquer" or a similar algorithm technique, for those exceptional profit margins, as well as letters of marque, *in personam* jurisdiction and *quasi in rem*: life?

However, grow a less volatile brain structure, especially during those early formidable years, and many economies might eventually collapse from lack of retributions both major and minor, from petty spite, which that quickly leap into a variety of cultural and conventional wars. Economies might collapse from lack of pillage, one after another, from one raid after another, in what seems as if an endless series of raids, on versions of self, the *hominin clade*, social constructs and nature, and done so with a variety of different styles that add a shiny new veneer and slogans-of-the-day from top-down systems, which often include buzzwords, fancy labels, and bling to provoke anima and animus, provoke animadversion or impose a system, provoke the brand, fan base and flash mob with a guerrilla or viral marketing promotion, of promote another super trope, or another high-octane nightmare, and it is usually sold as a vital, as another system to end all other systems?

However, it often produces another layer of gnarl or gristle, of tough, tendinous, or fibrous matter, another entanglement, which that represents the classic approach and favorite tool, to use impulse and smolder with very few options, such as fight, flight or surrender, or better yet buy, buy into a program or script then sign a few very complex long-term contract, with ever so small fine print to entangle?

So, it might be best to avoid this exact science, avoid those whisperer coolant skillsets and wide scale usage, especially during those crucial years of early brain structure development and mindset formation, as it might lead to a tipping point, to a golden age of peace, which could break that classic primordial spell, that petty style and major source material for the big ugly, and break that disruptive wave, which relies on an easily tippable being and other social constructs, as well a prickly me, the frantic me, often in crisis and exceedingly stubborn to stay that way, stay in that escalation cycle, as expressed through a hydrodynamic Rayleigh–Taylor instability which swirls through civilizations, through gender, family, tribe, team, politic, enterprise, religion and race, and because a golden age of peace could cause a profound economic collapse?

Regardless, as well as here and now, and with a deep sophisticated high-octane exhaust rumble, that tricked-out iridescent burnt orange muscle truck exits New Hope, enters Route 202, then eventually travels pass Suffern, Woodbury, Kingston, and continues north, while Agrippa consumes the last energy drink then one beer after another, and focuses on bitter memories, which causes her to smolder then mumble about this and that.

Then moments later, she speaks in a very loud declarative speech, a soliloquy, as if still in the armed forces, and among raw recruits or fellow hardcore commanders, and the speech consists almost entirely of foul language, quite, which contains five straight minutes of not repeating the same foul word, and says in that bold cuss master tradition used by military commanders, a tradition that continues to this day among certain warriors who curse above and beyond everyday foul mouth themes.

In fact, it represents a high cultural style, as odd as that might sound, within this low-brow art form, sort of a sweet science of exceptional foul-speak, designed to shock and provoke the senses, and yet when done in a certain way, it can reveal a well-seasoned mind, certain refined judgment, sentiment and taste, even scholarship, yes, that sounds odd, and done so with a well-crafted mastery of aesthetics, of nature, art, beauty, taste, and especially the sublime.

Offshoots exist. In fact, most have long-standing traditions, such as a warrior poet who is someone tough and courageous in battle and yet has another dimension, a profound cultured being with a well-seasoned and agile mind, as well as a person capable of delivering a fistic lesson or spinning karate chop to the throat, and another, and another, or reveal some extraordinary scholastic insight, for instance, contemplate the big questions of life and the universe, as opposed to a savage or common thug or the well-educated version.

However, Agrippa has none of those advanced poetic skills, yet does qualify as a cuss master and by necessity, in order to survive. Especially within the military, because women must make more than a few adjustments, a few compromises, and sometimes they must use very crude tools to avoid showing any hint of weakness, which would invite an attack by the enemy and even one's own system, well, as tough love, or so they say. As well, women must hide certain refined culture, which includes symbolic nicety tokens of consideration and those other crucial elements of a truly civilized system, such as a sense of compassion and mercy for the weak, victim and prey, which, oddly enough, represents two components of true greatness, two of those pesky things.

Here and now, and after exiting onto one rural secondary road after another, and through sparsely populated areas, Agrippa continues essentially north northwest, drives through the sticks, the boondocks and remote places far from civilization.

Eventually the truck rumbles up and into a pristine moonlit forest of cedar, yew, cypress, spruce and pine, as well as into the hills and pass an occasional rocky stream; then the road narrows, requires plenty of quick and awkward driving maneuvers here and there, with difficult turns and elaborate switchbacks.

In due course the road narrows even further and takes on a very remote feel, then within minutes it leads up and up into the mountains, into the majestic, into a place that has a sublime and prehistoric feel, and of certain trees, shrubs, ferns, as well as an occasional patch of fog, which gives the forest a certain ethereal atmosphere of the transcendence, of a better place, fit, free and fair, of original intent, and a fresh start.

However at 2:00 a.m., the circadian rhythm creates a triple witching hour from melatonin, liquor, and habit. As all those sleepless nights of tossing, turning, grumbling, smoldering and cursing from the prospects of bankruptcy, as well as betrayal, all take their toll, or put another way, they demand a toll, a withholding tax, or quite possibly a severance, sin or death tax, or what maybe an eternal tax.

As a result she begins to lose focus, the vision blurs now and again, then rapid blinks help, as the truck enters and exits one forest section after another, which each time produces a whoosh effect then dust, debris and fallen leaves rustle in her wake, as eyes close and open with a special pattern.

So, to stay alert and fill the moment, she turns on the radio, and what might be "Max Manus OST – 18" by Trond Bjerknes plays.

However, it only creates a feeling of alienation, and of someone who barely survived a war, who feels numb, damaged, spent and systematically ground down, as if the system has ground things out of her, such as joy, charm, fascination, imagination and zest for living, and into a state of mind with few choices.

Moreover, things around her begin to change.

They take on a pale, empty and surreal look, as if at the very edge of existence.

So much so, grogginess causes her eyelids to grow heavy and slowly bat.

As, they seem easy to close and bring a certain relief, comfort, as well as peace.

However, they require a great struggle to open each time.

As a result, the task of staying awake becomes her central focus. It becomes a real struggle to open the eyes and stay in this world, to drive, to pay the tax, such as spark a revolution then pay a special toll or tax, a withholding tax, or a farming tax system, with natural tension between state and the farm, or container and product, the self, such as a revenue issue if you will, or ataxia, and not a tax-free threshold, yet the continual price of admission, and a full reconciliation seems to get further and further away—that heavy burden.

So much so and each time these eyes shut, it seems as if the universe collapses; it ceases to exist, and eventually a new one buds into existence.

This open-and-close pattern continues, as if along some great wave, one after another of destruction, creation and expansion, and so forth.

As, some of these places seem quite brief and elusive. While others feel extraordinarily vivid, even peaceful and inviting, for instance, "Come a bit closer—yes, more, and stay for a while, stay forever, for an eternity, or better yet, stay in this timeless place that transcends, a place not restricted to a particular time or date, or absorb back into nature, into the stockpile."

However, something happens—something.

More and more these places seem irrational, excessive, crude and treacherous.

Eventually the truck moves through a rare section of road with streetlights, and one by one each passing fixture casts very distinct light and shadow into the truck, especially into the passenger side.

So much so these shadows move about, as well as fade in and out of existence.

As a result, her focus shifts from the road to inside the truck.

And she seems transfixed by these passenger-side shadow casts, especially all those patterns, which appear on the passenger door panel as if a portal, an opening in some great wall or important structure, such as a building, fortification, community, history, tell or system, with an exceptional view that reveals hidden aspects, reveals a profound mystery.

All the while, her eyelids grow heavy. And even the simplest movement takes a great deal of effort and tremendous concentration.

Moreover, that side of the truck becomes a story unto itself, a third act and great mystery.

So she explores, as if a third culture person, psychonautic, transformative, grok or kythe agent, or equilibrium refinement within that great phantasm expanse of supra and subspace, and yet it feels as if a cave wall, possibly Plato's cave or some mystic grotto, one that seems ancient, oddly illuminated and a quite familiar place, such as a place-based education, or of primes and places, as well as an important telling, or teller of an election, amendment or possibly a dangerous mine, where a pioneer might carefully dig at the substratum for an idea, spark, zap or a Bethany solution, for a last possible second effort, because of procrastination in a very narrow field of time, and that final deadline, that final *verbum sat zapienti est*, to rise from the rut: rise!

With a sense of awe, she studies these complex images, these AB hylomorphs. As, they explain a few Franz Kafka notions, Schröder–Bernstein theorem for measurable space, indexicality, as well as distinct branches on her trouble tree, and that tree common space associate with contemplative practice, as well as lateral roots that branch to unrealized resources, highly specialized biological scripts, atavisms, exaptations, *weltanschauungs*, internal gardens and understudies of potential sparks.

All the while her brain searches for something, which seems elusive and beyond a full fathom, just beyond reach, beyond transliteration and a private revelation.

Moreover, and to reach beyond, her brain waves occasionally shift to invoke a major mental adjustment, to petition for help, as well as support, to appeal to the internal coalition, for a great effort at this frontier, and with an earnest request for a full fathom, with a unihemispheric slow-wave sleep, something to improve the sleep-deprived driving, such as a sleep and release to enable more maneuverability, to enable a deep power shell effort, to explore the great frontier, and then hemispheric roles shift into a profound configuration, as the paired opposites reassign vital responsibilities and allow a bold venture, such as how it was done during the golden age of the aquatic apes?

Moments later, the sound of a very powerful distant explosion catches her attention for a few seconds, a sound from the heavens, the star-filled sky.

However, the eyes and brain want that elusive full fathom, then "Bang!"

CHAPTER

With tremendous force, something crashes through the passenger side windshield, which causes the truck to wildly fishtail out of control.

So much so, as well as moments later, the truck grinds against a steel guardrail, which sparks again and again, then a thick tree branch whacks the truck with enough force to pulverize things, and this happens three times.

Eventually, a tire blows then shreds, and rubber strips fling.

Again, the truck grinds that guardrail, which causes sparks, and again, and again.

Moments later, another tree branch whacks the truck and pulverizes things, and another and another until bang, which causes the truck to leap up and over that steel guardrail then down the steep mountainside.

And all along the way it runs over things, as if in a tremendous battle, over shrubs, small trees and rocks, which whack the truck or gouge underneath, yet none slow that rapid descent.

CHAPTER  19

Then the truck runs over more shrubs then a sizable tree, and another, as well as very large rocks that bang and gouge underneath.

Moreover, and from one side or the other, an occasional tree branch whacks the truck. So much so and each time, they create tremendous dents and pulverize aspects, such as a door handle, trim and glass.

Moments later, the truck takes a mighty leap then sails off a precipice.

CHAPTER 20

Finally, Agrippa appears fully awake with wide eyes. Although limbs seem frozen and she sits speechless, the mouth forms an "Oh!" position, the classic "Oh, my God!" expression, as if rediscovering faith, yet which version, because within any religion profound divisions exist, major schisms, as well as denominations, and any given religion can have as many as 50,000 denominations or more, each quite sure it represents the best way, each with a unique perspective, such as schema, orientation and value system, its own zeitgeist or localized solution, of divergent thought, as if an agent of innovation. Or they differ, as if a visionary, truth-telling sage might, or poet trying to reach accord with nature, with the universe, and not as a pale copy of a copy, not a distant memory, such as a drudge, though done as a good shepherd might, or maybe a hippie religious teacher or the eccentric mentor version, as if a local scout, at the great frontier, or as a wasteland elder in search of the one true light, the one true full-spectrum event, of move from the darkness into light, into an indestructible place, garden and eternal home?

Regardless, the mouth freezes at the first stage of "Oh!" as the truck falls, and falls, and oddly enough her hands move to the traditional ten-and-two steering wheel position, the often taught position, and something she stubbornly refused to do in the past, because of, well, whatever, maybe stubbornness, pride, bravado, or from justification based on exceptionalism, skill and a belief in quick reflexes, and all reinforced with a mantra or two.

In fact, year after year she refused to drive with the classic ten-and-two-system, even as family and friends warned then eventually nagged, and nagged about reaction time danger, from her easygoing lap-high two-finger-style.

However, stubbornness matters—it really matters—and that trait exists elsewhere in nature, such as within gender, family, tribe, team, politic, enterprise, culture, religion, race and within other constructs, other forms of individualization, other localized solutions, especially ordinary atoms, as well as ideas, universal truths, aspirations, precepts and practices, even within the quest for dignity, freedom and justice, as opposed to standardization, or else, bada-bing bada-boom, with a full emphasis on boom, to jolt, or smash.

Sometimes stubbornness defies convention, the system, defies the large-and-in-charge, or Mr. Big, or Miss Big, or the man or woman behind the man, or the ultimate authority, the da chief, or the load-bearing boss, or champion planar. It even defies universal law and the classics of a stable configuration, such as how to properly sit, as well as travel in high-dimensional topology, in spacetime, and discreetly, as a best-effort grok or anchor in the great spectacular, in the big ugly?

For some, stubbornness or the process associated with "no" represents a favorite device or tool. As certain people, phenomenon and noumenon often deploy it as a reflex, or reflect an intrinsic system, as if that default position in people originates from a second internal decision-making system, for instance, the second brain if you will, the gut, as in do bacteria rule and manipulate the mind?

Have the meek already inherited people and other living things, have they already inherited the earth, the first ones, have they always been in control, especially control of personality, emotion and mood? And are animals including humans merely borrowed scenery or stagecraft, and some more so than others, easy to borrow, as well as control? Such as, those who rely on a gut decision-making system, who might represent a borrowed heap of opportunity, as compared to the senior executive function, abstract thought for complex problems, symbolism and the subtle? Moreover, do these houseguests rule the self, and who is the real indentured servant, as within the human body, bacteria and prokaryotic microorganisms outnumber by a ten to one or so ratio? So human cells represent a very small minority within the body, within the great empire of the self?

Regardless, and midflight, the truck pitches slightly forward as it continues to fall, and fall towards her inevitable death, to a rude and sudden impact, which would jolt wit and realized gains, from the body acquired during that great unbroken chain of generation after generation. Whether it is a bible-thumping 10,000-year chain or so, or some other cultural version, or a four-billion-year version, of anatomically modern human and human predecessors, such as a hominidae great ape, primate, mammal, amphibian, bilaterian, animal, multicellular life, complex cell, cyanobacteria, simple cell then gunk, or the technical term might be a biogenic glop, within a variation of Hades, within a hellish early conditions on Earth, as well as an extreme bombardment, and that entire precarious unbroken chain over time, which led to the eventual creation of a childless Agrippa.

Just as importantly, the impact might abruptly reduce her into a crude lump of baser material, into a phylogenetic glop, or punctuate her equilibrium at the minimum.

So the ten-and-two driving system now seems quite reasonable. As hands firmly grip those traditional steering wheel positions, maybe to ensure a smooth transition, which goes to show that even certain stubborn people and systems can change. They can atone when at the great frontier, the great threshold adventure, at the enthalpy threshold that tests and puts the identity in full foreclosure crisis, which might lead to the classic unemployment or underemployment equilibrium. Because one must start at the very bottom then aspire, as well as branch with new ways and means, with new primitive contracts, some of the original contract types, to bargain for a soul, and with considerable tradeoffs, as well as implications of mission drift, such as a drift net, reservoir, station then trike.

With that, the truck impacts a steep mountain slope.

Then it plows over one shrub after another then a sizable tree, and another and another, as well as large rocks, which bang and gouge underneath.

Then on any given side, an occasional branch whacks the truck here and there. So much so and each time, it creates a tremendous dent and pulverizes things including the last door handle, trim then glass.

Moments later the truck takes another mighty leap. Then it sails off a final precipice: Agrippa!

CHAPTER

Eventually, and as a direct hit, the truck explodes through a red barn roof then one floor after another, which causes considerable debris to fall through, such as shingles, beams, joists, studs, as well as panels, braces, purlins, struts, posts, flooring, then hay, chickens, ducks, a beloved pet goose, feathers and plenty of dust.

Lastly, a squirrel falls within that pile.

Moments later this creature alerts, as if saying, "What-what-what?" and the classic squirrel twitch-twitch-twitch.

Then it climbs the rumble, the heap, above civilization.

And there it grooms with tiny hands in an effort to remove rubble, remove fragments of same-old, same-old, then looks as if saying, "What-what-what?" as well as the classic squirrel twitch-twitch-twitch.

CHAPTER 22

Elsewhere, the Punker Buster must quickly decide whether to go back and clean that initial bunker hazardous waste, which pollutes the local timeline or worse, chase those things along that passageway, decipher that cloaked gained species mystery conducting secret experiments, repair more underground sections that maintain forest shadows, snares, pits and other wiles, repair more worldwide abilities to deliver retribution against trespassers, or repair the future, repair the throne, the official residence and fortified crown, which has a human aspect, yet of supreme technocracy and unquestionable glory.

Meanwhile, and elsewhere, that chthonic throne again resembles a being, as well as thing, and appears at an odd stage, at the border of a great threshold adventure, and many aspects of this throne and underground system appear in full crisis, as if at an enthalpy threshold of an identity foreclosure, a critical phase transition during the great identity versus role crisis of the self, at that natural barrier, with the mystery of various internal and external separations as well as all those nuances, and where many things will not reconcile in conventional spacetime.

Just as importantly, that profound throne crisis continues, which creates an intractable EXPTIME—hard balkanization, feudalism, the great survey, stratified sampling, and accidental sampling, also known as "the grab" or opportunistic sampling of just in case.

Often, as an idea, person or thing progresses, the mission drifts or feature creep occurs, and the more elusive original intent becomes two steps forward, one step backward, or worse, drifts into someone else's domain, into the surly.

And this especially seems the case for overall system stability, as well as endurantism, which better accommodates the theory of special relativity, specifically when a person or enterprise takes an idea then applies it to real-life dynamics and scalability, the classic problem, and those pesky things, as well as system bloat with "ad hoc, informally-specified, bug-ridden, slow implementation," and other unforeseen things built into nature, the mostly hidden.

As life has too few straightforward approaches, lines, paths or options to a solution, and can a person walk on a truly straight line, really, or draw one; and yet they expect a system to move that way: that frequent misalignment or mystery?

Just as importantly, as well as here and now, many underground throne system aspects continue to vie for full control, or is it *c'est la vie, tranche de vie, eau-de-vie,* a buzz, or buzz-saw over other parts, especially the weak, the easy to overrun, with an exigent circumstance, with emergency powers, such as the classic style of a very powerful aspect, "I can change the rules at any time or place, regardless of logic as well as reason?"

So, just like that, more significant parts of the throne system are under new management, as an all-powerful person, family, tribe, politic, race, transnational or other construct might take over a town, city or nation-state, or a group of transnationals take over a large nation-state, sometimes with brute force, with a spinning karate chop, and another, and another, or with a buzz-saw, yes, yet most often with ever so sly infiltration, especially between things, between vital segments, or a batch insert, or modified a key aspect of the "set, process and thread," especially the *mise-en-scène,* to control the message.

And, aspects of this underground bunker system use a series of feints, tricks, tricks of the mind, such as cognitive bias, to provoke other underground subsystems to panic, to overreach.

Of which, this often seems the case, especially for those less able or not designed for direct confrontation, for combat, as well as open warfare, such as Dacian warfare, or the latest stage of the never ending escalation, of truly unconventional and asymmetric warfare, especially the psychological warfare of economics, which focuses on frequent use of thrownness, phase transition, seam management, emergence, swarm behavior, spontaneous symmetry breaks, convection cells, and real-time stochastic calculus.

As, internal forest system aspects grab and fight-it-out, the classic frontier style of grab as much stuff as possible, that frenzy, as well as very personal attacks, which seem so quick, raw, and savage, and what has really changed in the last 250,000 years: tools and devices, that form of endless escalation?

As a result, many throne system aspects try a compel underline twist of separation, and freedom.

However, in general and throughout history, many systems resemble the mafia, such as once in even on a technicality or by way of a desperate local weakness, deliberately make weak by one means or another, and the device or construct owns you for life, owns the people, land, sea, and air, the atmospherics, the airwaves, and all are considered property of the system, yet rely on semantics, a shallow language game, such as state, religion or some other construct, and of equal importance, it attempts to own history?

Yet it often calls the process some other names, or euphemisms, which refers to taboo topic, such as a blaspheme, sacred or inviolable, all of which translates to no way out, ever, as if eternal, and that represents a popular management style throughout history of the human species and other animals, as well as the history of atoms, and chemical elements, yet humans were supposed to be above all that, above nature, at least according to history?

Just as significantly, more throne aspects seem almost human, as well as techno glory, and not bling, not a shallow version, yet true glory, though now confused, disoriented, isolated then forsaken, and in a profound crisis—such as, will they survive from all that experimentation and fandom, as well as from this new golden age of biological, chemical, material and subspace manipulation?

CHAPTER

Regardless, the Punker Buster appears indecisive about whether to go back and clean that initial bunker hazardous waste, which that pollutes the local timeline or worse, chase those things along that passageway, repair more underground sections that maintain shadows, snares, pits and other wiles, repair more worldwide abilities to deliver retribution against trespassers, or repair the future, repair the throne, the official residence and fortified crown, which that has a human aspect, yet of supreme technocracy, of unquestionable glory.

As the cleanup would take a considerable series of time-consuming efforts, because the polluted smolder and ruin has a chaotic quality especially when approached; as well, there's the issue of how to dispose with the proper material handling methods.

Indeed it would require a meticulous effort, as this bunker system has a considerable amount of smolder and bits of unusual rubble, of "final days" ability, or end of days, end of time or eschaton, the final events of history, and ultimate human destiny.

Just as significantly there seems so much of it, which would require a careful effort, careful not to trip and drop any of it.

In addition, the process must occur in ever so slow stages, with special handling procedures.

And tradition dictates a shortcut, bypass, combinatoric, parallel metaheuristic, "WP:SHORT" or with some other quick approach, such as a surge, swarm, or saturate it and apply overwhelming force, because as a small amount of force is good, so overwhelming force must be great, truly great, at least according to the history of civilizations, to the thematic style of bang-bang-bang on something until it fits.

Then the Punk Buster considers treating the universe as if it represents a version of mind, or more likely the mind mimics the universe, or all mimic a container, such as the supreme bulkhead or bulkheads, the supreme stack or the quintessential metastack.

Regardless, the Punk Buster must quickly decide one of those five choices, all of which seem quite bad in their own special way.

However, and from hazardous waste proximity as well as a sudden shift in material temporal inflection, the Punk Buster drops that vital handheld device then staggers back again, and again must, one by one, drag those bears to a safer distance.

Just as importantly, the one-of-a-kind handheld device had shattered, and the pieces seem beyond repair and resemble a pile of plastic and metal junk.

Then moments later and elsewhere, the entire throne and many bunker residences shudder again and again, as a human might; and then many aspects seem almost human—confused, disoriented, isolated then forsaken, and in a profound crisis from all that threshold experimentation, which produces a profound sense of alienation, as in a secular version of "Why have you forsaken me, oh Lord?" from a major crisis from all that threshold experimentation, as well as from the universal expansion process, which produces a deep sense of alienation.

As a result, and again, other system aspects panic at that threshold, at that great precipice.

CHAPTER 24

Mid-morning, in eastern Sussex County, Delaware, the Buick caravan exits Route One, turns left onto Rehoboth Avenue, and drives pass the public library then into a quaint small seashore town.

As a result, the smell of barbecue arrives.

So much so, it causes the visitors to alert, notice, and fascinate, as others eat mouthwatering pulled pork sandwiches, world-class lasagna made with fresh mozzarella, parmesan and ricotta cheese, or stuffed bell peppers made with rice, lean ground beef, basil, marjoram, olive oil, and generously topped of ever so fresh parmesan cheese.

Then more heavenly smells arrive, such as wave after wave of newly made pizza, a real pizza, not the industrialize version, such as a franchise or institution, and based on a chemist notion or theory of how to save a few coins, a so-called better-idea, a quick modern fix, based on a found molecule or two, or polymer, not an institutional technique, such as from a new age food-flavoring company, a specialist, based on life in an institution, that bubble, who make a cardboard whatnot, and the type that cools and turns into what?

What is that thing?

What are those new age pizzas?

Institutions often make pizza, not with an old-school baker, not with a classic artisan, not with real old-school techniques based on an exceptional tradition, based on the very best Middle Ages tradition, or Assize of Bread and Ale, or some other exceptional old world natural tradition.

Here and now, these pizzas are made with real homemade ingredients.

Then more smells arrive, of calzone and *stromboli*, an Italian turnover filled with cheese, typically mozzarella, as well as the finest Italian meats, such as salami, *capicola, bresaola,* and on occasion, vegetables, filled with the best of the best, yes!

Beyond that, other people carefully enjoy other things.

They enjoy and tend to hand-dipped ice cream, and do so from one angle after the other, to alternate; and some slowly spin the cone with a continuous lick, well, to maintain a certain shape, style, symmetry, and for a practical reason, to manage the drip, to not become a drip painting.

However one person becomes a work of art, and passing people notice, many find joy, point until the wife notices then offers him an evil eye, as well as a fully animated lecture about this and that, especially about old unresolved issues, and some of these issues seem older than the hills.

Just as significantly, other people have a unique lick style, verve, or *con brio.*

In fact, one person paces about, as if a major event, yet another steps side to side, while another tippy toes, and one person ignores the pesky aspects, sees a considerable drip too late then overcompensates, and enough so the delight tips over and meets the grass.

Other people enjoy *gelato,* frozen custard, Italian ice, sherbet, Popsicle, or a chocolate ice cream sandwich or two, as they can be addictive and quite easy to eat one after another.

Others eat *halo-halo,* or *dondurma*, and all the while many people try to eat fast enough, so a single drop does not touch the hand, or worst yet, another drip painting, on the new shirt or shorts.

"Damn!"

"I told you so."

"What!"

"You know."

"I have no idea what you're talking about."

"Really, no idea, none?"

However, something else happens, the brain freeze dilemma, with one person then another.

"Oh."

"Ah."

"Ouch."

"Double damn!"

"Hey, watch you're language."

So, rapidly eat, yet not too fast, not too slow, and watch the drip.

"Okay, I got it, I got it" then seriously try the fastest possible speed, and can a person eat faster, just a bit?

"Nooooo!"

Meanwhile, the gal pals, called "frenemies" by Agrippa, include Vera, Tommy, Emma, Zoey, Benny, Mel, and yes, Samantha, see the boardwalk, as each highly stylized Buick muscle car arrives in side-by-side parking spaces.

"Ah, yes!"

"Finally."

"The promise land."

"I believe."

"Me too."

And after that long drive from New Hope, Pennsylvania, they step out then stretch, really stretch, in search of satisfaction.

So much so an arm reaches, trunk twists, and leg extends: for the best technique.

And what is the best technique after a long sit, a long drive through space?

What represents the best methods to find real relief, as well as satisfaction then mellow with a well-being glow?

How does a person find that position then glow, as well as generate a halo, an original glory, a nimbus that surrounds a person and radiates beams of everlasting virtue and majesty, an aureole of unknown origins, or poetic truth, or gloriole, which resembles a totality, or a restored state, and also when the mind and garment act as one? As they related to the classical abstract Latin noun of *velificatio*, a certain billow effect from the breeze, and the way it was supposed to be in the beginning, with a swirl of new ideas, possibilities, events, expansions into the great mystery.

As, that state appears in art, the classics, especially during the Renaissance, Renaissance Humanism, Neoclassicism and the Age of Enlightenment, and the Romantic era version. Where, a person resembles truth, beauty and mysterious beam of completeness, of totality, a majestic glory, become a fully realized redemption, the source of a great culture, become the source of a truly great civilization, as well as a vapor, the atmospherics, and ethereal yet vivid universal dream, of a psychonautic, that sails through distinguished states, properties, *sui generis*, especially the *qualia*.

So, stretch.

"Yes," as they enjoy the fresh ocean air, as well as classic boardwalk smells, of "Yes," soul-satisfying food.

Then Tommy says in a major decree, of not quite a Decree of Memphis, of Ptolemy V, and as arms stretch out, "Ladies, ladies, we have arrived, and I now fully understand, as well as give into the madness!"

And the girlfriends give her a very strange look, and again, a full double take, as there might be something wrong in the universe, something serious, quite, a major adjustment issue, or special phase alignment, a thing, or an equilibrium refinement, equilibrium stage, and the ladies eventually shrug, as life often has these special days.

So with real gusto, as well as full unity, they cheer several times, as if one with the universe, and in a profound event, a full atonement, a special buyback event, a fountain of youth, and again, and they become well-beings indeed.

In fact, they seem to reach that mental state, at the same time then look about tell jokes, glow, and beam smiles.

Just as significantly, their style turns heads, because of the two-tone Elvira-like updos, vintage fire engine red cat sunglasses, over-the-top casual 1960 versions of highly stylized skirts, blouses, pants, Givenchy Vogue Paris, Vogue Couturier Fabiani, and Guy Laroche Vogue Paris, as the current cool weather permits such a fashion statement, "because the girls are back in town," of what might be, yet a female version of "The Boys are Back in Town - Thin Lizzy": "so, spread the word."

And they continue for some time then eventually Emma senses just the right moment, which seems often, and any excuse to launch into a celebration, search deep into everyone's eyes, hug one person after another, and want to hold hands.

In addition, she calls for a group hug and Tommy cringes, in fact her eyes roll, then closes as she says, "Here we go again.... Let me guess, kumbaya."

Everyone takes that call as a question, put up for a vote, as if a genuine democracy, and one by one they vote with a show of hands.

Vera says, "Yes, without a doubt."

Emma bounces with elation for a resounding, "Yes!"

Zoey does a stylish twirl, curtsy, then puts an index finger under her chin and says, "Leave no doubts, yes."

Benny beams and exuberantly says, "Oh, hell yes, welcome to my world," then does a special happy dance, and a dance not done in human history, and for very good reasons, in fact, too many to list here and now.

Next, a unified Mel and Samantha do an elaborate ever-so-cool over-the-head synchronized z-shaped finger snap routine, along with, "Can do, and think happy thoughts."

Well, that causes Tommy to reach a limit, a bright redline, as both arms fully extend, and pat the air, to slow things down, "Hold on, sistas! I didn't mean it as a question, as an Athenian democracy."

Too late, the gals converge into a tight group hug, which traps Tommy with momentum, and her eyes roll to show a mixture of hesitancy, grump, discomfort, and wanting to avoid, yet eventually, and reluctantly she surrenders, as they squeeze and squeeze, which causes her to utter, "Yeah, yeah, kumbaya! Let me guess, bake a pie, eat a pie."

Soon, Tommy warms a bit, yet still shows signs of awkwardness, especially about the outfit, which shows as being self-conscious with each stiff movement.

However, Mel and Zoey appear in their element, their world, or aesthetic style summary.

In fact, if they could remake the universe, because this represents a good place to start, a new beginning. As both savor these highly stylistic moments, and gush, bubble, chat then show one considerable pose after another, yet they do as any respectable scientist might, of someone who greatly respects the scientific fields, respects the history of ideas, yet does so with style, as well as flair, with context, and not as an ever so dull abstract, not a well-intentioned nerd or geek construct, not an abstract or theoretical, with no substantial visual cue, or cues, that might feed the full imagination of people, feed them vital sustenance, as compared to popular trivia, and the often shallow pop culture or cult, yet sold as vital, as another spectacle or bling of superficial, of sensory candy, such as follow the Nielsen ratings, or equivalent, follow the bling, for a network bonus, regardless of implications, and what can lead to excess, to the shallow language game, into no more excuses?

Soon, they turn to Tommy, who forces a polite smile, tilts the head slightly and says with a long emphasis, "Nice," then shifts to a grumpy manner while pointing to everyone's fancy hairstyles, then her own, "Yeah, yeah, up-d-dos, great, look at me," but that mood quickly disappears and eyes widen, "Oh, look, food!" as Tommy sees and smells fresh barbecue that transfixes, then moves her head about for better angles, to keenly studies people who carry huge plates, piled high with barbecue, homemade potato salad, and sweet jersey corn on the cob.

Of which, she says slowly and softly, "Excellent," then quickly and loudly announces, "Good bye, ladies, unity in numbers, fight the power," and bolts.

Then Emma follows; Tommy immediately notices and thinks, *Oh, trouble*, but the sheer gravity of heavenly barbecue tows Tommy towards paradise.

There, she quickly enters a line and shifts about with excitement at the prospect, even moves from side to side, with a mild dance action in full anticipation, which that seems quite uncharacteristic, a dance move, golden smile and eyebrows wiggle, and again.

Moments later, Emma stands behind her, while Tommy savors in her imagination.

So much so, eyes widen; lips practice then she smiles, nods, and quickly says, "Yeah-yeah-yeah!"

Soon lips form the letter "O," as in "Oh my."

Then more hypnotic aromas arrive, in waves, from pizzas made in a genuine brick oven.

In fact, the pizzas call, in their own way, with bright, vivid and compelling notes.

As a result, Vera, Zoey, Benny, Mel and Samantha notice, turn then bolt towards the food and ogle row after row of mouthwatering pizzas, and nearly every known variety, with toppings from heaven.

Benny says, "Holy smokes!"

"I agree."

"Oh, I'm in love," and they imagine each slice.

Soon, these ladies collect piles and piles of food then eventually arrive at a picnic bench with gained treasures.

In fact, the piles seem more than enough to feed all of them, and several times over.

"To hell with a diet!"

"With starvation."

"Yes."

"And suffering day after day."

"And crunching and crunching on raw vegetables, on Veggie sticks."

"Yeah!"

"And tofu."

"By the way, what the hell is tofu?"

"Curds."

"I thought so; curds, as the name speaks for itself, curds, a special reward, after a long day among the modern toil and trouble."

"Yes, as a new-age indentured servant, in this brave new world, or stark expanse, at the edge of poverty, a paycheck or two away, such as a modern version of the poorhouse.

"Yeah."

Then they recover joy and ogle massive food piles then share, eat, swap stories, poke fun and admire the view, the shore, with an epic expanse of nature, of opportunity, and more than a photo opportunity, a new chance, a fresh start and path into the future, into the paradise, as well as original intent, and that gentle enclave that represents the history of everything.

Just then something happens.

Two kids arrive then motion to the gal pals and other strangers, to gather.

"Yes," gather right here and now, perfect strangers, "come closer," and still "closer."

"Yes."

The kids, nearly twelve, are Donatella and Auslebenstein—well, the father named him Auslebenstein, but the mother calls him Belebenstein.

However, you know kids and that rebellion thing, plus kids often feel more conscious of peer pressure, especially from the petty association, with nicknames and singsong rhymes.

So, the son only answers to a name he picked, Pomer, named after a famous German swashbuckler, a rogue and true trickster, however a better version, one more sophisticated, cultured, reasonable, and exceedingly kind to the disadvantaged class, to people who need a sensible opportunity to aspire, as any given system often offers people a list of very bad choices, with certain paths that represent shallow, false, and petty, or crude, warped, and barren, or offer a disaster, another quagmire sold as vital, and of the first magnitude, yet same old, same old, just new faces, new players or locations, again sold as vital.

And a person must follow, live and grow along that path, grow in someone else's dream, then struggle, and often grow inside a cruel and unusual situation, as well as all that multidimensional pressure, and it eventually takes that person far away from their full potential.

So Auslebenstein has a role, a life mission: to tweak the system now and again, the powers-that-be, such as large-and-in-charge, or Mr. Big, or Miss Big, or the man or woman behind the man, or the ultimate authority, da chief, or the load-bearing boss, or champion planar, or the big ugly, as well as system, especially the stuffy class, gentrification, *gens* Julia, Aetheling, and others. As they often become stale, as in a noblesse oblige stalemate, and that high-wire act, which needs fine-tuning, especially regarding clever and yet practical inventions in aesthetic accord with nature. And where is the real sense of exceptional, to resolve truly great issues, particularly for the disadvantaged class, the people stuck in someone else's bad dream, stuck in a quagmire, an unfold and repeat, a catch-22 logic?

So Donatella and Auslebenstein have a true mission: create a bold future that honors the classics, that system, and something practical, and yet with joy, compassion and mercy, instead of all that system glum, grump, frump and mugwump, and a world system that in many respects seems stale, a poverty of ideas and thoughts, a systematic rut into local communities, a top-down regimental style that often makes matters worse, as a plow, a crude or noble plow, and one that concentrates tremendous power into a very deep rut, a feudal rut, a secular version of "sacred" that translates into "This is the one true way, so, keep digging, as we will guide you"—where?

In the past, as an act of revenge, and when his parents call him Auslebenstein or Belebenstein in public, especially in front of other kids, he and Donatella adopted a theme song, which might be "Don't You Just Know It" by Huey Piano Smith. And it serves as a tool, a device that pokes at the very serious and no-nonsense parents, as well as the stuffy system—then the kids would arrive home, unite and barricade themselves in a room, then meticulously develop a protest plan, against the system, against the powers-that-be, and for a totality of slights, and the parents would bang and bang on the door to demand full obedience, as well as unconditional surrender and respect, or else.

But each time, the door would eventually swing open and that song played on cue, and loudly, then he and the sister did a very serious yet silly, fully animated variation of a *Pulp Fiction* dance, and what might be a Chubby Checker twist, as well as some other fashion-forward ultra-cool dance style. In addition, they did so dressed with highly stylized fashion forward retro fifties looks, as ultra-cool Teddy Boys, both of them. Moreover and on occasion, she dresses as the ultimate Greaser Girl, with a tight skirt, or one that hits around the thigh or full with flounce to the knee, and maybe with a petticoat underneath, to add volume, and on occasion, with a white bobby socks fold down.

So, and each time, the kids would protest with song and dance, as if a truly great and joyous victory, against the system, and in a cool, as well as ever so sophisticated way, at least from their perspective, retro cool, yet it simply infuriated the parents to no end, who alternated in cycles of flabbergast, sizzle, and mumble about this and that.

However, for the kids, ah, they found total joy, paradise, and some secular form of Gan Eden, Avalon, or another official transcendent paradise, and a place with compassion, mercy, and redemption—yes, even for the others—and a place where toes could wiggle in ultra soft dew-covered grass, to, well, measure their full potential, as kids.

Here and now, at the shore, these parents fully realize a public protest is coming, especially as the kids cue other kids, who have a boom box, a mega system.

All of which causes Vera to pause, look, wonder then edge closer, as do Zoey, Benny, Mel, Samantha, Emma, and Tommy.

Then the two kids continue to motion, "Yes, come closer, and still closer," to the gal pals and other strangers.

Moments later, as well as, on cue, that song—which might be "Don't You Just Know It" - Huey Piano Smith—plays.

And the kids dance as well as sing a fun, elaborate and popular dance routines, which triggers something, as a stranger joins, then another and another, until the situation takes on a flash mob aspect.

Moments later, something happens, something quite rare indeed, which causes the gal pals surprise, intrigue then total fascination, as jaws drop.

Tommy joins the dance, moves to center action then sings a key musical part, and with full gusto, with an artistic style, as a true exceptional, then as a special delight, which seems ever so charming.

All of which generates an extraordinary sight indeed, of a two-tone Elvira-like updo, vintage fire engine red cat eyeglasses, organic bubble gum, 1960s ultralight weight two-piece suit, as it's a bit chilly this time of year, brisk in fact, so Lanvin Castillo, Vogue Paris original number 1213 seems quite appropriate.

And soon, this event has the look of an extravaganza, show of shows, especially as a five-year-old girl, Jennifer Congrego, arrives, she from Houston and wears her best floral Sunday dress, as well as white socks, with cute ruffle trim, and black patent leather shoes, which that projects an image of a "true young lady" in all respects.

And she eventually stands next to a boulder.

CHAPTER

Just as importantly, a rope drapes around that boulder—and not an ordinary rope, but the type a person might see on a shrine, for example a Shimenawa rope made from rice straw, or a rope worn by someone who dresses for a special occasion, such as for an initiation ceremony. Although it seems more similar to a tassel, one worn by a chancellor at the University of Oxford or by a foreign minister, as well as one closely associated with a tenacious defender against accusations, a fair hearing, especially against tyranny, thugs, and chaos in whatever form.

In addition, the elaborate polymath rope configuration shows a separation of powers, transformative agents yet borderline life, and something worn by a certain personality type, a person with keen interests, as well as curiosity about the underlying universal principles, such as how things work, the mechanics, and as someone who chronicles events, as well as tracks who recently conducted wide scale experiments, on the various populations, especially on people, and who used a technique known as the "gene drive system," to propel a gene of choice through one population after another, such as "delivering through the Cas9 protein and guide RNA, or a similar process," to the "cash cows," if you will, for lack of a better phrase. As no gene drives have yet been officially tested in the wild, at least according to the-powers-that-be, as that would represent an irresponsible act, to treat the population as theatrical property, very much so, and especially these detected genes, which that are not minor ones, but ones which might reshape the course of human history, change destiny, and quickly amass great wealth, as well as create massive income disparity that represents a topic best discuss in the open, and not in a small circle of privilege, such as inside the dark art of politics, especially regarding the sale of creeds.

Just as significantly, the five-year-old girl leans ever so close to the boulder then whispers something for the longest time, then points here and there with a certain specificity, which implies another best-effort explanation of how the universe really operates, then even more details, such as the structures, mechanics and processes as told to her, and by whom, which she points to.

And of equal importance, she adds her special observations then does so in a way that seems to charm that boulder, which tries to remain devoid of motion.

Moreover, this process continues.

Then, the conversation seems to have a give-and-take quality, an exchange, an ion or as if an exchange student, as she also listens with great interest and a wide-eyed "Oh, really?" which has an ever so cute style.

Yet that boulder does not move—well, at least from the perspective of everyone else, as angles matter, especially *qualia,* as well as the willingness to shift, to the best psychological states or altered state of consciousness, or techniques, for any given situation, as well as adjust the internal storyboard, and if need be, the battle cry of freedom.

Moments later, the little lady kisses that boulder—she delivers a transformative kiss, the rare type, a once-in-a-lifetime, if you are ever so lucky enough to receive, and at the same time, on delivery, one of her feet lifts from the ground, that special type of charm, such as to charm the spirit, as well the personal termination and bow shock then ethereal.

However, and not far away, her parents see, reel, gasp, dread, and fully exasperate, again.

Also, they lose their bearings then lecture her with exceptionally harsh words and wild gestures, as if her actions bring dishonor, ruin and shame, as well as reveal a pernicious family defect, a defect that extends back generation after generation, maybe to Cain, or some other equivalent, in another culture, and the parents continue with that theme for a considerable amount of time, of "Blah-blah-blah," especially their utter frustration and perplexity, as "Little ladies don't do those sorts of things, ever. And what were you thinking?"

It resembles another phenomenon: when Agrippa was born with two mighty fists, and those doctors and nurses made the newborn more presentable, as well as moved exceptionally close then made ogle noises, those classic "goo-goo gaa-gaa" baby talk sounds, to charm her, as well as showed those faces, those exaggerations baby girls receive, those "Oh, she's so pretty," "She is such a wonderful darling!" and "She's so cute!" and "How did you get so cute? Come on; tell us, how did you get so cute?"

Then, the little baby girl seriously considered their efforts, seriously pondered, squinted a few times, then released a single finger—yes, the finger, that finger—which completely shocked then disappointed the doctors and nurses, who, in fact, and based on this action, "Well, she might not be a little lady after all, or a princess," as in, "They never do those sorts of things, ever."

Right now, the five-year-old girl Jennifer Congrego seriously considers and measures everything the parents say.

In fact, she listens to each and every word, as well as phrase, again, and watches all that over-the-top body language, such as arms that gyrate, as well as a series of crazy looks and their feelings of bewilderment, disillusion, exasperation, anguish, agitation, bristle, rebellion, temper and full denunciation, and that process repeats.

Moments later, the little lady again has a series of realized sparks. So much so, a broad smile arrives, and in a playful manner, she wiggles eyebrows, as a trickster might, with insider information, keen perspective, and sense of proportion— as perceptivity can allow vital context, to the data reference stream, and metabase, or trouble tree for some, which depends on the personality, as in style really matters, especially when processing real-time data. Where some people store things in heaps, in data structures that consist of emotional piles, and some in heaps of raw feelings, bounded in an interval hierarchy, or doubly chained trees of absolutes and perfections, as in "All or nothing," a "Give me liberty or give me death" storage system—well, often a metaphorical death, a symbolic construct, until the "me" locates new bearings, such as a tree of virtue and vices, and everything else sits atop, as compared to an objective cluster, stored by practical facts. And some people store based on a dancing tree, or a whisperer of joy, or a figurative system of human knowledge, or by color, or freshly baked goods, or chocolate products, or panic is the norm, those memory systems. Or some people store based on an obsession, for instance the me, a highly superior autobiographical memory, or shoes, sugary treat, starch, religion, politics, whatnot or other stuff, such as crispy bacon. Or they store by grump, as if a professional grump, a cruel and unusual, who have special tells, give cues of their ever so cruel nature, as people store based on a vast number of systems, which that assign value and priority?

Regardless, the parents are "not amused" by this little lady— "If she really is a little lady."

In fact, they stare at her with a very serious look, again, designed to deflate her willful charm, and they use the "fear of God look," a formidable weapon, from the Old Testament or some other religion, which that uses a beam of shame, hellfire, and brimstone, the classic evil eye, as in "Obey or else," similar to the "end of days," or your last few living moments, which seems to work.

So much so, the five-year-old loses that fresh brilliance.

Then, her charm fades.

Eventually, the lower lip quivers.

In fact, it truly quivers.

Then, the little lady loses vitality—she withers, and something else happens.

She loses that special charm, and once gone, things like that rarely return: life!

However, something else happens—something.

That boulder stirs ever so slightly, again, and not in obvious ways, not visible to classic human sense—as it stirs as if inside, a portable secular aedicula, a shrine, and not the classic type or shape.

It stirs inside what resembles a mobile constitution, a complex superstrate as well as substrate, an empire if you will, with various temporal inflections, or serious temporally managed threshold states, which that separate the past, present, and future, the quintessential stack, and as if a coalition, and as if certain aspects of this boulder are elsewhere, the alterity or entanglement, and maybe part of the quantum entanglement system, as well as the "mythology of lost," and that narrow path to an island, or through a special sequence of hatches, windows or states, or flash-sideways, yet all also known as the parent issue, or container, or apparent, or visible, yet nearly all sit as a dynamic invisible, as well as a hidden gelatinous effect, for lack of better phrases.

However, if taken as a unified whole, this boulder resembles a truly great artist—with a storyline that easily detaches and can set into various forms of music, constitutions, perspectives, settings, architectures, as well as community, emergent phenomena, theatrical property, and moduli space.

Moreover, this thing or creature seems to ponder the five-year-old situation again, as well as the fundamentals, and does so with a complex series of internal sparks, which that crackle within that mind, and a mind resembles a great phantasm, with a very unusual biology and other aspects not easily quantifiable, as a different type of contemplative tree, deep belief network, as well as over net, with certain guiding stellar principles, catalogues and atlases, which have a certain theme, for instance, stay ever so true to oneself, elevate to a noble purpose, keep the objective faith and never panic, ever, or use a *beot*, a ritualized boast of grand stories, about the self and past glorious deeds that promise destruction, to civilize.

Just then, and with an ever so slight shift that no one notices, it looks toward the serene blue expanse of sky, to the heavens, and again studies something beyond the Sloan Great Wall, then Giant Void in NGH, followed by a nearby hidden threshold event, less than forty feet away, a transcendent state, then towards that forest, towards that hidden throne, and a place that gives the full impression of unquestionable glory, a throne that has an imperial quality, and full aesthetic of a supreme technocracy.

So much so, and in a very discreet manner, the boulder crackles, percolates, measures, weighs, and renders a full judgment—as this resembles a hidden initiation ceremony, an official event, one might associate with a chancellor equivalent at University of Oxford, Cambridge, or Bologna.

All the while, that little lady's lip continues to quiver, and quiver.

So much so, eyes well, as that shaming event burrows into her mind, burrows into her *psyche*, as well as soul by design, and incinerates the region responsible for charm and innovation.

It crisps that region of divergent thought, that synectic dream weaver, that region devoted to oblique and lateral strategy, as well as the exedra aspect of a subconscious conversation pit, and the lip truly quivers.

CHAPTER

Moments later, that rock creature projects an exceptionally subtle beam at the little lady, projects one not noticeable to the general public, and one that has a nootropic effect, as well as the benefits of salt, a special version, and how both best function, as a sapient, prudent, shrewd management of practical affairs, as a prudent investor of vital circumspection, piquancy and permanence, which also helps regulate engaging provocative charm, and the lively arch charm device of wit, of the ability to reach beyond the quagmire.

And, that subtle beam works a special region within her mind, as if to *werc*, or *ergon*, or cultivate subspace, the universal entanglement of local, as well as insert an impossible, to create an identical copy of an arbitrary unknown quantum state, and yet eventually does, as the little lady's lip stops quivering, and she stirs, regains vigor then inflates until something happens—something.

So much so, a golden smile arrives, something true and special, as well as an absolute sense of joy, and to make matters worse, she wiggles her brow in a playful yet stubborn manner.

Again, that infuriates her parents to no end, and who each broadcast a speech, a soliloquy, on how they walked ten miles to school, and back, uphill, both ways, and then they speak at the same time about separate topics.

Just as significantly, their heads bob to accent this and that, which resembles two people in a profound mental loop that may well be a rut within the conventional mindset or system, of an often tried path, which that seems to get deeper with each plow effort, and according to that same borrowed script, as well as baggage, tethers and blinders. The type borrowed from someone else, who borrowed from another person, and so forth, and so on, of trapped and fully exasperated people, in a collectively exhaustive system, yet urged to go faster. Or, it might be system-speak, to create loyal consumers or slogs, and a catalog associated with entanglement, frustration, agitation, exasperation, indignation and blah-blah-blah.

Likewise, as the parents loop in that mental schema, and one at a time, older siblings eventually join in and complain in their own way about something, about their side of the story, which has fully pressurized them with all those conflicting scripts, which to a person without a restored dream weaver function, without objective judgment, all those complaints resemble noise, discord and confusion. As a result, each might need more than a special reference desk solution, or reference library, or more than the reference planes associated with celestial mechanics, such as a special view of the heavens—it might need a very special dream weaver, to understand, or a zany inventor, with "six thinking hats," with those six classic skills, or another version, or a Zen survivor, visionary, truth-telling sage, good shepherd, wasteland elder, yet trickster, that sort of tradition or motif, or as a badass teacher, a very gentle soul until you threaten the students, and something based on the classics, or the best version of a zombie survival guide, or *Skeptics Guide To The Universe* and not a *Faux To Guide*, yet something to restore original intent, context, objectivity and practicality?

In addition, and to the little lady, all that noise, discord and confusion again reminds her of Wolfgang Amadeus Mozart, and the movie *Amadeus* as told with a flashback by his peer and secret rival Antonio Salieri, as well as an entangled state, or estate.

So much so, and on her face, a smile appears, about how a duet becomes a trio, a trio becomes a quartet, quartet becomes quintet, and so on—apparently, this phenomenon transcends opera, and it has other applications in nature, in the universe, then at that very moment, it is as if the universe operates as a harmonic wave, and yet a union of paired opposites, dynamics, companions and the dependents, and yet all connected in a single unified wave function, a mostly hidden ontic wave, a hydrodynamics Rayleigh–Taylor instability, with that swirl of turmoil, byproduct and distribution, and so on.

And just then, as well as above it all, a melody arrives, which seems pure, noble, free and fresh, as if it were a series of exceptional poetic phrases, above a dramatic structure, as an uncommon narrative arc of exploration, with three acts: life!

Meanwhile, all family members grumble about this and that, in their own way, as if in their own secular or mobile niche, impluvium, or portable aedicula—as each of them broadcast departed glories.

And then abruptly, the parents tow this little lady along the Rehoboth Beach boardwalk, if in fact she is a little lady.

Then, once at a considerable distance, the little lady turns and waves goodbye.

In addition, she beams a golden smile then in a playful and stubborn manner, wiggles her brow, as if a true trickster, an agent of innovation, as well as change, of change data capture, of change the base rule, or: change the beat!

Or, she might Harlem-shake, at just the right time, at the threshold, of a great adventure then make an ever so smooth transition, into a promise land.

Regardless, the parents notice that brow wiggle then sputter, reel, fully exasperate, engage a tow device, and in a remarkable way, that large family gesticulates along the boardwalk, until they eventually disappear.

CHAPTER 27

During that little lady family event, Vera, Tommy, Emma, Zoey, Benny, Samantha, and Mel notice, and yet it represented the type of thing most people hear, see and follow for a while then shift back to their own lives, own mission, to that long overdue mini vacation, as a change of pace, change of scenery, as well as a real and substantial vacation, and not a quick rest or getaway, not a pit stop or three-day weekend, also called a vacation express, which consists mostly of packing, traveling to the airport, waiting, shuffling, grumbling, arriving, unpacking, depressurizing, paying tourist rates, grumbling, remembering frustrations, preparing to leave, packing, traveling to the airport, waiting, shuffling, grumbling, arriving and unpacking, well, because a real and substantial vacation, on some regular timetable, serves a vital function in nature, and an effective vacation seems quite rare indeed.

Just as significantly, these gal pals eventually notice Samantha, who relaxes, really relaxes, as if the weight of past events lifts, especially that fiasco, the mansion fundraiser, and botched effort to secure a mortgage for Agrippa, who faces a pernicious bankruptcy, eviction, poverty and total disgrace.

However, the friends carefully avoid the subject, the elephant in the room, in order to not embarrass Samantha, or spoil the fun, spoil a pristine day, with a spectacular expanse of ocean, sky, fresh air, excellent food, as well as a genuine sense of peace and well-being.

Moments later, something happens.

And the gal pals look at Tommy then cringe. Because they know what will happen next, the inevitable. As life is filled with direct people—okay, blunt, clunky, and who are known to galumph into a subject, or barge, and embarrass others, as well as have no reasonable internal filter, as if they cannot edit themselves, their thoughts, and do not have the ability or willingness to deploy subtle ways and means, when entering a subject or place.

So, they barge.

Then Tommy launches into the peaceful setting and says, "Look, I know what was said about Sam, and yes, written in those blogs and especially the gossip rags, yet it didn't happen that way. Anyway, do you believe everything on the internet, in the newspaper or on TV, really?

"The media and people in general pick an event aspect, then put a frame around it at just the right angle, to highlight points that match their mindset, and motive, their cognitive bias, such as what will sell to their audience, and reinforce a message they want to send.

"Every person or system has an agenda, which is often hidden like an iceberg, with the vast portion underwater, and what sits above the water is often masked, to lure you closer.

"It's just one perspective, yet they want you to think it's 'the perspective.'

"There are billions of people, and each person has their own slant on the universe.

"A person or system sets the edge, the angles, options, and degrees of, and often overlays black or white, and not a full spectrum.

"And they'll tell you it's the definitive one, and the only way to see it, be it, live it, and often frame it as us versus them, or us versus it, the subhuman, as in, here comes their primary tool of thump, of brute force, the mob, chaos, and another yet another endless cultural war.

"And it often starts with an evil eye, or some other related look, a look to smolder then crisp an ideal, person or thing.

"Regardless, your internal alarms should ring as soon as they display any of the classic signs, such as loud, hyper, twitchy, dominant, absolutely certain and insistent you agree with them, especially right now, which represent a classic sign of a narrow mind event, quite, and one that offers few choices, and often ones that reinforce the quagmire, or quickly neutralize efforts to escape, such as new ideas, of the millions or so options, or chastise a single step towards the quagmire exit."

One after another a friend adds, "Amen."

"You tell em sista."

"You're preachin' to the choir."

Then Vera leans in and whispers to Sam, "So what happened really with the banker?"

Others turn then edge closer.

Tommy says, "I tell ya: Sam noticed Seska, Mero, Livia and the reporters sneaking up the main mansion staircase, and they dragged the banker along. Then she tried to stop them and explained which sections remained off limits for the fundraiser, yet they repeatedly ignored her, so she followed."

Vera deflates, lowers her head and confesses, "Yes. I saw it, eventually followed; yet, okay, I was afraid to say anything."

Tommy seriously considers then says, "Now that I think about it, I'll bet they never had any intention of giving her that loan."

"Maybe it was a scam."

"To get her savings."

"Or a conspiracy."

"Or blackmail?"

"She'll forfeit that deposit?"

"$653,000."

"Holy smokes!"

"Now I really feel sorry for her."

"How could she afford that kind of house?"

"Saving, as well as reenlistment bonuses; she was a Navy commander, plus credit card cash advances."

"She was scammed."

"Twenty-day bridge loan—what the hell kind of loan is that?"

"Manipulated and tricked."

"Hey, by the way, have you noticed those credit reporting services, something about them, such as try and remove an obvious error, and it seems nearly impossible."

"I think the system is rigged."

"Yes, it has an agenda, but for who?"

"The credit card industry?"

"The credit industry."

Others nod in full agreement, "Yes."

"Maybe we should call her?"

As a result, the group winces then pictures Agrippa cursing exceptionally salty language. And insults that could easily stagger and drive back the most feared, such as drive back James Harrison, Clay Matthews, Ed Reed, or Ray Lewis, Jack Lambert, Dick Butkus, Chuck Bednarik, Jack Ham, Ray Nitschke, Sam Huff, and even Bill Romanowski, who would flinch, slowly back away with hands patting the air, as in "Whoa, whoa, hold on lady, you must have mistaken me for someone else," realize the danger then fake an injury, for a timeout, or drag a best friend into danger then quickly exit alone, without ceremony, without the vital ritualized sequence, to open a rarified event or space, and he limps on the wrong leg, yet mid exit, suddenly remembers, and curses beyond all ability to reason then adjusts to the other leg, for a wholly dignified exit, well, because, no one's perfect in any given situation, put on the spot for the best possible answer, and wholly dignified, because someone might record this event, so, an explanation, to family, friends and especially the kids might require an exceptional linguistic feat, a high-wire act with considerable gestures.

Here and now, and as a result, the friends look at one another, consider calling Agrippa, to offer sympathy then flee in various directions.

First, Tommy abruptly disappears. And the likely destination might be a miniature golf championship, at a nearby local replica of the Ladies' Putting Club in St. Andrews, Scotland (Carlson), followed by a maniac, as well as bug-eyed white knuckle drive, in a regional go-kart competition.

Emma follows.

However, Tommy turns and says, "No way sista."

Elsewhere, Reece and Vera find a fast exit, to an antiques roadshow, in search of redemption and glory.

Whereas the two scientists disappear, and will likely go on a helicopter coastal tour then visit a local winery, in search of a balanced, charming, and expansive spirit, which might recreate the Areni-1 experience, or some other Late Chalcolithic event.

In contrast, Benny scouts the Farmer's Market then Dewey Beach, to skim board, or a best effort at, and "oops," and again then what represents the best technique, to skim through time as well as space, with ever so smooth adjustments?

Then later, she searches for trinkets, and the sights, which consist mostly of people watching, of ogling ever so compelling fashion statements, of what makes something a true classic?

And okay, well, she stares at one spectacular body and face, after another.

And what makes someone special, those mysteries, which causes her to astonish then mumble, and that probability represent jealous barely audible impressions, a mimic with considerable head movement, and again, with a less than flattering impression of the perfect, a snooty, snob, of someone superior with an overbearing manner, as well as presumptuous claim.

Then Benny continues to estimate what that person might say or gesture, which seems to represent personal baggage, cues, of subject and viewer, of ever so complex stuff, especially if read between the lines, and of things accumulated before birth, from progenitors, from source material, from the very early days of all living things, from the meek, who merely want a fair hearing, want an ability to express the reasonable, now and again, as if casting a vote in a Gerrymandered system, and yet often cutoff, such as by the powers-that-be or an expressed DNA segment, by an acidic product, a rude local claim, within the local entanglement, of the great string theory yet as a supreme bulkhead, or thread that lace into the stack, the supreme stack, the protocol, or ultimate function, as well as container?

Yet, this is not the right path, at least according to Benny, not the way it was supposed to be, from the beginning.

And, it is not a "08 - Lovely Day."

Yet Benny quickly realizes her error then seems determined to make improvements and have a lovely day.

CHAPTER 28

Elsewhere, and inside that partially collapsed red barn, the only sign of life is a chicken, which seems quite indignant about unjust aggression, then clucks about the rubble.

And when the dust eventually settles, it pecks about for something, for morsels, for a small portion of food, such as a scrap, anything, maybe a treat, maybe something very appetizing to a chicken, for example a tidbit, an attractive, one delightful, and what might lead to a feast.

Moments later, as well as deep within the rubble, something moves, struggles, and eventually a pet duck struggles free, especially to regain dignity and honor, then waddles around with a certain style, as if an exclusive, aetheling, socialite, or tastemaker.

CHAPTER 29

Elsewhere, underground and with only bad choices, the Punk Buster steps forward to manually repair bunker systems, yet moves sideways in time, to another timeline, which greatly perplexes, causes a profound stagger, and quick-steps back, as there seems a considerable number of temporal fractures, as if a "drawing of the analytic extension of tetration to the complex plane," yet all hidden from sight, or put simply, narrow windows into these various aspects, of flash somewhere, often in a loop, or worse.

In fact, it seems quite a tricky venture edging in various directions, as it often leads to profound disorientation, as well as a precarious edge of crumble then steep drop, into no more excuses, into the impossible mystery.

So, there appears no direct path, no clear route into those heavily polluted bunker sections, as one wrong step in most directions and a person would trip into a theater, of one version of another, and lose constructs, frames of reference, a deep belief network, and whole categories of thought, or gain a species, such as a cloaked shadow, just to name a few potential problems, or worse yet, such as thrown to the very edge of the universe, to a final frontier, or out of the universe, as a reject or rejection slip, of sail on, sail away, yet all of these problems sits as a dynamic invisible, for lack of better phrase.

And upon returning from that sideways flash in time, the Punk Buster recovers then notices a cloaked shadow quickly arrive, as if a priority interest, and it moves well inside personal space.

Yet the Punk Buster does not reveal this understanding, as these types of things often happen in free enterprise; they arrive, search for informatic, cash cow and/or treasure then leave.

Just importantly, why start a war unless thoroughly investigated, the full implications, and more than a peer review, as well as a solid end game, as it is quite easy to start a war, yet quite difficult to win, well, unless it is intentional, an industry, in need of a cash cow, for example *The Mouse That Roared,* wink-wink.

Just as significantly, why destroy what might become a cash cow?

Moments later, it completes these secret observations and that bunker pollution, yet seems perplexed at the entire situation, as well as ever so vigilant, that someone might follow then it departs.

So, and because of the complexity, the Punk Buster procrastinates, postpones the most difficult task until last, gathering then carefully disposing of that waste material, and careful not to trip.

As a result, it carefully exits that bunker then eventually chases those things, along one passageway after another, which leads towards underground systems that maintain forest shadows, snares, pits and other wiles, as well as the throne.

However, and along the way, the Punk Buster must stop and repair vital systems here and there, which consumes a considerable amount of time, as this entire process, to fix all critically damaged forest systems, might take days, weeks or more, and it seems unable to catch those things, which have quite an elusive ability, as if specially breed for this sly new age metagame.

As a result, the Punk Buster becomes quite suspicious then mistrusts more things, as eyes carefully study the surroundings, and look for certain visual references and theatrical cues, as well as a cue mark, or the sweet spot, an ideal place in the frame of reference, system, setting and cycle then looks for manipulation.

And it taps the back of the left hand three times, and again, taps left of right, the left brake, the left-handed material index— well, to see if it creates an instantly awaking moment, in a sick bay or some other place, such as a limbo, a secular or sacred version of purgatory, or intermediate state, maybe a bardo or liminal state, middle ritual, mid threshold, or within a special rite of passage, to atone, or some other segment within the great monomyth.

However, it does not, nor does another elaborate technique.

And this problem does not resemble an in-the-moment binding of events, such as how someone might tamper with the mental system, for instance during the survey, and when a person looks at events in real time, and multiple brain aspects monitor the sensory streams or drafts, and tag things in memory, tag cues in that special workspace in the mind. Such as how someone outside might tamper with that mindset, that process or function, might tamper with firmware for lack of a better phrase, and memory. Of which, the observer might enter more than a catatonic state or psychoactive trance, and from the likelihood of a hidden neurogenic or particle beam, and not likely from a psionic event.

All of which at the minimum might disrupt or modify the thalamus, or equivalent, as if a delta wave effect, then that person or thing slips into a profound and persistent vision, or shared daydream, or worse yet.

However, subtle cues here and there indicate no such manipulation, and no superimposition, temporal stub, and no sunken kingdom to reemerge, or a different face, different space event.

CHAPTER  30

Elsewhere, Mary drives through one pristine old-growth temperate coniferous forest segment after another, of yew, spruce, fir, juniper, pine and eventually arrives at the sculpted thirty-two-foot high iron gate and limestone wall bordering the mansion property.

And the huge house appears in full view, with many similarities to The Breakers, a Vanderbilt mansion with terra-cotta red roof tiles and Indiana limestone walls.

However, this Gilded Age home has only twenty-two rooms and consumes 18,000 square feet.

Just as significantly, the landscape contains large weeping willows, majestic oaks and mature red maples, as well as plants in full bloom, which include a wide variety of rhododendrons, laurels, and dogwoods.

In addition, all add to the overall charm, and give the place a certain poetic beauty, especially from the symmetry of design, foliage, and vivid colors.

It gives the place a certain image of prosperity, progress and peace, a place in full accord with nature, as if it represents an unofficial paradise, with a deep foundation, an earthfast, a substantial situation, post, or an effort to address a theory of everything, an Age of Enlightenment, as well as what a person might expect within the golden age of the classical and Renaissance gardens, a place that might lead into the transcendent, might trigger a full restoration of glory, the original long lost glory now found?

The view activates a full imagination, especially from one adventurous footpath after another that leads to one not-so-secret garden after another, an st-connectivity, context-free grammar or an exceptional Risch algorithm field, such as a cultivated crop, or trial garden, and each garden with a microclimate, as well as stylistic allure that has full potential, with potential acoustic gain, or gain from accurate feedback, where some appear spacious, grand, and noble.

Others sit in small niches, such as inside a small bamboo grove, or under the full protection of a weeping willow in bloom, or between huge ceremonial boulder crops, for example, an ancient yet uniquely complex rock culture, a prehistoric tribute yet an ever so advanced therapeutic space, which form a poetic megalithic boulder garden shrine that enables rare and sacred space to form, and where anyone of these places a person might sit, meditate, and ponder the great mysteries of the universe, as an explorer, third culture person, psychonautic, transformative, grok or kythe agent, or as an equilibrium refinement then notice something special.

Many of those picturesque gardens have their own unique style, and with colorful bloom, that includes shrubs, subshrubs, and especially distinct thematic herbal sections, many of which sit in spectacular elevated beds, elevated in unique stages, as each stage seems to represent a vital aspect, represent context as well as substantial support, and with no significant or apparent waste.

In addition, these appear as if more than persistent biological interactions, more than mutualistic, commensalistic, parasitic, and something quite different, such as if other categories of being, and not a common ratiocination groupoid or Abelian group.

These gardens show a series of evolutionary updates, as if each represents a well-being indeed, or natural expression, or efficient extension of the mind, and at the same time more than ingredients for an exceptional elixir, atonement, or sacred marriage, and not a trope, or corruption of nature, from a frivolous inserted often said vital.

And each colorful flowerbed, with distinct thematic herbal sections, elevates in stages, as if to convey specific nuisances within secular and sacred space, as in philosophical and therapeutic nuisances, to cultivate, redeem, regenerate, transform, evolve, and expand the mind, as in a place pristine, vivid, free and fair, a place wholly natural and absolutely fascinating, especially as a place for artists, poets, scholars to sit, and ponder truly great questions, and even a place for romance, yes, such as romance of Palamedes, or an admirer, and again, fate drives them together, such as she is not my girlfriend, finishing each other's sentences, everyone can see it, like an old married couple, office spouse, or a complex triangle relationship, or a place for science, if you will, and sit as a super geek or nerd.

Just as importantly, these gardens seem to represent a special position, in relationship to that forest old-growth tree, the one with a human aspect, and not in a conventional sense of body, mind and soul, but ineffable and primordial, as if a missing link.

Although, Mary has no comprehensive insight about these things, just a full appreciation of the idyllic estate, with a series of favorable impressions, about the landscape and mansion, yet they instantly disappear as she wildly sways from one vehicle side after another, to avoid hitting a boulder, which that precariously leans into the driveway.

And then the car swerves here and there to avoid the velvet green lawn, avoid damaging it, which appears fragile and soft from a previous rain, or rain delay, or rain ritual.

This time, another special rope drapes around that boulder— and not some ordinary rope, but the type a person might see on a secular or sacred shrine.

Next, Mary eases along the driveway of antique white pea-sized gravel, as the wheels crunch more so on contact, and all the while she looks about for Agrippa's truck.

Then unable to find it, she stops, exits the car and eventually knocks on one of the massive hardwood front doors, which has an abbreviated theme, similar to those thirty-two-foot high iron gates, as well as immense limestone wall that borders the property and shows impeccable sculptures, based on the phase transition theme, especially seam management, which includes norm of reaction, phenotypic plasticity, genetic hitchhike, acclimatization, stages of existence, crisis of the self, as well as what a person might describe in the study of thermodynamics— when matter transforms from one phase or state to another, which includes those four discrete states of solid, liquid, gas, and plasma, as well as low-energy states classical and modern, along with very high energy examples, and with a special section on the bimodal, and especially on aetheling principles. Moreover, these themes pay a full tribute to the cradles of civilization, as well as ancient schools of thought in Greece, India, and other parts of Asia, along with their insights, tools, parables, precepts, and practices.

No one answers.

So, she patiently waits, looks about then knocks with a modest fist bang, the type which avoids the label of a savage, as well as ignorant.

And that fails to stirs anyone inside.

Just as significantly, Agrippa has not answered the phone since that wild fundraiser fiasco and fistfight with Tommy, a knockdown, drag-out fistfight, which quickly morphed into a combination pit fight, Muay Thai and Greco-Roman event. Where they tied up then struggled in close-quarter infighting, and each of them landed a series of brutal elbows then delivered a series of spinning back fists, and each time knees buckled.

Both of the ladies alternated and spit out a bloody tooth or so, as well as fought, huffed, strained and searched for an opportunity to deliver the pure power of a spectacular knockout.

However, they occasionally clinched and utilized various grips to gain control, such as "S, T, three finger, as well as the Gable grip," and all the while they struggled to gain an advantage, anything, even a slight one.

They separated and a superwoman punch-buckled Tommy, yet she grabbed and clinched with one method after another, with Thai, collar and wrist, collar and elbow, double under hook, body lock and double wrist control.

Moreover, Tommy and Agrippa switched from one hip technique after another, to maintain balance, as well as made one attempt after another at a decisive judo throw, one that would at least knock the wind out of the other, break the momentum, or better yet, score a complete knockout on ground impact, or against a tree trunk, or that boulder.

In that previous fight, and eventually, Tommy delivered three solid spinning elbows, and Agrippa reeled then grabbed, to recover then ultimately saw an opportunity and delivered three brutal forearm uppercuts, and each time it rocked Tommy, who staggered then saw an opening, and the fight transitioned back into a good old-fashioned fistfight, a toe-to-toe slugfest.

Then each of them connected with one solid punch after another to the chin, which abruptly snapped the head back, to see stars, and the type of punch that would knock out an ordinary human being, in an ordinary situation, but the pump of adrenaline, rage and betrayal, as well as departed glory added fuel to the fire, added propellant.

Since that fight, Mary has not seen Agrippa.

Regardless and with a fist Mary knocks again, then harder.

Not much later by cell phone she calls, and with each cell phone ring she keeps an ear to the door then carefully listens, yet hears nothing.

Eventually, a low cell phone battery compels her to stop and save remaining power.

So, she knocks again, waits, then circles around the house, passes colorful flowering shrubs and beds of fragrant peppermint, lemon balm, lavender and blooming fennel as she lightly taps on one window after another.

Ultimately, no one answers.

As a result, and with a last effort, she circumnavigates the house and moves pass large weeping willows, oaks, red maples, rhododendrons, laurels, dogwoods and flowering shrubs.

Then with no sign of life inside, Mary phones one more time and places an ear to a mansion window, which creates a smudge, the type another person might find quite annoying, and represents a rude act.

A sound arrives, yet not from the house.

Moments later, the phone fails.

"Damn, hell's bells."

After pushing the power button, shaking the phone and a few rude finger taps, the power light blinks for a few seconds then the system completely fails.

A few solid fingernail taps do nothing, well, except create scratches that appear significant and permanent.

"Double damn!" then she grumbles, and says things not spoken by a lady, and shakes a mighty fist toward the heavens, specifically towards heaven number 955 or the equivalent, and then tries to remember the angle of that last ring.

To her surprise, and off to the rear stands a small building, which appears mostly obscured by overgrowth, and it represents a carriage house, constructed from the same mansion material of brick, concrete, Indiana limestone, steel trusses and a terra-cotta red-tiled roof.

Just as significantly, tracks lead to an open door, and inside sits Agrippa's badly mangled truck, with completely crisped tires, as if driven on mile after mile, until worn down to mostly bare rim, yet the person continued to drive, which must have caused considerable rim sparks, scorches and eventually blackened aspects.

Just as significantly, the rims sit at odd angles and must have given a wobbled ride.

Also, the truck body has tremendous bends, gashes, pits and tears.

Even the spectacular hardwood-paneled truck bed has been battered, until only a few rickety planks remain.

Of more importance, traces of smoke rise from the engine then something sizzles and occasionally the truck pops, from twisted metal and plastic, as a powerful smell of a burnt rubber, plastic and oil vapors swirl through the air.

Moments later, other sounds occur, "Ping, ping, ping," as something makes a distinct rhythm, which, in many respects, has a comforting effect, very, because the pace seems ever so peaceful and natural, the type of sound that allows the mind to drift and drift, to a better place, to a substantial, true, fit and inviting place, along a clear path, to a promised land, and a place of limitless potential bold, bright, and free, such as free, prior and informed consent or a free-mind well-field system, or at least as a free-mind phonation.

And yet, as gasoline drips and eventually forms a small puddle on the concrete floor, a telltale vapor rises and moves through the air, as if a subtle spirit on the rise, or a John Locke notion of liberty, a universal, of freedom, as well as social contract with the system, with what matters, as well as the universe, such as an ever so smooth phase transition, where the conscious gradually unfolds, as a legato, or evolution, or blank verse?

Moments later, various crushed truck structures laboriously moan and groan.

Occasionally, things pop, and then the entire truck shifts slightly and again, then again, as something sizzles within.

So much so, a thin wisp of smoke rises, whirls, and fills the air with a very pungent smell of burnt oil, plastic and now gasoline.

Eventually, Mary hears a groan, finds Agrippa inside the truck, groggy then carefully attends to her by examining injuries and measuring vital signs.

In spite of plenty of cuts, scraps, bruises and a possible concussion, Agrippa eventually tries to walk it off, with a classic female macho style, yet instead wildly staggers out of the truck, only to tip over a table, with a galvanized tub that contains a trowel, hand cultivator, shears and clay flower pots, which causes all of these things to loudly bang about, as she dangerously stumbles on a few rakes.

Ultimately, she tries to stand still, but has a profound sway then speaks with an incoherent mumble about this and that.

So Mary compels her to lie down and rest, or at least sit, so she can continue checking injuries and vital signs.

Moments later, the nurse reaches for her phone, turns it on only to receive a low battery icon and says, "I'll call an ambulance, back in a moment; whatever you do, stay still."

However, Agrippa grabs her sleeve enough to rip it, and says; "No, wait" then points to the passenger seat and says, "The cave, the AB hylomorph."

And lying there is a twisted mass, a considerable, a massive otherworldly creature or thing that barely moves, and again, while gasoline drips on the below concrete floor, and into a puddle that generates a telltale whisper, a vapor on the rise, a subtle spirit on the rise, very, or a John Locke notion of liberty and no more excuses.

For Mary, this creates a holy smokes moment, especially from the sight of that considerable repulsive passenger side thing, as well as the combustible smell, and instantly, ten years of her life leap from the body. Just like that, gone.

CHAPTER

Nonetheless and moments later, something happens, something beyond innate, impulse and reason.

As it might represent a single point meditation, a spontaneous sacrifice, an exception to life, to self-preservation, such as when someone runs into a burning building, regardless of a certain disfiguring and gruesome death.

As a result, she scrambles into the wreckage, over chunks of shattered windshield bits then pries away various sharp, mangled and smoldering truck parts, then squeezes and squeezes between jagged edges to find someone in a suit, a feudal superior for justice.

In fact, it appears as if a combination JIM ocean diving suit and something else, something odd, something a bit less bulky, much more mobile, highly stylized, and with extraordinary, as well as meticulous embellishment, as if a haute couture merged Baroque, Plateresque and cult, yet represents an outline of classical studies.

Just as significantly, the main colors consist of black with golden bronze accents, and all of which gives it a distinguished look; a certain brilliant nobility, or noocracy, or elite theory.

However, the collision decimated a considerable amount of it.

As a result, the nurse looks in amazement, as whiffs of smoke emanate from the suit, hot to the touch.

After edging closer and still closer, she notices a man inside, who lies unconscious, as much of the helmet and a considerable portion of the suit have been rudely sheared off.

Mary carefully reaches in the suit, avoids jagged smoldering edges, checks vital signs and quickly examines him with a cursory check, and he appears relatively stable.

As she cautiously backs out and turns toward her car, Agrippa grabs her by the right wrist, and not with an ordinary grip, with an ultimate grip, and she says as a true threat, "What are you doing?"

"I'm calling an ambulance, for both of you."

And as she tries to move, the grip tightens.

She tries again and that grip becomes quite powerful, then freakishly tight, in fact crushing.

As a result Mary says, "What? I've got to call. Both of you have concussions, and maybe broken bones." Then she explains the danger of blunt force trauma, such as internal bleeding and what happens if a compound fracture goes untreated.

Her friend refuses to release that freakish grip.

In fact, the face shows determination and ferocity, as eyes that bulge.

Then a struggle ensued, which escalates.

Whether it is from multiple concussions, betrayal or lack of sleep, Agrippa takes on fierce mindset.

And they struggle in a clinch that intensifies then all hell breaks loose as the best friends since grammar school become surly, snappish, and quite bitter.

All this fury, the feral outpour, shocks Mary, as she by nature represents a laid back person, known as a coolant, unflappable, drama-free and quite patient under pressure.

Regardless, they struggle and it completely unravels her in such a profound way.

Eventually things settle, but Mary insist insists on making that phone call; however, Agrippa refuses to permit any outside intervention, and that triggers another round of struggle and savage fury.

This cycle repeats again and again until Mary exhausts, surrenders, and slumps then ultimately settles for an agreement, to at least move him into a room, near the library.

And one by one, with a makeshift stretcher, Mary carefully drags each inside then rechecks vital signs, looks for broken bones and attends to gashes, contusions, cuts, scrapes and bruises.

Again Mary looks toward the phone, Agrippa sees and another fight erupts as they struggle.

However, all that fury truly unsettles Mary beyond description.

And eventually she fully surrenders then begrudgingly pledges complete discretion, yet afterward mumbles about the mortal danger, life, reputation, career and a friendship, and a friendship seems to extend in one direction, as some friends take and take, and it seems difficult to satisfy them.

In fact, this uncomfortable dilemma weights on her mind, yet for now she will stand by her friend, as long as no one is in critical condition.

As a result, Mary focuses on making the best of a bad situation, as none of the choices seem agreeable, and all have serious consequences.

She considers quickly borrowing a few pieces of equipment, from work or the graduate nursing school she attends.

Maybe quietly slip into the training facility during off hours and discreetly borrow a few things, such as the portable x-ray machine specifically designed for field use, "Yes, ever so discreetly."

CHAPTER 32

Still hidden deep within a forest dense thicket, Bonnie maintains a comprehensive stealth and continues to recover from that tremendous sign impact, that direct hit which created acute aches, sharp pains, and profound winces, as well as fear about serious internal damage.

She appears slightly improved then looks about for the dog, which lies eight feet away and has considerable damage, from the bear attack, that frenzy, and yet seems stable.

In fact, it slowly raises its head, looks at her, lowers head on to extend paws, and closes eyes, as if to recover.

As a result, she says, "Now that's what I'm talking about: distance, and respect of personal space," then a grumpy face reinforces the message.

Just then her stomach loudly calls then rudely rumbles over a considerable internal distance.

More compelling, the stomach growls in that classic and universal query, that song, food, food, food, now, feed me, or feed me to something, I just want to be part of the food chain, part of the process, part of the great machine, which constantly and restlessly churns and churns, and a system never fully satisfied, never paid in full, never fully squared, and I want to pay the price of admission, to the big show.

Then she seriously considers borrowing a substantial number of those prepackaged meals, the MREs, also called combat Meal Ready-to-Eat, or self-contained individual field rations in lightweight packages.

However, it seems vital to do so without detection, as well as in a respectful way, respect the property of others.

So, Bonnie carefully looks for danger, slowly changes angles, as well as levels then decides to exit into the open, which causes acute aches, sharp pains, and profound winces, yet eventually arrives at an MRE case, one that has a dirty combat boot print, and she borrows a wide selection of these meals, nine in total, especially the ones labeled "delightful," and also borrows that heavily ornate bottle, the old one, the Three Sovereigns and Five Emperors.

In addition, she borrows that foreign diplomatic sack, as well as a small empty four-ounce tin can with lid, LED flashlight, powered by one AAA battery and various filled plastic bags that say, "Burn for sensitive and classified documents," as they might prove helpful, plus would extensive homeland system really mind, under these circumstances?

And often, she carefully listens for forest movement, for twigs that snap under footsteps then slowly looks about, at various angles.

Not much later, Bonnie hastily writes a note, with blackened bits from that flamed out and previously shook shaken spear, and expresses her version of a polite IOU, which does not contain any cleverly turned phrases, based on the 1600s, with no acute sense of self and existence, no well-constructed sonnets, to please an often vain self-absorbed patron, no strictly regulated da-Dum, to praise and dance or mock and dance.

Instead, she writes, "IOU—Thank you," and adds a classic happy face icon with a tongue that flaps, to convey a tasty treat.

Not much later, and with dog under an arm, she slowly hobbles south then eventually locates another forest entrance, barely, the dark hidden type, one for an ever so slim rabbit, and the type a person might dive into then shimmy and belly-crawl into the trouble.

However, a smell arrives, a sickly sweet perfumed.

Just as significantly, it seems quite unsettling, and offers a delayed jolt to the mortal coil then produces an odd whole body shudder—a series of painful quakes, as if the body considered with a set of primal as well as long-dormant senses, and those issue a warning to locate an exit then stampede towards, even if it means acute pain and toil, as well as a total loss of dignity, a loss of hard-earned rank and community standing, now lost in an instant because of the ways and means, which might look quite unusual, and not according to the script, and something that would surely earn a certain reputation, as a verb, as a cautionary action, and one that eventually appears in the Oxford dictionary, after considerable, as well as fully animated debate, of gestic, and among well-respected linguists, among super geeks, of "I have the power and glory," also called wordsmiths, who bang and bang in their way on a subject, okay, and often with obsessive ways and means.

Moments later, the smell foreshadows a gruesome death.

So, in a best effort, hampered by plenty of tremendous aches, cuts, scraps, bruises and possible concussion, Bonnie quickly hobbles back, to a safe distance.

And just as importantly, only a very foolish person would venture into that place, that treacherous forest, something a certain type of guy would do, or teen, or a big burly galoot, or palooka, especially on a dare, or a bet, often for a very frivolous reason, and not something done by a well-seasoned mind or wit.

Regardless, she best effort sprints—okay, hobbles—with that diplomatic bag and dog under an arm, then belly-dive leaps inside the dark narrow passage, which on impact creates a holy smokes moment, of pain and stars, yet eventually she shimmies through dense toxic thorns shrubs.

However, the passage narrows, and hook-shaped thorns precariously catch her clothing, snag then poke sensitive skin, and pierce a few times, pierces the theatrical scenery.

Eventually limbs swell, as claustrophobia and panic arrive.

Then, she backs out, yet ensnares, more so, on sharp thorns, especially the sack, which often requires a tremendous pull action, to free.

So, with her only realistic option forward, again, she best-effort shimmies pass past one hazard after another, along this tight passage, which that contains holes here and there, and likely snake and rat holes because of obvious hints, from an elaborate underground labyrinth of intricate passageways that exit in nearby locations, and as if a creepy community, with unique as well as repugnant specie smells.

So much so, hair stands and individualizes on the arms, neck and scalp. As if each hair casts a vote, in their own way, which translates into stand and run, as fast as possible, somewhere, anywhere and now, yes, right now, go-go-go, which causes her heart to pound, and really pound, as those considerable thumps add to her disorientation.

And to make matters worse, things move within these holes.

They seem to shift about and search for something, quite possibly for opportunity, for just the right savage leap, and deadly nip.

Soon, and while edging forward, she mumbles and grumbles, about personal baggage.

Meanwhile, her limbs continue to swell then develop a freakish appearance.

The type of condition a person should not look at, and especially dwell on, as it might cause disorientation, panic, surrender then a dangerous state of shock.

Or, at the minimum, the mind might unravel and think wild thoughts about these grotesque limbs. It might unlock memories and personal baggage, unlock all those flaws and imperfections then flood the mind with vivid images and other wholly irrational things, for instance life as an outcast, again, an outsider, and a true freak, to become the other, to become an it, a thing, and how choices narrow, and narrow. Until, a person becomes isolated, or worse yet, forced and herded into a sideshow, as much of life sits inside one side show or another, with reluctant(s), or freaks, so they definitively say, and forced to join a classic sideshow, a P. T. Barnum event, or forced to live in a cabinet of curiosities, such as *Wunderkammer*, or maybe a modern-day version of the Black Scorpion, the Jim Rose Circus, a lollapalooza festival, or maybe into an old-time revival show, with a colorful barker, on a local circuit, which visits very rural towns and isolated places that do not receive much fresh air, by law. Where, in that show, and for a single admission price, it enables people to buy a ticket, for a cautionary lesson, of enter the big top, or a tent, and gawk at human oddities, at the freaks, the working acts, at the others.

Regardless, she continues, to painfully struggle, with the dog under arm, and especially struggle with the diplomatic sack, which trails and often requires a yank, now and again, to free.

Eventually, the tight passage opens into an area about twenty feet across.

Just as significantly, and often, an impulse arrives, to look at those freakish limbs.

However and each time, the eyes avoid, as the mind fights this impulse, and looks elsewhere, anywhere seems fine, as the mere sight might trigger disorientation, shock then death.

And yet often, the eyes flick that way, as if trying to gain a quick glimpse, and as if controlled by reflex, or the great subconscious, or by aspects of, or an aspect of, the microbiome, well, that looks out for itself, rather than the self, the collective, and as if it or they take control over an occasional look, as in "We do not completely trust the self," the state or federal system, or single-party rule, or party system, or the power-that-be, the boss man, Mister Big, or Miss Big, large-and-in-charge, too big to fail or free enterprise.

Often, this represents a time people suddenly remember something, such as God, family, friends and other serious neglects, such as other constructs?

And, it frequently resembles an urgent bargain, a three-for-one sale, which includes relief, promise and interest in a better life, also known as a "midnight madness sale," yet held regardless of the time, and with everything open at bargain basement prices, for instance an eternal commitment, a willingness to trade creed, destiny and soul for immediate relief, as well as for a better and more fully realized potential. Such as the way it was meant to be, before all those pesky life distractions, as well as the thrownness of life.

So, this last-second bargain normally includes content of character, bedrock principle, and especially "oh so stubborn habits," and all with a newfound golden truer than true faith, as well as sincerity of a "last-minute contract renegotiation." Where, this time represents a definitive commitment, the contract, and not like the last eleven bargaining sessions, those last crises, and this one will finalize those index of character issues, and all those often ignored and pesky things, for example codes of conduct, which includes faith, devotion, respect, compassion, mercy, civility, justice, freedom, and even glory, as well as a reconciliation, of those ten sacred rules for some, and the Carlin three for others.

Again, Bonnie seems distracted by that impulse to look at those grotesque limbs, which that resemble an impulse people have, when they drive by an accident then slow down, to look. So much so they really slow down and try to take a few good long looks while still driving at a considerable speed. And often, they rubberneck a few times while awkwardly pumping the brakes, just in time to avoid creating a major accident; that irony, as they hope to see something, anything, just something, someone they know, God forbid, a family member, friend, coworker, or frenemy, "Yes, oh yes, a frenemy, and badly hurt, really bad, as if karma delivers a full impact." Or, they might see a celebrity, a real celebrity, someone with star power, a diva, "Yes, but not a typical diva, not the me-me-me, look-at-me type, and who will say anything for attention or to win an election, not those quick change artist, especially the ones who, regardless of the group they pander, the professional panders—okay, maybe them, especially in an ironic situation, such as a bold moral crusader, an absolute, caught mid seven deadly sin or two, also recognized as a capital vice or cardinal sin, and bonus points if caught doing an exceptional combinations not thought humanly possible, and caught in a memorable position, such as something that would YouTube quite nicely, or frame quite well in a textbook—well, as a cautionary lesson, of hypocrisy, the list of, as often, the loudest barkers of absolute hellfire, or some other cultural equivalent, or purism eventually trip, for example, those who speak with a style, of step on an ant, or on the less fortunate, and they speak or rant with an ever so certain style, of the highest standards, and often do so as vain, pompous, grand, high speech, long-winded, or as a Pyrrhic victory leader, or as a jabberwocky, with ever so shallow thought, in search of sheeple, yet trips then justifies, such as blame the others, that rubberneck sight?

Eventually, she stares at those limbs, and notices the swollen freakishness, especially all those obvious and subtle aspects.

Then, as if struck by a lightning bolt, Bonnie begins slipping into a state of shock, where her mind, body and soul undergo a rapid depersonalization, derealization, numbness then detachment.

However, the dog revives, as well as notices then licks her face, which causes another form of shock.

And eventually in stages, utter disgust arrives, which may have a certain medical recovery value regarding a potential shock victim.

Then she ultimately says, "Don't do that—never, ever. Are you insane? Go away. Go-go-go, be gone!" followed by a distressed effort, from bruises, to wipe away every molecule of dog slobber.

Nonetheless, the dog moves eight feet away. Where, it finds a comfortable place to recover then lies with head on extended paws.

There, eyes carefully look at her, as well as measure aspects of that condition, and wait for a real command, for a real mission, and a command said in the proper way, according to a specialized stack protocol, or a one MC full stack alert, or at least one from the prescribed reading list, as she seems literate and reasonably educated, even well-studied then the dog reconsiders.

Regardless, a profound hunger arrives and she considers the MRE, which needs water and fire.

So, she cautiously searches for water, which leads pass those previously fortified nests with improved drainage, added coverage, to make it "near impossible to dislodge those eggs," as well as added style and flair, as compensation, and that process gave the nests an "ultra-retro hip look, and yet fashion-forward, a timeless look, because style matters—it really matters?"

Just as significantly, those previous modifications "made them windproof, stormproof, maybe even hurricane proof— well, maybe not hurricane proof. Regardless, these nests and eggs had no significant chance of falling."

Once done, Bonnie says in an annoyed, fully animated and highly stylized way, "Done, as in *finito*. Goodbye, as I will never return, ever, and of equal importance, find a calendar and record this day, as well as time—wait—or record it in something permanent, for example: chisel it into an enormous block of granite."

However, here and now, as well as upon close inspection, hatched baby birds chirp and seem hungry, very, which the arriving dog also notices.

In fact, this truly perplexes Bonnie, who carefully looks about for the mothers, waits patiently, then sits and waits even longer.

Nothing happens.

Meanwhile, the baby birds flop, struggle and chirp for food.

All of which she considers, as well as other dangers then says, "Oh, my, so many bad choices. Let me think—hmmm, baby birds: tweeties with no mothers, and my previous handling of those eggs might have created this situation, might have left an offending human scent."

So, she turns to the dog and says, in a fully animated, as well as highly stylized way, "Okay, okay, I have a plan: food—a few bugs, worms and grubs then I'm gone, done, as in finite, goodbye, as I will never return, ever."

And while trying to avoid hidden coiled snakes, which might leap with fangs and deliver a quick nip, deliver death, she carefully reaches under rocks, logs and piles of leaves, really reaching into one place after another, stretching then rooting about.

After twenty minutes, she finds a considerable amount of tasty treats—well, things birds might love.

Then a capital idea arrives, "In fact, I'll stockpile them."

So, Bonnie weaves a small wicker-style basket, adds two narrow slots at the bottom, fills it with a wide assortment of earthworms, bugs, grubs, as well as other juicy birdy treats then climbs the tree, as aches and pains greatly slow the process, which requires a frequent pause to recover, and yet she eventually attaches that shared device to the nests.

"Now that's a substantial stockpile."

Of which, and with a considerable effort, the tweets consider, peck and eat.

"Okay, I'm done, and with a clear conscience," so she carefully descends, with a frequent pause, to recovery, then departs the area in search of water, for the MRE, with dog trailing behind.

And yet within sixty seconds, something rustles back there, which causes her to stop, slowly crouch into cover, and eyes widen, to look for better angles.

Yet, during a considerable amount of time, nothing moves.

Then more time passes, which has a distinct feel, as if particles of time, granular aspects, yet something else effects the timeline, the local version, that loses sync, as if an event might push the local area somewhere else, into an exception, construct, frame of reference, deep belief network, case study or new category of thought, or push the local sideways in time, or into a parallel verse.

All of which causes her concern, then distress, yet curiosity, as well as fascination.

Enough so, she slowly returns with cautiously placed steps, with ones that avoid crisp things underfoot, such as leaves, twigs, and branches.

Moreover, each effort through foliage tries to cause the least amount of disruption and visual clues.

Accordingly, she avoids foliage breaks and ground disruptions.

On arrival, Bonnie finds that birds and food have gone, everything—no birds, no wide assortment of fat earthworms, tasty bugs, juicy grubs and other birdy treats, none.

An ever so slow climb, with frequent pauses, verifies, "Not even a feather or bug wing. Ready?"

So she descends and thoroughly examines the ground within a forty-foot radius, which finds, "No bear tracks, in fact, no animal tracks whatsoever, or overturned leaves or twigs, or sign of a winged predator, —damn! What the hell is going on?"

As a result, she unsettles. "Now that's freaky. Not a single feather."

So, Bonnie slowly crouches, scans and waits a few minutes, then with dog under an arm and a painful style, she flees south— well, hobbles.

After reaching a safe distance, she searches for water, finds a very small artesian well and scans for trouble, yet finds nothing, not even with a painful crouch or look at various angles then levels, as there appears no signs of movement or tracks.

Just as significantly, nearly twenty feet away and slightly elevated, sits a good shelter location, near water, tinder and kindling, where she considers two ways to make friction fire, with a fire-plow, which requires her to rub a hardwood stick tip against a softer wood base, with a repeated downward plowing action, of back and forth, in a narrow softwood channel, until it pushes out small particles of softwood fibers, that pile, and eventually smokes into an ember, hopefully.

Her second option represents a five-piece bow drill set, which consists of a relatively flat stone, to act as a socket, a control of downward pressure on a straight hardwood stick that will act as the drill, against a flat softwood slot, and a bendable bow stick with strung string, from her shoelace.

So, Bonnie gathers material for the bow drill set then tests material for dryness, by holding the wood to her cheek.

Once selected, the set undergoes construction, and within ten minutes she leans down on the socket and drill stick, while producing a back and forth action with the bow, which causes the drill, tightly looped by string, to spin back and forth into that softwood slot.

Eventually, soft wood fibers build then smoke rises, and the small pile grows then eventually smolders.

As a result, she gingerly moves a small half-inch smoldering pile into a tinder bundle, then offers an intermittent air puff, just enough air to ventilate an ember, which glows brighter and brighter then bursts into a flame.

Much later, coals form, and she makes a considerable quantity of char cloth, which will make building the next fire easier, as well as faster, with swatches of red shirt cotton, put inside that almost airtight can then cooked over campfire coals.

As the cloth cooks, smoke vents then eventually slows, and once done correctly, it reveals something light, charred, and a simple spark would cause it to immediately ignite.

Afterwards, she stores the results in that small container, then dry location, inside a "Burn for sensitive and classified document" bag, wedged among various papers, then diplomatic backpack, along with emergency tinder for later use, for a just-in-case moment.

And with the hard work done, she tests the artesian spring water for fitness, for clarity, smell then a risky single shallow sip, which feels cool.

So, after waiting, another sip considers the full metrics, and another.

Then this water suggests a certain something, which seems clean and bright.

Not much later, the full effect arrives, which adds considerable perk.

In fact, it instantly satisfies and brings a smile, "Ah. Damn, that's good water!"

In fact, it produces a balanced satisfaction, then eventually restores as if a tonic.

Enough so, a full smile arrives then elation, mindfulness and that same peculiar side effect, a keen understanding of connotation and denotation, as well as the degrees that exist in between.

"Oh no, I hope it doesn't have the same effect as that other water source, with all those pesky side effects, that ability to think about profound issues, and with power shell data dives, into the mind, into ever so deep mental states, and remote memories, memories connected by an ever so weak thread, those hard to reach places, and especially activate a profound moral code, of conduct, virtue, and moral excellence, and that mission for the collective, for the history of ideas, and civilization."

Then Bonnie looks about for risks, as well as a comfy place to sit, prepare breakfast and organize this long-awaited meal.

All the while, the dog studies this activity and moves from a sit to a lay down recovery position, with head on paws.

As a precautionary measure, she gives him a certain evil eye, a malevolent glare, which if need be, would serve as a death ray, a beam of destruction, to incinerate things on contact, to crisp things, or melt steel, or at least, the willful aspect of a canine mind.

Then she mumbles a series of colorful sayings, not fit for print, and especially not said by a lady, a true lady of exceptional distinction, with a mind, body and soul seasoned with an exceptional understanding of art, aesthetic, and science, of advanced culture.

In fact, the dog appears educated; in fact, well educated, yet not to her, and it seems immune to the evil eye, that elaborate belief system and skillset, as that look has no effect and he lies attentive, peaceful and occasionally blinks.

Regardless, her attention turns to carefully examining each of the three meal types labelled "Four fingers of death, black bean and rice burrito and chicken fajita."

Four fingers of death is not the real name, as someone placed a handmade label over the original title, and with a fingernail, a few pick attempts fail to remove it.

Regardless, Bonnie considers it a term of endearment and says, "That must represent a charming way of saying delightful, as well as a savory indulgence."

So, she smiles and imagines each variety, the taste, texture and absolute satisfaction, then chooses chicken fajita.

And like all three varieties, it sits inside a dark chestnut plastic package that says, "Ready-to-Eat, Individual, U.S. GOVERNMENT PROPERTY COMMERCIAL RESALE IS UNLAWFUL, FLAMELESS RATION HEATERS ARE PROHIBITED ON COMMERICAL AIRPLINES UNLESS SEALED IN ORIGINAL MRS MENU BAG."

She says, "Flameless..., what the?" then seems delighted and opens the meal, which causes content to spill out, including various packets, some big, some small.

"Holy smokes, it's like Christmas, excellent!" she exclaims as eyes widen.

These items include single portion packets of instant coffee, iodized salt, two bright-green Chiclet-like things, mini tobacco sauce bottle, moist towelette, brown spoon, beverage base power, the chicken fajita packet and other things, as well as a "MRE (MEAL, READY-TO-EAT) HEATER" in a single-color camouflage green packet.

Apparently, adding water triggers the chemical heater, and instructions seem easy enough, even for a person who knows no English.

She says, "Cool. I'm game," and with a single motion tears open the packet top, places the chicken fajita packet in this bag, pours water inside, folds the torn packet top closed, slides it into a carton box, sits that box upright, and at a slight angle then eagerly waits.

Minutes later, something happens.

As telltale signs appear, Bonnie finds this process absolutely fascinating then charming.

In fact, she ignores acute aches and pains then barely stands up, from the nervous energy, from anticipation.

Yet the recovering dog continues lying and intently looking, with only the eyes following her every move.

Then something strange happens.

She hums, followed by smiles, and percolates.

As the minutes pass, a fidget arrives, which moves her in a left to right action, shifting weight from one side to the next, then with an exaggerated playful side to side hip action, regardless of discomfort, as joy apparently saturates, "Oh yeah, chicken fajita, fajita!" in a louder than reasonable, as well as playful, announcement.

"It's ready."

Normally, a dog would perk up with the first food cue, of culinary delight, and ears would raise, tail wags.

In fact, inside someone's house, the tail would really wag, and often knock over a consider amount of things, framed family pictures, of clear the deck, and knock over a flower vase or two then cup of grape juice, a difficult stain, and other considerable things, from anticipation.

Plus when excited, dogs slobber.

However, this dog shows none of the classic traits.

Then she juggles this package, "hot-hot-hot," opens, smells, ignores instinct and devours.

In fact, everything in that original package that could be eaten she eats with gusto, and sounds support that process, which include deliberately eating in a very sloppy way, with joy to the nth degree, with gusto, as well as making all those sounds and other phrases that seem wholly unintelligible and exceptionally crude, "Hmm, nam, nam, nam," and all done as she occasionally flashes a very naughty smile, of a true rascal.

Then well into the meal, she pauses, considers something then offers some to the dog.

However, it shows no interest, none, nada.

"Okay, your loss," then shrugs.

Eventually, she eats everything, even the hot sauce, by tapping out that tiny bottle content directly into the mouth, every drop, with zero waste.

CHAPTER 33

Deep underground, and along the way, through one tunnel and bunker after another, the Punk Buster repairs vital systems, which consumes a tremendous amount of time.

And just importantly, it seems unable to catch those elusive things, which grow bold in numbers, and this entire bunker complex repair process could take days, if not weeks or more.

Regardless, all these efforts bring it closer to the main bunker command center, as well as throne.

However, procrastination, regarding the initial bunker damage, might create the ultimate demise, and it might have been best to first clean that hazardous waste, that considerable amount of smolder and bits of unusual rubble, which often represents the "mythology of lost," as there appears no direct route through this complex state, or state-transition equation, or put another way, state's rights yet the quantum entanglement system, and of the Greek word δρᾶμα, a dramatic branch of, well, and poetic meter, of set, setting, fundamental rules of nature, system, symmetry, symbiosis, "set and setting," as if the term, to trip, really trip, trip into one theater or another, and that narrow window into, or flash-sideways, yet also known as the issues of a parent, container, or apparent, or visible, yet most sits as a dynamic invisible, for lack of better phrases.

Just as significantly, it pollutes the local timeline, the temporal inflection, and pollution does that, has a noxious quality, such to $\sqrt{dar}$, to hold, or *deréti*, to slow maturity, and substantial adjustments, or reasonable tacts, inside the stream, for a sagacious truth or more, a permeation, a fix, of the soul, the StreamSQL literary wit, inside the complex algebraic stacks, among all those scripts, and partition elements.

As often, life consists of many bad choices, very, which consume large amounts of time and resources, as well as frequently has profound implications.

And in this case, most have a chaotic quality, as well as "end of days" risk, end of time or eschaton, the final events of history, of human destiny, and ultimate fate of the universe, such as the big rip, or rip the fabric of this universe, the fabric of spacetime then collapse the supreme bulkhead or metaverse, or supreme bulkheads, collapse the supreme stack, such as how to remove all that space in between everything, and do so at faster that the speed of light, with a special warp bubble pierce, with the harmonics and overtones of deflation, as well as spacetime symmetry, and from procrastination, on occasion, regarding the decisions that seem little, the time-consuming ones, put off until the last possible moment, from procrastination.

CHAPTER

Regarding Bonnie, stubbornness does run in her family, especially her mother, a world-class version—in fact, you may have met that type of person and wondered, really wondered.

However, Bonnie had been the exception, a person easily wounded, and more than willing to retreat from confrontation, or surrender then go along with the situation, to maintain the peace, but each time and underneath it all, those feelings went unresolved then eventually pestered the mind, and often.

Where, a person can become stuck in a loop, and similar to how an image, phrase or song becomes stuck, for one reason or another, and what is that process, that loop?

As if the mind is stuck in a place, region, or a conjunction fails, or limited to a set of, or stuck in a stage, or temporal loop, a stubborn bit, parity bit, or a two-bit heap of what, of gristle, of bias?

And a person or system often seems stuck in a certain segment of time or technique, as well as space, and while in that stage, such as something is missing, a vital aspect, a protein, connection or idea, or a vital aspect of the mind seems barren, destitute, or "tangled up in blue(s)," or part of the executive region has withered or overinflated, such as the unfortunate version of pride, of pride before the fall?

And for some people and systems, resistance, stubbornness or "no" represent a favorite tool, or default position. As certain people, phenomenon and noumenon often deploy it, as if a reflex, or it reflects a vital intrinsic, or represents a default position of the second internal decision-making system, such as, when asked a question, they quickly impulse "no," as a blurt, even before the facts arrive, maneuver through each chain link of reasoning, each segment, let alone rigorously measure all those aspects in real depth, all those layers of complexity, as well as implications.

And you may have met those people and systems, been in a meeting with, such as a brainstorming session, where they quickly hijack the process, especially when someone is mid thought or sentence, especially the first sentence, and before everyone has had an opportunity to express an option, as the process does not get very far, because it is quickly seen as "a waste of time," letting a person speak a complete thought, and they quickly maneuver the process, back into the loop, rut, quagmire, and want to know, "why stop digging, and why not dig deeper, or surge, or swarm, or double down, as if a no-brainer?

As if they rely on a second internal decision-making system, one that can decide in a flash, a moment, nanosecond or attosecond, and does society often pressure a person into that style, that state, or thinking technique, to the basics, for instance, the second brain if you will, the gut, as in do bacteria rule and manipulate the mind?

And have the meek already inherited the earth, especially people? Do the first ones rule, and have they always been in control, the simple life, as well as the crude, cruel, irrational and treacherous, and will continue to do so as long as organisms exist, and are animals including humans merely borrowed scenery or stagecraft, and some more so than others? Such as, those who rely on a gut decision-making system or a borrowed heap of opportunity, as compared to the senior executive skills, abstract thought for complex problems, symbolism and the subtle? Moreover, do these houseguests rule the self, and who is the real indentured servant, as bacteria and prokaryotic microorganisms outnumber a human within the body by ten to one or so, and human cells represent a very small minority within the body, within the great empire of the self?

As some people become stuck in a stage, or fantasy, reality tunnel, niche, bubble or neurogenic trap, such as fetch a bubble or insert old data, and enter each brave new world that way, as same-old, same-old, and seem exceedingly stubborn to stay that way, stay in the fray, turmoil, in that escalation cycle, of tit for tat, the "got yah," based on a technicality, or a puritan moral infraction, as they often find something, or put another way, a trivial pursuit of an impossible standard, which leads to yet another great ugly.

And many people seem genuinely surprised when it happens, the implications of same old same old from poking the others, who often take great offense, reel then protest or have no interest in maintaining the great human species rut, the quagmire or cruel and usual, and have no interest in digging faster, or it adds to another golden age of escalation, swirl, and aftermath, similar to a hydrodynamics simulation pattern of the Rayleigh–Taylor instability, that swirl of turmoil, byproduct and distribution. As that process takes on a certain style, and the fundamental pattern repeats through the history of civilization, as well as nature, of mission creep, and tremendous collateral damage.

People often seem surprised by all those complex terms, conditions and promises in life, of *Will you love and obey me forever*, which often seems one way, the devotion, or some other phrase that denotes structural integrity, the physics, which is often asked by spouse, family, friend, tribe, team, school, politic, enterprise, institution, religion and certain schools of thought, as well as race, all those elaborate contracts, as well as conflicting scripts, serving all those "masters," for lack of a better word, at the same time, those supreme loyalties, and jump through all those hoops, such as here and there, then sign more agreements, with subtle or obvious gestures or until the hand cramps, becomes a claw, from I promise forever—yes, forever, then you might get that gift, that substantial treasure, maybe, but at what cost, as a person or system moves about with that very complex tethering system, which often pulls a person or system far away from their original intent or natural aspiration, and with even more restricted degrees of freedom.

It is as if these social constructs run out of ideas, or reveal a poverty of ideas, or rely on poverty, such as impoverished major segments. So, follow a script, a trope, and not based on stubborn facts, or durable facts, as well as full context and truly peer reviewable, which eventually results in an overall process and system, which has a certain flatness, or seems as if a faithfully flat scheme, or schemes, of generic property, generic flatness or a flat cohomology, and a faithfully flat fundamental descent that fades into a sober yet ever so complex reality of stuck again, in a quagmire.

However, her mother represents the meticulous alpha type, an intellectual yet bare-knuckles, and quite a colorful character, which is a story unto itself, similar to the movie *Knuckle*, a film about the secretive world of an Irish traveler, and bare-knuckle boxing.

Whereas her father is also stubborn, yet the exact opposite of her mother, as a distant, a person of few words, an enigmatic. And he gave her that nickname, the Mighty Sparrow and was a hunter by profession, not a big-game hunter per se, not like those portrayed in Hollywood, not those classic images of Clark Gable in *Mogambo* or a thinly disguised account of John Huston in *White Hunter Black Heart*. However, *The Ghost and the Darkness* might be a bit closer to what her father did, except without a gun.

His mission was to track and capture animals of prey, ones that display exceptional cunning, cruelty and mayhem; ones that killed locals as if a sport. And he specialized in bears, crocodiles and lions, such as animals that prey on the indigent, especially in the Third World, and only using primitive capturing skills, gathering local and natural resources, and rarely killed them, yet did so with honor when absolutely necessary. Just as importantly, his approach was systematic, the long game, well-organized and on the cheap, using no metal during the capture, and did it alone, with no fanfare, no tribute, no glory or ego, no "mano a mano," not a guy-testosterone style, of gristle, or *danegeld*, to prove this or that.

Why her mother married him, let alone anyone, remains a great mystery. For most of Bonnie's life, her mother forced him out, further and still further. He went from the next bedroom to another floor, to the other side of the house, then to a cottage, on the very outskirts of their rural property. Well, it was less of a cottage and more of a one-room shack—okay: a shed. As the mother clearly viewed him as some type of Greco-Roman wild man, German *wilder mann, wudewasa, Wodwo,* medieval Green Man or more likely an outright savage.

On many occasions, he could often be found meditating in an underground cave, one with three very narrow and convoluted rock fissures leading inside. However, in order to enter the cave, one had to dive underwater, down eight feet, into a black cedar water spring.

On the whole, his movements were highly stylized, codified and symbolic. In many respects, it had a similar theme and structure of a Japanese tea ceremony, *ikebana, noh, kōdō,* as well as elements of The Eleusinian Mysteries, especially when preparing to enter sacred and rare space, which, as a young kid, Bonnie closely watched as a third culture person, watched his specialized practices of stillness, movement, generative and creative.

Just as importantly, as well as here and now, Bonnie continues this forest mission, and then hobbles south with a renewed sense of energy, determination and what seems an indestructible interest, those property markers, those small metal geodetic survey plates inscribed with property details, as each sit on a concrete post, so, pry them off and return.

Along the way, and for the first time, she finds a small game trail that, although a tight squeeze, which often requires crawling by belly, leads out of the forest, to the south eastern corner she rounded on her initial search for a forest entrance.

With a held breath, as well as scramble through that exit, it appears quite clear how a person could easily miss this narrow low entrance, covered by thick layers of dense foliage, as the thorn passage barely lends itself to travel by belly, in either direction.

"Nice. I like."

And moments later, she gains distance into the open, keenly looks about for danger, at one angle after another and levels, then with a held breath running style, dives into that same forest entrance, and once completely through the passage, rises, dusts off the self and travels in an even wider loop that will eventually take her north-northwest to avoid those previous barriers.

As a result, Bonnie cautiously travels west northwest, moves through thick foliage and occasionally says with a smile, gusto and a special style, "Chicken fajita, yes, fajita!"

However, that charming state of mind suddenly shifts to something else, and she says softly, "Fajita...," as a frown arrives from that institutional product.

Elsewhere, and after adjusting her two-tone Elvira-like updo, as well as vintage fire engine red cat sunglasses, Quinn, who has some resemblance to the model Lynn Amelie Rage, loudly announces, "I made it! I'm here!"

Then a smile beams and arms fully extend to the world.

However, all of the gal pals have long gone, disappeared, in one fast exit after another.

"They must have forgotten about me, right? I distinctly remember mentioning it, in fact, in great detail."

So, she exits her car and stretches, a full stretch, one that really extends, as well as twists here and there, to bring a full sense of relief, from sitting during that long drive.

And her face shows the "Oh, ah" ecstatic of one twist and stretch after another, "Oh, yes," so much so, limbs and fingers tremble.

All that stops at the sight of those Buicks, which that sit neatly parked side by side, and saying in an extended way, "Yes!" as if winning the lottery, then she approaches and keenly peeks inside, one car after another, careful not to put fingerprints on the window or paint, as all cars seemed waxed, as well as fully detailed, and, well, people can be a bit jumpy, or testy, if you lean on their property, such as property rights and the property bubble.

However, it becomes quite apparent the ladies have long gone, and just as significantly, all of their parking meters have expired.

So, after going back to her car, digging for coins in the glove compartment between seat cushions and under seats, she finds and inserts money which extends parking times to the maximum, then notices something else, shrugs, considers and extends the times for six other cars, followed by a step up onto the boardwalk, to fully realize the magnificent 360-degree beach vista, and that special lifestyle, of freedom.

And after adjusting her two-tone Elvira-like updo, as well as vintage fire engine red cat sunglasses, this pristine day becomes fully apparent, as a scan in all directions reveals a spectacular expanse of ocean, sky, fresh air, excellent food and tranquility.

In addition, the air has a certain charm one expects, especially from freshly made calzone, *stromboli*, lasagna, and rows of mouthwatering pizza, with apparently every known topping.

Then, the heavenly power of barbecue arrives as people walk by with piles and piles of food, of gained treasures, which causes her to ogle, imagine and move lips, to simulate eating a banquet, within reach, yes, easy reach.

Elsewhere, Bonnie says, "Oh, my stomach! I don't feel so good. Fajita...," then feels puzzle, concern, more discomfort.

Moments later, a considerable frown appears.

C<small>HAPTER</small>

From an ad hock military base, and with no identification marks, a Bell Boeing V-22 Osprey aircraft prepares for takeoff.

And onboard sits a well-armed commando team, with one member who spits tobacco to the side, which, well, represents nothing new, as you might have heard this before.

Regardless, other team members notice, yet say nothing, and show steely combat veteran looks, of veterans who have gone through hell a few times, through smolder, as well as utter ruin, and done so because of the constitution and oath to defend, yet behind the scenes, behind the curtain, forced to because of a powerful special interest, an elite interest, as well as for a climbing political animal or two, often trying to fortify a resume, an exit strategy, such as an ever -so-soft landing into real money, and done so as a proxy, or for political brinkmanship, or cruel-and-usual by nature, or for a good reason, to deter savages.

Nonetheless, each commando would have no second thought of delivering a fist, a fistic event, a solid punch or more to the face, if the spit stained the combat boots, or uniform of glory, of everlasting.

Meanwhile, the captain receives a phone call from a Congressional broker, an ultimate insider, who orders them to "Standby," as the vinculum calculates, also known as a thinkculum, a specialized system, a big O notation algorithm or equivalent, which engineers and formulates political events, meetings, talking points, spin methods, political calendars, bill schedules and votes, which *de facto* represents the most influential aspects of the new age free enterprise system, as well as another aspect, the full impression of a pay-to-play system, and those players receive the highest priority.

And the system generates a complex formula, as well as produces terms and instructions, well, which often slows an opponent, slows a competitor on cue, for a patron, yet that purpose or origin is not often known, until an objective history reveals and squeezes a competitor for money, or out of the industry.

In addition, this specialized-big-O-notation-computerized-algorithm-based-system delivers daily internal and external media spin, delivers churn for each stage within the hour, day, week, month, year, and the message contains carefully timed instructions, buzz words, catchphrases, rumors to float, lists of approved praise or insult, and who delivers what, as well as sayings to manipulate and reinforce loyalty, as well as new ways and means to redefine a word, such as how to apply a stigma, a stain, how to leave a mark, or visible impression, leave a trace on something, such as a toke, symbol or brand, on fandom, and often leave permanent damage on the others, the outsiders. And show a normal human trait of the others; yet portray it as a world-class blunder, often with a sleight of hand, turn of phrase or keen revision skillset. And mostly, stir true believers with "end of days" or some other cultural equivalent, with fear and paranoia, as well as other topical "red meat issues," or another dietary functions, such as a deficiency, and often to agitate and destabilize the opposition, yet destabilizes the self, as a very profitable industry.

And just as importantly, trade ultimate insider information, such as when to buy and sell financial instruments, contracts, companies, institutions, key positions, levers of power, and often done so as manufactured profit, as a manufactured haste, waste and chaos, that style.

The thinkculum specializes in creating a string of well-timed crisis, with a precisely calculated pause in between each, to maximize effectiveness. All of which gives this method an artificial accordion feel, of cycles, or waves, yet the new age artificial version, especially to pressure the markets or constructs—well, to manipulate the betting line then extract profits from that "The Long Tail" statistical window, followed by restarting the entire process, over and over again, in artificial waves, as a big squeeze technique, yet one refined into a sweet science; well, sweet to some, yet often hell for the considerable others.

And more importantly, this process becomes a high art form, such as Artemisia, yet an Artemisia absinthium abuse, as a science, where many economies run on tricks, sugary treats and artificial ingredients, so to speak, and run on a mixed metaphorical, or trope, or factoid, run on a planted story or two, which often serves as a foundation then another and another, layer after layer, of gnarl, of gristle.

The thinkculum instantaneously calculates a forest solution, which includes targets, descriptions, locations, entry and exit points, diversions, backup plans, pricings and terms, for this pay-to-play scheme, as just another among hundreds of local, regional, and worldwide daily schemes, or quick shortcuts, to maximize profit. As if maximum profit represents a sacred event, a sacred moment or process, a way of life, especially in search of a great treasure, a ten-bagger or more, and all of these represent in the metagame, all players, places and things, and often adjusted in localized speak, in coded ways, the ever-so-shallow language game, in the tree of linguistics, the ways and means, to ultimate insider, to very wealthy contributors or patron saints, and all as part of the metastack, or metagame, the long game, or put another way, a differential game of continuous pursuit and evasion, and the play of one game develops the rules for another game, as well as mission, design, function, content, timing, and so forth.

Or imagine, the thinkculum as the most advanced set theory system to date, a metatheory, or several complex developmental stages beyond the Von Neumann–Bernays–Gödel set theory, index of cycle by time, pattern recognition based on physiological psychology, stagecraft, theatrical scenery, stage placement of *mise-en-scène,* and not a poetic version created by the best artist, in full accord with universal law. However, it was created by a super geek, an ally or yes-person, a disposable contract worker, someone that formulated a not so grand unified theory, based on system dynamics, based on complex numbers, on real numbers and imaginary numbers, a new theory of computation, yet the same old same old, to defend a Rayleigh region, an aspect of, defend a complex configuration that seems simple enough, such as a certain way of life, a philosophy, set of ideals with distinct thematic sections, thematic interpretation, transformation, and yes, complex effort to maximize profit if you will. As styles matter, style makes a good fight, and often based on a wave, a rogue wave, freak, monster, killer wave, or a simple wave packet, yet wave—particle duality, and on an occasion, with a major shift now and again.

Yet and often, the thinkculum does not respect the fundamental rules of a durable system, a reasonable approach, reasonable life, an elevated place above the quagmire, as well as without the cruel and unusual; quite the opposite, which is, in fact, the typical method, the common, because of the style, as well as the quarterly profit system or other artificial social constructs, other reasons or justifications.

Regardless, as well as here and now, the system distributes operational details to the commando team captain, who also notices the split incident, again, and steely looks of tough veterans, of soldiers who have gone through hell a few times, through smolder, as well as utter ruin, and often done so for a climbing politic animal or two, a device, and each commando would have no second thought of delivering a fist, a fistic lesson, a solid punch to the face, as that spit nearly stains combat boots, as well as a uniform of glory, of everlasting.

However, these six well-armed commandos give the full impression of distinct subsets, within various foreign agencies, which represent the new age interdependency, sold as vital, sold to nation-states and elite multinational corporate coalitions, which also seemed trapped as well as, and reliant on cheap money and easy access to special banking privileges, a special system window, of easy credit, well, to maintain a system, maintain the too-big-to-fail preference, and life inside an institution, "Oh, boy!" with the snarl, the gristle, within all those complex nests, within one another, and nests often well protected from the norm, from the really fresh air, and reliant on forced air, on air forced through vents, as opposed to fresh, and fresh according to those twenty definitions or more, with all the pros and cons.

And these commandos may well represent specialized commercial factions of CBI, SIS, ASIS, BND, NSS, and BSS, as often governments gives the full impression of a proxy, for free enterprise, dragged them into one quagmire after another, of very special interests, elite interests, or various aspects of government resemble another version of free enterprise, another common commercial interest of the day, and often quite desperate, yet sold as vital, as well as sacred, and enforced with a hyper style, yet is just another common effort, another version of escalation, and deeper into the great quagmire?

However, here and now, something seems slightly off, too accurate, too precise, possibly their commando uniform, bearing or index of character, which seems too precise, too super clean, and near perfection.

Maybe you have seen those types of people, things, or situations; too perfect, or close to perfect, such as perfect-pitch, perfect-fifth, or a perfect ten, citizen, couple, system, or a universal constitution, or universal wave function, or theatrical property, yet not a founding myth.

Regardless, they recheck silenced weapons and adjust especially made parachutes, designed to open well below 400 feet.

"Here, here, and here," says the captain to highlight mission details, "These represent drop zones, and once you land, move to your designated targets. Remember, navigational systems are not reliable in this region, not even a simple compass. And you must capture or destroy five Alcatel-Lucent 7950 XRS-style internet routers, collaborative filter devices, as well as the tunable metamaterial containers that house them."

After system checks, the Bell Boeing V-22 Osprey aircraft engines start, and one after the other eventually ejects white smoke.

Within minutes, the craft gains full power, lifts then rotates toward the destination, The Proving Grounds, home of the original DARPA, not a want-a-be, home to one of the scariest freaks ever associated with the field of PSYOP, a specialist in asymmetrical clandestine warfare, phantom warfare, including tradecraft, boots on ground and "techno" skills, especially cyber warfare, as well as "anti– and retro–bot asymmetrical warfare," a specialist in escalation.

Moments later, one commando after another tells an absolutely filthy insider joke, and not ordinary jokes, but true classics, then the captain edges to a private aircraft section and has a lengthy phone conversation with a powerful patrician, someone people might say represents an exceptional German mystic, an unknown superior initiator, and yet a superior judge, although not one who controls traditional court proceedings.

As that patrician stands inside a hallway of his German garden-mansion, and one quite similar to *Grüneburgschlößchen*, Frankfurt, one of the many Rothschild-style mansions, and not a Gilded Age version, the *nouveau riche*, yet this one has many features a person might expect in a secular temple, if you will, or tome, a sacred precinct with special rules, and surrounded by an extraordinary forty-acre garden, in fact, a picturesque place of colorful bloom, which includes shrubs, subshrubs, and special herbal plants, yet not a virtuous treatise of medicinal, tonic, culinary and aromatic expressions, nevertheless what one might expect within the golden age of classical and Renaissance gardens.

In fact, it gives the place a certain image of prosperity, progress and peace, a place in accord with nature, as if it represents an unofficial paradise, a deep foundation, yet earthfast, and a substantial post, a place that might lead to the transcendence, might trigger a full restoration of glory, the original long lost glory now found.

However, a closer look at all these fine details gives the full impression it lacks something vital.

And elsewhere, as the aircraft nears those targets, the captain turns to his men and signals one minute, then sends a brief text message to that patrician then network of patricians in Florence, Zurich, Ravensburg, Augsburg, Ingolstadt and Chur, as well as Strasbourg, Budapest, Vienna, Prague, Oslo, Stockholm, Neuilly sur Seine, and Saint Cloud.

Seconds later, he yells, "Jump! Jump!" and two commandos leap.

Moments later, "Jump! Jump!" and another two leap, then he and the last member pause, then leap.

Elsewhere, Mary rechecks Agrippa and the unconscious man for vital signs as well as broken bones, and then carefully attends to cuts, scraps, bruises and contusions.

Just as importantly, she detects no sign of internal bleeding.

However, this whole situation creates an uncomfortable dilemma, and she again considers calling an ambulance then anguishes, mumbles and grumbles with curse substitutes then quite foul animated language, not fit for print, especially by a lady, then eventually decides against a phone call, and will begrudgingly abide by that agreement, for now.

Yet in order to more accurately access his condition, she must remove that whatever, a diving suit?

However a careful examination, of fully articulated joints and breather system, shows no apparent way to remove it.

No knobs, switches, latches, levers or buttons seem apparent—none.

So, she steps back and looks from other angles; as a result, each step creates distinct crackles and crunches on the dark Brazilian cherry wood floor.

Regardless, "There must be a latch, somewhere," she concludes.

Although taps here and there reveal nothing, nor do hand slides across the suit's pitted surface.

Eventually when the index finger reaches and lingers between the second and fifth rib, a dim blue light appears for eight seconds.

And more attempts produce the same effect.

However, a combination of touches, taps, pushes, pokes, slide attempts and even a few rude fist pounds here and there fail.

Soon, fatigue arrives, as well as a few frustrated huffs and unladylike gestures.

Then among the stacks of unopened moving boxes she plops down, puts feet up and wiggles into a very comfortable position, then wiggles toes, and verifies Agrippa sleeps, as she might leap at the sight.

After settling down and pondering nothing special, a bag of Bazooka Bubble Gum becomes apparent, a rare version indeed, because it contains no artificial ingredients, as well as sweetened with cane sugar.

And eventually, one below average-sized bubble arrives after another.

Yet when the first decent one slowly forms and bursts, a realized spark, "about schema," arrives, about organization, the fundamentals of an organized system, as well as oblique strategies, which generates a broad smile followed by an extending "s" version of "Yes."

As a result, she takes his right gloved and touches it to that spot, between the second and fifth rib, with a common hand scuba signal for decompression, and it does a considerable something, such as a decompression party yet it does not open.

"Hell's bells," then, one diving hand signal after another fails to open the system.

However and by happenstance, leaving the pinky in that spot for a time, leaving the baby, the future, the eternity aspect, causes the blue light to flicker then something whirls inside the suit, clicks and releases all suit latches.

Then with a twist and yank, each heavy section slides off, such as the remaining sheared helmet, one shoulder to arm's aspect after another, primary air supply, back-up air supply, command center, waist to chest, and waist to legs.

Eventually, the equipment builds into a floor pile, left of that massive ornate library fireplace.

After taking pictures from as many angles as possible, as well as for maker markers, symbols, such as hieroglyphic characters, stubs or leaky abstractions, Mary checks him for identification, yet finds none, no wallet, no name tag, no "I heart mom" tattoo.

In fact, he has no tattoos or distinguishing marks.

Also, and clearly, all of his clothing labels had been removed.

However, he does wear a considerable medicinal skin patch system, a very complex one with elaborate connecting wires, as well as something unrelated to a quit smoking effort, or for any other conventional aliment.

The system appears homemade, and it has no manufacturer details, yet the device does not appear as if a crude effort.

However, and on the floor sits a large flat pouch, and based on the found location, it must have fallen out of the chest assembly.

Just as significantly, and inside are absolutely fresh one hundred dollar bills, grouped in a traditional pack of fifty, and thirty packs in total.

As a result, she perplexes, looks about, especially out one window after another then turns on the television and scans local stations, yet sees no mention of anything, which might explain this event—nothing, no bank robbery, no strange sighting, no missing person alert, no warning of a desperado, and "come to your senses."

"Nada," even a scan of other channels offers no answers.

As a result, she says, "Now that's just plain weird."

And for more clues, she inspects each money pack with a quick thumb scanning motion, which reveals a wave of spectacular new money smell, and eyes widen.

"Oh my, that's ever so fresh."

Then she opens a large number of packs and counts, which proves quite difficult, as new money does that, it sticks together.

In fact, it takes a considerable effort to verify each bill, which might represent a deliberate technique to slow down, well, a cash-based transaction, as the system is desperate for informatics, then a weird feeling arrives from the idea of her fingerprints as well as DNA and fibers on nearly all that money, as police, especially the FBI, are in a very bad mood lately, and they will dust for fingerprints in search of the classic villain, for thugs, mooks, and evil minions, especially for organized crime, as well as accomplices, for troublemakers, the greedy—okay, or newbies, particularly the symbolic for "no more excuses."

Moments later, someone bangs on the massive front doors, really bangs in very loud way, as if pounding with a mighty fist.

Mary thinks, *And the shoe drops.*

Then long pause, *Here comes the pain.*

Elsewhere, at that garden-mansion, and one quite similar to *Grüneburgschlößchen*, Frankfurt, one of the many Rothschild-style mansions, that powerful German patrician reaches for the hallway doorknob, notices something, stops, and waits without motion.

Just as significantly, he appears as if a direct descendant of Teutobod, of Jutland, and family, which eventually, as well as shrewdly, rose to power, mostly through sleeping partnerships of land and trade then expanded into banking, which eventually seized a continuous leading role as a family of first class patricians.

Then his eyes widen, nostrils flare as he waits motionless and without expression then, ever so slowly, scans the area, as eyes narrow and search for obvious, as well as subtle things, section by section, including above and below yet not behind.

However, everything seems normal and in the correct place, as this has happened before, several times—that feeling of something.

Moments later, a subtle hint of pine arrives, then cedar, storax, frankincense, and Indian hemp.

However, something else arrives—thistle, an Asteraceae, an inflorescent star, yet as if a complex polyphyletic or thistle sage, a salvia carduacea-style system.

In addition, that mixtures gain a certain intangible power, symmetry and depth, all of which conveys something quite practical, although a vague reminder of something else, for instance the epistemology of science, then evokes fleeting mental images of Plato, Aristotle, Roger Bacon, Francis Bacon, René Descartes, John Stuart Mill, and Jeremy Bentham.

Likewise, it reminds the German patrician of something beyond those, and quite elusive, but what?

In fact, it hints at the qualities of a psychonautic portable secular shrine, or transformative agent, and yet feels as if it might generate a hidden great event, with phantasm in back, something, such as influence on supra and subspace.

Moments later, something happens.

Elsewhere, after arriving at the door, Mary looks through the side curtains then at various angles yet sees nothing.

"Bang, bang, bang!"

And with a deep breath then shrug of the shoulders, she quietly says, "The end is near, jail then prison; yes, hardcore prison, and not a club med, not a German– or Scandinavian–style prison, design to truly rehabilitate, and where many prisoners have a key to their room, a studio apartment, with what people might say, right wing people, people who breath hell fire and brimstone, 'what the heck is going on?' not that version."

In fact, she would sit likely inside a true hell hole, a smoldering place, a pit, as the homeland system continues to remain in a very bad mood over the past few years.

Plus her fingerprints are all over that money, as well as DNA.

Then as the front doors swing open, two neatly dressed smiling ladies appear and say, "Jehovah's Witness."

And they immediately offer words of wisdom then say in unison, "Trouble is part of your life, and if you don't share it, you don't give the person who loves you a chance to love you enough."

Mary seriously considers then her head tilts a few times, looks about then says, "That's Dinah Shore."

They continue, "We're growing a strange crop of agnostics this year."

"That's E. K. Hornbeck."

"Then why did God plague us with the capacity to think? Mr. Brady, why do you deny the one thing that sets us above the other animals? What other merit have we? The elephant is larger, the horse stronger and swifter, the butterfly more beautiful, the mosquito more prolific, even the sponge is more durable. Or does a sponge think?"

"Henry Drummond?"

They continue, "Fanaticism and ignorance is forever busy and needs feeding."

"Jerome Lawrence?"

They continue, "A gem cannot be polished without friction, nor a man perfected without trials."

She puzzles, flinches, looks about and says, "That's a Chinese proverb."

One of them continues, "I would never have amounted to anything if it were not for adversity."

With that, Mary squints and seriously scans in all directions, for context, for stagecraft, theatrical cues, show controls or a playwright-associated metathetic then says, "That's J.C. Penney" and resolves the problem with a crisp twenty dollar bill, closes the door and mumbles in absolute disbelief, as well as grumps, "J.C. Penney, really?"

Elsewhere, that German patrician realizes a critical truth then it becomes more specific, yet not within sight, and it has a certain feel of a PowerShell, a transhuman, posthuman, and yet a WS-Trust hypnagogia, with a transitional state from wakefulness to sleep, yet a walled Accumulo NoSQL garden, if you will.

As a result, his eyes widen and nostrils flare then he slowly scans the area, as eyes narrow and search for obvious and subtle things.

Yet everything seems normal and in the correct place.

So, he reaches for that same doorknob then midway freezes, and waits, and really waits, as if in an iānuae threshold, a well-known port, or well-known binary, and carefully scans in a way that shifts back and forth, from questioning to studious of the smallest details, and all done without blinking—as the eyes often narrow and methodically scan section-by-section, even above, below, yet not behind.

Eventually, he carefully back steps to gain safety, and further, then once at a considerable distance and out of that field or event horizon, scans the area, as if a scout at the frontier.

However, nothing seems out of the ordinary. Nothing, and even as the nose takes a few cautious samples and the mind considers all evidence, as well as what might seem trivial.

Then as he nears that door, and reaches out, and things darken around the periphery then remind this person of living in a cave, in a very familiar place, a place-based education, of primes and unusual places, possibly Plato's cave or some mystic grotto, and one that seems ancient, oddly illuminated, and more importantly, a telling, or teller of an election, amendment or possibly a dangerous mine, which a pioneer might dig at the substratum, or search for a Bethany-style solution, yet finds procrastination, the self and crucial syncretism sparks, of *verbum sat zapienti est*, to rise from the rut, rise from the rutway.

And moments later, this German patrician frequently experiences a sense of tremendous awe, which causes mouth and eyes to widen, as this person quickly looks for AB hylomorphs, for Franz Kafka notions, Schröder–Bernstein theorem of measurable space, indexicality, as well as human aspects, and not in a conventional sense of the body, mind and soul, for instance, something you might find near a very specific well of souls, and that phase transition not easily quantifiable.

All of which causes a strange and extraordinary thrill, a marvel, as well as mystery, which shows on the face, and the internal body alarm warns of exceptional frontier danger, and yet, as if at a threshold of sheer greatness, that thrill of a cliff, of real danger then rise into greatness, and yet something to not trifle with, ever, then the process causes this person to transition through various emotional states, which include flabbergast, "ah-ah-ah," then difficult to catch a breath, puzzle, fear, hot and cold flashes, shakes, very, then a trap, also known as an exception, fault or synchronous interruption, then petrify followed by thrill to no end at this great mystery, and that cycle repeats several times.

Eventually, this German patrician quickly steps back to gain safety, and further, then once at a considerable distance, out of that field or event horizon, scans the area in great detail.

Not much later, he slowly travels to the right, to a nearby door, and cautiously reaches for the doorknob then midway freezes, and waits, really waits, and something else happens, quite an unusual feeling.

So he burst inside the room.

CHAPTER

Elsewhere, Mary remembers her plan regarding that comatose man, and slowly opens the front door, carefully looks about for trouble, quickly enters the borrowed hospital van, then slowly backs it up, to the front door.

Eventually, she reaches above the truck bumper, for a metal down ramp, the portable type, storage under the vehicle, which slides out and down.

Not much later, she straps an unwieldy x-ray machine to a dolly then, with a serious-heave-ho-effort, it rises yet greatly wobbles and needs a bear hug for dear life, as damage might represent the beginning of the end.

In the meantime and elsewhere, that German patrician burst inside the room, a conservatory of iron and mostly glass, a greenhouse for citrus, which requires a special warm environment, and the place also contains rare tropical plants.

Then he meticulously scrutinizes section by section then slowly steps back and out.

Moments later, he travels left of that problematic door, to a nearby door and cautiously reaches for the doorknob then midway freezes, and waits, really waits.

And something else happens, an unusual feeling, a critical truth, and something one might feel at a well of souls, and that phase transition, something else not easily quantifiable, yet an identity foreclosure then species dysphoria.

As a result, his eyes widen, nostrils flare, and he waits motionless then ever so slowly scans the area—as eyes narrow and search for obvious then subtle things.

Yet everything seems normal and in the correct place.

So, he bursts inside that lumber room.

Elsewhere, Mary stabilizes the expensive machine.

Then with a hip action, which causes the dolly wheels to edge onto the metal down ramp, she says, "Peace of cake," and smiles that becomes a full beam.

So much so, teeth appear then the maximum number, which have a certain appearance; in fact, quite nice as all seem remarkably fit, well-maintained, and have a superb symmetry.

Yet in that brief moment, the heavy as well as unwieldy x-ray machine accidentally rolls down that ramp; as a result, she imposes a freakish bear hug grip on both dolly and machine—too late, as midway down and still many feet off the ground, all tip to the right, off the ramp.

CHAPTER 37

Meanwhile, the patrician bursts inside that lumber room, a room well-heeled people have, to store custom furniture, such as built to match a theme, yet a place for things not needed now; however they have tremendous value, so, a treasure room, with only one substantial way inside, and often lit by natural light, such as a narrow slot or more, although not large enough for someone to shimmy inside, and outside that slot often leads to the forbidden garden, a place other people rarely see, for any number of reasons, such as a sanctuary, and the best possible quiescence.

Or, it represents a work-in-progress, and effort to restore the *apokatastasis*, a *diaspora,* such as the soul or paradise lost, or heaven on earth, yet other people might misunderstand, which seems to represent the norm of people who see very little of any given situation yet jump to a conclusion with a heuristic, a mental shortcut, or often based on a cognitive bias.

Just as importantly, here and now the scan moves a few degrees at a time, left to right, as well as the ceiling then floor, yet not behind.

And he finds nothing as a result, exits, and returns to that first door, the one with a tremendous mystery, and moments later, a subtle hint of pine arrives, then cedar, storax, frankincense, and Indian hemp.

However, and again, something else arrives—thistle, "yes, an Asteraceae, an inflorescence star, yet as if a complex polyphyletic or thistle sage, a salvia carduacea-style system."

Then he slowly reaches for the doorknob and says, "It leads everywhere, yes, everywhere," and eyes widen at the threshold, then role confusion arrives, as well as "What have I become?" that danger.

And so much so, that a reasonable person should carefully step back, far back, and especially out, of each event horizon stage, out of that theater, and narrow path or window into everywhere, or flash-sideways-lost, as there also seems a considerable number of temporal fractures, as if a "drawing of the analytic extension of tetration to the complex plane," yet all hidden from sight, here and there, or put simply narrow windows into these various aspects, of flash somewhere, often in a loop, yet as if yet another television episode, at some fundamental threshold, or worst, at the very edge of existence, or out of the universe, as a reject or rejection slip, of sail on, sail away, from the stack, or supreme bulkhead.

Then his soul shivers and eyes widen, at that very edge of true greatness, the cliff, or final precipice of existence, and a thrill arrives, over whelms, and he frequently experiences a tremendous sense of awe, which causes mouth and eyes to widen, as a person might exit the evolutionary tree, the tree of life, and become what, not a local, global or universal, not the over– or undersoul, become what?"

Regardless of the danger, this German patrician bursts inside that room, yet beyond that special state.

Elsewhere, and with a freakish bear hug grip on dolly and expensive machine, Mary continues to tip over, in a bad way; as a result, all tremendous ground impact on her.

Meanwhile, the German patrician bursts inside that room, an enfilade, a suite of rooms, ones that feature grand European architecture, a place with two parallel axis of rooms, and rooms with a similar style as *Studiolo* of Francesco I in Palazzo Vecchio, Florence, with spectacular vistas, often a private art gallery or two, or *Wunderkammer,* as some aristocracies prefer to live among exceptional art, of one type or another, live within or connected to, by way of a state apartment or more, and very impressive places.

Yet with a burst inside that room he finds an enormous buzz of guests, in various clusters—all of which gives the full impression of a spectacle, a show of shows event, filled with bright lights, as well as live chamber music, and quite possibly Joseph Haydn String Quartet, in C, opus seventy-six, number three, "Kaiser."

Overall, these guests spark, delight, gush, and chat about the enfilade, the spectacular vista of rooms, which mostly consists of a private art gallery, as well as elegant throw rugs, furniture, curtains, chandeliers and indoor palms, yet done as a complete set, as a unified theory, the atmospherics, and a case study, as well as the deep mathematical beauty of life, the phenomena of existence.

And this seems the case, as a considerable number of these people believe so, especially ones relatively new to this lifestyle, and they also exchange shared hopes, as well as dreams then meticulously flatter one another with a give-and-take manner, gush even more, sip rare spirits then imagine a bright future.

However, a smaller number of people, some with a family line, hundreds of years inside the aristocracy, seem stoic, matter-of-fact, aloof, detached, indifferent, and far less impressed.

Yet, a considerable number of them show disdain and grump, as a professional grump might, or as a glum, grump, gripe might, to spoil or decimate a situation, as if a favorite style, the histaminic, as a considerable number of this subset resemble fashionistas and hauterflies, then take great pride in well-crafted nips, pecks, and blunt critiques—as everyone and everything appears fair game to this criticism, which eventually intensifies, as if to wither a target, wither it out of existence.

And this subset does so with a certain cold, barren and desolate style, a classic version of the modern ugly, a certain guy thing, yet women also have a version, and with a coldness, as well as the shun process, maybe with a quick alliance, a quick negotiation, to negotiate someone out of the social network, out of the community, out of history, existence and the timeline. As if they never existed, were never born, and often done so as if a favorite tool or system of compliance. Again, it represents a reoccurring theme through the history of ideas, and this style is often deployed by many other aspects of society, not just aristocracy. As some family heads use that favorite technique when they impose a system, as do a tribe, team, gender, political party, economic system, religion, race, and other social constructs. And they do so as if life operates in a vacuum, has no symmetric aspects, no trophic levels, no consumer-resource systems, no ever so complex web, or biological interactions and no profound chain reaction. As a result, cruel and unusual does not seem so bad, especially the ripple effect, or that others will mimic this technique, see it as a tradition, rite of passage, or some other justification, or see it as an opportunity for chaos, to vent pent-up frustrations, at a gerrymander, of one type or another, as well as the lack of true mobility and ability to become a fully realized being, then the cumulative effect often and eventually triggers another great collective identity crisis, embitters the collective dream, the under– and oversoul?

Yet the overall guest mood represents an enormous buzz, of joy, as well as of opportunity, and in various fully animated clusters—all of which gives the full impression of a spectacle, a show of shows event, filled with bright lights as well as chamber music, and quite possibly Joseph Haydn String Quartet in C, opus seventy-six, number three, "Kaiser."

Elsewhere, Bonnie continues west by northwest and travels mostly through thick brush, but occasionally finds a small open area.

However, something rustles, which causes her to freeze, look about and try to locate it.

Then from behind, something sprints towards her.

And enough so, it rattles the woman into a repeated start and stop pattern, on where to run or jump, maybe jump up a tree, if that is humanly possible, but no trees seem close enough, only very tall and ultradense shrubs.

Instead Bonnie flees west, and all along the way, hurdles over one moss-covered fallen log after another, which requires a world-class technique to avoid the green slick, then she must zigzag pass one obstacle after another, except for wait-a-minute-shrubs, which she counterintuitively plows through.

Too late, something quickly closes the distance.

CHAPTER  38

Elsewhere, and after that tremendous equipment impact, Mary dies.

As that type of thing happens all the time—life.

People have accidents.

Or, a person might languish or fade in a ghetto or shanty town.

It happens to people in the middle class, as well as above, which many people might dispute, and show a quick willingness to trade places—duly noted.

Where many in general and in their own way languish or fade, and often in very complex situations, in a *de facto* trap, such as an oubliette, epiphanic or cardboard prison, and a place without real universal suffrage, a substantial vent, or substantial opportunities and real prospects.

Maybe of greater concern, they lack vital sustenance at a critical moment, or at various stages, or have a surplus of, such as "the intrinsic motivation and the sixteen basic desires theory," and need an individualized solution at each vital stage, as no two people are exact in the ways and means, nor have the exact same language, so they languish, fade or ruin in a way, at each of those moments.

And many of these people eventually crack from tremendous stress or simply disappear, even an entire generation—lost, or just as often, deliberately sacrificed by one system or another, or one social construct, well, as expendables.

It happens all the time—gone.

And of significance, will anyone miss Mary? Will they truly miss her? Or will she quickly fade from memory?

That happens to many people, tribes, ideas, cultures, and religions said vital.

As well, it happened to many human species and varieties?— quickly forgotten.

And for many of them, it is as if they never existed, as they depart without a ripple in space or time.

In the meantime, Bonnie runs into a small clearing, and from behind, a rabbit run by her, that same bunny rabbit, the ever so cute one, same markings, and with the dog in hot pursuit, as well as apparently fit.

Then the rabbit shows brilliant maneuvers, smart pivots with one well proven angle after another, again and again, and easily avoids the dog, as if to deliberately toy, as if it knows that dog could never compete at that level, ever.

Just as significantly, and often, the dog seems wholly unprepared for these brilliant maneuvers, ultrafast reaction times, as well as world-class accelerations and abilities to easily elude at will.

Eventually the dog has a flashback, to a bookshelf, another bookshelf, to the ugh, not the favorites, not the preferred reading list, which includes an assortment of works from Lorine Niedecker, Carson McCullers, Willa Cather, Emily Brontë, Charlotte Brontë, and occasionally Flannery O'Connor, Maryse Conde, Toni Morrison, Gertrude Stein, Iris Murdoch, Virginia Woolf, or Mary Shelley's Frankenstein with those lessons, which warns about unnatural modes of tinker, production and reproduction, or Emily Dickinson selections that convey her bitter, relentless, and measured wit, or any of the other fifty books on that shelf, that jubilee, a fresh start, or emancipation of all slave types, even wage slaves, and the restoration of alienated lands, omission of all cultivation land, such as a time of special solemnity, a special plenary indulgence, or a religious song, to foretell a better world, a better way of being, and not this industry of constant pit, such as pit one against another, for a few coins, or that other strange trait, a primitive blood sport pleasure, from the suffering of others thought reasonable, from the pleasure of someone else's stumble, from a relative moral human code, with has a certain temporal, as well as local inflection.

As a result, the dog has a major flashback, to the other book shelter, the ugh and essentials, to stochastic, to a Kolmogorov, Markov jump process, as well as discrete and continuous games then it realizes something, finds a new set of gears, as well as exact angles, precise timings and a bold speed.

Then it matches one virtuoso rabbit maneuver after another, and just as importantly, based on subjects it thought of as ugh, and contrary to how dogs think, such as no great interest in the abstract, the obtuse, which many humans seem quite fond of, creating abstract ugh, as if they lack of a vivid imagination.

Regarding here and now, it has a flashback to the other bookshelf, and finds a series of cues then true canine greatness.

Of which, the rabbit immediately realizes those adjustments and that shallow game limit, such as when something snaps and becomes part of a metagame, the long game, or put another way, a differential game of continuous pursuit and evasion, and the play of one game develops the rules for another game.

As a result, it makes a brilliant series of adjustments then pivots even deeper into the forest, with the dog in full pursuit, with a now superior canine mindset, of the long game, which many humans often dismiss; the long game, for a few coins, for the shiny, for bling, or a sugar treat, or equivalent, such as a starch—yes, that effect on the mind, of starch, potato chips or glucose, a must-have—or worship a star, celebrity, someone with star power, a diva, yes, but not a political diva said vital by the system, by the monopoly, not the professional panderer, but someone on the A– or B–list, maybe C—although, and come to think of it, D-list has those oh-so-juicy scandals, and anything to feel alive during this slog in the massive underclass, the underutilized, the expendable.

Then rabbit and dog disappear, with that new dynamic, that select pair of opposites, yet dynamics, companions and the dependents: life?

Chapter

Elsewhere, something secretly scans that German patrician, as well as enfilade, for signs of a special gene drive system, for someone or thing propels a gene of choice through a population, and just as importantly, as no gene drives have yet been tested in the wild, or so they say.

Then moments later, that German patrician, the homeowner, bursts inside the enfilade, a suite of grand European architectural rooms.

And he moves through the crowd, towards his state apartment, which sits on the far side, discreetly behind center axis, and in such a way, he can easily come and go, such as during a post-meal lull, for a brandy, bitter, *digestif, aqua vitae*, gentian spirit, or popular grog, for a vital spark, a potent drink, which might rejuvenate the mind, body and soul, and one that could serve as a proven tonic, one said effective, efficient, precise and balanced, one that will charm the spirit then immediately perks, restores, and produces a balanced satisfaction with newfound freedom.

And late at night, that person can sit among exceptional art, among the sublime or deep mathematical beauty of a *sui generis*, a class by itself, the unique, and do so in peace, as many Germans seem quite sensitive to noise pollution, and need a considerable amount of peace and quiet, especially late at night, from the enterprise system, from industrial clunk, and neighbors.

They need relief from wave after wave of circuitous, clamorous, crush, as well as clatter, clang and contradiction, and one presaging crisis after another, such as barking dogs. And these people in general heavily regulate those types of things, such as how long a dog may bark, as well as soundproof playgrounds, and when the country should close down nonessentials, to relax and find cool relief.

Or late night, this person can sit among art, among the aesthetic, especially ideal proportions, of a well-being, place or thing, or a zeitgeist, if you will, then formulate the ability to determine a nation, or determine an era, or, okay, settle for a classic alcohol buzz, to numb the trouble tree, the mind, mental baggage, numb a persistent personal demon, a tenacious pest, as if a nuisance tax.

So, numb with alcohol seems quite reasonable, especially a certain region of the brain, such as the aspect stuck in a loop, a true obsession?

Or better yet, quickly down a few drinks then utter a battle cry of freedom, "Freedom reigns! Freedom," as if a freedom reins or some other precarious substitute, of just another tenacious tether, another complex web or entanglement that represents a claustrophobic trap.

And especially avoid being exposed as a great pretender.

Such as, if a person looks in the mirror at just the right moment and angle, they might see the true self; see a lost opportunity, at a major threshold, or reference point indentation, or reference class problem. Yet that person quickly hides among the scripts, or quickly picks a script then act, and often with a very fake manner, as the great pretender.

And as this German patrician moves through the crowd, towards his state apartment, with a genuine sense of concern because of those hallway events and forest mission, one sizable group of guest after another surge towards him, as clusters of fully animated joy, as well as buzz, which in stages eventually overwhelm him, especially as it seems quite difficult to maintain a polite mood and small talk while quickly moving through one group after another, as if tethers.

So much so, speed slows, as more people crowd closer and closer.

All of which creates claustrophobia and eyes widen, as this situation might irritate him beyond reason, beyond that sweet spot in the mind, that region, and it does, especially from the noise, and each wave of people cause pressure to build.

Of which, he tries to suppress those internal feelings, and stay strong while still moving forward.

And yet he occasionally seems quite abrupt with a guest here and there then nips, and in a way that seems hasty compared to the overall festive mood, to the joy and to people who praise, ask a considerable number of questions, as well as simply want to share hopes and dreams, with a give-and-take manner, but mostly as if a soliloquy, a speech.

As people often do, they vent then go on and on about something, about their individual path, and from their unique perspective. As no individual seems exactly the same.

And often, they leave no significant room in the "give and take" process for "take," no regular pause, no choice, no way out.

In addition, many of these individuals gush forward, with what resembles a bright future filled with well-beings.

Needless to say, the patrician feels caught in a Rayleigh–Taylor social swirl, of byproduct and distribution, which represents a situation quite contrary to his nature, all that tremendous pressure.

And how does someone remain ever so cool and calm under pressure, and not become rapid with unpredictable mood changes, of impulse, of a considerable fight-flight impulse, that quickly reduces thought, to a very narrow one-dimensional range of choices associated with a snap decision, such as strike or escape, or the classics of peck-peck-peck, which often starts as grumble then gains energy into a considerable gruff? As compared to an exceptionally cool bearing under enormous pressure, and one that a person can easily shift perspective, abilities, and resources, as a master mechanic might, with an ever so smooth style, to select the most appropriate tools, compared to showing each transitional seam, each weakness.

Then if need be formulate a fresh approach, and something that solves yet does so as a poetic deed or act, to atone, such as in a situation, a family situation, later that night, or some other vital social construct, to resolve the next level, next vital stage, as well as remarkable improvement, and solve as a true virtuoso might, without exposing the seams, such as with a "strong seam management technique, on both sides, to enclose the raw stem or edge, the raw nerve."

And in doing so, the fresh approach might spark then illuminate some greater truth about perspective, the progress trap, max Q, and when to sit in a cool stream, as compared to heal something with a nip, a common nip, or remarkable one, such as a clever slight, designed to nip the *psyche*, the soul, in a cruel and unusual way.

How does a person remain nimble and not snap, not show a "tell," with all definitions of the word, such as show a profound secret: show a systemic weakness, kink or kluge?

This patrician seems quite strong, as well as powerful, yet not the flexible version, and flexible under a wide range of conditions, of various pressure types, and of dynamics.

Which could result in a few problems, as much of life functions with complex interdependent scripts, as well as timing, and often has a randomness of no rhythm or reason. Plus no system is perfect, regardless of what system commercials promote, as each has a price or kink, an unfortunate twist, as well as wake of destruction.

As things do not always square, especially an idea, belief system, or plan, or things at the subatomic and subnuclear scale, for instance, an eventual curve, when a thing needs to be very straight or flat, at the endpoint. Or those couplings do not quite meet at a common energy scale. Or the dynamics of a "wave translation" conflict, which compete; those engines of uncertainty, change, randomness and chaos, as well as all that atomic vibration, which leads to an opinion: no wonder people, places and things fall apart.

As any given thing can have a serious design flaw, also called "the oops moment," or represent individualization, which has existed since the very beginning of time, since the beach ball universe unpacked, in an instant, as well as other problems, such as the oscillation between complex states, superposition and the perpetual unique stamp on a system, a temporal stamp, such as "Made in Podunk," or a one-horse town modern equivalent, or next to a mud hole said "great" then system members must chat that message on cue, or else.

And yet, people, as well as systems, fully expect thing to remain ever so straight, as well as true, yet life is as much a wave as well as a particle, and building on a wave, such as a delta wave, a profound and persistent vision, or shared daydream, requires a tremendous feat, and a reasonable, as well as open mind.

Here and now, the patrician's speed slows through each cluster of people, while the live chamber music continues with quite possibly Joseph Haydn String Quartet in C, opus seventy-six, number three, "Kaiser."

In addition, these guests continue to spark, delight, gush, and chat about the people, as well as the enfilade, the spectacular vista of rooms, which consists of a private art gallery, elegant throw rugs, furniture, curtains, as well as chandeliers.

And this seems the case with a consider number of people, especially those relatively new to this lifestyle, atmospherics and subtle adjustments, as they offer meticulous flatter to the host, as well as one another, with a give-and-take manner, about shared hopes and dreams, yet mostly give a soliloquy, a speech.

And when do these people rest, as well as *maybe they deserve a rude nip or two.*

Yet, a considerable number of clusters seem stoic, matter-of-fact, aloof, and far less impressed, while others show open disdain, as a professional grump might, or as a glum, grump, gripe, to decimate, as if a favorite style, a histaminic, as fashionistas and hauterflies might show great pride with a well-crafted nips, pecks, and blunt critiques.

Elsewhere, the dog eventually returns, which causes Bonnie to mumble, shake her best fist, growl and show an evil eye, a certain menacing look that transfixes, and one that could crisp things along that line of sight—incinerate things, or at the minimum, it could shame, by burrowing into the doggy mind, as well as *psyche* then incinerate that mental region responsible for charm, intrigue, divergent thought, as well as oblique and lateral strategy, if in fact a dog has such a mental place and ability, then she mumbles foul words no real lady would ever say, at least in public.

Regardless, the dog stops, perks and proudly approaches her, with tail a-wagging.

As a result, she says, "First of all, stop following me. Secondly, are you insane? Never, from the unknown, run at a person like that, ever."

Then her mood shifts a few times.

"Oh, my stomach, I don't feel so good," and says with a soft realization, "That damn fajita," then her best fist rises high into the air, "Curse the sinister devil who created it. I curse the manufacturer, the institutional process!"

Then her attention shifts to the dog, "Oh, where was I? Do you have any idea how dangerous that was? Whatever you're doing in your doggy world, leave me out of it."

Bonnie points south "Go away, go-go-go!"

It sits.

She puzzles, "Really?"

"Stand!"

It lies down.

"Sit."

It stands.

"Roll over."

It hops about like a kangaroo.

"Climb that tree."

It stands on two legs, then just as quickly sits and refuses any more commands, as this person may have no real education, especially if she attended a corporate university, or diploma mill, or majored in underwater basket weaving, or, yes, liberal arts, such as a "foofoo" subject, a little bit too frilly.

And with each new command, nothing happens.

Of which, this causes Bonnie to mumble in frustration then say "Lazy suffering."

And with that, the dog perks, recalls, quickly departs into the dense brush, and eventually rustles in the distance then beyond reason, if a dog might have that ability.

Elsewhere, Mary groans then leg twitches, and again.

Moments later, fingers twitch.

Meanwhile in the dense forest, and at a considerable distance, more things rustle then become a considerable struggle, as if true chaos, which causes Bonnie to crouch, look at various angles then seriously consider a fast forest exit, and stampede towards, even if it means a total loss of dignity, of self-respect, because of the ways and means, which might shock the script, and leave a lasting mental impression, of panic. As fear can easily burrow into the *psyche*, especially into the personal baggage, and panic from that plow action, through wait-a-minute shrubs, which will damage and eventually create grotesque swelling—such as legs and arms becoming thick ghastly things, and something not quite human, again, become a thing, or an it.

Then something plows towards her.

And enough so it rattles the woman into a repeated start and stop pattern, on where to run or jump, maybe jump up a tree, if that is humanly possible, but no trees seem close enough, only very tall and ultradense shrubs.

Elsewhere, again Mary groans then leg twitches.

Not much later, fingers twitch, and she says, "Oh, that's gonna hurt in the morning!" yet remains pinned by the heavy machine.

Just as importantly, finger curls, legs slightly move then toes wiggle, to confirm a few more working parts.

Well, that happens all the time, a person thought dead, and word quickly spreads among the community.

Just as importantly, some cultures would rush to bury a person, fast, and dig a deep hole then bury.

Why are they in such a rush? What are the real reasons? and not the fast talk version, the talk technique designed to crush all real debate, that fast talk style, to brand a person as an outsider, and the "You are either with us or against us" style, of black and white, stay on the script, another "no-brainer," and yet the mind is capable of developing a tremendous number of options, especially with medical advancements, as well as a major paradigm shift. As a person may lay dead, in that very specific stage of the great arc, and yet may in fact live in a version of the limbo, not the classic version, and may do so for a significant amount of time, and in varying stages, as the ultimate test, if you will, and more than a leaky abstraction.

However, and the most important takeaway message, a being in that state might simply need a new container, and fast, and not a new set of clothes, yet something fashion-forward, such as a modern vessel with a new form of sustenance, plasma or electricity, for instance solid state and battery-powered, such as a tiny penny-sized nuclear battery, which produces energy from the decay of radioisotopes, or a Multi-Mission Radioisotope Thermoelectric Generator, developed for NASA deep space missions. And a person might need not want the same-old, same-old, another complex coalition of the so-called meek gut bacteria, who may have never lost control over the earth, and use people as mere stagecraft, which includes theatrical scenery, property, wardrobe, and sound: so speak!

So, instead, select a modern vessel based on bold imagination, and new ideas about the dead, and are they really dead? As in—yes—that classic sense, the classic body has died, or is that person waiting for their prodigies, or is it progenies, to solve one of the great universal mysteries, solve the next stage, and what really remains after death, in those various stages, and how to recover the exceptional aspects of body, mind and soul then transfer it, the uniqueness, as if a one-of-a-kind device, and save the scripts into a more durable container, and do so quickly before the internal barriers or connections leak, or fade?

So, put the self, the coalition, into something more rugged than flesh, bones, and the current coalition of mostly bacteria, and put it into a tool or device, a very smart device, and something free from the microbiome predicament, with all that crude clamor, crave and obsession, especially from yeast, starch and sugary treats, or inflation, for an aspect of the traditional self, when alive and kicking, mostly kicking, mostly war, with a very brief peace yet loudly announced, such as "See, I fixed it, so stop nagging me," of an ever so long procrastinated home project, which needed a simple fix, of reasonable, of well thought through, and not another clunk or shallow fair haven, that right or left thump, or beat, such as a beat box, or beat the root, or beat the core?

However, a modern vessel is unlikely, unless it represents a cash cow, "moo," a major profit center, or of greater importance, a lost sacred cow, now found, or, well, unless created for a megalomaniac, narcissus, or government, yet from behind the curtain, a special interest or two, sold, yet again: sell a creed?

And they might create a more mobile version, yet with a mandated backdoor(?), which eventually translates into an ultimate insider benefit, that look, that exceptional form of inflation, of escalation, that chase, and, well, eventually, the horde, yet based on a *Return to Tomorrow* in *Star Trek* theme, another distinguished place with the essentials or indispensables of tomorrow, such as the dawn of a new civilization, a new way of thinking, yet often, and required, by a special law, or bubble, as the same, or block, on cue, or else?

However, it seems unlikely a modern vessel, at least according to history, as an open mind seems vital, and ever so serious concern, to explore based on vital, yet often, it arrives at the same old storyline, as if a loop, a string, of "same-old, same-old," with minor adjustments here and there, with new players, yet same theme and tweak, to tweak the chaos, tweak the beat in more ways than one, and a desperate search for the elusive, for unobtainium.

So, bury a dictator fast, the faster the better?

Regardless, as well as here and now, Mary wilts under that tremendous equipment pressure, which might puncture an organ or two.

CHAPTER 40

Meanwhile, in that dense forest, and at a considerable distance, something plows toward Bonnie.

And enough so, it rattles her, as if the end nears, and into a repeated start-stop pattern, on where to run or jump, maybe jump up a tree, if that is humanly possible, yet no trees seem close enough, only very tall and ultradense shrubs.

Eventually, the dog struggles through dense brush and arrives, as if a perk beyond reason, if a dog has that ability, and returns to Bonnie with a willow branch.

Which causes her to double take, high energy sputter, and eventually find considerable relief from all that danger then she puzzles, seriously irritates, and says, "I didn't say Lady Suffolk," which represents an excellent reason why a person or being should not rely so heavily on a favorite tool, such as single book, bookshelf, or philosophy?

Then "fetch" and she tosses a stick well over forty feet, which arcs and lands in dense brush.

Which causes the dog to launch, disappear, seriously dig with a great effort then it eventually returns with a gun silencer, and a version unlike any known style or function, as if twenty years ahead, from DARPA, ARPA-E or HSARPA.

"What the hell...?"

Elsewhere, something flings one blanked commando after the other, out of the forest in a huge arc.

And eventually, each rag doll neatly impacts that sign, "Bang, bang, bang!"

Then not far away, the captain scrambles to send a text message, and moments later, other sounds occur, "Pfft, pfft,

pfft, fshht, pfft, pfft, pfft, ffft, ffft!" as something snatches a commando by a dirty combat boot, rudely drags that person over very rough ground, bangs against rocks, trees, then pulls underground, bangs even more rudely and moments later, flings that blanked category of being, the warrior, along a great arc, out of the forest then catches and repeats the process with another intruder, and another.

Eventually, and one after another, each neatly impacts as a direct hit, "Bang, bang, bang!"

CHAPTER

Meanwhile, and in his earpiece, the German patrician receives a forest mission update, which causes eyes to widen, from *of how is that possible?*

As this mission had all the right components, it had an exceptional plan, team, resources, and timing.

All during the time, he attempts to suppress feelings with a best effort, because of the situation, the guest, as the face shows perplexed, baffled, concerned, worried and trapped then dismay, provocation, irritation and revenge.

Regardless, some of these feelings leak onto the face.

In addition, he develops a better crowd escape system, such as squeeze through the tightly packed crowd with "Sorry," and "Pardon me," and continues to maneuver between more and more people then really squeezes through, "Excuse me," "Pardon me," and "Oops, I didn't mean to touch you there—honestly, I like you; in fact a lot, yet not that much," then accidentally touches another person, in a less than appropriate place.

Then the patrician maneuvers through hedge fund managers and venture capitalists, who seem delighted.

In fact, most of them beam, chat, and joke with just about anyone, and regardless of class, gender, age, dress, or body of politic.

Moreover, they continue to alternate with praise, sips of spirit, and breath, as well as seem ever so fascinated, because of the various ultra rare groups, symmetry, due proportions, set construction, moduli space, in addition to the extensive travel circuit potentials, of new people and communities, those beyond their normal annual migration route, beyond the traditional pattern, beyond the World Economic Forum, Milken Institute Global conference, Allen & Company conference, TED and dreary Foggy Bottom meetings said vital, those predictable meetings, with so many very needy politicians, such as the professional climbers who each toil four hours a day in their own private yet party boiler room, a phone booth, for direct solicitations, of dialing for dollars, which to some people feel as if just another cult, an *argumentum ad hominem*, based on a stale script, a logical fallacy, a dusty creed, that uses an ever so shallow language game, a stale process, while powers-that-be create yet another tempest, for what feels as if an endless number, to fix or prevent a self-made crisis? All of which in fact appears to offer a side benefit, build a resume, find a future job slot, as a proxy for a competing power, for too-big-to-fail, and find an ever so soft landing, into luxury, "Yes, ah," such as a skybox, yet a niche among chaos, the modern version of Dante's *Vita Nuova and Divina Commedia*?

Here and now, these hedge fund managers and venture capitalists mumble, "Thank God," or some other cultural equivalent, less jet traffic, especially for private jets, and where to park them, close to these events, as things have escalated beyond reason, such as the Super Bowl, Masters Golf Tournament, Wimbledon, Monaco Grand Prix, Concours d'Elegance, Royal Ascot, Triple Crown, and the four fashion world capitals of "Milan, Paris, New York and London," as well as "Portugal, Rome, São Paulo and Berlin" and the food and wine festival migration, which includes Aspen, South Beach, San Diego, White Truffle and other premier events, and with an ever so brief stop at the Cannes Film Festival then devote far more time at Cannes Lions International Festival of Creativity. As those travel circuits, those often elusive searches, represent a considerable effort, to find the right crowd, in the ideal circuit, such as private, inclusive, discreet, as well as discrete, a safe haven, sanctuary, and maybe "A Home in the Meadow," someplace elsewhere, and "Away, away, come away with me," that search, that elusive circuit, which mysteriously shifts, and is never quite the same. "Why?" And yet, once there, it resembles a great nexus of rare space, of warm, inclusive, free and fair, of "Away, away, come away with me."

Here and now, the patrician neatly moves through one tight pack then another unusual cluster of people, a transformative star-making system or event, as if a studio system, and a rare look behind the curtain, so to speak, at the process, as well as functions, a quick look at their secret techniques and ultimate insider languages then pass a very unusual person.

And yet, the patrician notices yet does not slow, primarily because of hard-earned momentum, by inertia, which might happen to people and systems in general, trapped by momentum, and often, it takes a considerable amount of time and effort to see, to enter any given moment then fully register things in the mind. As there often appears a wait-state, such as one-wait-state, at best, in the everyday dynamics, which refers to delay, to reaction latency, through internal filters.

Just as importantly, many people go through life not fully awake, and they move through much of life groggy a bit, or with a certain mental fog, or a restricted attention span, or as twitch-twitch, or the uppermost mental facilities seem quite distant, or a considerable number of mental aspects seem offline, and what causes that, those barriers and is there a cycle, or cycles? Such as, is that person coasting, or on autopilot, or traveling in a furrow, ditch, or narrow channel, and of habit, yet often, of grump, and "Yeah—what?" such as drive home and not remember any significant detail. Or, a person walks from one end of the house to another, then once there, cannot remember the trip or purpose yet bumps nothing, on the tree of habit, tree of life, tree-depth, tree-graded space or on the mental table of judgment? Or more importantly, the fact that no one can arrive twice at the exact same point in universal space, which might represent some of the disorientation, going to a new place every second inside the universe.

Regardless, as well as here and now, with the patrician, the sight of that very unusual person does not fully register as an exceptional.

Yet that type of person seems quite rare indeed, for several reasons.

Mainly, because it seems quite unusual to see a well-being, and very much so, a complete person, and yet as if some complex domain, or a superior domain host, as well as a civic virtue, in fact, a first contact specialist, and the way it should occur during a foundation event.

That person resembles the type one reads about in news articles, and is quite possibly a plenipotentiary, or stateless elite, or Davos person, not a hard money lender or young Turk, or thyristor, polysemy, groupoid, or an impossible object, or hermit as opposed to an eremitic, a person with real wealth, and not stuffy money, or new money, not a new arrival, who has not had a chance to acclimate—well, to the environment, the atmospherics—and not grasping for stuff, or grasping for replacement genes or the next best thing, such as starch, or new and improved whatnot, whatchamacallit, or for the thingamajig. This person is not a frantic me, not raised during the critical childhood years as a cog, or professional grump, or as a glum, grump, gripe that decimates as a favorite style, the histaminic, or a tightly wound histone of repression, or a churn, who often specialized in plowing through the poor, middle class or peers for profit or sport, which often displaces a generation or two, displaces them in time as well as space, or treats them as expendable, as just another thing, with often one cruel and unusual idea after another.

Regardless, the forward momentum takes the patrician through aristocrats, which include Livia and Mero, through *sprezzatura*, nonchalance, an effortlessness that conceals the true art of construction, as well as underlying desires. And as if it represents a careful balance through life, yet above it all, with an ever so smooth glide through the temporal stream, and in a humble manner, when possible, even as their minds often dwell on this secular form of cavalry. As this event has so many common people, crude people, people new to manners, and money, the new age version, of first, second or third generation money—the modern version, as in modernism, with that restless examination and experimentation, of what feels as if every aspect of life, in search of better way, which all that wasteful effort, that churn, and a style that also shows a few great pretender, with certain looks, scripts and techniques, as compared to old money, old wealth—very, and enormous wealth.

And many of these aristocrats have a considerable fortune, from legacy, and some earned with an exceptional style, culture, intellect and wit, with a certain bearing, precept, high honor, and ethos, or guiding beliefs and ideals, well, a considerable number of them.

Yet a significant number of them represent genuine rascals, of the highest order, wholly unredeemable, and kept afloat by complex legacy rules, by schemes, for example a scheme-theoretic image, or put another way, they have a timeless look, because style matters—it really matters, and more than you could possibly imagine?

Then this patrician shifts strategy through the next swirl.

So he stretches for a potent drink then notices something elsewhere, as if a vital, a great mystery, which causes that crowd to wonder then look as well, as he departs towards, which represented his preferred path all along, as the next tact.

And this technique proves so efficient, with the least disruption, and only a negligible turbulence once through, he uses it again, and again, as well as along the way, adds a distinguishing quality, an ever so personal charm, as well as unique signature move, the type that often defines a person in the best possible light, as a natural.

And all of these techniques resemble maneuvers, as if a sailboat principles of tact, at a precise angle, of physis, to create the best possible effect, such as a peaceful departure or a tremendous wake.

Just as significantly, it works quite well, as each maneuver greatly improves, and takes him easily pass past elite members of the Russell and Aldwych groups, congressional committee members, an acutely self-confident Sloane Ranger then venture capitalists, Washington power brokers, special interests and proxies for shadow then with an even greater ease pass elite nerds, as well as super geeks, such as members of Defense Advanced Research Projects Agency (DARPA,) ETH Zürich, Pierre and Marie Curie University, University of Copenhagen, Karolinska Institutet, University of Tokyo, or Tekes—the Finnish Funding Agency for Technology and Innovation, Defence Science and Technology Organization, Defence Science and Technology Laboratory.

Then he passes Seska von Sonnenfels, a woman who resembles the 1940s' Jean Patchett, as photographed by Nina Leen, in that famous picture of her wearing a checkered outfit, with matching hat, long gloves, and book in hand—a clever person, as well as a bit dangerous.

Lastly, he passes through another group with Gus, a minor congressional aide, a person who ascribes to a golden rule of never underestimate the power of anonymity, and the ability to hide in plain sight, especially when maneuvering among people with enormous wealth, influence, privilege, position, reputation and connection, and of equal importance, never underestimate the addictive impulse created by power, money, and fame.

So much so, fame, when combined with ambition and money, often creates the classic recipe for disaster. It often triggers a primitive impulse, to satisfy an insatiable aspect of the body, mind and soul, and that which cannot quench in conventional spacetime. It can trigger a primal greed, inflation, and a powerful drive to surge, clamor, and grab—where a person becomes truly reckless and is managed by primitive aspect of the brain, managed by an insatiable savage aspect, and a mob, which prefers to spark and surge forward with a certain greedy, ugly, and sinister style.

That minor congressional aide specializes in anonymity and the discreet application of power, wealth, privilege, position, and connection. One of the most difficult skill sets to acquire and deftly apply in life, truly a lost art, to have enormous power, influence, connection, as well as remain vital, and yet barely visible, such as the type of person with very little backstory and a keen ability to keep it that way, with a discreet craft of appearance and movement—in fact, ordinary, a nondescript person, and yet, fully and deftly in control, with the ability to steer events through very subtle hints and movements, which burrow into the subconscious of others, and eventually trigger a plan, path, and action.

Put another way, and for lack of a better phrase, this style or technique by Gus has a Jedi mind trick aspect, though one more similar to a liminal master of ceremony, for the phase transition, and with far more nuance, and very little to do with an implanted mimic instruction. As he deploys some type of metaphysical and universal shared wave system, maybe with technology, which ritualized space and focal point, as if participants are one and the same, for those brief moments, but do not know it, and something partially described with the concept of atonement and being at one, a function of harmonics.

All of which, regarding Gus, might start with some type of well-timed ritualized quiet and barely detectable breathing trick, presence, mood, mindset, as well as subtle clues vaguely similar to Anapanasati and a few other very old-school systems.

Is it a religious tool or device, or secular, or technology-based, which activates the fundamental laws of biology, chemistry, economics or systems in general, as well as the physics of spacetime?

Regardless of the mechanics, this trick or technique by Gus seems to evoke a heuristic event, a speedup effect and decision shortcut, which, in retrospect, gives the appearance of a deliberation process that feels cautious, prudent, clear, efficient, effective, practical, as well as a decisive application of power, yet leaves no significant trace of the source—all of which comes across as a truly lost art.

Imagine a high diver, a person who stands on one of those very tall diving towers and jumps from that great height, falls then lands in the water without producing a significant ripple. Moreover, that person departs and people do not recall the jump, yet do remember the heuristic effect, and most importantly they attribute it to themselves, which then triggers determination, grit, inflation, pride, and the me component.

Just as importantly, here and now, the patrician does not notice the Gus Hermanos technique directed at him, and exits to safety, beyond that enfilade system, a suite of rooms, a place with a two parallel axis system of rooms, and he did not have to fake a minor injury, which represented the next tactic, and anything to plow through that dense crowd.

Moments later, he enters the discreet apartment entrance, eventually exits this amazing retreat, and travels a hallway then ultimately enters a control room.

CHAPTER 42

Elsewhere, Mary initiates an equipment rocking action, which feels quite painful, from all that weight as well as sharp machine edges that dig into her vitals here and there, as they might puncture a lung or some other organ, and that causes eyes to widen, body flinch, alarm and overwhelm.

So, she stops and tries to catch her breath, as the machine sits heavy on the lungs, on the ability to breath, which requires a quick, as well as ever so shallow breathing technique, to avoid passing out, and yet she eventually passes out.

Meanwhile, the German patrician embitters among his staff, then boils and caustically rants, which has an abruptness, which that seems cold, cruel, materialistic then defiant and petulant, as he ridicules nearby a financial day trader as grotesquely inept, as a "*schwachupdate kopf,*" and pushes him aside to see if those forest routers still operate.

And, they do as an elaborate bank of flat screen monitors shows real-time stocks, stock options, currencies and futures contracts, such as equity index, interest rate and commodity.

Just as importantly, each screen rapidly updates the latest information for his European bank, with a longest-standing patrician-class affiliation and a fast proximal server, which has the minimum data source delay, the minimum intermediaries, or "middlemen, or barnacles," if you will, and all of which have a certain agenda.

These screens update and track scalp-trade-positions, track an intra-day speculation system, which usually has the trader hold a financial position for seconds or even minutes.

Another series of screens track their shave trade positions, a method which allows the scalping speculator to jump ahead by a tenth of a cent or more, for trades often completed in less than one second.

A companion system actively searches for potential trading setups, which represents any stock or other financial instruments in a state of tension or crisis, as in ready to price-accelerate regardless of direction.

The German patrician adjusts that system, which shows his overall financial position, the entire investment portfolio, and it reveals a tremendous amount of leverage, of debt, and from people who could demand immediate repayment, such as no more excuses, regardless of your reputation.

And of equal importance, the patrician expected major financial markets to flinch, panic, buckle then collapse, which would allow an easy profit scoop, yet nothing happens.

More time passes, and nothing.

Just as importantly, his costs to hold these positions soar, and losses quickly build, because ultrahigh leverage works both way, a fast path into financial paradise, the secular version of rapture, or fall into hell, into fire and brimstone, as well as the angry mob, and people who would love retribution, as well as sweet revenge against the powers-that-be, for a lifetime of slights, from a condescending and patronizing apostle of culture, of special privilege.

As a result, the patrician flinches, grimaces, waits, sweats, panics then frantically wave a market exit signal, to unwind those exceptionally complex financial investments, and fast, which the traders do, as he sends warning messages to Ingolstadt in Upper Bavaria, Chur, Switzerland, as well as what might represent something formally known as a charcoal burner cell.

Too late, those five Alcatel-Lucent 7950 XRS-style forest internet routers activate and send data bursts into the sky, to satellites then worldwide markets.

They reveal those awkward and heavily exposed financial positions, as well as attempts to quickly unwind the ever so complex.

And, all that frantic financial activity attracts predators, especially algorithms designed to locate and react within a few milliseconds then savage a vulnerable position, which represents a new version of war, of mortal combat.

Elsewhere, Mary regains consciousness, tries to catch her breath, as the machine sits heavy on the lungs, heavy on the ability to breath, and this weight feels as if it might again puncture something, and again, such as an organ or two.

And all this weight requires a new quick shallow breathing technique, to avoid passing out, and she nearly does as lights dim, yet a rock back-and-forth effort causes the machine to move more and more, though pain intensifies, such as at any moment, something internally might burst.

Then the rocking action gains considerable momentum.

Eventually, the expensive machine rolls off her and impacts the white gravel driveway, which causes internal machine parts to bang within.

Meanwhile, the patrician motions to his team to call exclusive clients, which consist of ultimate insiders, of patricians and elite corporations, such as venture capitalists, private equity firms, securities broker-dealers, and credit insurance providers, as well as various funds that includes hedge, money market, exchange-traded, credit and investment, also known as the shadow banking system, and urge them to sell fast.

Often, these clients depend on artificial financial maneuvers, on a last-minute effort of one variety or the other, to generate a quick profit, or appearance of, such as paper profits, and often with accounting tricks, as well as off shore maneuvers.

Just as significantly, many of their clients rely heavily on one type of thinkculum or another, on an internal version or special financial-political-ultimate insider system or two, which offers an exclusive previews and offers, before the others.

And often, thinkculum systems use a shock-the-market-effort to sell urgent whatnot, or sell the end-of-days theme, again and again then profit from the flinch by others, especially the poor, middle class, and even upper class outside that exclusive loop. Many of them sell panic then profit from each disruptive wave, and do so with an accordion style to squeeze markets, which also creates financial trading profits, to help improve quarterly and yearend corporate financial statements, because rush and chaos sells.

Just as importantly, many clients depend on these artificial shocks and maneuvers, the classic divide and conquer, especially on less mobile wealth, less dynamically able.

As many systems and clients rely on drama, on dysfunction, alienation, identity crisis, and bankruptcy then exploits the gap for profit, exploit the turmoil; exploit a disaster for profit, which represents a lucrative industry at the threshold, as well as tremendous incentive to destabilize. So, create a series of scripted crisis, often based on the political calendar, and crisis designed to generate a tremendous buzz, the "Big Mo," or big momentum, such as how to herd cash cows into profit centers, and based on swarm behavioral techniques, those best cycles that exist in nature, as well as the artificial ones created by newbies, by the young Turks, who experiment with poke-the-system. Yet it is much easier for them to poke the others, such as people, places and things less able to defend themselves, to show the establishment a thing or two, about the true nature of real power, tremendous might and how to create the biggest swarm, for instance a revolution, or at least do so as if interviewing for the next job, and anything to exit the political party boiler room, that phone booth, for direct solicitations, four hours a day, of dialing for dollars, which to some people feels like just another cult, an *argumentum ad hominem*, based on an exceptionally stale script, as well as process, a logical fallacy, a dusty creed that uses an ever so shallow language game.

Regardless of that, organizations that rely on this drama-based system, and even after pay-to-play participation costs to get a first insider look, well, that technique has generated enormous profits.

However right now, their trade positions experience enormous pressure.

In fact, losses build up and ever vigilant clients quickly notice and clamor for answers, for themselves as well for all the clients they resell an exclusive-first-information-look, and still further down that line, that pecking order, the privileged, such as platinum, gold, silver, bronze and so on, yet not necessarily based on those exact metal names, as escalation and the inflationary aspect of language has lowered real value, meaning, or ability to perk. So, often, newly formulated titles take their place, and on a timely basis, to index for language inflation, and based on the ability to impulse a person or system into believing the magic, the buzz, the artificial whatnot.

Just as importantly, the further away a person sits from the financial information source, such as this new age gloriole, this perk, a mystery of origin exists. And the longer it takes for notification to arrive, and at each stage, a certain distortion can occur, such as shortcut, generalization, trope, or substitution, of each local agenda, and often done with a poverty of thought, based on speculation or bias, with a certain *pathos*, patina or residual. And of equal importance, people as well as systems rarely seem interested in the true material origin, the completeness, the balance, as they often seem more interested in a quick confirmation, of self and/or system, the bandwagon, the razzmatazz, with a quick answer, and close enough, as well as satiation of a stage, or fantasy, reality tunnel, niche, bubble or neurogenic trap, such as fetch another bubble or insert old data inside?

Regardless, as well as meanwhile, as each level receives the bad news, they clamor and rant, as in me, me, me, as if their version of me sits at the center of universe, and all 300 sextillion or so stars orbit, and adjusts to their every whim or wish. Where, a sudden move left or right, and the 300 sextillion heavenly stars move in full accord, from the gravitational effect or maybe from a magnetic personality of the greatest me?

Elsewhere, and eventually, Mary stumbles to her feet, checks one limb after another, with a flex here and there then pokes at one organ after another, at each that might have burst, and how would someone know?

However, she seems quite pleased at no significant damage then with her best fist, curses the x-ray machine, and with language not fix for a true lady, and just as importantly with a quick search, she finds no real machine damage, just minor aspects, which would easily disappear with a vigorous rub, which does not, and again with vigor, so, maybe with spray paint, the inexpensive type, as she is on a frugal budget from astonishing tuition costs, and would anyone really notice a few scratches, nicks, and scraps?

Eventually, and with a heave-ho, she straps the machine to a dolly, struggles and moves this unwieldy thing along the white gravel driveway, which, on occasion, nearly tips over here and there, as well as requires a freakish grip, a feral, and her back, "Oh, my!" as it hurts beyond description. And ask anyone who has had a bad back, because it seems quite difficult to locate a comfortable position, let alone walk up right.

All of which gives her an odd gait, and the driveway gravel resists all along the way, promotes instability, and her fear that someone might arrive at just the wrong moment, "such as an eager witness, someone determined to capture a YouTube moment, and become an internet micro celebrity, or better yet, turning that into a big business, as they capture a desperado, and "come to your senses," plus "my fingerprints are all over that money, as well as DNA."

So, she bear-hugs the machine, holds on for dear life and prays, to Avalon or some other forms of paradise that transcend, or to one of the nine hundred and fifty-five distinct heavens. And she does so with a mnemonic device then waits for the awkward machine momentum to stabilize, and then she restarts.

Eventually, and once inside the room, she positions that x-ray machine at the unconscious red-haired man, who resembles a Thracian, a freed man, a peltast, such as an Agrianian peltast then examines Agrippa.

All of which finds no significant damage.

Then the sight of that money worries her, the absolutely fresh one hundred-dollar bills, grouped in a traditional pack of fifty, thirty packs in total.

And where is the best place to hide money—in an underwear drawer, under a mattress or pillow, in the wall, under a floorboard or in plain sight?

As a result, she perplexes, carefully looks out one window after another for trouble, and with a spray window cleaner spritzes, scrubs fingerprints off the money then eventually stuffs it in the freezer, while remembering the wild-eyed Agrippa rants of "the sky yet from a grotto, allegory of the cave, AB hylomorph, Franz Kafka notion, Schröder–Bernstein theorem of measurable space, indexicality, yet someone you might find near a well of souls, and that ever so smooth phase transition of things not easily quantifiable."

Again, the local channels mention nothing, nor do cable outlets.

So she expands the search to online newspapers, for any mention of an accident, robbery or scientific test, something, anything, yet finds nothing.

As a result, a mumble, "How's that remotely possible? Now that's bizarre."

Moments later, someone lightly taps at the library window, which causes Mary to jump, see Taters, panic, as well as hem and haw with unusual body language.

And eventually, she opens the window and says, "I..., well..., ah...," to think fast, think of something, anything, "Ah..., I...," then proceeds to speak without forethought, which has a nervous rush, a babble quality of "Agrippa was in town and a funny thing happened, you know, you'll never guess."

As usual Taters says nothing, then tries to climb inside, struggles, nearly falls backward a few times into a colorful flowerbed with distinct thematic herbal sections, a spectacular elevated bed, which convey specific stages and nuisances within secular and sacred space, as in philosophical and therapeutic nuisances, to cultivate, redeem, regenerate, transform, evolve and expand the mind, as in a place pristine, vivid, free and fair, a place wholly natural and absolutely fascinating, a place for artists, poets, scholars, to sit and ponder truly great questions, and even a place for romance, yes, such as romance of Palamedes, or science if you will, and sit as a super geek or nerd.

Ultimately, she climbs through the open window, dusts off the self as well as crumples, looks about in a very careful survey then intently studies every word of Mary, and especially the odd body language.

In fact, her method of observation seems quite particular, keen, astute and analytic, as if judiciously following each reasoning chain, the link, the firmaments then carefully weighing each branch, as well as the essential facts within, and more so than most people.

Just as significantly, her demeanor shows powerful thoughts that shift, as well as the subtleties and phantom aspects of intellect, followed by one keen sparks after another, of realized kernels, which give the full impression of a very profound apothegm, maxim, proverb or truism will arrive, and yet she vocalizes none.

On a good day, she says the bare minimum, a word or phrase here and there, such as, "Oh, I see…," or "Really…," however not today.

As a result, Mary feels more awkward from the silence, and impulses to fill the vacuum with something, anything, yet this story might cause her to tip over from a nervous high-wire act of here and there.

So she says, "Okay. She saw this guy and realized … they dated before … really. Well, sort of dated, as they were only five years old and neighbors. You know, kids. And their parents were best friends as well. As a result, it was a longtime no-see-moment, and they chatted and chatted; you know, a catch-up moment, a long-lost thing. Can you imagine that?"

Tater continues to study and measure.

Mary thinks *If I could only stop talking… please stop talking.* However this spontaneous story gains a certain momentum, an escalation to a life of its own, which happens to people, as well as systems, more often than not, as it seems easy to start something based on an idea or principle, and yet it becomes exceptionally difficult to resolve, and do so neatly, with a soft landing in sight, or insight, and with few unintended consequences.

Mary continues and says, "She decided to show him the house—you know, proud of it. Well, on the way here they had an accident: the truck crashed … yes, really," as eyes widens, "and both were injured, yet are much better now. And they're resting, so we shouldn't make a lot of noise…, you know," and again eyes widen.

Tater says nothing then to the absolute shock of Mary, she checks the vital signs of both, yet does so with an unusual medical technique, not a western medical style, but some other elaborate method to measure well-being.

All the while, Mary cringes, panics and expects very bad things to happen, especially with Agrippa sprawled, battered and asleep in the corner daybed.

And as Tater monitors, the zombie robot queen awakens, sees, eyes narrow and jaw clenches then says, "Prepare for a good old-fashioned beat down," followed by a growl and clenched fist promises of pain, "and relay that to Benny, Emma, Reece, Vera, Mel, Zoey, and the other girl, whatever her name is, the one that always hangs around, oh yes, and especially to Tommy, Samantha, and Seska, yeah Seska," and that last name really causes her blood to boil.

As a result, Tater recoils to a safe distance and reaches inside her bag, the one that is not a Louis Vuitton, Burberry, Ted Noten, Yoga-a-GoGo nor Longchamp, yet a simple Betel aluk bag from West Timor, in which she digs and digs.

Meanwhile, Agrippa boils and struggles to rise.

However, each attempt to leap with fists of fury fails.

In addition, as if a bolt of lightning, pain shoots and arrests. Muscles ache. Bones protest and each time she lets out a sound, "Fff!" a profound huffing exhalation, as in *Ulysses* by James Joyce.

All the while, Tater searches in that bag and really digs beyond things.

Meanwhile, another attempt to leap fistic fury produces a state of mind, which combines the questioning sound of "Nn," as in *Finnegans Wake* by James Joyce, with pain so pronounced that it causes a cadence of spasms, as well as delirium, which eventually leads her to wither and wan into an enfeebled stupor, then in due course, leads back to a full consciousness, and in that pronounced cycle a few times.

And yet in that near-unconscious stage, she still mumbles a promise of an exact Old Testament retribution with hellfire fists.

Moreover at each low point, sheer willpower and determination reanimates her one distinct stage after another, with true grit.

Eventually, Tater finds ibuprofen, fifty, 200-milligram caplets, along with a bottle of water, the tiny size, a mere five ounces, yet one from a famous mineral spring, one known for water, which serves as a proven tonic, such as a tonic accent and chord, or a tonic *sol-fa* script equivalent, and water says to be effective, efficient, precise and balanced, as well as one able to charm the mind, body and soul.

Of which, she offers, and just as significantly, does so with a genuine look of concern and willingness to help.

However, Agrippa erupts and says, "Get out, now! And never come back, ever."

CHAPTER 43

Days later, Agrippa has improved; gained mobility, with far less aches and pains yet hobbles, and has an occasional bout of dizziness from sudden movement, where she must stop then grab and hold something, and hold on for dear life, as if a life-span.

Regardless, eventually, and as a mumbling grump, she trudges down one hall after another, then into that enormous mansion kitchen with exquisite flooring tiles, cast-iron stove, elegant hardwood cabinets and a centrally placed hardwood worktable, with a marble top, sink and exceptional kitchenware.

Yet she has no specific plans, just breakfast, then pulls out various ingredients, which include Russet baking potatoes, salt, pepper and three oils that consist of olive, canola and grape.

Moments later an idea arrives: crispy golden hash browns.

And with the help of a few more ingredients, it takes a small amount of time to cook, cool and quickly eat then she considers and says in an extend way, "Nice; however I want more, something else—but what?"

As a result, the imagination activates, "Something tasty, easy to make and with a bright bold flavor, oh yes!" and she says with gusto, as eyes widen, "*huevos rancheros.*"

Within minutes, the ingredients are assembled and ready, which include chopped tomatoes, jalapenos, refried beans, tortillas, eggs, and a pinch of sugar.

After cooking the eggs, they are placed atop oven-warmed tortillas, along with generous spoons of toppings, then slowly eaten, as if savory bits of heaven, "*huevos rancheros.*"

Afterwards, she prepares a persimmon-pomegranate fruit salad, one made with Granny Smith apples, fresh mint, a bit of lemon juice and a kiss of honey then leisurely consumes, thinks about each bit, agrees, and completes the meal.

Outside, at the front door, Mary knocks, waits, knocks again, waits then maneuvers around back, passes one flowerbed after another then on a side door floor mat, meticulously cleans her feet, enters a side door, travels one long hallway after another, and eventually locates Agrippa and immediately check bumps, as well as bruises, at ever so tender locations here, "Ouch!" and there, "Hey!

"Morning."

Agrippa replies in a disinterested tone, "Yeah, yeah, great."

"How do you feel?"

"So, so."

"How is he?"

"I have no idea."

"Really, you know the danger? He may have a concussion and needs constant supervision. Did he regain consciousness, move, open eyes or say anything?"

Agrippa does not react or seem concerned.

Mary says with a sense of urgency, "We have an agreement, and more importantly, I have a moral imperative. Beyond that, it's my reputation."

Yet this does not generate a significant spark of concern.

"So help me, I make that call."

Agrippa snaps and tests, "Really, and do what?"

"I can't stand by. Don't force my hand. I will personally remove him, and within forty minutes he'll be in the hospital."

That creates a tipping point, as things instantaneously erupt into a loud argument then furious struggle.

Chapter 44

Again, both struggle.

However, all that fury truly unsettles Mary beyond description, beyond all known language, especially from the suddenness, rapid escalation into feral, as some people are not built for all that fury, which truly unsettles her to no end.

And eventually, after a one sputter after another, as well as inability to respond, at the level, in that state, that narrative structure, as a literary element, she fully surrenders, and feels quite bad, as a failure, and someone who could have been a better person, with a calm, serious, search, in the pocket, as a quarterback might under tremendous pressure, yet she buckled, as does a nation, or system, at the threshold.

Then much later, off to the side, in private, and after yet another compromise, Mary calls, "Hello, Mel?"

"Yes," Mel Horar-Caldo answers.

"It's me."

"Oh. Mary."

"I need a special favor," then she says, stretching the words, "A big favor. I need your help, and done with the utmost discretion. Okay? Your lab processes blood work, right?"

"Well, yes."

"I need blood work; in fact, comprehension-type panels."

"Wait, you're a nurse at a hospital. Why can't you?"

"Well, that's an excellent question—I'm in a difficult position."

"How so...? Oh, wait..., that guy, yes, the one staying with Agrippa, really?"

"What! You heard already?"

While adjusting her two-tone Elvira-like updos then vintage fire engine red cat eyeglasses, she says, "Hell, yes, things like that travels fast, and sparks fly."

"Apparently Taters can talk, imagine that.

"Look, I need a few discreet tests, okay? Is it possible, a favor for me? Please?"

"Well, that's a bit risky, as our laboratory work is, well, I can't fully disclose, you know, we have a major homeland security contract, but I'll try, and how soon do you need it?"

"With all due speed."

"By the way, is he still unconscious?"

With that question, Mary begins an impulse, again, "Ah," a storyline without forethought, which represents the history of civilization, off the mark, such as an idea without a considerable introspection, or understanding the profound implication, or spontaneous asymmetry break, or thrownness, "He has no insurance and is unemployed. So Agrippa is helping him, you know?"

"Really?" she says with a full understanding. Agrippa does not act that way, ever, yet Mel seems quite interested in this mystery, and is more than willing to listen, "That's nice. Okay, make a list and drop off blood samples at my house, as early in the morning as possible, okay?"

"Okay, thanks, and I really appreciate this, more than you know, and discretion remains vital."

"Yes, exactly, on both sides."

After Mary disconnects, she talks to herself, "I have to stop doing that, babbling on and on, blah, blah, blah. They dated at age five years old, kissed, former neighbors, longtime-no-see moment, parents are best friends. What the freakin' hell? What is that, the spontaneous break, Agrippa is helping him? Somebody, stop me, please!"

Then Mel turns to Zoey, yet her real name is Izo Zkiak, "That was Mary."

"Really, no way?"

"Yes … way. That guy now lives there, in that mansion?"

"No way he does? Say it isn't so, hospice care?"

"Agrippa is helping out. That's nice ... wait, that doesn't sound like her. He's been in a coma, how long?"

Zoey says, "It's more likely she beat him unconscious, and now feels guilty, feels remorse, now that's a first ... oh, wait, or more likely, a court order compelled her into charity."

"Oh, I fully agree, yet don't say that."

"Okay, okay, lunchtime?"

"Agree. Wait, is that soup? You know how I feel about soup, Zoey."

"It's a broth."

"Yeah, hello, broth is a soup."

"What, broth?"

"Yes."

"No. It's barely a soup, and I thought you had a thing for gravy, and what does gravy have to do with soup, let alone broth?"

"Well, well ... I."

"Here we go, sista, you need help. How could you possibly make a leap from gravy to soup, then broth? That's a mighty leap?"

"I ... ah."

"Do you need therapy or ... wait ..., better yet, find your own way out, maybe aversion therapy?

"Here, start right now, with broth. Go ahead, Mel, try, here," and she pulls out the steaming cup of homemade vegetable broth.

Mel's eyes widen and she considers the phobia with intellect, as a scientist, of course, and with four-dimensional thought, with as few heuristics as possible, and for very good reasons, because history is filled with people as well as systems, which relied on shortcuts, on assumptions that proved costly.

Yet eventually she leans back, further and further, into a very unfortunate posture then steps back, as her hands stretch out, as if a deterrent, and pat the air, "Wait a minute, let's not create a hasty event."

"What?"

"Life," a shrug follows, "a biological thing."

"What the hell are you talking about?"

"I might lack something, a set of proteins or enzymes, or a certain vital brain structural aspect, or too much of something, or a cerebral knot or two, or an inconvenient twist of some strategic connections here and there that leads to a dead end, or to a puny, crude, warped brain region, barren of vitality, or in short, a mere lump of DHA goo, or a feeble grey lump of gruel, as well as grout, or the original form of real hasty pudding?"

"Sister, you need therapy."

"I … I…," which resembles someone cornered, and who seems ready to raddle through a string of excuses and justify, and some pull from thin air, from vapor, or ethereal aspects of the soul and oversoul.

Clearly trapped, she stops, sparks then smiles. "Okay, okay. I will…, I'll drink that stuff, right here and right now, hand it to me," as bravado emerges in stages then ever so cool swagger here and there, of retro hip.

"Really, Mel, seriously, this represents a Hallmark moment. Just like that, you've grown … see, anything is possible."

Then as Mel prepares to sip it, she makes a series of complex body adjustments and says, "Okay, before I do, one moment."

Then she leaves the lab and returns moments later with a chocolate ice cream bar, double chocolate, and not an ordinary treat, something widely considered an exceptional delight.

"Here—if you eat this, I will drink the broth."

Zoey stutters, "I … I…."

Mel says slowly, as her eyes widen with full realization, "Yes, I thought so…, and I'll repeat the offer one more time…, slowly…, just in case my pronunciations were off: if you eat this double chocolate ice cream bar, then I'll drink the broth."

"But … I."

"I'll tell you what: I can make the process a bit easier," then she exits for a few moments and returns with a cup of mango Italian ice, all natural ingredients, in fact, organic. "There, a milk treat: Italian ice, and if you eat this, I will drink the broth."

Both of them wait for each other to flinch, to back down, and they carefully look at one another, study the face, ever-changing body language then eyes that widen, as well as the ladies hem, haw, hinder, and refuse to surrender, which, again, resembles the history of … what?

Next, they lift and offer a spoon of food to each other. "Come on, you can do it, overcome your fears, your phobias."

Zoey sparks then says, "Okay, okay, we'll agree to disagree," then, "or better yet, I'll eat my mango lunchtime treats in the lunchroom and you'll sip on the broth here. Agreed?"

"Yes, exactly, I agree," and they do so, as procrastination?

Elsewhere, and two days later, Mary returns to the mansion and, as of yet, has not called an ambulance, as that sudden Agrippa confrontation unsettled her to no end, that feral action, which burrowed into her mind, as a "burrowing vehicle," to "avoid, traverse, neutralize or defeat."

Some people are not built for all that fury, that suddenness, yet she seems determined to make this situation right, somehow, someway, and arrives at the mansion side door, carefully wipes her feet on an elaborate Herringbone doormat with extensive side bristles, which enable a person to thoroughly clean a shoe top, side, and bottom.

Afterwards, she travels through the house by way of one long hallway after another until reaching the library door, which receives several light knocks then turn of an elegant brass knob, made of an alloy, of two thirds copper and one third zinc for medical reasons, as opposed to stainless steel.

Once inside the immense room with a heavily ornate stone fireplace as well as dark Brazilian cherry wood-paneled walls, floor, recessed bookcases, and all with remarkably detailed intricate carvings, which have a similar theme as the outside front gates, property walls, and massive front doors, she expects the worst, expects a tremendous struggle and escalation, from bad to worse, to harsh then feral.

Yet Agrippa sits in front of a desktop computer screen, looks, types, well, more like pecks a few keys here and there, with a slow two-index finger style, as well as a considerable number of pauses to locate each key.

In fact, she seems wholly occupied in an online search, and often digs through a considerable pile of elaborate handwritten notes then eventually notices Mary.

"Hi. I knocked."

No reply.

"How's everything?"

Agrippa replies in a low-key matter-of-fact voice, one without lifting her head from an ocean diving suits search, "Fair."

"Did you sleep well?"

No reply then moments later Agrippa faces Mary and says with an intense demeanor, "Now this is truly weird. I've gone through a tremendous amount of material and can't find anything regarding this elaborate diving suit system. Look, these represent the leading manufacturers, their catalogs," and she points then browses through one online source after another then google others. "None, nothing even remotely looks or functions like that. And just as importantly, no one notices his disappearance. Nobody, and I've gone through the local, regional, and national papers—nothing."

Mary says, "I've searched as well, and nothing.

"Have you eaten?"

No reply.

"Do you frequently check him, the health status?"

With that, Agrippa snaps out of that mindset and offers an intense look.

And that causes surprise, anticipation, as well as Mary to step slightly back then says, "Regardless, frequently check his vital signs, and he needs a timely rotation, because bedsores are a real possibility, as they represent a very serious matter, on back of the head, elbows, hips, calves, ankles. Bedsores can be fatal. So, he needs a rotation every few hours. And, have you bathed him?"

As a result, Agrippa's look becomes an evil eye, a malevolent glare, which, if possible, would serve as a death ray, a beam of destruction to incinerate things, to crisp things, or melt steel on contact, or create eternal smolder.

Nonetheless, Mary exits and eventually returns with hospice supplies, such as food, feeding tubes, sponge bath supplies, waterproof bedding, and a hospice care book, a how-to-book for the average people, and then she awkwardly drags in another portable x-ray machine, for teeth.

Moments later, both ladies pause, turn and look about.

"Did you hear that?"

244

"Yes."

"What's that noise?"

"Where is it coming from?"

"I heard it before, on my last visit."

"Really?"

"Yes."

Eyes narrow and slowly look about then the ladies carefully move to various locations and listen for the best possible angle.

"There it goes again."

"What the hell is that?"

"I have no idea ... mice in the walls?"

"Hardly—they have a distinct sound, a scurry, a light, quick movement. This is something else, as if prying, sawing and hammering?"

Mary goes from room to room as Agrippa considers a nearby Major League Baseball bat, then dismisses the idea for the notion of a good old-fashioned curbside stomp, and do so as a seriously irritated person, with sizzle, real sizzle, as eyes bulge then seriously redden from a deranged mind stomp, of clinical insanity, of crave, to settle an old score with robust energy and enthusiasm, and with real style, the type where an arm grates off to the side, as a counteraction, to maintain balance with each tremendous stomp.

Or she might use some other lesson to get respect from this intruder, maybe a fistic lesson, to lay a fist on someone, for transgressions, well, to civilize the intruder, to pound them into compliance, and the victim eventually says, "Okay-okay, I'm sorry, my mistake, you win, and your system is the one true system, the one true apostle of culture, or the secular version, or the best cultural solution, or the supreme mission," then heaven opens and trumpets blare, to usher in that golden age, and let it be duly noted a fully animated curbside stomp did it, the kind where an arm whips about in the air for balance, as well as bonus points for style, or some other classic method to civilize, to build a great society, for instance with the cruel and unusual.

In the next room bed lays the unconscious man who resembles a Thracian, a freed man, a peltast, such as an Agrianian peltast, where both ladies meet, as well as struggle, to listen at one angle after another then ear to the wall.

Eventually, the sounds stop.

In addition, a considerable amount of time passes, and nothing happens, so they shrug it off then Mary exits and begins a full examination of the Thracian, pulls off the sheet for a top to bottom inspection, and expects gross neglect.

Yet he has no bedsores—none.

In fact, he has had a bath, recently, and smells of the finest soap, the type which a single bar costs over $240, such as an ultrafine Viennese soap.

Just as significantly, his chestnut hair, including beard, have been trimmed and stylized into a European style, ultra-cool and with real flair, of ever so cool, which has some similarity to the Bronze Head style of Seuthes III, found in Golyamata Kosmatka.

In addition, the sheets have been changed and they seem quite fancy, in fact overly, and new with a ridiculously high thread count, as well as so soft, and the bottom sheet has a pastoral scene by Frederic Edwin Church, *The Heart of the Andes*, 1859.

Just as importantly, this man has been well cared for, and has sapphire-blue eyes.

"Oh, I see," and Mary looks at all the ever so fine levels of care, as well as room details, the special arrangements then says, "Nice job, now that's impressive."

Which Agrippa shrugs no idea or interest, not even a remote concern, yet Mary notices none of that then says, "Keep up the good work," completes the examination and finds no major injuries, just the coma.

So they exit, and once in front of the computer, Agrippa sparks to her real interest, "Oh, by the way, I found a confidential online fingerprints identification service," and points to the kit page with an overnight delivery option, which is "discreet, has excellent customer feedback ratings, and provides fast results, see? Can you help me fingerprint him?"

Mary recoils from the idea then rolls her eyes, considers, carefully peeks out the one window after another then eventually replies, "How much worse can it get?"

A few moments later, Mary realizes and says, "Once they find out, the homeland system, and they will, as in 'No Morsel Too Minuscule For All-Consuming NSA,' they'll drop a building on us then another and another, to show the others, as a lesson for the nation, in fact for the entire world."

Next, Mary draws one blood vial after another then scrubs two cotton swab inside his mouth and places them inside a kit then both ladies wrestle that x-ray machine into place, realize something, then search and eventually locate a three-prong plug adaptor.

As the machine warms, Mary studies, adjusts settings then says to Agrippa, "Step back, way back—no, further. In fact, move over there. Good," and she takes a wide range of teeth images then says, "Seriously, I doubt any of these images will help."

"What? Why? Dentists keep records...."

"Yes, I know, however did you look at his teeth, really look?"

"No."

"He has perfect teeth, perfect pearly whites, in fact textbook, just the right size, shape, zero filling and no chips, wear marks, caps, crowns, bridges; none, perfect, and just the right color."

They slump.

Eventually, Agrippa says, "Mary, I need another favor?"

As a result, Mary reels, fully animates and says, "Really, a favor? Come on, I've already gone too far. In fact, you put me on the spot, invoke the childhood friendship card, jeopardize his life, my career, driven away all of our friends, who, by the way, have gone out of their way to sacrifice for you after you leaped to buy this huge house and you take and take. By the way, when do you give back? And they worked very hard for you, and I'm 100 percent.

Agrippa reels, riles, sputters and proceeds to mislay vowels when speaking, "Chhhht," of disbelief and absolute indignation, "hnh," of contempt, "fff," a huff, as in *Ulysses* by James Joyce then "pfft," of brushing off someone or something.

"What, no vowels, none?"

With that, Agrippa reddens, exasperates, sputters, makes an intense pressure sound, "Mmm," then "I ... well ... ah ... I ... I...."

Because of this, Mary says as a major pronouncement, "and there you have it, I, as in me and mine. How is it that everybody else is wrong? Everyone else needs to change, make adjustments, and you just keep rolling along?"

More sputters.

"Do you have anything else to say—anything? What … no fistfight? None…? Are you sure?"

Agrippa reddens into gristle, into a dangerous mindset, quite, as if ready for a fistfight, a "kickass and chew bubblegum;" yeah right, "kickass and take names," leap into an old-fashioned fistfight, with a superwoman punch then a pit fight combination, such as a Muay Thai and Greco-Roman event, with close quarter in-fighting, a series of brutal elbows, a series of spinning back fists, and spit out a bloody tooth or so if necessary, then search for an opportunity to deliver pure power, of a spectacular knockout, or make one attempt after another at a decisive judo throw, one that will at least knock the wind out of the other, break the momentum, or better yet, score a complete knockout on ground impact, or against some other solid object, those impulses.

Yet eventually she wilts just a bit, and again, until the head eventually lowers then says, "Somehow this entire process got away from me; the mansion—everything. I don't know how, where or when, however things unraveled fast."

From that admission Mary shocks, as this represents a first, and does not know how to react, then searches for something to say, only to quickly abandon one idea after another and finally says, "Okay, okay, understood … I'm culpable as well, and could have done much more."

Just like that, an awkward silence arrives.

And in a series of efforts, both look for something to say or do.

Both try to find a place for their hands and feet, which seem awkward as well.

So, to avoid a hallmark moment, because Agrippa is not that type of person, and the admission represents close enough for now, Mary shifts into concern, as well as worry, "Yes, I saw your desk day timer notes, the appointment. You're going to a diving suit manufacturer tomorrow, asking questions?"

"Yes."

She says emphatically, "Really?" then steps back in serious doubt.

"I'm careful—very—posing as a buyer, looking for a custom diving suit, and here are my deliberately vague drawings, as well as a list of the needed features."

"You're kidding. That's dangerous with a capital D, a red flag."

Agrippa shows no sign of wavering from that strategy, none. As a result, they stare at one another.

No one moves.

No one gives ground.

Eventually, Mary says, "I see. Okay.

You'll need a babysitter."

For Agrippa, relief arrives and tension fades as she says, "Yes, and I am so sorry about this whole mess, this situation. I got caught up in the events, the hype, yes, the overreach, and no budget, no reading of fine print, hell, I didn't even open the property map in advance."

From that admission Mary shocks, another first for Agrippa, and does not know how to react, and searches for something to say, then abandons one idea after another, as these admissions seem wholly out of character.

"Should I call Reece, Emma, Vera, Benny, Zoey, and Mel?"

That creates a tipping point and Agrippa smolders, reddens into gristle, into a dangerous mindset, very much so, as if ready for a leap into an old-fashioned fistfight, a "kickass and chew bubblegum," yeah right, "kickass and take names."

So Mary immediately realizes when to count blessing, those previous Agrippa admissions, and how "the entire process got away from" her, regarding "the mansion," as well as "regrets," about "everything," as some people have a certain personality, show no interest in hallmark moments or that process, and take more time to adjust, admit mistakes and reconcile.

Then Mary quickly adjusts tactics and inserts, "Oh, babysitting I can! However, I'll need to bring my niece with me tomorrow. Is that okay if she stays with me here, for your weekend trip? Well, because my sister really needs a break...."

And that interjection technique, the interjectional theory, to quickly bridge a considerable gap, with thrownness, with a spontaneous symmetry break, for a smooth phase transition, that statement technique causes the dangerous gristle to lose energy, lose that mindset, as Agrippa eventually says, "Ah...."

"Yes, my sister really needs a well-deserved break, needs peace and quiet, a fresh start."

"Oh. I see."

"Okay?"

"Sure, okay."

C<small>HAPTER</small>

L<small>ate</small> the next morning, Mel knocks at the mansion side door and again.

As a result, and eventually, Mary arrives, slowly peeks through the door curtain lace and says, "What the ... no way? What are you doing here?" and she refuses to open the door, "no way, ever."

Regardless, Mel does her signature move, an abbreviated cutesy, flashes a playful smile, then says, "Yours truly in person. The test results, you said 'in a hurry,' right?"

"Yes, but ... but, why come here ... you know?"

"Oh, come on—she left early this morning, right ... that trip?"

"But ... but...."

"I thought you wanted fast test results, you know," wink, wink, "about the guest."

Mary stands speechless as the jaw drops and she misplaces her vowels then alternates between shock and fear, "Hmmhmm," an expression of surprise, "dddrrr," a partially paralyzed mutter of fear, "chhhht," a disbelief expression, "rrrrrrr," an audible shudder of horror, "hnh," a disbelief huff and "I ... I ... how?"

Mel says, "Oh, okay, move your head up for the next question: is she gone?"

Mary nods.

"Gone for the entire weekend?"

Mary nods.

"It's cold—can I come in?"

Mary shakes the head no.

Regardless, Mel enters, as Mary eventually snaps out of that state then says, "that meant no, as in never," and commands, "Careful—wipe your shoes on that special mat system."

"Yes, sir," then she meticulously does and enters the mansion, offers with a bright smile, studies each and every detail in that spectacular room then says, "My first visit since the great war. Holy smokes! that was ugly event."

"How did you know?"

"Not important—here are the blood and fiber test results," wink, wink.

Of which, and just a bit, Mary loses balance.

"Can I see him?"

"What?"

"Come on, what's the harm, I gotta know, gotta see," and Mel walks the hallway, peeks in one room after another, then notices a locked door and jiggles the elegant brass knob made of an alloy, of two thirds copper and one third zinc.

"That's it, right, he's in there?"

Then Mary lowers her head.

"Can I see, please?"

"Never."

"What?"

"Never, ever, plus she might return at any moment."

"Really, tell me more?"

"If she saw you here, she'd go insane, berserk, and kick down one door after another, to warm up then with a single punch, knock you out of the timeline, and into forever."

"Me?"

"Yes."

Mary looks through one window after another for danger, grimaces, then puts her head into her hands and says with regret, "Someone save me, take me away, 'there's no place like home, no place like home.'"

"Come on, it's not that bad. What can it hurt, just a quick look? And I never knew she dated him—really, dated? She's too surly and impossible, who would ever date her? Come on, open the door," then as if to charm, "You can do it, come on."

Filled with dread, regret then surrender, Mary says, "Okay, okay, okay, say nothing," and with an ever so serious look, "as in, never ever say a word to anyone, got it?"

As a result, Mel raises her right hand, straightens posture, and shows an ever so serious look, "I solemnly pledge to maintain this secret, forever."

So, with a key turn, Mary opens the dead bolt, door swings open and they enter, look then say, "Oh my," as both heads tilt from one side to the other then eventually straighten, and both say the same thing, at the same time, "My goodness!"

Mel says, "How's that possible? He's unconscious and all; wow."

"It happens more often than not. You get used to it."

"How?"

"Professionalism."

"Really?"

"Yes, you become oblivious."

"Really?"

"Yes, focus on something else, look elsewhere."

"Okay."

"It's natural, a biological thing."

"I see."

"You're still looking."

"No I'm not. Okay, okay, I am."

Moments later, Emma, Benny, Reece, Cub, Vera Breden, Zoey and Tommy peek inside the room then say, "Oh my, look at that," as heads tilt from one angle to another.

The woman named Cub checks her elaborate backpack computer twice then says, "It's safe," and just as significantly, this woman has some traits of artist Nathalie Mieback, as well as a poet, math forecast specialist, of someone who understands resonance-phenomenon-natural frequency, collectively exhaustive events, oneiromancy outlier events, open source higher-order functions, and has advanced zombie survival guide skills. Which, the latter does not refer to the classic voodoo or cult zombie, but how any given system might train members into meekness, and/or to be a follower, with no executive thinking skills, or an ever so shallow version. Well, and she also organizes "zombie walks, pub crawls," for charitable and political causes, to raise awareness about zombie rights in a soulless ancient and modern systems, of the Big Show. As people are often treated as if mere stagecraft, theatrical scenery, theatrical property, or a principal with the least privilege and relegated a role, an ever so flat script. For instance, defend an idea, belief system or powers-that-be with that shallow language game; that chase, or defend a virtue, or an internal meek, such as bacteria, virus, viroid or metazoa, or some combination, which steers the agenda and defend as fandom with all those traits of same-old, same-old, the history of civilization, of ideas, life, yet often as a trope, in an common quagmire?

And Cub occasionally plays a mandolin in the David Grisman folk style or performs as an Occitan troubadour, to a very select set of exclusive clients, and often sings a solution created by very complex algorithms, from that elaborate basket backpack computer, which contains colorful lights as well as posts, wires, detailed notes, embedded messages, insertions, and strings.

Her name represents a short version of Somni Cub-Cullera.

Regardless, Mary sees the crowd and says, "What the hell? What are you doing here? Are you insane? Have all of you lost your collective minds?"

They notice none of that and head tilts here and there.

"Snap out of it. Look at me!"

And they eventually do.

"What are you doing? Are you crazy? Agrippa will go absolutely insane, and then one at a time to each of you, she will deliver a fist then bloody elbow."

Tommy extends hands to pat the air and says, "Calm down, Nurse Ratched, this isn't *One Flew Over the Cuckoo's Nest*. We know the zombie warrior queen is gone."

And for a considerable amount of time, Mary flabbergasts and reminds them about the danger, then all of them loudly argue round and round, which vents years of pent-up frustrations, even grammar school issues, as apparently some people carry certain events for a lifetime.

Just as importantly, here and now they vent with tremendous gestures and phrases, as everyone at just the right moment tries to fit years of issues and questions in such a small time span: life?

All of which might remind of Wolfgang Amadeus Mozart in the movie *Amadeus*, as told with a flashback by his peer and secret rival Antonio Salieri, as an entangled state, or estate. Of how a duet becomes a trio, a trio becomes a quartet, quartet becomes quintet, and so on—apparently this phenomenon transcends opera, and it has other applications in nature, in the universe, then at that very moment, it is as if the universe operates as a harmonic wave, and yet a union of paired opposites, dynamics, companions and the dependents, and yet all connected in a single unified wave function, a mostly hidden ontic wave, a hydrodynamics Rayleigh–Taylor instability, with that swirl of turmoil, byproduct and distribution, and so on.

Moments later, a melody arrives, which seems pure, noble, free and fresh, as if it were a series of exceptional poetic phrases, above a dramatic structure, as an uncommon narrative arc of exploration, with three acts: life!

However, none of the ladies concern with this phenomenon, which that transcends all thought and instead focus on self-interests, and quite loudly, as well as with over-the-top gestures.

Until Mary looks down and sees plenty of footprints, serious stains on the expensive dark Brazilian cherrywood floors from people who failed to carefully wipe dirty shoes.

She points, inflates with a mixture of puzzle and world-class upset, then says, "Now that crosses a bright red line," and readies to go truly berserk.

Enough so people notice, back away, pat the air, and loudly express regret.

In due course, she calms and says, "Shhh, shhh, be quiet...," with an index finger to her lips. "My niece is asleep in the next room. Beasts, be still.

"Okay, I want everyone's full attention. Clean your shoes then the floor, fast and be gone, go away."

As a result, they clean in an earnest way as well as systematic way then Mary locks that bedroom door.

Afterwards Emma says, "Can we see your niece? Please, please, please?" which causes everyone to join the chorus, with certain unified over-the-top gestures, and again, as if a history of certain notable art films.

Regardless, Mary says with skepticism, "Really, why would I introduce my niece, to a bunch of barbarians? You rush in here, create chaos, and now want a reward?"

Too late, Emma barges into the room and says as an announcement, "She's awake!" then receives a world-class hug from the sleepy little girl.

"You have got to be the cutest little girl I have ever seen!"

In fact they all agree, as heads nod at this wide eyed, slightly pigeon-toed young lady in a floral dress, white socks with ruffles, black patent leather shoes and hair tied back.

Then they say, "Aw!" then ask her one question after another, "How did you get so charming?"

"Can I hug you?"

"I want to comb her hair."

"Can I comb your hair?"

"Do you know how cute you are?"

Then with all smiles, as well as pictures, they take turns hugging her, followed by a group hug then hug each other, which causes Mary to cringe.

"Can I take her home with me? Please. Will you be my sweetheart?"

Even Tommy shrugs and wants a hug, which means something is truly wrong in the world, in the universe, as if the norm has shifted.

Moments later, Emma turns to Benny and says, "I want a baby."

Mel chimes, "Me too," which causes others to notice, stop and look.

Benny says, "Really."

"I'm very serious; I absolutely love kids, those fat little cheeks, arms and legs.

"Just as importantly, kids gravitate towards me and they smell so good. Kids love me. I'm the mommy type, single status notwithstanding," and her head lowers, as if in defeat.

In fact, the niece fully agrees; Emma and Mel are truly wonderful then she hugs them.

As a result, all of the ladies melt, except Mary, who sizzles beyond rhythm or reason.

Just then, someone bangs at the massive mansion front doors, as if with both fist, which causes the ladies to freeze, look at one another, and consider a leap out of the bedroom window then run for dear life, and not run like a girl—you know, where the arms do that funny thing and move in that unusual way.

Then just like that, Mary's eyes roll up as she passes out, falls backwards, then impacts with an ungainly thud, as feet fly high into the air, something no woman should experience, especially when wearing a dress, an impeccable one from Brunello Cucinelli, Akris, or is it from Chloe of New York City?

Regardless, Tommy yells, "Pizza party!"

Of which, it causes Mary to eventually revive, mumble an elaborate curse as if to evoke special celestial powers, yet eventually resigns then lower her head.

"Five pizzas—I ordered the variety!" then Tommy pulls out a generous tip and says, "Perfect timing," and closed the front doors.

Moments later, and as they open one box after another, steam rises, as well as heavenly goodness, each a republic of goodness filled with aromatic notes, which allure these ladies then a woman named Quinn arrives, by way of the side door, and with exceptionally clean shoes, and she eventually circles the gal pals, stands alongside, walks in between them various times, chats with no one in particular yet goes unnoticed.

Again, someone bangs at the front door, really bangs, with a mighty fist.

As a result, the ladies freeze, stop eating mid slice, look about, then deep into each other's eyes, back at the pizza, then towards each possible exit, such as a door or window, just in case, and they seem more than willing, to dive out a window then run for dear life, and not run like a girl, you know, as it might create a certain reputation, which could last a lifetime as people often rely on labels, on short cuts.

Tommy boldly announces, "A Chinese food party!" then she gives another generous tip to the delivery person and passes paper plates, forks, and napkins, as they celebrate, except Mary, who sizzles then puts her head filled with regret into her hand

and says, "Someone save me, take me away, there's no place like home, no place like home."

Moments later, more food arrives, "clearly a Thai party *leitmotif*," which triggers loud theme appropriate music, and that causes Mary to be flabbergasted beyond her senses, beyond all known language.

Not much later Agrippa phones, which Mary notices, and it creates even more serious distress, in fact a ghastly end-of-days look, end of the world, the apocalypse, or some other cultural equivalent.

And like any reasonable person, she refuses to answer the call, and again, which offers a bit of relief, until a text message arrives, of an early return, and that jolts her back into the end-of-days.

So, she immediately turns to the crowd and says in a stern warning, "Everybody needs to stop what they are doing and start cleaning up. Gather all pizza boxes, cartons of Chinese food, all those dirty plates, cups, spoons, knifes, napkins ASAP. Gather every telltale sign and clean this, as well as that."

"Message received?"

They settle, stop and grumble.

Based on a whim, Agrippa phones Reece.

No answer.

She calls Vera.

No answer.

At the house, and as each cellphone rings, Mary's eye widen, she over animates, gestures, leaps toward and waves off, with a warning, do not answer that call.

Afterwards, Mary asks everyone to "Go home, go away. Go!"

They intently listen, nod in full agreement, offer genuine comfort to her, even hugs, as well as longing looks then restart the party, which surges, fills the air with more music, singing, dancing, cheering and admiring, well, as if a major festival, a national folk, holiday or mela version, and the ever so cute little niece dances center action, and charms everyone, well, except Mary, who mumbles words not fit for print, at least by a lady, then she eventually surrenders, which causes the head to lower in full defeat, as the party roars.

CHAPTER 46

The following week, Agrippa needs another favor, and Mary knew this was coming, after noticing the desk day timer, with an elaborate list of dates, names, long distance phone numbers, and questions spread over the next few weekends.

In anticipation, her head shakes from "Oh my," as mixed feelings rush forward, of concern, regret, frustration and fear, of being caught, especially about that theme party, and possible mansion damage she missed, as often the little things, such as simple clues, ultimately reveal the truth.

Yet here and now, Agrippa explains as well as gestures in great detail about her master plan, elaborate theory then begins to talk-and-talk-and-talk, as a soliloquy, as if no listener needed, and a considerable number of people do that, they just talk-and-talk.

As a result, Mary drifts into a state of mixed feelings, into a trapped numbness, where all these things serve as weights atop her coffin, or tremendous weights that will sit atop a red brick building, which powers-that-be will drop on her, as a betting sport, to make an example of her.

That realization, as well as cumulative events, sit heavy, and she drifts down into another world, into a netherworld, and that ether with a certain *mythos*, then mythopoeic thought, a primitive dread, of forlorn hope, and "desperate or extremely difficult enterprise," as her eyes dart about and look for a system exit, from this legacy.

All of which Agrippa does not notice; then she reaches the front door, ready to depart cross country, which Mary sees and eventually shrugs surrender.

Then just like that, Agrippa leaves according to that mission statement.

And nearly five minutes later, someone loudly bangs at the side door, which causes Mary to utter, "Say it isn't so," then down the long hallway mumbles this and that, of things not fit for print then peeks out the window to see Mel, Benny, Emma, Reece, Vera, and now Samantha, yes Samantha.

"Not a chance, ever. Go away!"

Which cause them to smile and peer inside the window, even press faces to the glass, and do what people often can, especially when they have a known advantage—they press forward, such as life?

"I say again, no way, never, ever, and go way!

"If she finds out, each of you will need to spit out a few bloody teeth, and who knows what she'll do to you after that, such as a single punch which will knock you out of the timeline, and into forever, such as a clamorous version, where you'll become a feeble drool, a mumble."

They say, "Don't worry, we'll stand by you—that's what good friends do."

"Great, that's a real comfort. Now I feel much better."

"Really?"

"No, I'm being sarcastic; I'm a skeptic, a Kant, yet with other sensible and intellectual faculties; who knows that secret joke, of the soul, and justification, the constructs, the moral rules, often articulated 'in terms of rights and duties.'"

"What?"

"Regardless, go away."

They look at each other, suggest things, think over, and seem quite proud of themselves.

Yet in disbelief, Mary waves them off, as they tempt fate, seem quite cavalier, and maybe four horsemen of the apocalypse, plus two newly sworn members, sworn to chaos, "And where is Seska; yes, Seska?"

Of which Mary seriously considers for some time then snaps to reality.

Yet they say as a playful choir, "We're still here," then flash world-class smiles, of real joy, and how often does a person experience that, in this new age; find substancial satisfaction, such as blissful consciousness, and that substantial glow of peaceful, sane, composed and orderly, of an organized harmonic joy?

"Really?"

"Yes."

In disbelief, her head shakes and eventually lowers.

"Open up, Nurse Mildred Ratched. We are here to see your niece."

Then Mary quietly grumbles a colorful curse not fit for print and eventually opens the door.

"Samantha? Why not bring Seska too?"

"Wait, wait, it's not like that. She had no part in that fundraising fiasco."

"Really?"

"Really."

"Regardless, my niece is not here today."

And in complete disappointment, they shift about, turn to one another and vent, then Vera says, "Why?"

"I'll see her tonight. Wait a second—none of you move. I need a big-time favor, big … don't move," then she disappears down the hallway, rapidly gathers textbooks, supplies and knapsack then returns.

"I have graduate school classes today, in fact every weekend. And who among you would like to babysit, right now?"

No one responds, in fact they have a wide-eyed panic look, from the distinct possibility of having to bath that guy, and Agrippa might arrive mid bath, "oh my."

"Okay, raise your hand, and will that volunteer please step forward."

No one moves.

In fact no one blinks, as all have wide eyes, and it seems quite important—do not flinch, in this situation, or much of life, or show any sign of weakness, at least according to human history.

"Let me repeat: will someone please step forward?"

And they quickly stammer as well as utter words, such as utter free and bound morphemes, along with other unusual sounds, which soon become quite odd, as if the sum of those noises have a life of their own, which happens now and again with a song, with music, as if all represent a being unto itself, and this event seems to eventually create a distinct pre-Socratic soul.

Of which, and at a considerable distance, as well as in stealth, a boulder creature duly notes, a creature with all the classic characteristics of a boulder, which include quite porous and pitted material, as well as other solids and volatiles that contains various chemical elements and compounds. In addition, it has an odd biology, for instance extremely long and complex biopolymers, the type produced by living organisms, of polypeptides, nucleic acids, and more specifically, deoxyribonucleic acid—DNA. All of which suggests this four-foot wide and six-foot tall boulder might breathe, and yet it has other aspects not easily quantifiable, such as out-of-phase matter.

"He needs a bath, food, and moved about, now and again, to prevent sedentary problems; as well, the sheets need changing.

"Okay, somebody step forward."

Either Emma took one giant step forward or everyone else one giant step backwards.

However, Emma seems unaware for the longest time before she realizes.

"Oh my!"

Regardless, Mary sighs relief. "Great! And Emma: I thank you with all of my heart!" then she gives her a warm look as well as hug. "It's simple: all the supplies, bedding, and instructions sit on the nearby table. And here are the house keys, especially that room key, and the groceries sit on the kitchen table, if you're hungry; yet after, meticulously clean all evidence. Leave no trace whatsoever and I'll arrive in time to relieve you; in more than enough time, so don't worry—any questions?"

Emma flabbergasts, which shows a percolate appearance, of one impulse after the other.

Regardless, Mary continues, "It's a noble cause; be a humanitarian."

"What!"

"Yes, and think of it as an act of kindness, of sympathy."

"Really?"

"Yes, which represents one of the best human virtues, as well as a path into a better life, as a stoic calm; yes, with goodness and peace of mind, which represents a virtue in full accordance with nature."

Just as importantly, the others see this narrow opening then loudly agree.

In fact they promote, with either sympathy or as a clear opportunity, well, for a fast ever so smooth exit, as the Agrippa war wagon might arrive at any moment.

Then with all expediency, they exit and leave Emma standing there, as car after car quickly drives away from the mansion, along the driveway made up of antique white pea-size gravel, which creates a distinct crunching sound from wheel contact.

Then cars exit the sculpted thirty-two-foot high iron gate, with limestone wall bordering the property, and enter the single lane road then disappear into the pristine old-growth temperate coniferous forests, of yew, spruce, fir, juniper, and pine.

All the while, Emma looks at their departure, and a minute later she still stares.

"Well. That was a fast exit. I feel abandoned, very. In fact, none of them wanted to stay with me—none? Am I that repulsive, really?"

And she seriously thinks about it. "They fled from the repulsive, a great ugly?"

With that, it becomes quite personal then, as if nipped, as well as wounded, which immediately isolates her from everything else, then weakens the self, weakens her integrity, as well as significance, and as if this feeling radiates from within, especially from the head and chest region.

"I don't understand," and Emma tries to remember anything that might have offended them.

"Have they ever said anything, stated outright, dropped obvious hints, offered subtle clues?

I don't think so."

Then she continues to look about, as if in *nonesmanneslond*, for lack of a better word, a very old English word for a barren region, and for very important reasons, as something can only travel so far, through time and space, to the border.

Regardless, and moments later, a cool mist falls, which has a light, clean and uniform aspect, as particles feel small, and ever so delicate, when they lightly touch her hair, face and shoulders then eventually the event delivers a steady Scotch mist.

And during this Emma feels stuck, displaced, which seems eternal, as she looks about unable to see the future.

Of which, and at a considerable distance, as well as in stealth, that boulder creature crackles, percolates, measures, and duly notes then looks towards the forest.

For her, things now seem unfamiliar, as nothing calls out, and her cell phone has a full charge yet no phone number comes to mind: no person, place, or thing.

However and eventually the past arrives, and it contains regret. As one spark after another illuminates a memory, a situation, of one unresolved problem after another, which seems quite vivid, and each seems to make the overall situation worse, as if the game of life, the system, the ability to recall has now been rigged, to go down, and down into a quagmire.

And each attempt to locate something positive, the bright side of life, even a moment, only adds fuel to this feeling of displacement, separation and isolation.

To make matters worse, she clearly remembers all those quick-witted comments people said when they introduce her to others, those warning about her, "She's the hugger, loves to hug, a lot, regardless of who you are and whether you want a hug or not. Moreover, she will look deeply in your eyes while doing so. If you don't like hugs, avoid her. She won't take it personally."

And how many times have her friends said that to her and others? "Countless, as if I'm a bother, an annoying pest, a serious irritant.

That's me, the pest. I'm the problem."

And she remains stuck, as if in the eternal, and no matter where she looks, such as outward or inward, they all lead to the same place, a place without a future.

"I am the problem. It's me. And how many times have they warned me, it would drive everyone away."

However, something happens—something.

A breeze arrives, and her face shows a certain majestic sadness, a certain noble suffering, which seems quite profound, poetic and eternal, as if she continues to separate, in degrees, from family, friends, society, world and the universe.

Of which, and at a considerable distance, as well as in stealth, the boulder creature crackles, percolates, measures, and duly notes.

With all these grim notices, she could become quite emotional then rant, complain, blame the others, point to this and that, as well as unravel then cry.

Instead, a cool and calm demeanor arrives, eyes widen and she says "Ah, yes, I see; this must be the place, the identity in full crisis, the great threshold adventure."

And, just like that, all four metaphorical iron bands restricting her heart, her mind, release, those mental restrictions: the baggage: those mental constructs.

With that, a certain freedom arrives, as well as relief, and she takes deep breaths, notices fresh air then landscape, which contains large weeping willows, majestic oaks and mature red maples, as well as plants in bloom that include a wide variety of rhododendrons, laurels, dogwoods and aromatic beds of peppermint, lemon balm, lavender and fennel.

Six hours later, Mary returns, carefully wipes the shoes on that elaborate doormat system then enters the house and calls out.

Yet no one answers.

And, after carefully moving from one room to another, pausing, slowly looking inside each, looking for details, she finds no one.

So, she calls again.

No one answers.

Then a whiff arrives, which seems quite elusive, as if an elusive muse.

Soon, Mary realizes a savory pot roast, with carrots, onions, celery, and small new potatoes.

"Oh my, say it isn't so—I love pot roast!" and she eventually enters the kitchen and finds Emma.

"How did it go?"

"Okay."

"Really?"

"Yes."

"Did you bathe him?"

No answer.

She checks then quickly returns, and says, "He's been bathed and has new bedding."

No reply.

Moments later, Mel knocks at the side door then cautiously enters, stops, returns, carefully cleans shoes, reenters and says, "Hello, hello!" then makes her way through the house, follows the savory delight and eventually finds the ladies, as well as food. "Oh yes, food, food, food! I love pot roast! Ah ... may I?"

And they do, which soon sparks Mel's interest in the secret babysitting rotation schedule, especially after Mary promised her niece would arrive as often as possible.

"Excellent, I love that little angel, and she's so charming!"

As a result, they enter the library, and the secret rotation schedule quickly fills, based on Agrippa's detailed day timer calendar and elaborate notes, as Mary scans then meticulously plots every detail in her own private notebook, and says, "Remember, I'm the front person, the one always here; when she leaves, as well as returns, and there must be no trace of anyone else, ever, no strange signature scent, such as perfume or lotion, or left item—none, no cues whatsoever.

"Most importantly, I'll return with more than enough time to spare, hours ahead. And never mention this to anyone else, ever. Agree?"

Well, they completely agree, which seems not good enough for Mary until they have a formal ceremony, demanded right then and there, a pinky swearing ceremony, where all participants must improve posture, show a serious look then say, "Never, ever—I solemnly pledge to maintain this secret."

"Remember, we remain careful, quite, as well as low-key. And say absolutely nothing to anyone."

Again they fully agree, as every participant seems completely satisfied.

Yet, as they walk about the library, something occasionally crackles against the hardwood floor, that same annoying grit, such as particles, maybe sand, which Mary with a best effort sweeps then rushes to eat fast, eat that savory pot roast with carrots, onions, celery and small new potatoes, as well as a magnificent peach mango cobbler with a golden crust, which proves a crispy delight from real butter.

Elsewhere, something happens.

"Oh, that's good, really good," while nibbled bits tumble from the mouth as she eats-and-eats then giggles; from the sloppiness she says, "Sorry ... silly me, I'm normally not this sloppy. By the way, you look really good," as a flirt might say. "Why are you sitting so far away? Really, come closer. That's right. Can I run my hand through your hair and twirl? Do you mind?

"Oh, that's better."

And her partner must like it then responds by rubbing noses, as well as nibbling at her ear and neck.

"Oh, that tickles! You little devil ... but I like it, I really do," she says then chews, flirts and adds, "Your hair is so soft and silky. In fact, I like running my fingers through it. Do you mind?"

As a result, she receives a wet face lick, and again.

Which causes Bonnie to eventually awaken and focus; yet everything seems so blurry, and eye rubs eventually help some, as well as head shakes, then one squint after another offer more clarity, as bits of pine bark tumbles from her mouth.

All during the dog lay nearly eight feet away, with head on extended paws, as its eyes carefully follow her every move.

Eventually she wipes slobber off her face, realizes it was a baby bear cub, and she flees south through dense thickets.

Chapter

Over the next few weekends, Agrippa carefully investigates the man's identity; each new led, as fingerprints reveal nothing, nor dental records.

So, she focuses on that diving suit, which contains a wealth of parts, devices, compartments, and hidden functions.

Nearly all aspects appear custom-made, including the valves, anchor bolts, captive fasteners, Clekos, retaining rings, gaskets, screws, sprockets, specialty bearings, and compression coil, air manifold, heating coil, commutators, reservoir tanks, hidden hoisting rings, mooring clamps, a carbon dioxide scrubber, as well as what appears as if emergency panic control system for claustrophobia, which releases a gas, a complex sedative, yet as an atonement, at least according to Mary. And it "bends the mind," to "improve abstract thought, especially the executive function," and "a process that alters neurochemicals, such as neurotransmitters, enzymes and hormones."

Just as significantly, each effort to discreetly resolve all of these suit aspects only open more questions about its properties, the mechanical, electrical, thermal, chemical, magnetic, optical, acoustical, radiological and biological support systems.

Before each trip, she asks Mary to look after that comatose man, and each time Mary flinches, grumbles about this and that, which Agrippa does not see, hear, understand or accept, or she chooses to conveniently ignore.

Yet in the end Mary always agrees by default, maybe by not protesting loud enough or the right way, which represents life, as much of burden is placed on the protestor, and after a system collapses people often charge, "You didn't speak up!" and a charge often made by people or systems that act as if born yesterday, do not truly understand human history, especially human nature, top -down systems, concentration of power, stubbornness and obsession.

All of which puts enormous pressure on Mary, who already has a considerable number of problems, especially at work, as well as her efforts to earn an advance nursing degree, that seven-day grind, and from the bias against nursing doctorate programs. As no one explained to her in advance about the prejudice against the nursing field, the systemic aspect, the institutional bias, where many medical doctors show open contempt and prejudice against nurses, especially those who earn a doctorate in nursing practice.

And the mere mention of someone calling a nurse, "doctor" causes many medical doctors to cringe, knot, feel a slight then show open contempt, such as a primitive reflex to peck, bully and wound, as well as set the "record straight," and some of them take pleasure in subterfuge, as a trickster who deploys cruel and unusual methods, as a lesson. Yet if found out, they might call it tough love, which seems a reoccurring theme throughout human history, regardless of profession or system, a classic version of love, such as love me completely or else, or a love and devotion that travels one way, and is often seen in many other social constructs, which include family, friend, tribe, team, employer, town, politic, culture, religion, race, and gender.

As a result, all these pecks have taken their toll on Mary, on her point of view, as well as demeanor and self-worth.

Life has ground things out of her, ground charm out, as well as perk, and she says now and again, "Time spent babysitting time could be used elsewhere, such as a major reorganization of clutter, and sleep—yes, a peaceful sleep, maybe in a comfy chair, oh yes, in the backyard garden among aromatic beds of peppermint, lemon balm, lavender and fennel in bloom, in that Elizabethan Indigo-colored lounge chair, which has the full appearance of world-class comfort, the kind you sit in, sink down and say in an extended way, "Ah, now that's the way it should be—life, yes."

Regardless, she continues to secretly delegate babysitting to Emma, Mel, as well as Benny.

And once Agrippa leaves for the weekend, at that usual time and day Friday evening, then one or more of these substitutes quickly arrive to replace Mary, then Mary returns late Sunday morning well before Agrippa arrives late Sunday evening, which represents more than enough time to insure all is well.

However, as well as slowly but surely, Mary returns later and later, and on occasions, in the nick of time.

And Mary does not realize her surrogates often delegate responsibility during those days, and to people not on the approved list, especially when Mary fails to bring along that adorable niece, which was their main motive, a love of her, such as, how often does a person find true love, as opposed to settle for close enough, and someone with bad habits?

In addition, all their obvious and subtle hints to Mary about that subject, do not register, which might represents another example of human history, a fair, as well as reasonable notice, a practical request, yet no significant change to the system, and if so then a cosmetic adjustment, as Mary seems more and more preoccupied with her rut.

Just as significantly, and each time, the new secret delegation chain grows more complex, and as the weeks go by this circle widens to include Reece, Vera and even Samantha, then eventually expands even further to include, Zoey, Cub and Tommy, as well as their friends, and Vay, the quintessential "It Girl," one of those persons who can go by one name, which represents a curious phenomenon. How can a person gain worldwide recognition and do so with a single name? What traits have universal appeal? And what type of person can slowly move through the crowd, which cause social eddies to neatly pull people to and fro, as if a hidden misaligned gradient pressure, such as the baroclinic instability, for lack of a better phrase?

Just as importantly, this woman seems to be everyone's first choice.

However, Vay resembles the unattainable, the one people want to be near yet cannot have, which may represent a function of nature, such as the physis.

Just as importantly, much of life seems that way—where people must settle for a very pale substitute, for ideas, persons, places or things far down the ladder—and dozens of steps or more, and quite far from their first choice, from natural aspiration, especially vital needs, vital requirements—and people must settle for things not quite compatible, for things that do not quite fit or fully square, and does that phenomenon add to world turmoil, to the confusion, agitation and commotion of life?

Or said another way, and in the military industrial complex, or iron triangle terms with the acronym VUCA, does that phenomenon add to the volatility, uncertainty, complexity, and ambiguity, add to misunderstanding or poor communication, or result in the abnormal need for speed, to rush, for heuristics, for one shortcut after another, that obsession or need for sugar and starch, for a sound bite, or for something that must fit on a bumper sticker?

Long sought after, social circles want Vay.

So much so even women stir and lose their script in her presence, and they gush—really gush.

However, most people soon realize the near impossibility— and one at a time, a few of them might approach Vay, and each time a person walks towards her, and yet they end up elsewhere, from a series of subconscious mental constructs, which that trigger along the way, and formulate a complex solution without the normal level of awareness—the iceberg phenomenon—so much so the bulk of consciousness and formulation remains hidden. And more importantly, the solution deflects that person several degrees to a new path, which eventually arcs around her.

Worse yet, a person might arrive face-to-face then self-arrest with a mysterious state of mutter, babble, or ramble on and on, about this or that in a trivial pursuit. Or, they awkwardly use one very tired cliché after another, or become stuck in a series of gush. Or, worse yet, they become stuck in an exceptionally goofy mindset, and all that embarrassment might last a lifetime, even a few generations, where that person's name might become a cautionary verb, a warning told especially to toddlers, kids, and young adults who stray from a straight and narrow path.

Regardless, Vay as well as others babysit, based on elaborate switch techniques during any given weekend, and Mary seems quite oblivious, worn out and exhausted.

However and during one of her usual slogs to the mansion on Sunday, she jolts to find Quinn as a babysitter.

And Quinn eagerly greets her, seems ever so happy to help and says, "I'm here, everything is okay," then explains a remarkable list of her care accomplishments, as well as she made dinner, in fact a noteworthy one, and what a person might associate with true excellence as a chef, a chef *de cuisine*, or *sauté* chef.

Yet Mary carefully studies her head-to-toe then says, "I have absolutely no idea who you are."

"I'm Quinn, remember? We met at the mansion fundraiser, and few others times," then she continues to eagerly talk-and-talk, in fact, gushes and seems ever so satisfied, as a well-being indeed, yet Mary notices none of that.

For some reason—maybe it was the workload, tone, rhythm, topic, time of day, day of the week, cycle of the moon, or position of the earth as it circles around the sun, or position of the sun as it travels through space along with other solar interstellar neighbors in the Milky Way Galaxy, local galactic group, Virgo supercluster, local superclusters in the observable universe, or with relationship to other universes, multiverses, as the stack in the supreme bulkhead, or maybe a minor aspect, such as low blood sugar.

However, Mary hears blah-blah-blah and glazes over, mentally drifts elsewhere, and into a place where thoughts do not string together, where a person drifts away.

And for five minutes this woman, this well-being on the rise, joyfully goes on and on with happiness to finally be a part of their lives, to be accepted and included.

Eventually Mary says, "Okay, but I still have absolutely no idea who you are. And I don't remember any of that," which causes a spark in Quinn to slowly fade, slowly lose value, substance, and moments later become quite common.

Which often happens in life, to people, places and things, to family, tribe, team, political party, institution, religion, nation, gender, race and other constructs, such as other economic systems, to other systems of thought; quickly marginalized, gains devalued, rare opportunities often lost and will not fully restore once gone, and the boulder, which sits in comprehensive stealth outside a window, duly notes: "Another lost opportunity—gone!"

Chapter

In the forest, and moments later, a western wind arrives then whips through as menacing clouds build to great heights, eventually to an immense anvil shape.

Regardless, Bonnie seems preoccupied yet ultimately notices the wind however focuses on the nearby dog and gives him a stink eye, Hawaiian style, also known as the *maka pilau* or rotten eye then says, "For the last time: stay away! Or better yet, go, go, go!"

However, she notices something else about the dog.

It seems fully refreshed, in fact, well-fed, and has a shiny coat—a hell of a shiny coat, world-class—which gives the full impression of odd, well, primarily because it takes a considerable amount of time to look that way, mostly from weeks of eating heathy food, plenty of rest, as well as an elaborate bath then grooming, a lifestyle most owners find difficult to maintain.

Regardless, the dog hints at something, wants her to follow yet she refuses and instead wants to go north and quickly retrieve those mansion property markers then exit the forest.

Nevertheless, and after walking north for several minutes, towards what should be the first property marker, a profound hunger arrives then sudden energy crisis, then major, as lifting limbs seem a tremendous task, and walking becomes a true slog.

Even brushing aside dense foliage, navigating through thickets and avoiding wait-a-minute-shrubs seem exceedingly arduous.

As a result, walking resembles a low energy shuffle, with legs that barely lift.

Enough so, Bonnie look for a place to rest, yet staggers and stumbles, where lifting each leg takes considerable concentration and a great effort.

So much so, anywhere would do just fine—even collapse right here, as the dog follows at a safe distance.

Finally she barely pushes through dense foliage to find an open forest patch, nearly forty by forty feet, a "close enough," and drops that small foreign diplomatic sack with straps then flops down and rolls on her back, next to a small artesian spring, as eyes close and she mumbles, "Food, food, food. Feed me or feed me to something, I just want to be part of the food chain," then chants loudly, "Food, food, food!"

And yet she has absolutely no interest in the considerable number of carried prepackaged meals, those MREs, also called combat Meal Ready-to-Eat, or self-contained individual field rations in lightweight packages, labeled "Four fingers of death, black bean and rice burrito or chicken fajita," no interest in that dead weight.

All the while the dog studies her; while the voice grows weaker and weaker then she mumbles that slogan, "Food, food, food...."

Moments later the dog tries to wake her, and wants her to follow, and does so with a wet nose nudge to the face then a few times then ear, which normally annoys beyond reason, beyond belief.

Yet her eyes remain shut with each additional wet nose nudges, and they only cause Bonnie to makes a bare minimum of gruff sounds and motions, which gives the full impression of autonomic dismay, irritation then serious indignation sounds of "hun-na-hum," as well as similar vocabulary to drive the dog away, followed by a faint mumble of "Food, food, food...."

Which the dog keenly studies then compares to lessons learned, from that mansion main library shelf, books of the previous mansion owner who has gone ... where?

As it seems quite reasonable if you leave a dog, especially a well-educated one, you should explain the situation in great detail, and with vivid as well as appropriate language, in addition, explain the narrative structure, motif, folklore and new situation, the *umwelt*, as a common courtesy. And especially explain folklore, parable and the didactic story, a fascinating and intriguing event or thing, as humans often default to that state, that mindset, such as sugar, starch, or crispy bacon, and regardless of costs.

Yet people seem less interested in the complete cycle, of "live happily ever after," or reasonable as well as truly civilized, and seem stuck in an arc segment or two, in "limited awareness," "reluctance of the substantial and sustainable," especially "vital," and seem preoccupied with "experimentation," according to a mindset stage, and with no significant interest in the "complete third stage process," only a continuous loop though the first two stages, through to the "big change," the temporal stamp, stomp, or stub, to create a stub?

And the dog briefly thinks about lessons learned from the other bookshelf, the shelf of ugh, of ever-so-dry abstract stuff, such as poorly constructed language tokens, of compressions that human often create, well, from a lack of imagination, from a poverty of thought, which seem quite foreign to other humans, as especially a dog.

Moments later the dog exits into dense brush.

CHAPTER 49

Well over an hour later, something rustles in the brush, and again, which Bonnie fails to notice, from that serious energy crisis, which leaves her in groggy sleep, the type with an occasional autonomic gruff sounds and motions of dismay, irritation, then serious indignation sounds of "hun-na-hum," as well as other similar vocabulary, to drive the dog away, followed by a faint mumble of "Food, food, food...."

Eventually, the dog bores through that dense brush, to Bonnie then runs around her, as if exceptionally pleased.

Moments later, it herds five baby bunny rabbits to her; which, and they stop and do what bunnies do best: they nibble about, as well as on her clothing, as if food.

All of which causes Bonnie to wake, especially from those nibbling sounds, and reel up then says, "What the...," carefully studies then, "I can't eat a bunny rabbit, or can I?"

And she seriously considers for a substantial amount of time.

However, these creatures seem "so damn cute," especially as they hop next to her and nibble then one of them hops on her lap.

And all the while, she considers moral complexities, those degrees of, finds no solution, and grumbles things not fit for print, at least by a lady, then sleeps, as it requires the fewest calories.

Soon, a dozen baby bunny hop about her.

In fact, many eventually sit on Bonnie, hop about, then one sits on her head, her temple: *augurium*, the senior executive function, which causes her eyes to open and follow the details of every movement, every stage.

And after considerable thought, this woman growls, yet has no interest in eating them, which likely they know and as a result exploit her civility, her patience, which seems a universal phenomenon, the ever so cute often take full advantage of so many situations?

Regardless, and eventually, she chants, "Food, food, food. Feed me or feed me to something, I just want to be part of the food chain," which those bunnies hear, consider for an unusual amount of time, yet choose to nibble.

Not much later, she huffs a full resignation then drifts towards a deep sleep, regardless of the hop and nibble activity, even as one bunny nibbles on her ear, which generates a "By the way, you're not that cute, so, go away."

And eventually the dog herds them away, even the reluctant one, which apparently needs one nudge after another then a series of mild growls, and not the cruel type, not a threat, nonetheless one that conveys serious intent.

CHAPTER

Half a day later, and with a wet nose to her ear, and again, the dog wakes her, which causes her to growl and look, only to see a flock of baby ducks, the type most people might say "ever so cute."

And they march around her in a neat column; well, more like waddle.

As a result, Bonnies flinches, "What the...? I can't eat baby ducks, or can I?"

Then she seriously struggles with that idea, duck, only to soundly reject it then sleep.

The next morning, something rapidly approaches a sleeping Bonnie.

In fact, it increases speed while battling through one dense forest section after another and all the while making a bizarre sound, quite.

Eventually, it burst through the dense brush, and then the fully grown moo cow stops next to her position wearing a classic bell, which causes her to wake then reel, especially from the bell, as well as all that loud chewing and chewing: "Food!"

Moments later the dog arrives, and seems exceptionally pleased with a tail wagging, along with a small herded of moo cow.

Needless to say, Bonnie barely struggles to her feet, stumbles, steadies, fumes then moments later imagines things, imagines tasty recipes, such as "beef goulash with dumplings, or, yes, beef stroganoff, no, braised barbecued beef sandwiches, or, oh yes, corned beef and cabbage, or stuffed bell peppers, or lasagna, oh yeah!"

And she considers then formulates a detailed kitchen plan, with extraordinary details of step by step procedures, and how a cook should organize things, "yes, as organizational skills seem vital" and her eyes widen as she says, "Yes!" as the head nods.

"Come here moo cow; come here, come closer."

And, it causes that cow to stop chewing, look, consider for a significant amount of time then resume eating something, maybe a weed, at least what most people might call a certain plant, call a misunderstood thing.

So, she slowly approaches it with ever so careful steps, with ones that avoid crisp things underfoot, such as leaves, twigs, and branches then says, "I can explain, and to make a long story short, some of my best friends are moo cows. I come in peace."

And this causes the cow to stop chewing, look, consider, as "I come in peace" represents the classic line, and more importantly, the look of an invader, a barbarian or greedy con artist, a low-ranking bad guy, often nameless, such as bully or purest, the classic villain, or the tyrant, high king, Adipose Rex, rightful king returns or king mook.

As they have that look, and a native, regardless of the region, can tell you, "Here comes the pain."

And yet, the moo cow must know something, as it resumes eating another plant, maybe a weed, maybe a vital yet misunderstood plant, a solution, or breakthrough to a vexing problem.

And that enables her to arrive alongside that cow then consider it in great detail, as well as pat it here and there, which causes her eyes to widen from a keen interest, absolute fascination and anticipation of food, "a decent meal."

Moments later, that pesky moral thing pops into her mind, "decent," and in every sense of the word then it gains full strength, which causes her to mumble a curse, as if a sailor, and with words far too filthy for print.

All of which causes her to shrug, sit, despair then slump, and eventually wither into a major energy crisis stupor, which compels her to lay.

And not much later, the dog returns with baby ducks, which waddle around her for some time then a few of them hop up and consider her quite a reasonable place to rest, as if a paradise.

Meanwhile, her thoughts inflate and consider a more elaborate meal then eyes widen, mouth waters, especially at the thought of fixings, which include grilled potatoes and onions, wild mushroom stuffing, acorn squash with apple, and crispy coated Cajun fries, "Yes, a two-potato meal," as well as a seasonal dessert or more, with an appropriate wine or beer to wash them down.

Soon, a baby rabbit sits on her head, her temple then occasionally looks into her eyes, which widen, and that apparently crossed a bright red line, a moral exception, as she dismays, reddens, seethes then fumes beyond all reason.

Then she sits with a crazed looks of menace, of more than willing to do some serious damage, such as real hardcore damage, of clinical insanity, at that fine line between clinical insanity and true genius, at that ever so careful balance of when to pull back just in time, that precarious edge of crumble, where the soul shivers and eyes widen at that very edge of true madness, or greatness, at that stage of existence, and into no more excuses, into the impossible mystery of frontier justice.

Then, as if a dinner bell rings, "Yes!" she says, and with eyes that widen.

Yet moments later, a full revelation arrives, that pesky thing, morality, that little voice, the one that really knows how to quickly burrow deep inside the *psyche*, into the conscious and unconscious, into *das Unbewusste* and *das Vorbewusste*, one that knows how to spoil a party, then she cringes and says, "Am I a savage, a monster? Am I hideous, repulsive, and just another great ugly?"

With that, she gently shoos all of the creatures then "Go-go-go, be gone!"

And yet, it takes a considerable amount of time for them to leave, for their own reasons, if they have that ability, and uniqueness.

Eventually, that last baby duck waddles away then shimmies into the dense brush, yet over the next eleven minutes, she can hear an occasional quack and moo in the distance, which each time seems fainter, yet she cringes, tries to forget and conserve energy with sleep.

Regardless, and oddly enough, she tries yet feels too tired to sleep, which seems a contradiction, as most often, when quite tired, a person immediately relaxes then drifts, such as into another aspect, of physics or metaphysics.

And often, she mumbles, "Food, food, food. Feed me...."

Moments later, an idea arrives, and she reaches into her pocket, digs about, and pulls out a handful of critters from that bird episode, that compensation for disturbing those bird nests.

And she carefully considers each critter in great detail, and studies their size, shape, proportion, weight, as well as all those distinct features, the creepy bug parts of antenna, wings, thorax and legs then compares them to an MRE, also called combat Meal Ready-to-Eat, or self-contained individual field rations in a lightweight package, compares the dilemma, and which of them represents the most repulsive choice.

With a shrug, she says "Okay, I'm a savage," then eats a big juicy bug, which also crunches, and she thinks about the consistency, as well as taste then frowns, grumbles and curses like a drunken Marine on Friday night, eats more, grumbles then chews on a fat grub, a larva, as well as earthworms, crickets and termites until the meal concludes.

Surprisingly, a bit of relief arrives, which cause her to say, "Maybe eating critters is not that bad; in fact, it might be underrated, or berated by snobs, yes, the smug, by the high and mighty, the holier than thou."

Regardless, grogginess arrives and she sleeps, as the wind whips from the West then menacing clouds continue building to great heights, to billowy stacks in the south, east and north, as a late western sun lights them with spectacular shades of orange and white, which develop into a picturesque event then supreme greatness of nature, of the true power and glory.

Moments later it lightly rain then within less than a minute, dense sheets of water fall, in one distinct wave after the other.

Just as suddenly, it stops.

In fact, a certain peace arrives, quite, with a boxed effect yet unusually lit, as if a surreal poetical beauty of nature, exceptionally distinct, as even the foliage, color, and highlights seem remarkable.

Then moments later, minor-sized hail arrives, fraction of a pea, bits here and there, of ever so light pings, of gentle taps on vegetation, yes, of quiet charm, of peaceful and ever so serene.

Then golf ball-sized ones arrive, which pulverize vegetation, and another, and another, and soon that rate increases, and they pulverize aspects of the forest, and any given one arrives with enough force to knock someone out, cold, or into the next timeline, the next segment.

CHAPTER

Oddly enough, and upon closer examination, the hail contains distinct layers of white and transparency.

In fact, they appear as a remarkable stack, and some have as many as eight levels or variations.

Then moments later, that process stops, and more unusual sunlight arrives with a certain lighting effect, as well as a frog falls from the sky, and another.

Just a significantly, considerable ones arrive, not bullfrogs, not those monsters, but respectable-sized ones, which fall here and there.

In fact, some bounce off vegetation then hop about on the ground, then a sheet of rain arrives and abruptly stops, restarts and ceases, and over the next forty seconds, eighty or so frogs land about, then orientate, hop, consider whatever a frog considers, such as *What happened? Where is my lily pad; regardless? Where are the best insects? Who sits in my way? Am I getting too much sun? Oh, does she think I'm pretty: warts and all?* As well as other frog considerations, if in fact, they think with their own style, or maybe they have no feelings or significant thoughts other than instincts and reflexes.

As a result, Bonnie wakes, stares, double takes, then quickly gathers as many as possible and considers filling her pockets, stuffing them, which has more than a few disadvantages, and instead, locates those various knapsack plastic bags that say, "Burn for sensitive and classified documents," and carefully reads content then loads as many frogs in each one then knapsack, which also has a considerable number of disadvantages.

And after five minutes, all the easiest ones have been gathered, while difficult ones require a special effort, where she must shimmy low into a dense thicket, then shimmy more so, and reach then really stretch, fully extend fingertips, strain and strain, then shimmy the body with an extraordinary effort here and there, wiggle, really wiggle, strain even more, reach and reach then barely touch a reluctant one, which seems to have an agenda.

And eventually that style gathers a consider number, as winds calm yet more menacing clouds develop above, and build to great heights, to billowy stacks in the south, east and north, as a late western sun lights them, to produce more spectacular shades of orange and white which appear as a picturesque event then supreme greatness, of nature, the universe, as well as true power and glory.

Not much later, Bonnie sits, rests, organizes thoughts, cleans hands with a best effort, and not what most people might consider a reasonable way, not the average person, then she digs in a pocket for grubs, earthworms, crickets, termites, other tidbits, other heuristics, and eats one at a time, in a way that fully admires each, admires nature with its individual abilities, admires a local solution, crunch, and exaptation, as well as the best-of-the-best, such as make the best of a bad situation, or co-option, and just as significantly, she does not gobble, not as a greedy, not based on an inordinate greed-based defective protein or two, or lack of, which might create an excessive love of stuff, or to stuff until uncomfortable?

Well, she eats in a certain way, because dignity also matters, has a purpose, a function, even the symbolic type, as a lady, even with no witness, no dangerous people, and especially people who might gossip, the pernicious type, the ones with a mean spirit, the professional haters who look for any excuse to damage people, places and things, the type of people with an exceptionally crude soul, who specialize in "cruel and unusual," such as a certain cruel twist of separation. And it often seems the same people who wonder, "Why are people so overly sensitive, and not tough enough"—well, as in justify that style, that tough love technique, or so they eventually tact towards that justification, and a style which often uses an impulse of destruction, to improve something. Or so they say to build a civilization, to maintain it that way, with cruel and unusual, or explore the great frontier and other cultures with that same technique, with a lawn mower, or a "return to the good old days," to a rough and tough system, with less interest in profound implications or subtleties?

"Wait a minute."

And she finds more bits in her pocket, eats then says, "Okay, yes, yes, yes—I'm a savage! What would you do?"

In between nibbles, she looks around without searching, with a plain look without reason.

Then eventually, something sparks her attention, so much so, the leap up cause critters to tumble from her tattered redshirt, critters previously destined for dinner yet missed.

By the way, a side note, which shirt color best suits a person: blue, gold or mauve, as no one in his or her right mind wants to be a redshirt? However, the system often requires ideals, peoples, places and things to serve as a redshirt, the concept, yes, as a stock character, or dramatic potential or tact, as a mere step, angle or forlorn hope, and after a brief introduction, if they receive a minor courtesy, often not, yes, as a device for the Big Ugly, or the same-old, same-old, for nature and "bada-bing, bada-boom: life!"

Nearby stands a sizable oak tree, and underneath sits a mother lode of fallen acorns, which she quickly gathers, cheers, realizes the possibility of danger, carefully looks around, reduces the celebration to quiet cheers then does a fully animated nerd dance, which has an unusual style.

Just as importantly, the nuts have a tough, leathery shell and some tannin, yet remain rich in nutrients, such as proteins, carbohydrates, fats, minerals calcium, phosphorus, potassium, and niacin, as well as a nutty in flavor, if lightly roasted before grinding.

Not much later, she sorts them, puts bitter ones to the right, ones with more tannin, and soon the overall stockpiles grow.

Then Bonnie carefully looks about and listens for bears then finds two rocks, one flat, then removes her shirt and fills it with acorns, and in a swift series of blows, the acorn bundle content eventually pulverizes, which she sifts the results in that artesian spring, sifts to separate shells, and soaks the balance underwater, until the water no longer turns brownish.

As a result, memories arrive, of her father's preferred process and storage techniques, of how to maximize them, dry them in a way, which retains most of the original moisture, flavor and texture.

And if done correctly, to create the best long-term storage properties, up to six months; it would take as long as four weeks to properly dry, which would consume plenty of space, as well as need a close inspection, from time to time, for tiny worms, mold, and pesky squirrels: twitch, twitch.

Occasionally, he would sun-dry them, which extended shelf life, and would place the best green acorns on trays in direct sunlight for at least four consecutive days, and brought inside each night to prevent mold, and done so until they brown.

Nonetheless, danger, hunger, and those restless frogs compel her towards expediency, to the best short-term effort.

Plus, the thought of eating more bugs, "of chewing on more crunchy yet juicy bugs, as well as worms" or "those MREs, also known as Meals Rejected by Ethiopians and Meals Rejected by the Enemy," compels her to quickly prepare those acorns.

And while preparing, she considers what is worse: "earthworms, grubs, crickets, termites, frogs or chicken fajitas, black beans and rice burritos or four fingers of death, with all that processed food made from pulverized, denatured and fortified with artificial this and that, which no conscientious chief would tolerate, food that sits in the stomach as a lump of goo, a heap of institutional food, a classic example what often happens to an institution over time, a bureaucracy, committee, institutional logic, mission drift, which takes on a life of itself, and away from natural as well as original intent, and regardless of culture?"

And once digested, "The institutional food seems to travel for an eternity, or the opposite, as an express," and often does so as "a wholly unnatural," in what might become a digestive odyssey.

"It's a tough call: bugs or a lump of wholly unnatural goo."

Again, the dog motions for her to follow another place.

CHAPTER 52

Yet, she shows no interest and continues processing the acorn bounty, occasionally frowning at those restless frogs.

The dog persists, and again, and again, which irritates her to no end then she stands, feints to drive it off, yet to no avail, then she chases it off with an eight-step-go-away-surge and after the last step notices a nearby stream.

As Bonnie turns away, something catches her eye, and she takes a closer look, squints, gets close and kneels down for better angles, just as a fish takes a mighty leap, then another feisty flop.

"Oh my, fish sticks, or fish and chips" which causes her to perk up, and the stomach votes then whole body unanimously ratifies, with no dissenting votes, not even that pesky moral thing, that little voice, the one that knows how to burrow deep inside the *psyche*, to pester and peck from the best possible angles, and just at the right time to make a point, to gets its way.

After squeezing through dense brush eventually she arrives and considers methods to catch, then constructs a fish gaff, which represents a long stick with a sharp hook on the end, such as a broken branch junction that extends several inches, yet remains sharp, which represents simplicity at its best. As well, it is quick to construct, seems easy to use: just slowly ease it into the water at the proper angle and one that accounts for the prism effect then approach as another fish might, from the side with a calm respect, then once next too, and with a rapid jerk, snag that fish from underneath or gill and fling it out of the water.

All the while, the dog follows with fascination.

However, after standing in cold water for thirty minutes, and a considerable number of failed attempts by her, stumbles, and clumsy belly flops, she realizes the difficulty, as creeping up, easing a stick into the water, maneuvering it under the fish and that clean jerk motion proves tricky, quite.

So much so, she tires and simply flops down in the water, as the dog look on.

Moments later, she carefully looks around for danger, listens, exits the water and then a stubborn personality emerges, very much so, an obsession, of frustration, agitation, and mumble, of words not in the dictionary.

As a result, she expends a great deal of effort constructing a barbed tipped spear, which misses, again and again, as it might not represent the correct angle.

Then after constructing a trident, and jabbing here and there, it catches nothing.

All as frustration continues to build.

"No fishing pole, line, hook or reel."

"I want those fish sticks."

And because of dismay, Bonnie plops in the water, sits and considers.

Then she daydreams about fish sticks, the number that could and should be eaten in one sitting, and all the ways to enjoy them, especially "with ketchup or tartar sauce, yes," as well as "How many fish sticks can fit in the mouth at the same time?

I want those fish sticks."

Moments later, an idea arrives, and regardless of danger, the real possibility of snakes, as they prefer that location type, that position to nip.

CHAPTER 53

As a result, she sets homemade equipment aside then wades through thick water brush and finds a deeper section, one with a considerable enclave, where a person can quickly ventilate, hold a deep breath, then explore with a dive.

Which she does, yet seems unable to look inside the poorly lit hole for fish sticks, and a strain reach inside feels around, and again regardless of prime snake habitat.

Just as significantly, stubbornness does that, it can suspend the ability to reason, suspend logic.

And still unable to see inside, she rises, quickly ventilates several times, holds a deep breath, goes under then reaches inside and feels around for fish sticks, and for well over a minute to explores the entire area.

Empty.

In addition, this hole does not even have a snake, such as a water moccasin, also known as a cottonmouth, and not even a northern copperhead, or timber rattlesnake, to grab them mid strike, mid leap with fangs.

Regardless she tries again, feels around, as it is vital to feel around the murky water, touch then quickly grab one by the head with a fast reflex.

And how difficult could it be to grab a snake mid nip?

Empty.

So, she rises, breathes then moves onto another murky section, where the head can barely remain above water then arm reaches inside a passage and feels around.

CHAPTER

"Yes, something is in this one, maybe a snake; something big—very big," and Bonnie strains.

Then it bites her hard, and again, which causes her to reel a great distance, as well as her demeanor changes to wholly determined, as well as fully possessed.

"Maybe a snake, beaver or muskrat is in there, as it happened so fast," which shows as complete astonishment, and how could something strike that fast?

Yet she carefully returns and reaches further inside, reaches around then strains.

Moments later, it bites and she seriously reels back a great distance, is flabbergasted for some time, carefully considers the damage, the bite marks in great detail, then shows a demonic smile, of clinical insanity then sticks her arm back in that murky hole and fully extends, reaches, strains and reaches further.

As a result, it bites again, which cause eyes to widen beyond reason.

However, the stubborn thought of *fish sticks and tartar sauce* causes her to reach even deeper.

Moments later, a violent struggle begins, which causes her body to alternate between violent shakes, tremendous reels, then total chaos.

CHAPTER 55

Meanwhile, the Punk Buster repairs another vital underground section, which that maintains shadows, snares, pits and other wiles, other torments, as well as worldwide abilities.

And all of these repairs consume a tremendous amount of time, with one meticulous effort after another.

Yet these repairs should have taken days not weeks, especially if it had that one-of-a-kind handheld device, a smartphone-sized scanner, which that emits a tight complex energy beam to examine major event aspects, such as acoustical, biological, chemical, electrical, magnetic, mechanical, optical, radiological and thermal, and much more, for example, image schema, temporal inflection, alterity, bardo, perdurantism, endurantism, and behavioral cusp.

That device could scan, and more importantly, decipher problems and utilize advanced system techniques to detect event signatures, or unique aspects, such as event polymorphism, identification number, ingredient identifier, hit, hue or unique particle attribution.

In addition, that device tracks domestic and overseas events, especially well inside the ways and means of institutional machinery, inside Defense Advanced Research Projects Agency (DARPA), ETH Zürich, Pierre and Marie Curie University, University of Copenhagen, Karolinska Institutet, and the University of Tokyo, as well as key principal advisors to the president, the United States Global Leadership Coalition, shadow cabinets, corporate interlocks, digerati, elite members of the Russell Aldwych Groups, and special meetings in Oslo,

Stockholm, Copenhagen, Brussels, Vienna, Prague, Amsterdam, and Neuilly sur Seine, Saint Cloud, Strasbourg, Budapest, Madrid, Ingolstadt, and Chur, as well as certain vital aristocrats.

However, the Punk Buster dropped that scanner, which shattered into pieces beyond repair, into what resembles a pile of junk, a plastic and metal heap.

And it dropped the device because of that previous event, from a deliberate insane fury, from a juvenile bunker experiment, which tested boundaries of law, universal law and system theory, as if the universe was a bulkhead or series of complex algebraic stacks. And the test did so to manipulate subspace, the physics, tests stack theory, which seemed quite dangerous and unsettling. And it did so as if a game of chicken, that game theory conflict between two players or systems, as two free enterprise bunker or government aspects, to create a theory of everything, the ultimate theory, the all-inclusive explanation of the universe, of life, as well as the Grand Unified Theory.

As a result, the extensive damage in one bunker still radiates as well as pollutes the timeline of nearby events.

It corrupts that local temporal inflection, or function, and might push things sideways in time, or out of the local timeline, out of the history of ideas, which might have a considerable effect, as the universe often prefers a certain symmetrical structure, or distribution, such as a bell-shaped curve.

Yet what happen if the bunker event escalates then ruptures the universal fabric, punctures the fabric?

Just as importantly, the Punk Buster has not fully recovered mentally, recovered a vital K-wave understanding, as well as a history of ideas and special techniques.

Again, these repairs should have taken days not weeks if it had that handheld device.

And this problem originated from, well, because of a juvenile bunker experiment.

As any juvenile aspect, regardless of system or location, might rebel against the system, from lack of fresh air, exceptional water and/or freedom, might rebel against the top-down system, or because of a mid-phase transition, or the mental pruning stage, such as into a cog!

Or more likely, rebel from a lack of vitals and fed cosmetics, fed artificial whatnot, such as a flavor, product or service of the day, a fashion, maybe a flavor company special of the day to mask unpleasant off notes, and fed at that crucial junction, when an idea, person or system needs essential yet fed fluff, such as a molecule or string, a cheap polymer, fed to something or someone, maybe a generation, yet promoted as a vital, or else, as the only way, as a "no-brainer," however the consequences have a "reach-through-claim," or a physics version of product-by-process claim.

And, this narrow handheld device beam could penetrate subspace, and at just the right cyclical moment, between stages, between deployment, and that comprehensive beam educates space, as well as matter, into a charm set, with a special flavor. As if the device creates a lively arch charm of wit, a sapient, prudent, shrewd management of practical affairs, a prudent investor of vital circumspection, piquancy and permanence, which helps regulate chaos as well as the normal universal expansion process, and done so as if a theatrical cue, on that mark.

It does so as a playwright controls the storyline, controls the storytelling system, as well as backstory, especially the under and oversoul, to work under or over the set, and with the sheer beauty of science, of mathematical beauty, well, as support. And in part it does so as *The Dresser* might, as not just another theatrical stagehand, a device, technique, or just another something, a generic, a could-have-been somebody, yet expected to work as a shadow, or as a nerd, or just another geek, a proxy, yet semiotic, or hermeneutic. It does so as an elegant spokesperson for the self, nonetheless a mathematical representation of a complex role, a complex stack of deep math, and a monster group, which that deploys a friendly giant scheme based on string theory, on vertex operator algebra. And it does so as a host might, as a master of ceremonies or *compère*, and yet often a reluctant benchwarmer in someone else's storyline, especially on daily as well as frontier aspects, and things not in the classic "stall daily script" sold as vital.

Regardless, the one-of-kind device resembles a pile of junk, a plastic and metal heap.

And just as importantly, a considerable amount of damage still exists in various bunkers ahead, in spite of all those meticulous repairs over the past few weeks.

CHAPTER

In addition, the Punker Buster must quickly decide whether to go back and clean that initial bunker hazardous waste, which pollutes the local timeline or worse, or chase those things along that passageway or repair more underground sections that maintain shadows, snares, pits and other wiles, or repair more worldwide abilities to deliver retribution against trespassers, or repair the future, repair the throne, the official residence and fortified crown, which has a human aspect, yet of supreme technocracy, of unquestionable glory.

Then upon entering a long chthonic passageway, and further ahead, a thing quickly recedes then into another bunker, into a place devoted to Renaissance architecture with an occasional freakish item on the margins, well off to the side.

And further into this bunker, this place has an increasing amount of bizarre content, which represents a strange microcosm of curiosities, progenitor things, some transhuman or posthuman, and most look helpless, in fact quite pitiful and weak, as well as they motion for assistance, for "assistance in recovery," or a "recovery time objective," an elaborate "plan–do–check–adjust system."

However, when approached, they feral-attack, as if "attack-time delay," then *"Attaque à outrance,"* or a "sea of human attack," a fierce "melee combat."

Moments later, and elsewhere, the entire throne and many bunker residences shudder then alienate.

So, the Punk Buster increases speed through the tunnel complex, finds someone or thing which that manipulates various systems, and what a person might describe a misunderstood insider, a lovable rogue, or a terrorist; again it depends on perspective.

Regardless, and as the Punk Buster cautiously enters that bunker, the thing quickly recedes further into this dense packet room among other complex experiments, then eventually disappears along a series of chthonic passageways and one fortified bunker after another.

What Marcus Vitruvius Pollio of Rome might describe with the three qualities of *firmitas, utilitas* and *venustas*, or put another way, places that show a prudent, practical, balanced, efficient, and judicious style, a discreet, truly civilized place, with a calm aesthetic, as well as in full harmonic accord with nature, which might stand for a thousand years or more, such as the Tabularium, Curia of Pompey, Roman Forum or Rostra Vetera.

And yet here as well as there lay a considerable amount of black marble and cement mixture, to discourage Sulla aspirations.

Meanwhile, an underground forest passageway continues and leads through one heavily fortified bunker after another. Where content varies and have Renaissance architectural features and items of spectacular style, beauty, elegance, and things associated with discreet and impeccable taste, as well as an unquestionable understanding of art, especially aesthetics according to the ancient Greek term *askēsis*.

However, further into this bunker system sits an increased amount of content that seems bizarre—quite—and as if a strange microcosm of curiosities, yet normal for this bunker.

And things within this place have another world aspect, as well as primordial, yet universal, and some of these aspects maybe alive, maybe creatures and somehow related to humans, just a bit, as in barely, and as if progenitor things, which, on the whole, give an overall impression of missing links, of fundamental building blocks from the great philologic scripts, from that vast potential of the super apes and aquatic apes, of evolutional links in time, and those major junctions of alternate biological links, scripts and solutions.

Yet they resemble tampered versions, or what-if experiments, just because it can be tried; well, you know humans, as well as the history of experimentation, especially when they think no one is looking, or the system has no real checks and balances, such as the top-down system, the ones with the most coins and abilities, as well as secrecy, or mandate of clamor, which often sets the tone, the tenor. And when they create a bandwagon effect all around, with the big drum, yes: bang the drum, or transmit through the vital media complex, to gain the Big Mo, or the virtuous yet vicious circle, mostly vicious, or cruel and unusual: that feedback loop, of cognitive bias, cognitive distortion, with the forty or more bias types, which that maintain a certain system mindset, "maintain the bubble" or "fetch a bubble" or "insert old data," that type of room: so bang the drum, or play the guitar, as a guitar hero.

CHAPTER 57

Further along in this bunker, the walls and vault ceiling contain dense layers of *Wunderkammer,* or Leverian *façade,* contain dense mysteries, of microcosms within microcosms, as well as categories and degrees of existence, of crucial stages and craft from certain universal, as well as biological theater, or put another way devices, tools, agents, Accumulo NoSQL hylomorphisms, hirelings, pawns, spark reserves, as well as a few creepy industrialized sagacious wits, which resemble an ecstatic scop or sage, and who use a certain sly as well as malicious propaganda, to insert rot, as a professional panderer, a deception specialist.

However, a considerable number of things seem transhuman or posthuman, with colorful, irresistible and creepy gravitas, such as slowly back away from them, make no sudden moves or direct eye contact, and some appear to use Fluorinert as an experimental liquid breathing system and coolant, based on stable fluorocarbon fluid, which that seems to have side effects, similar to a modern drug sold as vital, yet not quite, and with a long list of possible problems, many scarier than the original problem: that new escalation.

Then once inside the next chthonic passageway and in the distance, a crowd of things form, notice, confer then rush into the next bunker, into a place devoted to the Renaissance, Renaissance Humanism, Neoclassicism and the Age of Enlightenment, and the Romantic era version, a place with certain truth, beauty and mystery of completeness, of totality.

And they quickly exit into another passage then bunker, into an ultradense collection filled with freakish items, bizarre content, especially from experimentation, as if a strange microcosm of curiosities with a considerable number alive, and who resemble progenitor things, many related to high level animals, especially humans, as many seem in a transhuman or posthuman struggle, yet most of the contents look helpless, in fact quite pitiful, yet "dangerously engaging," and be warned, "guard against being sucked into the mind games."

Of equal importance, this bunker gives the overall impression of things gone wrong, quite, as well as things kept there for an important reason, as a major storage facility, and members within seem to exist in an elaborate checks-and-balance system, with none of the members allowed out.

In addition, this ultradense community has some type of symbiosis, a persistent biological interaction among members, which maybe mutualistic, commensalistic or parasitic, or something quite different, such as an effort to create a series of evolutionary updates, quickly, for example a complex series of gene therapies, similar to CRISPR, for a major gene drive effort or more, apparently more, for a few additional coins, as if a race to the top, to alter the germline of organisms: animals, especially humans, and do so quickly at a much greater rate than nature might intend, which appears to have a serious effect on this bunker community. As they often pettifog and rapidly attack aspects of the community, versions of the self, the others.

All of which shows why this bunker resembles a series of "back out systems" gone wrong, roll-back techniques, such as when a gene drive system initiates then releases products or services into the stream, into life, into an algebraic stack, as well as the consciousness, and stream-of-being in search of special fruit, or the best thread within the forest, or wilderness.

However, the best systems in life can recall, can rollback, well, because of an "oops" moment, a mistake, which often happens, as the vast majority of products as well as services launched by life in general, such as species, even free enterprise or governments, fail, for whatever reason, and a staggering percent, as the rate of success for reinventing nature represents quite a tricky business, a considerable gamble, such as nation-building, which signifies a great idea, the nation-state system, a new germline, yet ever so tricky to maintain, because of factoids, as well as the "mythology of lost."

However, and more importantly, roll back the effort, or a "reversal drive" to repair the results, the damage from experimental tests, appears the greatest challenge, as nature has its own agenda, as well as functions, or history of ideas, and not history written by the winner, which often appears the human case. As the winner often writes a promotional document, a constitution, a certain mythos, or myth, theme, plot and storyline, and some are more sustainable than others. And a human or system often expects everyone to adjusting accordingly, well, to match that state of mind, to match those DNA issues, those birth legacy issues, or their preferred environmental version, which the powers-that-be drive, and often a quarterly profit system drive, or some other equivalent: that obsession, that institutional clunk, which pressures subjects to trigger gene sets off or on, to find a few more coins, regardless, and will not be satiated for any significant amount of time, because the lack of vitals, the fundamentals, the often ignored, and that viscous cycle, of save a few coins, as well as cruel and unusual?

Here and now in this bunker, a considerable number of these things motion for assistance, for help, such as help me first, and yet when you get too close, they attack as if a true savage.

Then when unable to gain a decisive victory, they change tact, adjust a few times then try to sell something, a ticket to this room, a slot, over there, which they point toward a cramped phone booth, to "dial for dollars" or some other support equivalent, which feels as if just another cult, or there, a vacant center bunker location, in a prime time placement, the ultimate test with a certain atmospherics, constitution, separation of powers, as well as a rough set category within the studio system, of the big show, as a hero's journey, yet do so with a subdued ego, the self-centeredness, and do so as if a *The Hero with a Thousand Faces,* or with the *Mask of Eternity*, which no one in their right mind would recommend, for any number of reasons?

Yet here and now, bunker members clamor a mission without a four-dimensional mindset, instead with one or two dimensions, or with a copy of someone's storyline, or a copy of a copy, yet not quite the same, with an abbreviated compelling version, missing a few vital aspects.

And all this clamor resembles a history of tropes with throwaway lines, or as bait from a desperate overpaid mobile landmark, with a fandom swirl in orbit, that atmospheric, which might change the balance of power, might shift the new world order, yet without a postwar plan or significant context. And frequently, they say the big ugly "was not so bad, not so crude or unusual." It was in fact as "a high concept, unique, and appealing idea," or "moral imperative and a special obligation," to follow, to obey this type of a leader, as if a cult?

Yet they do so as a dense collection, well, as backstage handlers ply complex tradecraft to them, apply special techniques.

And with a closer look these handlers do so, as if in competition with one another, and with differing agendas, and if studied in great depth, breath, as well as over time these agendas seem quite different, yet ultimately labeled the same, under the same banner: that strange use of language, where a considerable amount vocabulary accuracy seems unimportant, as long as a person or system says the buzz words or phrases. All of which shows a drift from word and phrase origin, the meaning as well as implications, and often when they make a statement, an insider or two must clarify to people beyond that coalition or bubble; they must translate in great detail, which often seems awkward and requires a considerable series of stages.

All of this resembles just another trope, misdirection or procrastination.

And when that persuasion technique does not work, they clamor then bunker handlers seem quite indignant then dust themselves off, their outfits then return to infighting, the art of, and among constituents in that special atmospheric, to maintain a linguistic shallow game spell, such as "for a swarm of bees," or "Lorsch bee blessing," and yet as if it might represent a "rumble and sway."

Yet it resembles an invocation.

Or, it might eventually call forth a swarm of bees, to move in a profound dreamlike trance in an effort to reach a full ecstatic accord with the universe, as part of a unique set, a topological group or automorph. And as if each bee represents a complex number, and yet as a harmonic and overtone molecular representation, such as the harmonic stringed just perfect fifth: that movement, or is it a bounded mean oscillation of accordingly yours—life?

Regardless, something seems wrong—quite wrong, such as a cheap trick.

Yet all of this activity seems normal for this bunker.

Then moments later and elsewhere, the entire throne as well as many bunker residences shudder again and again, as a human might; and many aspects seems almost human—confused, disoriented, isolated then forsaken, and in a profound crisis from all that threshold experimentation, which produces a profound sense of alienation.

So, the Punk Buster increases speed through the tunnel complex, one bunk after another, and finds that someone or thing manipulates various systems, which again might easily be interpreted as a misunderstood insider, and if you got to know better, a lovable rogue, a bit rough around the edges, a "rough guide," a person or thing that leads travelers or tourists through unknown or unfamiliar locations, or someone the system might label a terrorist; again it depends on the system mindset, the affiliation, membership, sympathetic syntopy of brother/sister species or social constructs, or justifications.

Regardless, repairs prove easy yet time-consuming, especially here and there.

CHAPTER

And once down another passageway, the main bunker appears then the throne, of what was unquestionable glory, a combination of a Napoleon, as well as the Imperial Senate's throne of Pedro II of Brazil and a secular version of the superstructure plus glory behind the chair of Saint Peter in Saint Peter's Basilica, Rome, similar to that golden luminous event of mega, yet a fully functional secular system, as well as with exceptional aesthetics, which serve full functions, as a tree of knowledge, the ultimate objective, and set inside theorems of complex geometry, of ever so complex manifolds, and maybe not stages of Gibbons–Hawking space, yet a superior class of Lie groups, of differentiable manifolds.

And this system deploys the science of a supreme technocracy, of pure mathematics, yet applied with exceptional beauty, and all that greatness of innovation, as in scientism, with a universal applicability of the scientific method.

It represents an evolutionary extension of the mind. Such as the way something might eventually overcome primitive structural disadvantages, of originating from a savage specie, that primitive baggage, that biota coalition within an empire of a self; the skittish, jealous and pettifog beings within, which impulse, such as a bitter shout at slights, shout at the devil, or some other cultural construct, or one created for profit, as an industry, to insert rot, for a few coins, or to flatter an unobtainable.

However, the throne now shows evidence of a pitched battle, of chaos, ruin and smolder.

As much of it has a wasteland look, of being bleak, exposed, and a barren gristle.

And with a detailed survey of that smolder, something lives, for lack of a better word, and it has a peculiar smell, of leek, evergreen, as well as something else, such as *in vino veritas*.

In addition, an ever closer look reveals a repulsive thing, a twisted beauty according to an ancient thought, an exceptional moral education, of a soul yet truly repulsive, as an unusual aesthetic, yet a major development of the body, mind, and soul, as well as beyond those traditional brain components, beyond the medulla, pons, cerebellum, midbrain, diencephalon, and beyond the telencephalon expanse, that last great effort, that major system distortion, opportunity, port and physical transport layer, as well as the implications of what that allows, as compared to what if one or more of the other aspects made a great effort, that expansion, or escalation.

In addition, this throne shows a series of real-time regenerative events, as well as segments, all of which give the appearance of tools, which support encephalization quotient and query skills of a resourceful, penetrating and definitive wit, regardless on their twisted gristle from serious damage; and above it all, a superstructure rose, a tremendous complex, which implies *The Nth Degree, Star Trek, The Next Generation* with Lt. Reginald Barclay, though this contains no holographic interface.

It resembles a deep state, a state within the state or shadow government, yet with brilliant separation of true powers. And the type that allows a deep data dive into cerebral forest, the contemplative tree and belief network, for a better exploration of options beyond that mindset, such as when considering things with another schema or rubric, with introspection.

And it allows a search or dive with a deep power shell into any given system, well, as a "senior executive" might to locate structural defects, to locate token bloat, bloatware, code bloat, or other system bloater forms, or tendencies to chase red herring, or as a cat that chases flicker, a phantom. Or, when the "executive function" wants to search internally for Parkinson's Law or the psake disadvantages, or to find the maximum number of options, including the prospect of a very bold system adjustment, which would require an audit of the active script engine, and that, represents no small feat. As systems have a certain momentum and resistance to change then have an impulse to double down or all in, such as follow a Nielsen rating or equivalent, follow the bling, for a network bonus, as head of a major media or corporate concern, and regardless of the implications. Because, if one is good, then two, or better yet, ten, must be great?

And just like that, this throne has the look of a being, a supreme technocracy, but not carbon-based, not that classic signatures of life, not those traditional biogenic substances, and yet it shows a symbiosis, a persistent biological interaction, which maybe mutualistic, commensalistic or parasitic, or something quite different, such as a series of evolutionary updates, and the way it was supposed to evolve before all those self-created petty distractions of attacking versions of the self, the others.

However, a closer look shows embedded regenerative biological components here and there, quite possibly exceptionally advanced beings, yet cogs, and not some ordinary creations, but some other category, and not a common ratiocination groupoid or Abelian group.

Regardless, this throne eventually gives the full impression of being heavily fortified, as well as of unquestionable glory, and true greatness of enterprise, and not necessarily free enterprise, as that current definition drifts, and seems exceeding vague, as if a justification.

And the throne shows science of a supreme technocracy and all that greatness of innovation, as in scientism, with a universal applicability of the scientific method, of true glory, of majesty, high honor, effective capital and certain personal privileges, as if a distinguished territorial warlord who has expanded even further, expanded fifty years ahead of everyone else, to create a truly great imperial empire.

And the Punk Buster, also known as the Neologic Freak, the Psychonautic, sits on the throne, attaches to it, thrills to no end, eventually overwhelms, frequently experiences a tremendous sense of awe, which causes mouth and eyes to widen, as this person looks for AB hylomorphs, for Franz Kafka notions, Schröder–Bernstein theorem of measurable space, indexicality, as if from another vantage point, such as the well of souls and that phase transition.

All of which causes a strange and extraordinary thrill, a marvel, as well as mystery, which that shows on the face, and the internal body alarm warns of exceptional frontier danger, and yet as if at a threshold of sheer greatness, that thrill of a cliff, of real danger then rise into greatness, rise, and yet something to not trifle with, ever, then the process causes this being or thing to transition through various emotional states, which include flabbergast, "ah-ah-ah," then difficult to catch a deep breath, which represents a "not quite Vader breathing style," with the inhale, hold and exhale in powerful distinct stages from the back.

Just as significantly, the face shows puzzle, fear, hot and cold flashes, shakes, quite then a trap, also known as an exception, fault or synchronous interruption, then being petrified followed by thrilled to no end at this great mystery, and that cycle repeats several times.

Eventually the full spectrum of unquestionable glory arrives, and the true greatness of enterprise.

And with that the system creates a more advanced metagame, a grand strategic system against shrewd animals, as well as things, and a robust net-centric yet very cold war, and what one expects in truly unconventional and asymmetric warfare, especially the psychological warfare of economics, which focuses on frequent use of thrownness, phase transition, smooth seam management, emergence, swarm behavior, spontaneous symmetry breaks, convection cells and real-time stochastic calculus, all done so with better heuristics, and even more data points.

It creates econometric indexes by time series, of the long game, or put another way, differential games, such as the continuous pursuit and evasion, and the play of one game develops the rules for another game, as well as mission, design, function, content, timing, and so forth.

Then from that throne, that power shell, or deep state, a state within the state or shadow government with brilliant separation of true powers deep data-dives into Tekes—the Finnish Funding Agency for Technology and Innovation, Defence Science and Technology Laboratory, Defence Research and Development Organisation, then Salzburg Research, Skunk Works, Mitsubishi

Electric Research Laboratories, Science Europe, as well as into Defense Advanced Research Projects Agency (DARPA,) Darktrace, Homeland Security Advanced Research Projects Agency (HSARPA,) Intelligence Advanced Research Projects Activity (IARPA,) Defence Research and Development Canada then a few others.

As a result, throne abilities continue to expand.

And eventually the Punk Buster thinks about intruders who systematically attack the forest system, such as ultimate insiders elsewhere, in domestic and foreign institutions, as well as other people who refuse to honor warning signs, such as Bonnie, the Mighty Sparrow, and people who might wander inside by accident.

Then the attention focuses on retribution, on a payment plan, if you will, for each of these special problems, each intrusion, and solves with a very precise method, to sting each person or system for transgressions, such as deliver a playwright into their system, "yes," a dynamic yet reoccurring productive wright, such as deliver a profound script, or large biomolecule, macromolecule or equivalent, which needs a special key, a password, a mathematical- algorithm-based one-time password, a one-time pad, to unlock the final procedures and findings.

And these people and systems are never quite the same, yet serve as a product, or part of a farm system, for a major league unto itself, to maintain that fifty years lead, and to help create the unified theory of everything, and just as importantly, a stable app, or "application to everywhere," as well as the ever so subtle, when need be, or disruptive, yet with considerable control of implications, the swirl, the turbulence, and products of, with subtle or gross tact, as well as various degrees of, in the wake or slumber, inside the well of souls, the supreme bulkhead, or supreme stack.

Again, and in general, the forest system seems to prefer one method—to enfeeble an intruder or sponsor, reduce him, her or system to a mumble, a feeble, such as a person, who would mostly sit and drool, or the equivalent, then once in a while has a wild-eyed-fully-animated notion, based on the farm cycle, yet cannot articulate a clear line of effort, and that effort shows very active and colorful delirium, of hallucinations, delusions, disorganization and confusion about preposition, postposition and circumposition, then the articulation slows to muddled speech, about a very complex content, about the next great zeitgeist or major breakthrough, such as a major mystery, an unsolved problem in physics, mathematics, chemistry, biology, medicine, or music theory, such as rhythm, melody, structure, form, texture, and especially harmonics.

Then at the key sequence of profound revelation, that person reaches a great mental barrier, realizes it then rants with wild-eyed delirium at the wilderness, at the frontier, and trapped in that endless cycle, or much worse.

Yet after everyone eventually exits, the Punk Buster secretly arrives then subject perks and say, "I knew you would return. They didn't believe me. They thought I was crazy, clinically insane. They want to lock me away, but you're here," and the Punk Buster directs a tight beam at the subject, in one stage after another, a stage-rigging system, yet staged trial, a show trial, as if a trial of Socrates or some other cultural equivalent.

Eventually something happens, that person finds a zeitgeist, yet does not remotely understand the process or results.

And the solution neatly fits into the complex puzzle, the "forest unified theory of everything," an all-encompassing, coherent yet practical system, which includes a unified field theory (UFT.)

Afterwards, the Punk Buster tests the person or system for a learned lesson, such as to not trespass, as well as respect the property of others, and are they more than willing to quietly retire, to self-exile, in fact, eager to flee far away, then up and up to a place just under a remote mountain crag and classic hovel, or some remote corner of the world—to Kataja, Nordaustlandet, Ejlinge, or better yet, to Ortac, or unceremoniously ushered into a life raft, because of those learned lessons, and with vital provisions, then cast adrift, maroon style, near a remote island such as Kerguelen or Bouvet.

If unwilling, or truly, the cycle continues, as a trial garden, a feeble reduced to mumble who would mostly sit and drool, or the equivalent then once in a while has a wild-eyed-fully-animated notion, as if a crop, or *kropf*, and that cycle.

Regardless, here and now, as well as on the throne, which continues to expand exceptional abilities, something happens.

Chapter

M oments later, the sixth hour arrives, a crossover trial before the highest blood pressure, or equivalent, and especially before the highest body temperature, then the Punk Buster realizes something: neglect, as well as procrastination, those pesky things, and the initial bunker damage, which could create the ultimate demise, and it might have been best to first clean that hazardous waste, that considerable amount of smolder and bits of unusual rubble, which, in a way, resembles the "mythology of lost," as there appears no direct route through that complex state or state-transition equation, or series of, or put another way, state's rights yet a quantum entanglement system, and the Greek word δρᾶμα, with dramatic branches, of, well, to trip, really trip, trip into one theater or another, or flash-sideways, or worse.

Moments later, evidence arrives of a polluted local timeline, the temporal inflection, and pollution does that, has a noxious quality, as well as to hold or slow maturity, such as an idea, stage, generation, or entire culture, slow substantial adjustments, or reasonable tact.

And just as importantly, life consists of many bad choices, quite, which consume large amounts of time and resources, as well as frequently have profound implications.

And in this case, it has a chaotic quality, as well as what might represent an "end of days" risk, end of time or eschaton, the final events of history, of human destiny, and ultimate fate of the universe, such the big rip, or rip the fabric of this universe, the fabric of spacetime then collapse the supreme bulkhead or bulkheads, the metaverse, the supreme algebraic stack, such as how to remove all that space in between everything, and do so at a rate faster than the speed of light, with a special warp bubble pierce, with the harmonics and overtones of deflation, as well as spacetime symmetry, and from procrastination.

Just as significantly, and unable to truly delegate, as that requires a certain amount of unconditional trust, which seems quite a difficult task—find a pure person, place or thing; the Punk Buster really struggles to detach from the throne in distinct stages, from that power shell, or deep state, a state within the state or shadow government, from the deep data dive.

And this being struggles to gain separation, with one twist of separation after another.

CHAPTER 60

With one struggle after another, it eventually separates then rushes through the underground system, through one passageway and bunker after another, and pass areas where someone or thing has manipulated various systems, which again might easily be interpreted as a misunderstood insider, and if you got to know better, a lovable rogue, a bit rough around the edges, or one might label as a terrorist; again it depends on the mindset, the affiliation, membership, sympathetic syntopy of brother/sister species or constructs of the various special privilege levels.

Regardless, the Punk Buster ignores those issues to gain speed; as a result, breathing labors, becomes forced but not quite Vader breathing style, with the inhale, hold and exhale in powerful, as well as distinct, stages from the upper back.

Then moments later, the entire throne and many bunker residences shudder again and again, as a human might.

And they seem almost human—confused, disoriented, isolated then forsaken, and in a profound crisis from all that threshold experimentation, which that produces a profound sense of alienation, especially the walls and vault ceiling of dense *Wunderkammer*, Leverian *façade* style, of dense mysteries, such as microcosms within microcosms, in categories and degrees of existence, crucial stages and craft, from certain universal as well as biological theater, or put another way, devices, tools, agents, Accumulo NoSQL hylomorphisms, hirelings, pawns, and elite beings as if cogs, as disposable.

Even the creepy industrialized sagacious wit, a scop or sage seems deeply worried then shifts to a certain sly propaganda, as a professional panderer, as a deception specialist, to whisper with propaganda techniques, with techniques of neutralization, and quick to insert bitter rot, and deliberately withhold maintenance in one form or another, for an "I told you" so moment, "I told you it would not work," as well as the type of person who narrowly casts that dream into space with a certain temporal inflection.

Regardless, the Punk Buster ignores those to gain speed, and all the while, laboriously breathes then rushes past more transhumans or posthumans with colorful, irresistible and creepy gravitas, and some of which, for the first time, inhale a new Fluorinert experimental liquid breathing system, of fluorocarbon fluid, then panic, from the normal impulse to breathe air, that reflex to gasp, as eye widen, as well as show being overwhelmed, bewildered then fear about serious internal damage.

Nonetheless, the Punk Buster continues pass past the helpless; pass the ever so pitiful, that motion for assistance and weak voice call for help.

Then something else happens.

And on occasion, if the Punk Buster strays from a certain straight line through one bunker after another, it triggers a raw feral attack by others, even against this powerful being, which would surely destroy each with a single chop, a 180-degree Jimi Hendrix style karate chop, as in the Jimi Hendrix Experience's "Voodoo Child (Slight Return)" —"Well, I stand up next to a mountain, and I chop it down with the edge of my hand," a type that instantly could pulverize, such as a large boulder into dust.

Just as importantly, it must maintain that path technique for another reason, to stay within normal spacetime, within a system, a "social construct," as that ability greatly narrows and becomes quite problematic.

And the safe path seems to resemble something, a process, a series of certain straight line segments, or more similar to a "straight line mechanism" theme, a linkage phenomenon, such as a series of hidden Peaucellier–Lipkin or a Sarrus linkage, those types of straight lines options, which seem to represent an ever so narrow window here and there, through normal spacetime, and inside each passageway and bunker.

So, stray through that narrow hidden process ever so slightly then experience profound nausea, disorientation, and much worse.

Chapter

Instead, and for speed's sake, the Punk Buster ignores all of it.

Moments later, the Punk Buster maneuvers through another passage and bunker then stops, because things seem odd.

As the bunker contains content, which appears surreal, disjointed, bizarre, lacks logic, and more so than normal, as well as in one grotesque gallery after another, in real stages of monstrosities, and when pure is not good, and all of which gives the full impression of a dreamlike, nightmare-inducing then high-octane nightmare fuel, of survival horror, yet not quite Lovecraftian or Tome of Eldritch, and yet based on the science of things not meant to be, or known, at least not this way.

Where, the distant future happens now, before people can truly grasp the full implications.

Moments later, something else happens.

Moreover, it seems difficult to describe—something.

Then the Punk Buster quickly looks about and meticulously scans a few degrees at a time, bit by bit, in precise degrees of freedom, as well as above, below and behind, yet finds nothing obvious or subtle.

Then it changes levels, as that might offer a better perspective, strains eyesight, and all the while prepares to deliver a 180, a swing around 180-degree style karate chop against whatever, and pulverize it into cosmic dust.

C<small>HAPTER</small> 62

Yet a meticulous scan finds nothing except normal bunker content, a world according to the juvenile, such as special cater techniques, to that audience mindset, to fill the void between the next great stage or transition, and pander to them with just the right sound, bling, and perk, to create a threshold adventure, to separate from the powerful, to another powerful, that quick dependence shift, to another guardian, or supernatural guide, or superstar *diva*, *prima donna*, *divo*, or *primo uomo*, an all-star, with a grand on and off-stage personality, with style, with an ever so special flair that can maintain fandom as well as the atmospherics.

However, a closer inspection behind the curtain reveals the hidden promotional system, the process and techniques, such as the science of what will mesmerize, and create a dependency, especially an addiction.

Yet further into the bunker represents the other end of a spectrum, something quite surreal, and dreamlike, then even further, nightmare-inducing, such as high-octane nightmare fuel of survival horror.

Again, the bunker content seems normal, relatively speaking.

Regardless, the Punk Buster has an urgent mission: to reach that next bunker with unparalleled destruction, of equipment that smolders, that sluggishly burns with a minimum of flame and smoke, yet a place with sections that have damage beyond description, and as if by some unknown process, as well as bunker sections which time may have "fractured," for lack of a better word.

Or it seriously damaged the temporal inflection, the bardo, perdurantism, endurantism, alterity or behavioral cusp, or damaged local aspects of the universal function, the supreme stack or the quintessential metastack function.

It may have damaged the local ability, as people often say the most important trait represents "location-location-location," a real estate term, that vital aspect, or that vital or vulnerable point, such as direct a powerful point particle force of complex pressure and unknown language, as if 50,000 languages spoken at once and directed at a universal pressure point, space or universal defect in spacetime, at the support aspect, or local engine, an engine that seems everywhere, well, the way someone brings down a high-rise building through the main support beam, to collapse as a wave function collapses.

Here and before, the damage may have pierced the fabric of this universal, or punctured it, and the ability to maintain a warp bubble, maintain universal expansion of the Big Bang until now, and something an articulate scientist, musician or poet might better describe, and with far more precision regarding all those obvious, as well as subtle, aspects, especially when something seems to transcend all conventional language and thought.

However, and on arrival, the Punk Buster appears to have underestimated those cloaked shadows, beings who now tinker with that central event, they "tinker with tomorrow" in search of a few more coins, or put another way, they tinker with a cash cow, which unfortunately makes the situation much worse from that "I got mind" mentality and "everyone is on their own," and "fend for yourself" for their own particular niche, or because of mission creep, and less concern about the totality or systemic risks, as well as implications—the domino effect.

In fact, the Punk Buster saw them as possible cash cows, or as a trial garden; well, and it might represent *vice versa* for that species, as they see a future opportunity to gain considerable benefits later, that line of thinking, as well as the ways and means of one cow is good, so ten or more specially manipulated ones must be better, that type of opportunity.

Just importantly, why start a war unless thoroughly investigated in advance the full implications, and more rigorously than a peer review system, as well as develop a dynamically mobile plan then solid end game, and not refight the last war, those memories, and not have all aspects mirror life inside a bubble, mirror an ever so stale system yet sold as vital, and full of yes-people, made desperate to stay on a tread mill, with complex contracts into one form of poverty or another, such as a poverty of thoughts, or the virtuous yet vicious circle, mostly vicious, or cruel and unusual: that feedback loop, of cognitive bias, cognitive distortion, with the forty or more bias types, which maintain a system mindset, maintain the bubble: that type of system, of bang the drum, or, play the guitar as a guitar hero.

As it seems quite easy to start a war yet quite difficult to win; well, unless it is intentional, an industry in need of a *The Mouse That Roared*, wink-wink, or for example, a cash cow.

Just as significantly, why destroy what might become a cash cow?

However, here and now, the triple witching hour arrived, and ever so close to the sixth hour, a crossover trial, a convergence, and part of that quarterly system ending, that deadline, which competes with tradition, fate, bad luck, and randomness of nature, as well as the thrownness, thrown into exceptionally uncomfortable situation, again, and when does a person arrive in the golden age of peace, a substantial time span, as well as prosperity, in any of these systems, and not a commercial break with an odd hyper style?

Of equal importance, these cloaked shadows step too close to that event, that end of days, and lose the cloak, realize this quite vulnerable position then they distress, well, seem quite distraught then mentally deranged, and eventually appear in a state of tremendous sorrow; yes, a certain majestic sadness, of noble suffering, which seems exceptionally profound, poetic and eternal, as well as in separating in degrees from family, friends, society, world and the universe.

In addition, the faces show as if truly alone and forsaken.

Then something else happens, a certain majestic glory, as a halo forms around them, an aureole of unknown origins, as if a poetic truth, a glory or gloriole; a transcendence.

Soon, a tremendous force pulls them in and out of sight.

Moments later the Punk Buster plans a careful route then steps around to solve procrastination, and it shivers, flabbergast, "ah-ah-ah," then finds catching a breath quite difficult, as well as puzzles, fears, shakes and feels trapped, also known as an exception, fault or synchronous interruption then petrifies followed by thrills, of joy to no end, at this great mystery, and that cycle repeats several times then eyes widen again, as if at the edge existence, or a cliff, a final precipice, which offers a precarious edge of crumble then steep-drop into an impossible mystery, or end of days, end of time or eschaton, into the final events of history, and ultimate human destiny, into no more excuses.

C<small>HAPTER</small>  63

Elsewhere, the woman named Cub startles.

And she still wears that elaborate basket backpack computer, which that has some traits of artist Nathalie Mieback, as well as a poet, math forecast specialist, of someone who understands resonance-phenomenon-natural frequency, collectively exhaustive events, oneiromancy outlier events, open source higher-order functions, and has advance zombie survival guide skills.

Which, the latter does not refer to a classic voodoo or zombie cult, but how any given system might train members into compliance, or meekness, and/or, to be a follower, with no actionable skepticism, no advance executive thinking skills, or they have an ever so shallow version to serve the rut, as if justification.

Well, and in the past, she also organized "zombie walks, pub crawls" for charitable and political causes to raise awareness about zombie rights in a soulless ancient or modern system, of the Big Show.

As people are often treated as if mere stagecraft, theatrical scenery, theatrical property, or a principal with the least privilege, and relegated a role, with an ever so flat script structure. For instance, defend an idea, belief system or powers-that-be, and do so with a classic "shallow language game." That chase, which often defies logic and reason, or defend a virtue that way, or defend the so-called meek, such as bacteria, virus, viroid or metazoa, or some combination which steers the agenda, and defend as fandom as well as atmospherics with all those traits, of same-old, same-old, the history of civilization, yet often do so as a trope, in an common quagmire.

And normally, Cub also tracks maneuvering among very powerful special interests, such as the cruel, unusual and hyper, especially interests that promote "all or nothing, my way or else," and doomsday, end time, end of days, or some other cultural equivalent, such as during an election, promotion, quarterly squeeze or other timeline, that process and industry. And they have the abilities to create the feelings of, which often means not necessarily an end of a local, regional or great power, a collapse, such as a too-big-to-fail, or end of a major event or cycle, a K-wave, and not the Big Bang cycle, not the Big Show.

However, more importantly, as well here and now, the backpack makes a considerable amount of noise and shudders then quite a disturbing cycle of clamor, of crisis, and one profound presaging event after another.

And so much so she must quickly abandon the backpack, gain a considerable distance, and it eventually becomes a thing, as well as great mystery, as if a sunken kingdom reemerges, and something a metaphysical poet or T S Elliot might better describe, yet the sounds become untranslatable.

And ultimately the backpack becomes almost human, yet an exceptional thing, as well as a *sui generis*, a class by itself.

Moments later, and of its own volition, it scans the surrounding space, as well as time, for a rollback event, and who could issue a major rollback of the universe, such as a true steward or trustee, an exceptional plenipotentiary, or special stateless elite, or extraordinary Davos person with a prerogative, an exclusive right to move toward the exit.

As all this takes place, and elsewhere, that huge forest old-growth tree shudders, the one which seems to have a human aspect to it, and not in a conventional sense of body, mind and soul, yet ineffable and primordial, a progenitor, as well as with traits associated with oak, peach, beech, hazel, ash, eucalyptus, willow, sycamore, almond, baobab and sandalwood, as well as acacia with thorny pods, shevaga, assattha, fig, kalpavriksha, thuja and yew, together with something unlike what a person might expect near a well of souls.

Again, the tree shudders, which causes something to fall, maybe a fruit, yet it resembles a special class of manifold.

However a close inspection reveals a world or universal line function, similar to a compass; and odd as this might seem, it looks edible, quite, or made into a liquor, especially a hard liquor.

CHAPTER 64

Regardless, as well as in that underground bunker, the one with unparalleled destruction, of equipment that smolders, that sluggishly burns with a minimum of flame and smoke, yet a place with sections that have damage beyond description, and as if by some unknown process, where all things might collapse into a single point, something else happens.

And yet, the Punk Buster becomes quite suspicious then mistrusts more things, as eyes carefully study the surroundings and look for certain visual references, as well as theatrical cues, such as a cue mark, or the sweet spot, an ideal place in the frame of reference, system, setting and cycle, look for manipulation.

Then it taps the back of the left hand three times, and again, taps left of right, the left brake: the left-handed material index—well, to see if it creates an instantly awaking moment.

Yet this does not, nor reveals a playwright or "Don't you tell me no truths, I want all of your lies."

Then it fully realizes true danger, which causes alarm as well as panic. And the mind loses ability to fully organize.

As a result, claustrophobia arrives, breathing changes, as eyes widen at that great threshold mystery.

Yet oddly enough and eventually the process has considerable charm, or ability to fascinate, as a compel, determine, compact, or compact operator of inseparable space, and a real possibility of into the original state, with a big crush, of everything into a single item, as compared to a compact of free association.

And as the end nears, complex pressure builds from an unknown language, as if 50,000 languages spoken at once and directed at a universal pressure point, at universal fabric, and appears ready to puncture it, or puncture the universe's ability to maintain a warp bubble, maintain that expansion since the Big Bang, and a puncture that will remove all space in between things. As if the universe is a house of cards, for lack of a better phrase, and most civilizations seem built that way, as well as other social constructs, with so many systemic risks.

And most things in the universe are quite empty, such as between atoms.

Just as significantly, there appears a significant emptiness between planets, solar systems, galaxies, and superclusters.

Just as importantly, here and now, a collapse would remove space between, and faster than the speed of light, with a special warp bubble pierce, with the harmonics and overtones of deflation, as well as spacetime codependency on symmetry, which represent crucial aspects to the Big Show expansion.

And in all fairness it was a spectacular thirteen-plus billion years, or a bible-thumping 10,000 years, or one of the million or so timespans, which other systems stated in absolute terms, such as quickly agree or else, and on cue, a mob arrived, with flaming pitchforks or some other cultural equivalent.

And civilizations had more than enough time to organize a reasonable system, as well as paradise on earth, such the golden age of peace, which could span a few hundred years, or more, a new Age of Enlightenment, a Renaissance, Renaissance Humanism, Neoclassicism, or the Romantic era version, with a full restoration of glory, the original long-lost glory now found.

Regardless, as well as here and now, things begin collapsing into a single point, which appears an end of the shallow language game, an imperfect thematic fractal variation that seems ever so familiar yet quite different than "Don't you tell me no truths, I want all of your lies."

Printed in the United States
By Bookmasters